Once Upon a Time in Paris

Also by Eliza Granville
FICTION (PRINT)
Curing the Pig
Gretel and the Dark
The Crack of Doom
The Dark Domes of Utopia
The House in the Riddle
The Tor
Until the Skies Fall

FICTION (EBOOKS)
Gretel and the Dark
South of Yesterday
The Crystal Singers of Iphicles
The Curious Ones
The Nine Witches of Glawster
The Snatchlings

Once Upon a Time in Paris

Eliza Granville

_____cHp_____
CentreHouse Press

Copyright © 2018, Eliza Granville
www.centrehousepress.co.uk | inquiries@centrehousepress.co.uk

The right of Eliza Granville to be identified as the author of this work has been asserted herein in accordance with the Copyright, Designs and Patents Act 1988

All rights reserved. This book is sold subject to the condition that it shall not, by way of trade or otherwise, be lent, resold, hired out or otherwise circulated without the publisher's prior consent in any form of binding or cover other than that in which it is published and without a similar condition including this condition being imposed on the subsequent purchaser

British Library Cataloguing in Publication Data
A catalogue record for this book is available from the British Library

ISBN 978-1-902086-21-7

Printed and bound by Lightning Source

Paris, 1695
Those were the days when fairytales were born –
In a nation that kept a peacock for its king
In a palace where buttons were cut from diamonds, walls
  built of mirrors,
In a city where the sun shone by night.
Believe that or not as you will, but
Those were the days when fairytales were born.

Chapter One

There was once a little princess whose parents showered affection upon her and declared that she was more precious than life itself. Alas, after some years the queen died and thereafter the king cared only for the princes, spoiled young wretches who teased and taunted their sister, calling her cruel names by day and by night. Since nobody cared for her, the little princess began to spend most of her time with a good fairy living in the palace's kitchen corner. But then a great wickedness came to the land, forcing the fairy to flee the kingdom. After this, the princess became so unhappy that she crept away and found a secret door leading to a high tower with narrow windows; there she stayed with only the spiders and mice for company....

There are no fairies here now, and all the spiders have gone, chased from their spinning as if they were maids on St Distaff's day; even the mice have deserted me. These days, my only companions are a crotchety old witch – she insists on being called Granny – who never stops chattering, and the ogre who climbs up several times a week, puffing and blowing because there are so many steps, bearing gifts, and speaking of marriage. I never utter a word, won't even look his way. My wedding will be sealed with a loving kiss not a contract of sale drawn up by sharp-nosed lawyers. The ogre demands to know what's to be gained by waiting. He'll never get an answer from me. Before she went away, the good fairy urged patience, promising that sooner or later a kind and handsome prince would find me, wherever I might be, and however carefully I was hidden away. Moreover, she whispered – very close to my ear – where true love exists my strange affliction won't matter in the least.

There was once an ugly princess, truly the ugliest, the most ungainly princess, seen since the world began....

Besides, at mealtimes, regular as a little monk to his prayers, Reims, my young jackdaw, arrives, strutting backwards and forwards along the window ledge, fixing me with his silver eyes as he waits to be fed. I'm teaching him to talk by repeating *they lived happily ever after* as I hold out each morsel. When he finally masters those words, Reims can answer the ogre for me.

As for the loneliness, it hardly bothers me. On a fine day, I swear it's possible to see to the very borders of this realm and with such a view it's impossible to be bored. There again, even in bad weather my grand theatre of clouds puts on a fine show outside my window, presenting an ever-changing cast of fantastical characters: bears and unicorns, dragons and griffins, quinotaurs, basilisks and, just once, a snow-white caladrius bird such as live in the palaces of kings and take away all sickness by staring into the royal eyes...though the witch saw only a broody goose. And there are plenty of books here. But I have another pastime, a gift, if you like....

It is said that there once was a king who celebrated his daughter's christening on such a grand scale, the food unutterably exquisite, the entertainment indescribably splendid, the gifts unspeakably lavish, that the entire city talked of nothing else. Or at least they talked of nothing else until the following morning when a new Pandora – one of those jointed wooden babies that display the latest fashions with such mute eloquence – was rumoured to be on view at Madame Bavard's establishment in the rue de Saint-Honoré. As is always the case with such an important royal event as the naming of a little princess, only the most gracious and wise fairies in the land were invited to be godmothers. Their presence added lustre to the proceedings. Not for nothing were they known as Les Précieuses, for bons mots tumbled from their lips without cease, sparkling like priceless gems. Naturally, these ladies expressed delight when the king was persuaded to read extracts from his latest poems. After an hour or more, when he finally ran short of words, the fairies roused themselves, clapped politely, and hurriedly moved to cluster around the cradle so that they might shower on the sleeping child all the usual gifts: intelligence, beauty, golden hair, straight teeth, violet-scented breath, grace, deference, charm, well-shaped hands—

"Pah!" snarled the oldest of the fairies, whose knees, though beautifully clad in silk hose, were playing her up after sitting still for so long. Her interruption meant that one gift was forgotten, but nobody remembered this until much later. "What does any of it matter? All your fine promises will come to nothing as soon as she's old enough to breed. I know what I know. Mark my words, the moment the girl hits thirteen, she'll be spellbound by some dashing young gallant and his promises of happy-ever-after. Immediately they're over the drawbridge of his tumbledown castle the enchantment will wear off. She'll see him for what he is – a veritable beast...."

The other guests tried to silence her with discreet nudges, pinches and pokes.

"A beast beneath his finery," continued the oldest fairy,

slapping away their hands, "at worst, a dissolute, pockmarked, humpbacked, bandy-legged penniless scoundrel, at best, a loud, coarse, gruff, demanding coq, with tight purse strings and a roving eye."

The princess stirred and whimpered. The king scowled. The christening guests coughed meaningfully behind their elegantly gloved hands, but the aged fairy had no intention of holding her tongue.

"Woe betide her when she discovers his dark secret: that small internal chamber, all splashed with scarlet thoughts, where he mentally stores a dozen or so other young women hanging like braces of brightly plumaged pheasants waiting to be plucked. From that moment on, she'll be his prisoner in all but name, cut off from everything that matters, lonely, lost to the world...."

Her words dropped to the floor like so many dead toads and rotting serpents. The princess howled. The queen wept. The king cursed. But then the seventh fairy, the one people whispered about behind their hands on account of her strong features and inability to drape a scarf with panache, stepped forward.

"If those things should come to pass," she said, raising her voice above the hullabaloo, "and qui vivra, verra – only time will tell – then my wish would be for this child to possess the twin gifts of curiosity and imagination, attributes that even time is powerless to steal. Whatever ills befall our little princess, a hunger to learn about other places, other people's lives, other possibilities, will allow her mind to travel to the four corners of the earth as freely as if she was wearing hundred-league boots."

Five of the fairies tapped their fans in recognition of the value of such gifts. The elderly one did not.

"Fat lot of good your wishes will do her," said she, looking down her nose at the seventh fairy's last-season petticoat and sturdy footwear, "alone in her grim castle at the end of the world with only the Beast, a wretched serving girl, and a potboy for company."

"Then my final wish for the princess is that she'll use what she learns to spin new stories. A tale, well told, is a lantern in the very darkest of places, brightening the world of teller and listener alike."

At the mention of dark places, the queen wept even more loudly. The king, on the other hand, swore a mighty oath to protect his daughter from all dissolute, pock-marked, humpbacked, bandy-legged penniless scoundrels posing as handsome gallants, even if it meant handing her over to the care of the good sisters of the Port-Royal-des-Champs Abbey – who knew a thing or two about depravity – the instant her childhood came to an end.

But tales, like tails, have unexpected twists, turns, knots and kinks—

"What are you scribbling away at today?" demands the witch. She shuffles closer. Her long nose twitches. "Can that be a love letter, my little pigeon?"

"Whoever would I send love letters to, Granny?"

The witch sticks out her claw. "Let me see."

"You can't read, Mamie." If she gets hold of my story it'll probably end up in the ogre's hands and that's the last thing I want.

"Ah, maybe not," she squints at the words, "but my fingertips can always tell what's been written by the feel of the paper."

"I don't believe you."

It's a conversation we've had before; nevertheless letting the witch boast about her magical abilities gives me time to edge away from the table and slide the page beneath a cushion. I'll burn it later…and toss the ashes out of the window for good measure. I rarely finish a tale, and almost never keep one. Stories, the kitchen fairy told me, belong to no one and to everyone, but travel on the four winds, forever seeking fresh tellers willing to infuse them with new life. Sooner rather than later, someone, somewhere, will breathe in the smoke of my tale, shape it to their liking, write an ending and pass it on. Stories are indestructible.

The witch cackles. "So it *was* a love letter. Why else would you hide it?"

"Oh, Granny, why do you say such things? You know full well that I've no one to write such letters to."

"Because it's high time you did." She turns her attention to my toilet table, with its many pots and jars – bottles of Hungary water, creams and cosmetics that I've no use for – boxes of this, and baskets of that, tut-tutting to find them still untouched, the scents untried and the jewellery unworn. "*Ma chère*, you promised to spend a little more time…."

"No, I promised to *think* about it." My fingers are covered with ink, but now isn't the time to scrub them lest the action be heralded as the beginnings of vanity. The witch rearranges my brushes and polishes the looking-glass with her sleeve.

"We could at least buy a little black maid to dress your lovely hair."

"My hair's fine as it is," I retort, pulling away as she grabs a handful, twisting it into a thick rope and sighing over the colour. "I've better things to do than waste an entire morning fussing over my appearance." Beyond the window, dark storm clouds are gathering; today the ogre will visit, but whether he roars and blusters or begs and pleads, my mind won't be changed. I'd rather throw myself after my unfinished tales, be torn apart by hovering birds of prey or dashed to pieces on jagged rocks, than yield to his wishes.

"A young blackamoor would have it curled and pinned up in the blink of an eye," argues the witch, "and she'd be trained in all the latest styles, with ribbons and lace and silk flowers and little wire cages and whoever knows what else. Ah, you can shrug, my lady, you can raise your eyes to heaven, but not caring how you look isn't natural in one your age."

"That may be, but I still won't have a slave." My hair hung past my waist when I came to this place, now it almost reaches my knees; if it grows any longer I'll be able to hang it out of the window and let the prince climb up to rescue me from this spellbound place. "Anyway," I add, hoping she'll take the hint and go away, "there's hardly room for two of us up here as it is." But instead of leaving, the witch settles herself into the most comfortable chair with a pile of mending and the smooth, egg-shaped stone she swears was given to her by a *fée*.

"Ah," she says, catching me looking at it, "this was a gift from a fairy I met by the seashore at home, many and many years ago. She was disguised as a little old woman that day. They often are, you know. 'Here, child,' she said, and this very stone appeared in her hand as if by magic, 'put this in your stocking and you'll never suffer from holes.' She walked away before I could thank her. Which was just as well, let me tell you, for before she disappeared I saw there were mussel shells clinging to her back while seaweed hung dripping from her shoulders like a shawl, and a couple of crabs scuttled at her heels like pet dogs. That's how I knew she was a *Grac'hed coz* – and everyone knows that fairy folk must never be thanked." Having pushed the egg down into the toe of the first stocking and stretched the worn fabric over it, the witch reaches for needle and thread. "I've kept this enchanted stone all these years, and the *Grac'hed coz* was right, I've never once had to endure holes in my stockings."

Her story changes a little with each telling: last time, a kelp-green cloak adorned with live starfish and cockle shells marked the seashore hag as a *fée*…and it's no good pointing out that it's the witch's darning skills providing the real magic. I content myself with saying: "It seems the fairies here must be more beautiful than those of your native country, Granny."

"Beauty is as beauty does." The light's poor and the witch's nose is now so close to her work that it's in danger of being woven into the repair. "Come, draw up that stool and sit beside me, *ma chère*. I've just remembered an old story from my homeland about a princess – with long golden hair exactly like yours – and a young prince cursed with head-to-toe trembling which can only be cured by finding her."

It's tempting. The witch keeps a great store of ancient tales from her native Brittany behind that knobbed and wrinkled forehead, but sitting at her knee usually means being stroked and petted by her bony hands. And, though she sometimes pretends to be kind, after all's said and done she is the ogre's creature, not mine. I swear she tells him everything.

"My story begins in a dark forest," she says, by way of encouragement, "where three young princes had gone to practise their marksmanship. It wasn't long before they met an old, old woman, just as I did—" She breaks off. "Come now, it's a long story. Sit here by Granny, make yourself comfortable and I'll begin."

My feet start to move of their own accord, but I've barely taken three steps when I catch the far-off boom of the tower door slamming shut. The ogre is on his way up. It's time to retreat to my seat by the window, fold my arms over my chest, and bite my tongue.

"You would do well to give him an answer," says the witch, who always listens at the keyhole and reappears the moment the door at the foot of the tower slams shut again.

"I never will." For the last hour, I've stared straight ahead, fists clenched, not moving, and with teeth gritted so tightly that now my jaw aches. "He won't get a word out of me. Leave me alone, if you please."

"This can't go on forever, *ma chère*. You're wasting your life waiting for someone who isn't going to come. And even if he did, who's to say that he'd stay true to you?" She fiddles with the ogre's latest gift – a fan with delicately carved ivory sticks, its leaves painted with roses, forget-me-nots, and small blue birds. The birds remind me of swallows; soon they'll rise from the ponds and lakes where they spend the winter and slice through the air around my tower swallowing fragments of cloud. "Now here's a dainty thing," says the witch, fanning her wrinkles. "It would be a shame and a waste not to use it."

I shrug. "Throw it into the chest with all of his other unwanted things."

The witch sighs. "If you say so." Then her eye alights on the box of *sucre d'orge* from the nuns at Moret-sur-Loing. "Do I see sweetmeats?"

"Barley sugar. I don't want the stuff. Throw it away."

She places the box on the mantelshelf without commenting, settles back into her chair, and takes up the partially darned stocking. "Come, sit yourself down, *ma petite colombe*, for it is high time you heard the sad tale of Princess Goldenhair – the one I spoke of earlier."

"Very well, Granny." At least a story will take my mind off the ogre, his threats, his prophecies, his promises, and the way he makes me fear my hopes are all in vain. Even so I keep my distance, only pulling my chair away from the window until it's near enough the witch to let me catch every word, but far enough away to avoid being clawed by her bony fingers. "There was this king," she begins, stopping to nip off her thread and hold the darned patch up to the light. "Where was I? Ah, yes—"

There was this king who had three sons, Cado, Méliau, and Yvon. One day, when they were in the forest, they came across a little old woman carrying a pitcher of water on her head. "Brothers," said Cado, "let's see which of us can put an arrow through the pitcher without hitting the hag." His brothers refused to try for fear of doing her some injury, but Cado's arrow found its mark, smashing the pitcher so that she was soaked to the skin. Of course, the old woman was far more than she'd seemed to be. "I will be revenged on you for this insult, Cado," she cried. "From this moment until you find the Princess Goldenhair every limb of your body will tremble as leaves on a tree tremble when the north wind blows." And instantly Cado began trembling from head to toe. The three brothers returned home and told their father what had happened. "Alas, my unfortunate son," said the father, "that good woman was a fée and no doctor can cure the malady she has laid upon you. You must now travel the world until you find this Princess Goldenhair. Where she lives I do not know, but here is a letter for my brother the hermit, who lives in the middle of the great forest, ten leagues from here. Maybe he can set you on the path." So Cado took the letter and began walking. Time went by and time went by and he came, shaking and shivering, to his uncle's cave. But for all his book learning the hermit could not tell him where to find Princess Goldenhair. "I will give you a letter for my brother," said the hermit. "He lives even deeper in the forest, fifty leagues from here, and has command over all the birds of the air. Maybe he can help you." With that he gave the prince a silver ball that would roll before him and show the way. Well, time went by and time went by until Cado found himself all a-tremble before the second uncle's hut. This hermit was also unable to tell him how to find Princess Goldenhair. But he possessed a magical silver flute and blew into it, summoning all the birds of field and forest, seashore and mountain. Not one of them could tell him how to find Princess Goldenhair. The last bird to arrive was a great eagle that knew of her palace and agreed to carry Cado on his back. Time went by and time went by and gradually the forest below them gave way to plains and then to a mighty ocean. "Princess Goldenhair's palace is on an island in the middle of this ocean," said the eagle. "When I set you down, you will see a fountain on the seashore, sheltered by a great tree. Every day, at noon, the princess comes to comb her yellow hair and admire her reflection in the fountain's water. Approach without fear, for she will recognise you and give you a pot of salve to heal your ills. In return, you must ask her to marry you. As soon as she agrees, call me and I will take you home. When they reached the island, Cado found the tree stretching over the fountain. There was no one beneath the tree but it was not quite twelve o'clock. Soon the princess arrived and she was beautiful as the day, with long golden hair that reached to her heels like a cloak. Her companion, whose hair was sparkling silver and who was also beautiful, followed close behind. Cado waited until the princess began combing her hair before approaching. "Poor Cado," cried the princess. "What a terrible curse the fée has laid upon you. Take heart, I will soon restore you to health." So saying, the princess gathered herbs and flowers, making of them a salve which she instructed Cado to rub into his skin. After a night and a day, Cado was cured and he showed his gratitude by asking Princess Goldenhair to marry him. She accepted, whereupon the eagle took Cado, the princess, and her pale companion upon his back and returned them to that part of the forest where Cado had insulted the little old woman. Here Princess Goldenhair presented him with a beautiful diamond ring, saying: "Never take this from *your finger. If you do, all memory of me will be lost as surely as if we had never met. Go now to be reunited with your father. I will remain here and build a palace where my companion and I can stay until it is time for our wedding. Then you and your father shall come for me." When she would not be persuaded to accompany him, Cado went home and was received with great rejoicing. "But where is the Princess Goldenhair?" asked his father. And when Cado explained, the king ordered his best horses to be harnessed to his finest carriage in her honour. While that was being done, Cado's sister noticed the diamond ring and was filled with desire for it. She led him into the gardens, sang softly to him until he fell asleep, and then slipped the ring off his finger. A few moments later, the king came to tell his son the carriage was ready. Cado rubbed his eyes and asked why he needed a carriage. "To fetch Princess Goldenhair," said his father. But Cado claimed he had never met such a princess and would not be moved. At that the king began to grieve, fearing that his son was mad. Later, when Cado showed no other sign of madness, he sadly came to believe that his son had become cruel and faithless.*

"So there we are," says the witch, rolling up the mended stockings in pairs, "my tale is done, and really the ending should be no surprise to you, for more often than not that's the way it is with young men."

"That can't be the end of the story."

"What makes you say that?" She pretends to examine her magic stone.

"Because Cado wasn't either of those things – he'd just forgotten…."

The witch cackles. "An excuse used by all black-hearted gallants since the world began."

"But it wasn't his fault. That wicked sister…."

Once Upon a Time in Paris

She rolls the egg-stone in her hands for a while, before admitting: "Well, it may be that the Princess Goldenhair gave him a second chance, though why she should I really don't know. The tale came to me so long ago, it's hard to remember."

"Please tell me the rest, Granny." I move my chair closer and let the witch run her fingers through my hair.

"Very well, *mon petit poussin*, as far as I can recall it goes like this—"

Time went by and time went by. One day, when the three brothers were hunting, they ventured far deeper into the forest than usual. To their surprise they came upon a wonderful castle. A beautiful golden-haired princess invited them inside but did not give them her name. Each of the brothers marvelled at her beauty and that of her silver-haired companion. When they returned home and told their father, he realised at once that it must be Princess Goldenhair but said nothing for preparations were already being made for Cado's marriage to another princess. On the day of the wedding, the Princess Goldenhair arrived in a gilded carriage so bright it dazzled the eyes. Her dress was of silk, ornamented with gold and diamonds, and her yellow hair flowed behind her like a train. When Cado greeted her, she took a beautiful diamond ring from her own hand and offered it to him, saying she was sure it would fit. No sooner was the ring on his finger than Cado recognised the Princess Goldenhair and remembered everything that had passed between them. He fell at her feet begging for forgiveness and they were married that very afternoon.

"There – does that ending suit you better, my little chick?"

"It's the proper ending, I'm sure." Whatever the witch intended, the story assures me that I'm doing the right thing by waiting.

"Such endings belong in old tales, not in real life," says the witch, glancing towards the stairs as if afraid the ogre might be listening. "If he exists at all, the one you dream of will never find you hidden away up here. He won't come, let me tell you. No good smiling like that – he won't. Better be sensible. Say *yes*. If you can't be perfectly happy, at least don't be poor. As a wealthy man's wife you'll never want for anything."

"He'll come," I insist, and stop my ears against the rest.

Chapter Two

On the seventh morning after Candlemas, Charles Perrault woke convinced he was still living in the old family house on rue Neuve des Bons Enfants. The unwelcome realisation that ten years had passed since moving to the rue de l'Estrapade plunged him into gloom. He scowled at his bedstead's footboard. Life, he was convinced, had taken several turns for the worse since taking up residence here.

As a young man – during those glorious years before the nobility started to abandon the Marais district for the newly fashionable Faubourg Saint Germain – he'd enjoyed a largely carefree existence with his brothers in the rue Neuve-Saint-Francis. Following his marriage, he'd set up home in the rue Neuve des Bons Enfants, a fine house, an excellent place for a young family, somewhere he'd never envisaged leaving. In fact, he'd commissioned costly paintings – from the best artists in Paris no less – to create a spectacular ceiling for a room there, his *Cabinet des Beaux-Arts*, when news came that the building was to be demolished. The king wished to create a new royal square: the Place de Victoires. That was in 1683, he thought morosely, kicking off the bedcovers; the fine Hôtel Perrault was reduced to rubble by 1685 without one of his beautiful paintings ever being put into place.

As for this present property, it was built into what remained of the ancient outer defences of Paris. Hints of the place's strategic importance lingered and Charles suspected some sections might date back hundreds of years, perhaps even to the days of Philip Augustus. The house was now far too big for the reduced Perrault family and the older parts – most of them, at least – were no longer in use. It wasn't its age that made Charles resent the place, nor its size or situation. The problem was that coming to live here had coincided with enforced retirement, unprecedented domestic discord, and never-ending ridicule from certain quarters within the *Académie française*. Only yesterday he'd returned from a meeting at the Louvre smarting at the digs and *sotto voce* comments – much of it concerning his alleged imperfect grasp of Greek and Latin – aimed at him by the supporters of his vociferous opponent Boileau. Charles sat up. His spine bristled. "*Ainsi voilà plus de vingt bévues que Monsieur Perrault a fait sur le seul passage d'Elien,*" he said aloud, adopting a falsetto voice the better to mock his detractors. "*Monsieur Perrault made more than twenty blunders when simply translating the passage from Elien.*" Blunders indeed – such accusations were outrageous: as was the case with any properly educated men, the Perrault brothers knew their classical sources.

Charles eased himself from the bed and shuffled towards the window. His grievances slithered after him so that he was still fretting and fuming, feeling himself ill-used and under attack, while throwing open the shutters. At least all was peaceful in the courtyard below. Even the discordant trundling of carriage wheels along the rue de l'Estrapade couldn't drown the sound of the year's first birdsong falling, almost liquid, from the budding trees or startle the lean squirrels nimbly emerging from hibernation.

His spirits lifted. The melancholic thoughts fled. Every man's hope was reborn with the approach of spring. He'd find some way to win back what he'd lost. And whatever misgivings he might harbour about this house, at least the Montagne Sainte-Geneviève was quiet, studious and respectable – and could never fail to be so for the area was home to the greatest minds of France.

He stood a little longer, watching pale sunlight struggle through a thick bank of cloud, likening it to the way inspiration tentatively emerged from the swirling mists of the mundane. A new determination seized him, for in his experience common interests almost always stimulated conversation. Although priding himself on his erudition, today Charles decided to put aside his biography of illustrious men and work on something lighter, a collection of sprightly *contes de fées*, fairy tales, no less and in prose, though it was not his preferred medium. A change, the old saying went, was as good as a rest. Besides, it was time a man's voice intruded to regulate the froufrou confections being aired in the salons as literature.

And who better? After all, he was a seventh child and, moreover – though his poor brother François died within a few short months – had been born a twin. Such details held significance for the illiterate peasantry and he'd long suspected that many of the salon offerings were simply vulgar rustic tales, gleaned from *La Bibliothèque bleue*, rewritten in flowery prose to incorporate modern notions of medieval romantic courtship. A cursory flick through half a dozen had confirmed those suspicions. Such wholesale borrowing was, of course, in no way comparable with his own acknowledged drawing on the work of the scholar Giovanni Boccaccio while composing *La Marquise de Salusses* – though it had to be admitted that the *idea* for his other two verse tales had been *sparked* by traditional narratives.

A pleasant thought occurred to him: this was not a lean day. Meat, eggs, sugar and cream could be used with impunity in the preparation of lunch, dinner, and in the selection of delicacies Charles enjoyed immediately before retiring.

Taking up his cane, he rapped on the floor to summon Poucet, his valet, with a porringer of broth. After partaking of *le petit déjeuner* and making his *toilette*, he'd retire to the library and begin at once. As he waited, Charles paced the floor, mulling over the form and content of his proposed stories. Certain themes dated from time immemorial, but his stance on literary progress was well known. He would look to the present not the past, to Christianity with its high moral expectations rather than classical times and the dubious morals of the ancient gods. As he'd written in *Le siècle de Louis le Grand*—

> Learned Antiquity, through all its extent,
> Was never enlightened to equal our times.

It was a sentiment he stood by, no matter the jeers and jibes.

Impatient now, he rapped again. Where was Poucet? What was the scoundrel up to? Throwing on his warmest bedgown Charles proceeded to the gallery, found it empty, and roared the manservant's name into the dimly lit stairwell. When there was still no response he was forced to descend two flights of stairs and, with a very bad grace, approach the domestic quarters.

The kitchen door stood ajar. Beyond, instead of daybreak's normal bustle and clamour – the cacophonous rattle and clang of knives, spoons, pots, pans, the hiss and sizzle of meat over flame, the dull thump of pestle against mortar – all was silence.

He peered through a crack and saw Poucet leaning over the table, having apparently been reading aloud from *Le Cuisinier français*, while the cook, Jacques, stood nearby wrestling with the knots of his apron strings, his pronounced sneer expressing heartfelt disdain for François Pierre's gastronomic treatise. There was no evidence of any breakfast preparations in progress. This morning Poucet looked as pale and stooped as a candle left out in the sun. By contrast, the ruddy glow of the cook's nose suggested another night of dissipation. Even so, it was with remarkable sleight of hand that Jacques caused both cards and dice to disappear from the central table as Charles strode into the room, stopping inches short of his flustered manservant.

"Didn't you hear me calling?"

Poucet hunched his shoulders and flushed scarlet. "B-beg p-pardon, sir, I was l-looking up a r-recipe f-f-f—"

"Since when do his wants come before mine, pray? And why are recipes all of a sudden your concern?" Charles turned on the cook, but decided against mentioning his flagrant disobedience with regard to games of chance in the kitchen. "Can you not read?"

Jacques glowered. "I'm no peasant. I can read my own language," adding a reluctant, "sir" in response to his master's frown. "But the writing is small and cramped for my overworked eyes. Leave me to prepare food as I see fit and no such help would be necessary. As it is, since you want everything done yon book writer's way and no other…." He shrugged and reached for a bronze cauldron, banging the vessel down with far more force than was necessary. "If you'll permit me to continue…." He gestured towards two brace of rabbits, as yet unpaunched. Their heads, hanging over the table edge, wept bloody tears into the small hollows between the flagstones. The kitchen cat circled, watching intently, from just outside the range of anyone's feet, skipping deftly aside as Jacques lunged at the costly volume and tossed it contemptuously onto a shelf.

Jacques was both exceptionally tall and astonishingly wide; to point out his failings took courage. The man was an excellent cook as long as he stayed reasonably sober. After that his penchant for knife-throwing came into play. He had other foibles, too. When it came to the person responsible for preparing one's food, one had to be careful. Charles bit back an angry reprimand

and instead cuffed Poucet. "Hot water!" he snapped. "And jump to it. You may lay out my blue brocade and the new lace neckcloth." Another thought occurred to him and he affected to peer into every corner and cranny. "Where are the females?" he enquired of the empty air.

A *gros mot* escaped from between Jacques' gritted teeth. His complexion darkened. His eyes bulged. Putting down his head, he bellowed like a great bull; corkscrews of ginger hair sprang from beneath the greasy wig concealing his bald crown; purplish veins stood out on his forehead. The two kitchen maids immediately scuttled in from the kitchen garden, wiping their hands on their skirts and coughing a little, smothering giggles as they took in their master's night attire. They were both chewing mint leaves. The smell of pipe tobacco clung to their clothes.

Wooden soles clattering down the stairs and across the stone floor announced the late arrival of Norik, a distant relative who'd stepped in to keep house for Charles – after a fashion – in the difficult days following the family's move from the rue Neuve des Bons Enfants. She wore a black gown so ancient it had now acquired the rusty patina usually seen on aged metal, together with a ferociously white linen turban and collar. The woman was dour and silent – at least when she went about her work – though Charles didn't believe she'd always been so. Every year that passed gnawed away at her height so that now she hardly reached to his elbow. Jacques could have picked her up with one hand, but wouldn't have dared to, for she had a dangerously sharp tongue on occasions.

"*Madame*," murmured Charles, and inclined his head. He immediately wrapped his bedgown more closely around his person. All old women were an anathema to him. He felt somehow diminished in their presence.

"No breakfast prepared," Charles pointed out, "no fires lit, no

Once Upon a Time in Paris

hot water carried upstairs – and yet you all find time for chatting and disporting yourselves." He looked from one face to the next, and then raised his voice. "Let me make myself plain. I'll suffer no repetition of this laxity. There are multitudes of unfortunates in search of employment. Henceforth each and every one of you will abide by the rules of my household – unless you want to find yourself scratching a precarious existence on the streets." He paused, letting his threat sink in. Life was difficult enough without a wife or unmarried sister to oversee servants, but for the unemployed of Paris it had become desperate. The city seethed with beggars, thieves, and whores. While most of the old Courts of Miracles – the putrid slums around the Filles-Dieu convent and the rue du Temple – had been torn down, vestiges remained. Just as before, the apparently halt, blind and hideously diseased vagrants who swarmed public places were unaccountably cured immediately they'd slunk back to their lairs there.

Nobody said a word. Nobody moved.

The air seemed to thicken and set. Both maids stood with downcast eyes. Norik's age-blotched claw hung suspended in the very act of reaching for a broom. Poucet stopped in the middle of pouring boiling water into jugs – even the steam seemed to cease its billowing upwards – the very flies clustering on a pan of humbles desisted from their sordid activities, and the cat froze, head raised, pupils dilated, scenting its prey.

A grunt from Jacques broke the spell. Grabbing the nearest rabbit, he turned his fury on the unfortunate creature, slitting its under-parts from back legs to breastbone with a sharpened blade held facing upwards. One maid began scouring a pan, the other fled to attend to the fires; Poucet followed after he'd first wrapped napkins around the hot handles of the jugs. Charles stepped back hurriedly as Jacques yanked forth a handful of the rabbit's innards. Under the table the cat inched closer, belly down, lashing its tail, and set up a low-pitched growling as the cook removed the heart and lungs from the carcass. Lifting a hatchet, Jacques chopped off the rabbit's legs then wrenched away the hindermost skin and fur with the swift motion of one removing a pair of drawers. Charles looked away as the hatchet was raised above the small neck.

"*Les lapins*," he murmured, wincing at the dull thud of steel meeting wood. One really should not have to witness such atrocities. It quite dulled the appetite.

"Rabbits, aye, as you requested," Jacques snorted. "To be served in a ragout – since I must abide by Varenne's methods – with orange juice, capers, and chives if there are any to be had this early in the year."

Charles nodded. "Good. Good."

It sounded well enough though nothing could ever match the grandeur of feasts at Versailles in those days when the Perrault brothers had the ear of the king. Every meal there ended with conserves and jellies presented in silver dishes: marmalades of *violettes*, candied pineapple, and *bouches d'anges* – ribs of lettuce in syrup, tasting so like angelica that they were called angels' mouths in spite of being aphrodisiacs. Louis had always been a prodigious eater. Even now, when dinner was served in the royal antechamber, it was said that the king never partook of less than twenty dishes and then left the table with his pockets stuffed full of candied fruits and hard-boiled eggs. Exquisite dishes, Charles thought dreamily, remembering roast beef served with smoked eel and horseradish, young turkeys cooked with raspberries, an entire wild salmon displayed on a fish-shaped block of salt.

"*Merde*," growled Jacques, wiping his bloodied hands on a rag before seizing the second rabbit. Charles beat a hasty retreat. Behind him someone snickered. Outside the door he paused, hoping to eavesdrop on their conversation, but nothing more was said.

Once Upon a Time in Paris

A few steps more, and he was standing in a large space, a type of vestibule, off which branched the stairway leading to more refined parts of the house. While familiar, this was an area he rarely visited and never lingered in, though he seemed to remember the children playing here. Disused and broken kitchen items were stored beneath the stairs and in the dense shadows to one side. Among the crates and baskets he made out a cracked *contrecoeur* – a cast iron fireplate dated 1608, with a design representing *Paix, Vérité, Miséricorde et Justice* – which he remembered in use at their previous home. There, too, was the *rouelle à corbeille pédiculée*, the ancient cooking-pot warmer, lacking a leg since his youngest son, Pierre, and a friend had used it for fencing practice, and a battered *pelle à châtaignes*, unused now, because he heartily disliked roasted chestnuts.

Behind the rest of the clutter, a spinning-wheel leaned against the wall, unused for so long – certainly not within living memory – that it was anchored to the ceiling by thick ropes of cobweb. His gaze travelled upwards, marvelling at the industry on the part of the spider and the lack of it in the under-disciplined housemaids, and stopped short at the sight of a key hanging crookedly from a nail. It was an ornate key, of a size that would fit neither the outer nor the inner doors of the main house, and he could not, for the life of him, imagine what it was doing there.

Charles was on the point of turning away, for Poucet – with his hot water and scented soaps, rubbing cloths, perfumes, pomades and the transformative magic of cosmetics – beckoned. He was almost sure – though it could not be, for that would require a light source of some sort and there was none – that the key was suddenly illuminated. He rubbed his eyes. This was what came of being denied his breakfast. One could not be too careful: such a lack might so weaken his constitution as to leave him open to any one of a dozen agues.

Despite concern for his health, Charles felt compelled to negotiate the crates of holed pans and chipped pots in order to stand directly beneath the key and squint upwards. The design was most unusual – the key's bow contained a heart surrounded by curlicues – and the faintest echo of a memory suggested it had once passed through his hands. Curious that he had no recollection of the lock it fitted. Perhaps it would come to him as the day wore on.

It was hardly possible, Lew had soon discovered, to get a decent night's sleep while lying on bare boards. Furthermore, his cloak, though of the best quality wool, still wasn't thick enough to keep out the cold night air of Paris. He lay shivering, thinking with regret of his goose-feather bed, once taken for granted – as were comfortable clothes and a full belly. This fabulously wealthy city didn't favour the poor. He'd come here seeking fame and fortune but ended up perpetually hungry, penniless, with only the clothes he stood up in. And to make matters worse, the rent being overdue, he was about to become homeless.

Lew forced himself to open his eyes and look around the tiny garret – hardly bigger than the carved chest in which he stored clothes in his bedchamber at home. This was a sorry place. The window was unglazed. The ceiling sagged at its centre, as though weighed down by despair. At intervals, plaster fell from the laths with muffled thumps. Mice ran races beneath the room's floorboards and *cafards* busied themselves in corners, though what mice or cockroaches found to sustain themselves on was beyond his understanding. To reach this dismal lodging he was forced to brave a rat-infested alley that even the daylight shunned, and approach slimy steps so steep it would be impossible to climb them without the aid of a rope attached to the wall by rusty iron brackets.

He thought wistfully of the family house, its perfect order, the splendid grounds, fertile pastures, and orchards with Normandy geese grazing beneath the gnarled old trees. Perhaps it was time to abandon his hopes, return home, bow to his father's wishes and marry the daughter of a neighbouring landowner. Angelique was a pretty enough girl, Lew supposed, pleasant, docile – and dull – but his feelings in the matter were beside the point. Since Angelique was sole heir to her father's estate the marriage would bring considerable wealth to Lew's family.

To weigh against that, he'd been offered a new commission – as a result of personal recommendation, too, which could only be a good thing – for a portrait of another old man, Monsieur Charles Perrault, a member of the French Academy. Their first meeting had not been entirely cordial. While Monsieur Perrault seemed impressed by Lew's finished picture of Monsieur Chantelou, he'd looked askance at the painter's shabby appearance, even going so far as to raise a perfumed handkerchief to his nose.

That was bad enough. It could be borne.

However, the real problem was that the modest remuneration from Monsieur Chantelou had soon been spent. Not a *sou* remained; nothing. For Lew to remain in Paris and continue striving for recognition as an artist would mean crawling to Monsieur Perrault, hat in hand, and requesting part of the agreed fee in advance. It was the only way to keep body and soul together, and at the same time have the wherewithal to purchase necessary materials. On the other hand, even if such a favour were granted, to receive so much less money at the end of the work would soon leave him penniless again.

The humiliation wasn't worth it.

It was time to concede defeat.

Lew rose and attempted to beat the dust from his clothes. Picking up his bag, he took a last look around the tiny room, slammed the door, and gingerly edged his way down the steps. There was a fountain in the square two streets away. If it wasn't too busy, he'd be able to get a drink and what passed for breakfast there before starting out on the long journey westwards.

As it turned out, only four people were clustered around the fountain, a woman who'd just finished filling her bucket, two urchins splashing each other – who soon scampered away in search of fresh mischief – and an old crone hunched inside a dark shawl.

"*Bonjour, Mère,*" murmured Lew, taking out his last hunk of stale bread. In the early morning light it looked even smaller than he remembered. Still, it was better than nothing. He leaned towards the fountain, thinking to soften it in the water, just as the old woman pushed back her shawl and extended a withered hand.

"Have pity, young sir."

Lew hesitated for the heel of bread might be all that stood between him and starvation on the road. Nevertheless he divided it in two, giving the larger portion to the old woman with a courteous bow. She devoured it so quickly – tearing at it with her toothless gums like a wild creature – that Lew broke the remaining piece in half and passed it over without a word. And after looking dubiously at what little remained, he pressed that upon her too.

"A blessing on you, young man. May everything you touch prosper."

Lew, whose stomach was rumbling a furious protest, nodded, smiled, and stared at his boots, wondering what madness had possessed him. When he looked up, the old woman had vanished. She'd disappeared so quickly he guessed she must have slid inside one of the nearby buildings, but was unable to work out which doorway had claimed her. Setting his bag upon his shoulder, he turned about, intending to make for Saint-Denis and the ancient road towards Le Havre that some called the Chaussée Jules César. With a heavy heart, Lew took his first step –

It was at that moment that something fell onto the cobblestones beside him.

Looking down, Lew saw a coin, moreover a *silver* coin, an *écu blanc* – what his grandmother used to call a silver Louis. He looked to right and left, before him, and behind, but the square was empty and unnaturally quiet. Not a bird sang. Not a dog barked. No upraised voices could be heard over the gentle song of the fountain's falling water. More importantly, no sound of pounding boots signalled someone hurrying to claim this treasure as their own. Lew scooped up the coin, and stood for a moment, elated. This was enough to cover his unpaid rent, pay for the costly materials, and still have something left over for breakfast.

It was a sign. The prodigal son would not be trudging home today. Instead, he'd stay in Paris and pursue his dream.

Even with a fire, the library was still chilly and before seating himself at the writing table, Charles stooped to warm his hands before the reluctant flames. His single Gobelin tapestry hung above the mantel, a prized possession, and justifiably expensive for even the most skilled weaver could only produce half a square *toise* of tapestry a year – hardly the measure from mid-chest to fingertips of an outstretched arm – woven in sumptuous colours from a cartoon by Le Brun, the king's own painter. Its particular appeal to Charles lay in the fact that, like a story within a story, this one showed tapestries within the tapestry; its very subject was Louis visiting Gobelin's manufactory on the banks of the Bièvre River.

Naturally, the eye was drawn to the king, standing left of centre, towering over his entourage, and to his legs, of which he had always been so vain, clad in scarlet *chausses*. Charles leaned nearer peering at the king's shoes with their ornate buckles and characteristically high heels, crimson to match the lining of the shoes' long tongues lolling against the royal shins. Whatever slurs were circulated by his detractors, the king's high heels were not worn to raise him to normal height: Louis le Grand was a tall man, unlike his brother, Philippe, the slight and pretty duc d'Orléans, depicted at his left hand. Jean-Baptiste Colbert – Charles' one-time immediate superior and the minister charged with the Augean task of swelling the king's coffers – had also been woven into the tapestry.

As always, Charles experienced a stab of disappointment that he himself never figured in any of the designs; after all, he'd composed the sixteen legends chosen for the Four Elements tapestry series in 1663. Moreover, he'd rendered the king a valuable service in safeguarding his popularity by insisting the gardens of the Tuileries remained open to the public – not to mention his suggestion that Apollo and the four horses of the sun be incorporated into the construction of the Versailles grotto as a tribute to Louis as the Sun King.

Charles grimaced. He turned, lifting the skirts of his *justaucorps* so that the rheumatic twinges in his back might be eased by the feeble fire. It seemed, in spite of his meticulous work in office, that the name of Charles Perrault was destined to remain virtually unknown. And, while certain of his literary endeavours were praised – and forgotten – others had been belittled by his enemies, dismissed as trifles penned by 'Colbert's spy' or, equally unkind, decried as composed by 'P******t, the tax collector's friend'. On inspecting the tapestry again, he comforted himself with the observation that all eyes of importance were directed to the right, to someone unseen, *unwoven*, while Louis gestured towards a newly finished piece of work held up for inspection as though soliciting a valued opinion on its suitability. Charles imagined himself quite equal to that role.

Having ascertained that the room was arranged to his liking, the recently purchased Aubusson carpet – in the new *grande mosaïque* design – lying flat and unwrinkled, the portraits straightened, stools set square with the windows, chairs placed precisely *so*, Charles finally seated himself before his bureau and inspected his writing materials, about which he was most particular.

His quill must come from a swan, never a goose. In part, this served as a tribute to the king, since these waterfowl were one of the sacred birds of Apollo, the sun god, who ascended from his birthplace in Delos riding a chariot pulled by swans. With this in mind, Louis had established a colony of swans between Paris and Versailles. Most hadn't survived for long, the Seine being both polluted and congested as a result of the vast number of vessels bringing goods into the city. The use of a swan's quill also reflected Charles' belief that geese were probably the most stupid, vicious, and ungainly creatures in creation, gathering in knots, cackling like nasty old women at their gossip – though there were certain additional reasons for disliking them so intensely. The quill must be the pinion, that is to say the first of the primary feathers. Furthermore, since he was left-handed, it must have derived from the right wing of the bird so that the curve of the feather lay over the back of his hand as he wrote, and thus did not obscure his sight line.

He took out his quill knife and ran a thumb over the blades – flat on one side, convex the other to facilitate the rounded cuts necessary for shaping, both sharpened as he had instructed – and placed it to one side of the sander and inkwell. For once Poucet had remembered to replenish both commodities. Only iron gall ink would do, purchased from Guyot's near the Pont Neuf.

Charles raised the lid and inhaled, reassured – first by the strong smell of iron, and second by the ease with which the ink flowed, that this was no inferior substitute. Finally satisfied, he took a deep breath and began to write—

> **The Shoemaker and the Devil**
> *There lived, in the city of Bordeaux, a poor shoemaker who, though skilled, could barely afford the materials of his trade, never mind enough bread to keep hunger from his door. He was a Godless man, giving to blaming others for his miserable situation. Regardless of the damning of his soul, first he cursed the priest. Then he cursed Saint Crispin and Saint Crispinian, his patron saints. Finally he cursed his Maker.*

Charles hesitated. He'd aimed to compose something refreshingly original. Now his hand hovered over the page as another dim memory surfaced. A peasant story from childhood – told to him, if he remembered correctly, by a visiting washerwoman – about a poverty-stricken shoemaker who was banished to the Forest of Retz after striking a deal with the devil. The incessantly wagging tongues of women at their menial tasks meant these tales kept travelling. Would anyone who mattered make the connection? A blot of ink fell. It was unlikely. Dismissing the old wives, he continued to write—

> *Late on the eve of All Saints' Day a swarthy stranger was seen approaching the shoemaker's hovel. Those town's folk who were still abroad scattered as he passed, for sparks flew from the cobbles at his every step and something snakelike dragged behind him, partially obscured by a voluminous black cape. The shadows thickened. A cloud of bats swooped low and the sulphurous stench of addled eggs hung on the air. A solitary*

beggar, crouching beneath the city wall, observed le Diable pass straight through the shoemaker's door but watched in vain for him to re-emerge. The hovel trembled. The church clocks failed to chime. When dawn broke, the sky was the colour of spilt blood.

In the washerwoman's story, her shoemaker was granted as many wishes as there were hairs on his head. As Charles recalled, the price was that for each self-serving wish one hair thereafter turned as stiff and scarlet as an unconfessed sin. It would be as well, he decided, to omit such a memorable detail.

Whatever bargain was struck, after that night the shoemaker's hair grew thick and coarse and low on his forehead. His eye teeth became long and pointed. Animals and small children fled from his path. It was whispered that at full moon he prowled the quaysides and lonely alleyways of the city seeking lost souls. He was never again short of the finest materials, silks and satins, velvets, calf leather. His business prospered until he employed twenty men and despite his physical shortcomings it was rumoured that women—

Charles hesitated again over the last word, afflicted by self-doubt. Leaving aside the dubious wisdom of writing on the subject of shoes, how would this tale, intended as a wry commentary on the excessive vanity of certain courtiers, measure up to the way in which the women's compositions were received, in particular those of Marie-Catherine d'Aulnoy? More importantly, could the planned end of his story be misconstrued, taken as criticism of the king? He wondered, not for the first time, whether there was any truth in the rumours that Madame d'Aulnoy had acted as a spy for Louis during her years in exile and, indeed, still did.

He mentally lined up the bare facts behind his small narrative. In the year 1659, Louis had travelled to Bordeaux, ostensibly on business connected with the forthcoming royal marriage to his double first cousin – such a plain young woman, such a hefty lump of a creature – but actually for the purpose of saying a fond farewell to his first love, the delightful Marie Mancini, one of Cardinal Mazarin's nieces, who'd been banished from court.

Resisting the urge to scratch beneath his wig – it had been deloused less than a week ago – Charles leaned back, closed his eyes and began stroking his jawbone with the feathered end of the quill. Marie Mancini had been eleven years of age when her mother brought her to Paris, an elfin creature, at the peak of perfection, the epitome of desirability. Others had mocked all seven of the 'Mazarinettes' for their dark complexions and slender figures, calling them 'dirt princesses, stinking snakes', but he'd been entranced by Marie's unblemished innocence, that pretty face, her tiny hands and, especially – how ironic in view of what was to come – by those delicate little feet. *How beautiful are thy feet with shoes, O prince's daughter!* He'd yearned to have glass slippers made for the child so that all might better observe the sweet curve of her instep, the little toes tight as rosebuds, and her nails like pink, translucent seashells. The young king had also been besotted: calf love, at once funny and tragic, and in that case unrequited. Now *there* was a fairytale with an unhappy ending. Ah well, it was a long time ago, but to get back his *conte*—

The shoemaker of Bordeaux went by the name of Nicolas Lestage and kept a shop in the rue de Parlement. In expectation of the royal visit, he stitched a breathtakingly beautiful pair of shoes for the king, honey-coloured silk richly ornamented with embroidered fleur-de-lys, burnished with gold, and lined with azure blue taffeta. It was whispered that the devil had a hand in the gift for they were a perfect fit *though Lestage had never taken a single measurement.* But there was more to it than that: Louis was bewitched by the shoes. They took the young king's mind off his farewells and reconciled him to marriage with the ugly princess. He even wore them to his wedding.

Lestage's diabolical triumph came four years later when he made the king a pair of boots – of all things *des bottes sans couture*, boots without seams – confirming the rumours of him being in league with the devil. How was it possible? Were they made from an elephant's trunk? Or fashioned from the legs of a hanged man? Or from the neck of a forest hind? Were they made of some new fabric that could be blown like glass? Nobody could work out how it was done. No matter: Louis commissioned a coat of arms for his newly ennobled royal cobbler, a boot surmounted by a crown on a blue background adorned with fleur-de-lys.

The name of Lestage's shop in Bordeaux was *Loup Botté*, Wolf in Boots, and, thought Charles, making a note of it in the margin, as everyone knows, the wolf represents the devil....

Charles laid down the quill and massaged his aching wrist. The room was still a little chilly, his breath lay on the air like a cloud, and he suddenly desired a jug of hot chocolate. It was one of the small luxuries he enjoyed, though many in Paris had turned against the stuff, in part due to the rumours. One had to be careful. Louis' first wife, Maria Theresa, had been passionate about chocolate. She'd brought with her a Spanish maid whose sole function it was to prepare this royal drink. Maria Theresa drank so much, it was said, that it burnt her blood and in 1664 she'd given birth to a chocolate-coloured daughter, who was speedily despatched to a convent.

And yet, in spite of her Spanish maid – or so the gossips would have it – Fagan, that vile little hunchbacked doctor to the royal family, had managed to hasten the queen's death by slipping poison into her cup. Charles shook his head. On that matter he had his own, unspoken, suspicions: Fagan and Madame de Maintenon were *amigos como cerdos,* as they say in Spain, *copains comme cochons* – tight as pigs, thick as thieves. The man was besotted by her. She'd ensured the physician obtained his prestigious position; he, in turn, enabled the ageing Maintenon to step into the place vacated by the queen. Yes, when it came to poisoning, there was usually a woman involved.

This time, Poucet answered his summons almost immediately – not a difficult task, since he occupied an uncomfortably hard chair placed next to the library door for that purpose – and began to prepare the chocolate in plain sight. Hardly had he begun when a commotion outside had the fool gawping through the window.

"What is it now?" Charles demanded. His irritation turned to alarm as the noises grew louder – yells and the sounds of running feet, followed by a thud that could only be something hitting a wall. "Is it a fugitive from the law?" He'd long lived in terror of the poor of Paris rising against their betters. "Is it robbers?" He looked in alarm at his precious tapestry. "Are we being attacked?"

"I d-don't know," breathed Poucet, gnawing at his knuckles, "b-b...." He gulped. "B-b-b—"

"Oh, *bordel il suffit juste de le cracher!*" bawled Charles. "For crying out loud, man, just spit it out!"

"B-but they're all out there, ch-chasing s-something."

"All? And chasing what?" Charles limped across the room and peered over his servant's shoulder in time to see Jacques, puce-faced and breathing hard, one hand supporting his great stomach, the other clutching a cleaver, disappear round the corner of the building. Behind him came old Norik, holding up her skirts and moving faster than he would have deemed possible. Bringing up the rear were the maids, clinging to each other and convulsed with laughter. "Chasing what?" he repeated.

A moment later Charles had his answer: the kitchen cat

appeared, making its second lap of the grounds, its jaws clamped round one of the unfortunate rabbits he'd seen butchered earlier. The cat was gaining ground in spite of its heavy burden. One leap, two, and it gained the roof of the wood store, from thence to the stable where it calmly washed its paws and chops before surveying the surroundings with an arrogant air as a prelude to dining.

"The c-cat," Poucet smirked as the kitchen procession hove into view for the second time, "all that f-fuss and it was j-just the thieving r-ratter."

They both watched as Jacques slashed at the air with his cleaver and let fly a stream of curses, before turning his rage on the three women. A shrill howl rose on the still morning air, and the sound returned Charles to the moment earlier when he'd stood staring up at the key. He shook his head, unable to see the connection.

"My chocolate, if you please," said Charles. "After that, you may go."

He considered the cat while sipping his delightful beverage, flavoured with cinnamon and a dash of cream. A clever animal, it had to be admitted, and cunning as any courtier: fawning one minute, clawing the hand that fed it the next. Certainly, in that sense, he was a cat fit for a king. The creature was a large and singularly ill-favoured animal with fishbone whiskers, rag-edged bat ears, and piebald legs that had once been described as resembling ermine boots by one more kindly disposed towards it than Jacques must be.

And with that thought, the pieces of the puzzle fell into place.

Charles nodded. There was only one person who could have described the cat's oddly blotched legs thus, just as there was only one lock the antiquated key could fit: that of the huge double doors leading to rooms closed up and abandoned several years previously, following certain unfortunate occurrences within the family. As a kitten, the ratter had accidentally been shut in there. For hours the entire household was forced to cover their ears against the animal's eldritch caterwauling as the din ricocheted along passages, creating unearthly echoes, without leading anyone to its source. This didn't explain why the key had been hung in such an odd place, unless it was a misguided effort to avoid a repetition of the noise.

And that reminded him – he still hadn't made a fair copy of that other tale, one about an equally clever cat.

Charles looked over his shoulder, checking that he was alone. Still not satisfied, he opened the library door a crack, making sure that Poucet had returned to his chair before unlocking a drawer and bringing forth a crumpled sheet of grubby paper, smoothing it out with a care which almost suggested reverence.

Le Maître Chat
Un meunier ne laissa pour tous biens à trois enfants qu'il avait, his mill, his donkey, and his cat. The division of goods didn't take long, neither notary nor attorney had to be called in. They would have soon swallowed up the whole pitiful inheritance. The eldest received the mill, the second son took the donkey, and the youngest was left with only the cat. The latter was inconsolable....

After reading it through twice, Charles finally decided *The Master Cat* was a tale not to be improved, though perhaps adding an alternative title, *Le Chat Botté – Puss in Boots* – would provide a witty allusion to the Bordeaux shoemaker's establishment. The work possessed a lightness of touch, liveliness – the words fairly danced along the page – he would go so far as to say it was touched by genius.

His hand hovered – surely a little touch here and there would not come amiss – perhaps a small moral in verse added to the end. Something along the lines of

> *However great the advantage*
> *Of enjoying a rich inheritance*
> *Passed down from father to son,*
> *Usually for young people*
> *Hard work and competence*
> *Are better than bequeathed property*

After a moment's thought, he crossed through *people* and substituted *men*. Even then he considered his work unfinished for – this being a *conte de fées* – to please the ladies, it should speak of love. Charles smiled to himself. Perhaps

> *If a humble miller's son can so quickly*
> *Win the heart of a beautiful princess,*
> *So much so that he is gazed at by her with eyes of longing,*
> *It may be because clothes, good looks, and youth*
> *Should never be discounted as a means of inspiring love.*

He conceded that the latter moral needed a little polishing, but there was still time to perfect it and make a fair copy of the entire composition before midday. Once that was done, his original version would be returned to its drawer and locked away for safe-keeping.

Luncheon, Charles conceded, had been superb. The rabbit flesh melted in the mouth, a fine king's cheese, sent direct from Meaux, was at a perfect stage of ripeness, and afterwards there was a frangipane *tourte* of which he was inordinately fond. Charles had not stinted himself. It was difficult to resume work. Perhaps he'd dozed a little. The next thing he knew, Poucet was standing at his elbow, coughing gently.

"Sh-shall I b-bring a side t-table, sir?"

Charles opened his eyes and closed his mouth. In front of him was a salver bearing the restorative he took mid-afternoon when his energy flagged. "No, no. I'll drink it now." He reached for the silver goblet, took a small sip, and asked, as was his habit: "What news?"

"P-poor B-Blanche...." Poucet attempted to lean against the writing table, but straightened abruptly in response to Charles' outraged glare.

"Who the devil—"

"B-Blanche, she's the l-littlest k-kitchen m-maid, threatened to l-leave your service after J-Jacques b-boxed her ears."

"Oh, he did – and on what account?"

Poucet smirked. "Ap-p-parently, she l-laughed too l-loudly at the sight of him chasing the c-cat."

"An empty threat, no doubt, for where else would she go?" Charles yawned. He drained the goblet and considered sending the manservant for another. Perhaps not: there was more to be accomplished today. "The woes of a kitchen wench are hardly newsworthy. Is nothing else happening in the world?" What he really wanted, but would never ask a servant for, was news of his sons – Charles-Samuel, so like his grandfather, old Pierre Perrault, who took his fledgling career as a lawyer very seriously and rarely made time to call, and the baby of the family, young Pierre, who hadn't been home for two days, the rapscallion.

"They're s-saying," Poucet hesitated. "It s-seems your f-friend M-Madame B-Bédier d-died unexpectedly and—"

Charles shuffled himself upright. "Marie-Violette Bédier?"

The manservant nodded. "The v-very l-large l-lady who was so p-proud of her y-y—"

"*Yellow*, yes, yes. Get on with it."

"Y-yellow hair that she r-refused to p-powder—"

"False vanity: it was still a wig." A wig, furthermore, that did nothing to remedy those monstrously equine features. Marie-Violette was hardly a friend, though she'd been a constant visitor in his first months of widowerhood, professing a desire to feast her eyes on baby Pierre's beauty, while openly befriending his other children and their nurse. At the time he'd suspected the woman of – well, never mind, it was years ago. He'd not been in the market for a new wife. "Madame Bédier was a dreadful woman. Rumour had it that she was bald as an egg."

"B-bald?" Poucet sniggered.

Charles nodded. "As an egg," he repeated, adding hurriedly: "Of course I never saw her naked pate with my own eyes." Madame Bédier was no great loss. An upstart widow from the provinces with more money than taste, she'd inveigled her way into the salons by slavish adoration of the self-satisfied Catherine Bernard who, incidentally, had a great deal to answer for after that pronouncement on *contes de fées* – 'the adventures should always be implausible, the emotions always natural', indeed. Pah! As for Marie-Violette's own ludicrous efforts at literature, *she* resorted to outright plagiarism, even stooping to— A small frisson of fear interrupted his train of thought. "What was the cause of her death?"

Poucet shrugged. "I h-heard it was s-something she ate."

"Poison?" Charles sat bolt upright, remembering the terror of a few years back during *L'affaire des poisons* when really one was afraid to eat or drink anything. His eyes widened. "Poison."

He peered into the dregs remaining in his goblet. Were those small deposits natural to the wine or something more life-threatening? He clutched his throat. Perhaps it was time to give up wine altogether. Proverbs 23, he told himself sharply: '*Look not thou upon the wine when it is red, when it giveth his colour in the cup, when it moveth itself aright. At the last it biteth like a serpent, and stingeth like an adder.... They have stricken me, thou shalt say, and I was not sick: they have beaten me, and I felt it not.'* Charles comforted himself with the realisation that the writer had continued: *'When shall I awake? I will seek it yet again.'* Then he recalled something worse.

During that terrible time, there'd been a soldier who claimed he could infuse a silver goblet with toad poison so that whoever drank from the vessel would die. Belot – that was the fellow's name – son of the evil sorceress La Bosse, so he probably knew what he was talking about. According to him, the method was simple: take a toad, whip it, force arsenic down its throat and then kill it in the vessel you wanted to poison. Charles flung his goblet back onto the salver, where it toppled onto its side. It was a beautiful piece of work, the rim decorated with leaping dolphins to honour the birth of the Grand Dauphin; what a pity he'd never be able to use it again.

"Are you quite w-well, sir?" enquired Poucet.

"Did you pour the wine yourself? Good. Good. But has my goblet been in anyone else's hands?"

The little manservant shook his head. "It's k-kept l-locked in the d-dining-room cupboard, with the r-rest of the silver."

"And do we know what poisoned Madame Bédier?"

"Sir, you m-misunderstood me – as f-far as anyone knows no p-poison of any k-kind was involved. It's widely b-believed she d-died of a surfeit." He coughed. "They say her ap-p-petite was—"

"Prodigious," finished Charles. Like a horse, he thought.

"Ap-p-parently, a c-countrywoman brought ap-p-ples to her door."

"Selling apples at this time of year? They'd be wrinkled as prunes." Unless, he thought grimly, they'd been stolen from the ice chambers at Versailles or some other noble estate.

Once Upon a Time in Paris

"That's the s-strange thing," said Poucet. "These were said to l-look f-freshly p-picked, the d-dew still on them. The s-story I heard was that the ap-p—" His mouth worked. "Ap-p-p—"

Charles sighed. "Apples."

"Yes. They're saying they were so b-beautiful – r-red one side, y-yellow the other, p-perfectly m-matched in size and shape – that M-Madame B-Bédier's cook turned them away, b-believing them enchanted, at which the woman began to s-sob and w-wail, calling on G-God and all his angels to b-bear w-witness that she was no s-s-s—"

"Sorceress?" Charles sighed again.

"No witch, yes. In the end M-Marie-Violette c-came to see w-what all the f-fuss was about. And the seller t-took one of her ap-p-ples and cut it through the m-middle. 'W-watch while I eat one half,' she said, 'and w-when you see f-for yourself there's no enchantment, you c-can t-try the other.' I heard M-Marie-Violette took the r-red half, said it was the m-most d-delicious ap-p-p-p..." he gulped, took a breath, and finished, "...*fruit* she'd ever t-tasted, and g-gobbled the entire b-basketful." Poucet lowered his voice. "They s-say she seemed to choke on the l-last one and b-began to f-foam at the mouth a l-little, and afterwards c-complained of s-stomach ache, but what I say is – so would a p-pig after g-guzzling down, well, they say it was almost a *minot* of ap-p-ples."

"That's three *boisseaux*," murmured Charles, relieved, even as he tried to visualise such a quantity; unless he was mistaken a *boisseau* measure held over twenty pints. "She was a glutton indeed." He righted his goblet and pushed the salver in Poucet's direction. "I'll take another, if you please." Picking up his quill, he bent over the second moral. That last line was still proving troublesome, but he was determined to perfect it before making the last of his thrice-daily inspections of the garden and grounds.

41

The Perrault residence was a fine big house, Lew thought as made his way along the rue de l'Estrapade – though one would expect no less from a member of the French Academy – and the air was mercifully fresh considering it was a scant ten minutes' walk from one of the most stench-ridden parts of the city. Lew was about to approach the front entrance when, with a wry smile, he remembered his recently demoted status and instead retraced his steps, heading for the rear of the property, parts of which seemed to have been built hard against what little remained of the old city defences, perhaps with an eye to economy.

Across the courtyard two young women – housemaids judging by their drab clothing – lolled against a wall, passing a clay pipe between them and drinking the smoke as might a couple of sailors. His painter's eye took in the scene: one maid was handsome, high-coloured, with glossy dark ringlets, while the other might have been her antithesis, a pasty-faced young creature with lank, tow-coloured hair and watery blue eyes. A battle-scarred black-and-white cat emerged from an outbuilding and minced towards them, stopping dead as it registered Lew's presence. As if at a signal, both women turned to face him. Only the fair-haired maid managed a timid smile; the other folded her arms over her chest and stared.

"What's that you're selling?" she demanded, eyeing his bag and the linen canvas tucked under his arm. Lew shook his head.

"Nothing, I'm—"

"Whatever it is, you're wasting your time, so clear off before—"

Lew raised his voice above the curt dismissal. "I'm not selling anything, Mademoiselle. I've come to ask if—"

"It's no good looking for charity here. Better scram before he," she jerked her thumb towards what Lew took to be the door to the kitchens, "takes the fire irons to your back."

Lew produced his most cheerful voice. "Mademoiselle."

"I won't tell you again, scrounger."

"Ladies, my name is Lew le Sauvage – a name with which the whole of Paris will soon be familiar. I am an artist, here to deliver the materials necessary for commencing work on Monsieur Charles Perrault's portrait tomorrow. Is there some corner where I might store these things overnight?" Whatever they came up with, it would be far safer than taking anything saleable back to his filthy lodgings.

"Ho," said the dark-haired maid, tapping out the pipe and stowing it away in a small leather pouch, "you've got a pretty face and a posh voice for a painter."

"Artist," murmured Lew. His mild correction was met with a shrug.

"My name's Blanche," volunteered her companion, "and my friend here is Escarlatta." She beckoned with a small hand, red and chapped from scrubbing, "I'll take you to Madame Norik. Perhaps she'll find you a space."

Lew started to follow, almost falling over the cat as it wove between his legs, leaving him startled, but not surprised, by Escarlatta's laughter. Her merriment died away as an elderly woman appeared in the doorway, a tiny, black-clad creature with a fearsome expression that reminded Lew of that habitually adopted by the harridan ruling over female servants in his father's house.

"Madame," began Blanche. The tiniest of hand movements silenced her.

"What's this?" Norik's expression changed to one of distaste as she looked Lew up and down. "No beggars here."

Lew stepped back sharply. "Madame," he bowed, shifting the canvas beneath his other arm, "tomorrow I start work on a portrait of Monsieur Perrault. I need—"

"You're the artist he spoke of?" Norik sniffed. Her sharp eyes lingered on his hands, which were in better shape than the rest of him. To Lew's surprise she reached out and fingered a fold of his cloak. It was old-fashioned by Parisian standards, but perhaps she appreciated its quality. Certainly her voice softened. "Tomorrow, that was the arrangement. Why are you here today?"

"I need a place to store my painting materials."

Norik pursed her lips. "You'd better come in."

Lew followed, ducking his head to clear the low doorframe. The regular *clack-clack* of her footsteps caused him to glance down. She wore wooden sabots, such as many countrywomen still wore at home, but hers were so dark with age they might have been coated with pitch. A second look showed him they were richly carved with a design of coils and spirals. He would have commented on the workmanship had it not been for the blast of heat – accompanied by a wealth of savoury aromas – that welcomed him into the kitchen. Two greedy in-breaths later, Lew saw the devil himself rise from before the stove – a massive man, shaped like a Bordeaux wine barrel that had sprouted limbs, topped by a bald head fringed with flame-coloured hair atop a complexion veering dangerously close to purple – and let fly a torrent of invective that seemed to be directed at the ceiling. Lew backed away, scuttling after Norik, who'd ignored the outburst and continued walking.

He caught up with her in a shadowed alcove that seemed little better than a dumping ground for discarded household items. With no proper workshop as yet, Lew had no option but to buy an expensive, ready-prepared canvas and now he anxiously smoothed its chalk gesso surface: the finish was brittle, one careless knock and it was liable to crack.

"It'll be safe enough here," she said, as though reading his thoughts. After carefully stowing his materials behind an old fireplate, Lew straightened to find the old lady staring fixedly at him. "How old are you, young man?" And when she'd been answered: "What did you say your name was?"

He shifted uncomfortably, stumbling over the lie. "Lew le *Sauvage*, Madame."

"Do you have a wife?"

Lew smiled and shook his head. "I do not, Madame. Time enough for marriage when I've made my way in the world." He started to turn away, but Norik nimbly positioned herself in front of him.

"And where are you from, Monsieur le Sauvage? You don't sound like a native of Paris. Who are your parents? Does your father follow the same profession?"

"I was born in Normandy, Madame. My mother died some years ago. My father is a...." He dealt the old lady a half-truth. "He's a farmer." She nodded tepid approval. "This is a fine house," he added quickly, hoping to change the subject. "Is the Perrault family a large one?"

Norik narrowed her eyes. "What's that to you?" The atmosphere turned hostile. "Who sent you here?"

"Nobody *sent* me," Lew replied, taken aback by her outraged expression. "On the contrary, I was sent *for*. After successfully executing a small commission for Monsieur Chantelou – one of your master's colleagues, I believe – he recommended me and my skills. I thought you understood that it was Monsieur Perrault himself who summoned me."

"Very well," she said, apparently satisfied, "but only Monsieur Perrault's commands concern you. Anything else here is none of your business whatsoever."

With that, Norik shepherded him back into the kitchen, where Lew was confronted by a slight fellow with wide eyes and a nervous smile. "This is Poucet," she announced. "He's the master's valet. He'll show you what's what tomorrow. We'll expect you at daybreak. There's the door. I'll bid you *au revoir*."

Lew mumbled a polite response but didn't move. In his short absence the central table had been laden with food: roast meat, pies and tarts, a generous wedge of king's cheese, and a jug of wine, filled right to the brim. It proved impossible to tear his eyes away. His mouth watered.

"By the spindle of Queen Pédauque!" he exclaimed, attempting to keep his tone jocular, "that's enough food for an infantry. How many are you feeding here?"

A chill silence followed. Little Poucet stared at him, his expression that of a startled rabbit. Escarlatta hid a smirk, but Norik's mouth tightened.

"More questions," she snapped. "You're a very nosy young man."

"Just damnably hungry," Lew said humbly. An entire loaf of coarse bread bolted down earlier hadn't satisfied his longing for a proper meal, and the admission was out before there was a chance to think better of it. His cheeks flamed. He eyed the door. To make matters worse, the monstrous cook slowly turned his great head – now covered by a greasy black wig – skewering Lew with a gaze that pinned him to the wall.

"Hun-gry?" The ogre mouthed the syllables disdainfully, as if it was a word in a foreign tongue. "Hun-gry?" Lew shrank as he lumbered forward, looming over him.

"No, really, I—"

"Hungry. *Pardieu*, I'd be asking questions too, if I ever found myself in such a sorry state." The cook let out a great thunderclap of laughter and Lew's knees buckled as an arm with the girth of a whole smoked ham descended on his shoulders. "Set your backside down, my lad. You'll eat well this afternoon."

"Not if the master hasn't said so," protested Norik.

"Let the lad be, woman. Feeding him won't mean any skin off your nose or anyone else's. Since our master's too grand to have leftovers served up to him, there's plenty to go round." The cook began sharpening a carving knife. "*Of pleasures the chief, is a fine piece of beef.* Lew will be one of us for as long as he takes making his picture."

"It won't do at all, Jacques," insisted Norik. "I shall have words with the master about this, see if I don't." Seizing a tray piled high with food, she clattered from the room, leaving Lew afraid he'd made an enemy.

"Don't take no notice of her," commanded Jacques. He tapped Poucet on the shoulder. "Shove along the bench, *gosse*. There you go, young Leonardo, squeeze in next to the nipper."

Lew hastily complied. Immediately in front of him was a basket containing a mountain of good white bread rather than the gritty stuff – *mesteil* they called it here, a grey mix of rye and barley and God alone knew what else, with only a token nod at wheat – he'd unwillingly become accustomed to. Taking out his table knife, he polished it against his thigh, reminding himself neither to snatch nor ask further questions about the Perrault household. He quickly discovered that Jacques' cooking was too good to waste time on conversation. Keeping his head down, Lew simply ate and drank whatever was put in front of him, rising – a trifle unsteadily – an hour later to take his leave.

Outside, a few snowflakes fell. His little sister – Oh, how he missed her – always swore snowstorms were caused by Old Dame Habonde turning her feather mattress and shaking her bedcovers. Lew wrapped his cloak around himself in an attempt to keep out the gnawing cold and almost went back, hoping the genial Jacques would permit him to spend the night close to the embers of the kitchen fire. Instead, he jingled his few remaining coins in his pocket and – deciding to see what the taverns along the rue

Mouffetard could offer – went on his way, stopping only to observe a curious piece of theatre being played out in the road immediately in front of the Perrault residence, before turning sharply into the rue Contrescarpe, picking his way between the piles of filth, his head once more filled with dreams of fame and fortune.

Charles stood at the front entrance of the Hôtel Perrault, noting that the weather had deteriorated. This morning he'd sensed spring on the air, now leaden clouds were billowing in from the east, borne on an icy wind that was rapidly growing in viciousness. The temptation was to scurry back inside and stay close to the fireside, but he'd promised himself to walk the property's boundaries, and at least a little further – conditions permitting – three times a day until the problem was resolved.

After blowing on his hands, he poked his cane into the small crevices at each side of the steps. Having discovered nothing, he made a slow circuit of the courtyard and garden, before stepping out onto the pavement and measuring precisely seven times seven paces in the direction of rue des Postes – examining the ground carefully as he went – before turning back and walking an equal distance towards the rue Saint Jacques.

On his return, there being no carriages, Charles trudged wearily along the centre of the road, avoiding the plentiful heaps of manure while peering to left and right, straining his eyes against the fading light. He was so deeply preoccupied by his dispiriting quest that the unearthly sounds of things unguessed, unseen, but nevertheless rapidly growing nearer, became for a moment the crying of lost souls, the Wild Hunt, the *Mesnée d'Hellequin*. Raising his eyes to the heavens, Charles saw it was only a skein of wild geese overhead, flying unnaturally low, heading for better feeding grounds. And as they flew, so they began to shed feathers....

But the feathers continued to fall long after the geese had passed by. With a sudden sick lurch at the pit of his stomach, Charles saw the swirling, whirling scraps of white not as feathers but as tiny pieces of paper, each hardly bigger than his thumbnail, covered with letters that never in ten thousand years could be rejoined into words, let alone sentences. After a few moments of ungainly lurching and reaching, he managed to catch a few of the fragments, which immediately melted against his hands. "Snow," he said aloud, watching as the wind, now howling in triumph, now shrieking with derision, swept the snowflakes up and over the rooftops. "They're nothing but snow."

Charles plodded towards his door, only then noticing a cloak-swathed figure, partially concealed by the building's shadow. It was a man, judging by his height as he walked briskly away, and moreover one who must have watched the entire leaping and snatching performance. This shouldn't be happening, Charles thought miserably. Nobody can understand the sense in the things I do – continue, and I'll become a public laughing stock or, even worse, find myself packed off to end my days, four to a bed, in the Hôtel-Dieu or some other madhouse. But what can I do to change this miserable situation? What can I do?

Chapter Three

It's almost midnight when the witch creeps in and stands over my bed, listening to me breathe. "Still can't sleep, *ma petite?*"

She squeezes my arm, as if judging its plumpness. I sit up quickly, remembering a picture glimpsed in childhood of a hungry witch pushing live children into her bubbling cauldron. "No, I long for ink-black darkness. Tonight the moon's bright enough to read by."

"Ah, she's coming up to the full. A dangerous time – men are readier to draw their blades on such nights as these. Back home, L'Ankou will be sharpening his scythe on a human thigh bone, but you're safe enough hidden away up here, my dear. Let me hang a cloth over the shutters to keep out the moonlight. There we are. That's better. Shall I bring you a draught of poppy in milk and honey?"

"In a while, Granny – first tell me about your L'Ankou."

"He's the collector of souls, my turtledove, an ugly old thing – tall and thin as an oak sapling, with long white hair but," the witch sets down the candlestick, "neither eyes, nor nose, nor a mouth. Plague and dearth live hand-in-glove with him." She sighs. "And I dare say he'll be coming for me soon enough. As a child, many and many was the time I heard his cart trundling along the track – *skreek, skreek* went the wheels – straight through the village in the dead of night, *skreek, skreek*. Some swore it was only owls screeching, others that it was cats making their wedding music.

They were all wrong." With that, the witch wraps her shawl more securely around her shoulders. "And I tell you this, L'Ankou's never short of work, especially when the moon shows her whole face to us." She pauses. "Of course, it's only at full moon that wolves leave the forests to prowl city streets in search of fresh meat."

"Into *cities?* Surely not."

"Yes, indeed – Lyon, Bordeaux, Toulouse, Marseille, even mighty Paris – they've all had their share of wicked wolves."

I can't help laughing. "Come now, Mamie, even you can't believe wolves would dare enter Paris."

"Maybe and maybe not…. And if not, then it wasn't always so. You must have heard of Courtaux the Red?"

"No. Was he a barbarian?"

The witch shakes her head. "*Un loup énorme* – perhaps the largest wolf the world has ever seen." She draws up a chair. "At the shoulder, Courtaux was three times the size of an ordinary wolf, let me tell you. His teeth were longer than a man's hand and his pelt was the colour of a cardinal's robe. Some say his eyes glowed like live embers." At that, the witch lowers her voice. I can't help shivering and sliding under the covers. "Many and many years ago, a bitterly cold winter night it was, and almost full moon, just as now, Courtaux led his wolfpack through a chink in the old walls of Paris, right into the heart of the king's own city. Oh, if you could have heard the howling and growling, the snapping and snarling, crunching and munching, the cries and the screams…."

Up come the bedclothes, right over my nose, only leaving my eyes uncovered. I want to shout 'stop!', but it turns into such a feeble squeak that she doesn't hear.

"Forty good Christians those wolves killed and ate, all seasoned with fresh snow. The people of Paris were terrified. Who could blame them when the streets were running with blood? And nothing could be done. Nothing could be done. Until," the witch pauses to cross herself, "a brave band of men armed only with knives and sticks, faith and prayers, trapped the wolfpack in front of the cathedral of Notre-Dame where Our Lady herself intervened, turning every last one to stone. I'm told you can see many of them to this day, lurking behind the demons waiting for the Last Judgement. Some years ago, I made the pilgrimage to see for myself, but the wolves are high up and even then my eyes weren't what they once were."

"All that must have been a very long time ago."

"It was in the times before the olden times, my dear."

"These days—"

"Oh, there are many sorts of wolves," says the witch, picking up a discarded stocking and casting about for its mate. "There is *always* a wolf. And there always will be since his form changes with the passing years. Anyway, however well any city is guarded from what lies *without*, still the bzou ventures forth from his fine house *within* at full moon in search of tender young prey."

"You mean the *loup-garou* – a werewolf!"

"Laugh if you must, my dear, the old stories don't lie. And I know one about just such a wolf. But it's very late – are you ready for sleep yet? Or shall I fetch you that draught of poppy?"

"Oh Granny, I'd rather hear your story first."

"Very well, though I'm sure it won't be new to you." The witch settles herself more comfortably, pulling a fold of my counterpane over her bony old knees. "It goes like this—

This woman had finished her baking, so she asks her daughter to take a fresh loaf and a pot of butter to her grandmother who lived in a cottage on the other side of the forest. The girl sets off, and on her way she meets a bzou. Oh, and he's a charmer, to be sure, all over velvet and lace, primped and pomaded, smelling like a garden of flowers.

'Where are you going?' asks the bzou, with a smile. 'And what's that you're carrying?'

'I'm going to my grandmother's house,' says the girl, smiling right back, 'and I'm taking her this fresh-baked bread and a pot of butter.'

'Which path will you take?' the bzou asks, 'the Path of Needles or the Path of Pins?'

'I'll take the Path of Pins,' says the girl, because that was the only one she knew.

'Why then, I'll take the Path of Needles, and we'll see who gets there first.'

Well, the girl sets off and the bzou sets off, but the bzou reaches the grandmother's cottage first. He goes straight in, does away with the old woman and eats her up, flesh, blood, and bone – except for a small slice of her flesh that he puts on a platter in the pantry, and except for a few drops of her blood that he drains into a bowl. Then the bzou dresses in grandmother's cap and shawl and climbs into her bed."

The witch raises the candlestick and peers at me. "Are you still awake, *ma chère?* You know, the rest of this tale can wait until tomorrow."

"I'm still not sleepy. Please go on."

"*Bien*, if you're sure. So—

When the girl arrives, the bzou calls out: 'Lift the latch and come in, my child.'

'Grandmother,' says the girl, 'mother sent me here with a new loaf and some butter.'

'Put them in the pantry, child. Are you hungry?'

'Yes, I am, grandmother.'

'Then cook the meat that you'll find on the shelf. Are you thirsty?'

'Yes I am, grandmother.'

'Then drink the bowl of wine you'll find on the shelf beside it, child.'

As the girl cooks and eats the meat, a little cat outside the door cries: 'What a hussy is she who eats the flesh of her own grandmother!'

'Throw your shoe at that noisy cat,' says the bzou, and the girl does.

As she drinks the wine, a little bird cries at the window: 'What a hussy is she who drinks the blood of her own grandmother!'

'Throw your other shoe at that noisy bird,' says the bzou, and the girl does.

When she's finished her meal, the bzou says: 'You must be cold and tired from your journey, child. Take off your clothes, come to bed, and I shall warm you up.'

'Where shall I put my apron, grandmother?'

'Throw it on the fire, child, you won't need it anymore.'

'Where shall I put my bodice, grandmother?'

'Throw it on the fire, you won't need it anymore.'

Well, the girl repeats the same question for her skirt, her petticoat, and her hose. Each time the bzou gives the same answer, and the girl throws each item onto the flames. As she comes to the bed, she says to him: 'Grandmother, how hairy you are!'

'The better to keep you warm, my child.'

'Grandmother, what big arms you have!'

'The better to hold you close, my child.'

Once Upon a Time in Paris

'Grandmother, what big ears you have!'
'The better to hear you with, my child.'
'Grandmother, what sharp teeth you have!'
'The better to eat you with, my child. Now come and lie beside me.'
'But first I must go outside and relieve myself.'
'Do it in the bed, my child.'
'No, I must go outside,' the girl says cleverly, for now she knows that it's the bzou who is lying in grandmother's bed.
'Go outside, if you must,' says the bzou, 'but mind you come back again quick as you can. I'll tie your ankle with a rope so I know just where you are.' So he ties a rope to her ankle, but as soon as the girl goes outside she unties the rope and ties it to a plum tree. After a while the bzou grows impatient and calls out: 'Haven't you finished yet, my child?' When no one answers, he calls again. 'Are you making a dung heap, my child? Are you making a dung heap?' Still no answer comes and he leaps from the bed, follows the rope, and finds her gone.
The bzou gives chase, and soon the girl can hear him on the path just behind her. She runs and runs until she reaches a river that's swift and deep and dangerous."

Even though I really want to hear the end of this tale, I can no longer keep my eyes open. The witch's voice grows slower, quieter, until it seems to be coming from a far distance and I sink beneath the sound of it into a pitch-dark forest where a young girl runs and runs and runs….

Today the ogre comes very early, bearing flowers and wearing a smile. To begin with he talks pleasantly enough about things going on in the world, distant battles, comic fashions, news of deaths and births…and weddings, which brings him, as usual, to marriage. Wrapped in my favourite coverlet, my hair still hanging loose, I stare straight ahead, hardly listening to his pledges and promises, until a small yawn escapes me. At that, the ogre clenches his fists, stamps his foot, and sits in grim silence for a very long time. I hate him. I hate him. Hate him.

As for me, I think about the witch's bzou tale, watch the clouds – for a few moments a splendid castle hangs outside my window, with turrets and conical towers resembling those of the Château d'Ussé, but then it collapses into a mountain range, breaks up and begins to drift away – and wonder why my jackdaw, Reims, has not visited me for almost a week. Suddenly, the ogre makes me jump by blowing his nose very loudly. Sniff, sniff, sniff, he mops his eyes and leaves without another word. I can hear him descending the stone steps. Sniff, sniff, sniff, down and round he goes, thump, thump, round and down – my hate nipping at his ankles – the sound of his footfalls growing ever fainter until it becomes the merest whisper cut off by the faraway boom which is the stout door at the tower's base slamming shut.

The witch immediately appears, popping out from her cubbyhole like the demon from an infant's *diable en boîte*. She peers around the room, examining every surface to see what gifts have been left today. Her greedy little eyes alight first on the *manus Christi* – lozenges concocted of sugar, rosewater and ground pearls, whispered to be efficacious in dispelling women's fidfads, and for that reason I shall grind them underfoot by and by – and then on the flowers.

"Ah, *des violettes!*" She sticks her nose into the basket. "Oh! Here, smell these violets, my dear. Their sweet perfume fair lifts the spirits, and from the look of you, that's just what you need."

"No. Throw them away."

"But think of the cost of them. Mark my words – these were grown coddled-up warm inside a glasshouse." She puts her bony hand on my shoulder. "Why the sad face?"

"My jackdaw no longer comes to the window, Mamie."

"That's no reason to weep."

I scrub at my eyes. "Everyone deserts me. Because I was born like this, my parents forsook me. Even my good fairy went away."

The witch pats my hand. "Your old granny is still here."

"What if," I can barely get the words out, yesterday my future seemed so certain, and yet now....

The ugly princess waited and waited. Years went by and her hair grew so long that it wrapped itself twice around the tower, and a great moat surrounded it, formed entirely from her tears.

"What if the fairy lied and the one I'm waiting for doesn't even exist?"

The ugly princess waited and waited. A hundred years or more passed. Still the prince didn't come. A great forest grew up, hiding the lonely tower from the world. No one remembered the ugly princess, except for old grannies who told her story on cold winter nights, crouched close to the fire. In time, the tower fell and the forest died, but the ugly princess continued to wait until she too crumbled into dust and was carried away on the four winds along with her stories.

The witch clicks her tongue. "Isn't that exactly what I've been saying all along? Listen to me, girl, for once in your life. Believe it or not, as you wish, but I was once a pretty young maiden dreaming of a handsome prince that never came." She dabs my cheeks with her apron. "And I didn't sit around waiting, let me tell you. No, not me – I went out looking high and low for him."

I risk a sideways glance at her. "And still you never found him?"

The witch shakes her head. Of course she *is* a witch, and must always have been so, but is that any worse than an ugly princess?

"In the end – like every other girl since the world was new – I settled for what was available. And that is what you must do."

"No—"

"Yes, I say *yes*. Youth is soon spent. Old age is at your throat before you know it, *ma fleur*." The witch starts to gabble, as if repeating something she's committed to memory and I can see exactly what's been going on. "Say *yes* and leave this lonely place. Say *yes* and grasp the small joys to be found everywhere that make life worthwhile…theatres, balls, shopping trips, excursions to the sea, the countryside. You see those violets – soon flowers as beautiful as these will be growing a thousandfold, massed free for the picking in the woods and hills and valleys. A few weeks more and there'll be primroses and *jonquilles* in the meadows, bluebells at the forest edge. Only do his bidding and he'll take you anywhere you like in his fine carriage and—"

"Did the wolf eat the girl?"

The witch stares at me, startled. "What's that?"

"He told you what to say, didn't he? Well, I'm not doing it. You can tell him the answer's still no."

"But you just said—"

"I only said *what if*."

"And you were weeping—"

"Waiting sometimes makes me sad, but it passes. And you'd better tell him that even if my prince doesn't find me, I'll never say *yes*." I take a deep breath. "Last night I fell asleep before you reached the end of your tale. I remember the wolf eating the grandmother. Did he also eat the girl?"

The witch grumbles and grouses under her breath. Instead of telling me the rest of the story, she starts fussing over the state of the floor. "What's been going on here? Look at this mess. Feathers everywhere – there must be a hole in that terrible old coverlet of yours. It's past time that ragged thing was thrown out."

"Never – this was left behind by the good fairy."

"Then it'll have to be patched. Now, lift your feet – if you won't move, I must sweep round you."

"I didn't ask you to sweep at all."

"Cleanliness is next to godliness, miss."

As so often, the witch croaks out a song from her homeland as she works, her voice cracking on the high notes. I don't understand a word but by the sideways glances, it's directed at me.

> "Ma breger din deus ma dim'iñ
> N' pregit ket d'toer mein-glas din
> Perak eta ma merc'h, perak eta?
> La-la lah-la-la
> Un toer mein-glas zo kroug-diskroug
> Ma gouezh d'an traoñ eñ dorr e c'houg:
> Oh, ya! gwir eo, ma merc'h, oh, ya! gwir eo!
> La-la lah-la-la
> Ma breger din deus ma dimi
> 'N pregit ket deus menuzer din
> Perak eta ma merc'h, perak eta?
> La-la—"

"What's your song about, Granny?"

"In my tongue it's called *Ur plac'h diaes da zim'iñ* – about a girl who refuses to marry. Hah! She won't have a roofer in case he falls and breaks his neck, nor," the witch ticks them off on her fingers, "a carpenter, an innkeeper, a weaver, a mason, a sailor – always some footling reason for delay. There, that's better. Now I need to sit down and catch my breath." She helps herself to the last of the barley sugar pieces and sucks noisily.

"What about the tale – did the wolf eat the girl?"

"That wasn't his plan." The witch shows her few snaggly yellow teeth. "You missed the best part. Where did we get to?"

I smile. "The bit about the dung heap."

"*Bien*. Well then—

When no one answers, the bzou calls again. 'Are you making a dung heap, my child? Are you making a dung heap?' Still no answer comes and he leaps from the bed, follows the rope, and finds her gone.

The bzou gives chase, and soon the girl can hear him on the path just behind her. She runs and runs until she reaches a river that's swift and deep and dangerous.

Some women are washing linen on the river banks.

'Please help me cross,' she says to them, looking over her shoulder. They spread a sheet over the water, holding tightly to its ends. She crosses the bridge of cloth and soon she's safe on the other side. When the bzou reaches the river, he asks the women to help him cross. They spread a sheet over the water – but as soon as he's halfway across they let go. The bzou falls into the water and drowns."

I'm not entirely pleased with the ending. "It would have served her right if she had been eaten. What a simpleton."

"Anyone can make a mistake," retorted the witch. "The simpleton is the one who does nothing to put her mistake right." A long silence followed.

"Don't let's quarrel about a silly girl in a story, Granny."

"I didn't think we were. But it still isn't natural, cooped up here like a hermit when a simple word—"

"Go away, old woman. What I do is none of your business."

"Of course it is. Like it or not, I'm the nearest thing to a grandmother you've got." The witch hobbles towards the door. "Don't worry, I'm going. No need to shout. One of these days I won't bother to come back. And what will you do then, miss? What will you do then?"

The old hag never stays away for long, more's the pity. I'm standing by my window, watching clouds drift past and thinking about the nature of wolves, the foolishness of girls, when back she comes with her poking and prying, no doubt intent on gathering bundles of my thoughts that might interest the ogre.

"Still waiting for your jackdaw, *mon petit grognonne*?"

"Don't call me that. The only time I'm a cross-patch is when you make me so."

"Ah." She doesn't bother to hide her grin. I pretend not to notice.

"I wasn't waiting for Reims, Granny. No, I'm looking out over the ocean."

"Is that so," says the witch and her grin fades.

"Yes, today I can see great waves crashing, small boats foundering upon the rocks."

She folds her bony witch arms across her equally bony witch chest. "Well, well, who would have thought it?"

"See for yourself, Mamie – but be quick, for the sky's darkening."

"Yes, yes, poke fun at me if it pleases you," she says. "I know more than enough about the sea, *ma chère*, having given her a husband and two sons."

It's too late to take the words back and too early to apologise. So I say nothing.

The witch sighs. "Since your bad temper is forgiven if not forgotten – but we'll say no more about that, for what am I, the worn-out shell of an old woman that stands before you, but a *bouc émissaire*, a whipping boy, a veritable chopping block on which certain others feel free to take out their anger – I'll tell you something about the sea that laps my country's shores while patching this tattered old coverlet of yours." She seats herself near the window with a basket of fabric – scraps of embroidered silks and satins, strips of fine linen, some crewel-stitched with fanciful scarlet birds, others scattered with flower sprigs, even some brightly printed Indian cotton of the sort that is now forbidden – and holds a needle up to the light, squinting horribly as she attempts to thread it. "Once my homeland was mighty Armorica, then *petite Bretagne*, but now, alas, we're only a speck in the eye of France. Some believe we lie at the end of the world."

"Are you speaking of Finisterre, Granny?"

"We say *Penn ar Bed*, but that's right. It's the place where a crystal ship comes to take the fortunate to the Island of Eternal Youth. There," she waves the needle aloft, "threaded at last. And a curse on old Father Time who robs a poor woman of her vision while she still has need of it. Where was I? Ah, yes. Our sea has her moods, sometimes generous and open-handed, sometimes a cruel widow-maker," the witch sighs again, "and once in a while she becomes a monster, biting into the coast, swallowing whole swathes of land, even a town. There was this king…

> *Gradlonvawre was his name, Gradlon the Great, and he ruled over the kingdom of Kern from his castle in Kaer-Ys. He had but one daughter and her name was Dahut.*
>
> *In those days Ys was the most beautiful and prosperous city in all of the surrounding kingdoms. Because the city stood perilously close to the sea, King Gradlon built a great wall to protect it, with a gate that was lifted only to allow ships into the inner harbour. That gate had a single key and Gradlon always wore it around his neck.*
>
> *Now Dahut was fair of face but not pure of heart. She drank and swore, and kept company with the most dissolute men of*

Ys. Every night she took a new lover to her bed and at first light she killed him. One day a knight dressed head-to-toe in black came to Ys. Oh, he was handsome with his blue-black hair and his blue-black beard. Dahut summoned him to her bedchamber but he would not go. And the next day, she summoned him, but he would not go. On the third day, when Dahut summoned the black knight, the scoundrel sent word that he would go to her chamber only if she took the key from her father's neck and opened the gate for his ship that was lying at anchor beyond the harbour.

That night a terrible storm broke over the city. Lightning flashed. Thunder roared. The winds howled, and waves as high as the castle battered the stout bronze walls safeguarding the city. Now Dahut, who'd drunk deep of the bloodred wine, did as the Devil – for it was none other – commanded. She went to her father's chamber. She stole the key. And she opened the gate. Whereupon great waves high as mountains broke over Ys and the city was lost. Not a moment too soon, Gradlon awoke and leapt onto his horse, setting his daughter before him. But as he fled, the raging sea snatched Dahut from his arms and turned her into a mermaid for her wickedness."

"That's a terrible tale, Granny? Is it true?"

"None truer, my dear, for my *mamm-gozh* – my grandmother on my mother's side – was the very one who told me." The witch breaks off her length of thread and holds up the coverlet. "There, look, a neat strip of pretty blue linen stitched with flowers where there was once an ugly hole. Even so, this old thing won't last much longer." She pulls at the threadbare fabric. "I suppose it could be re-covered. Is it worth it, I ask myself? But to get back to the tale of Ys, our brave fishermen often glimpse the castle towers beneath the water when the sea is calm. And on stormy days some have caught sight of the mermaid Dahut sitting upon the rocks and weeping for her sins, so that must also be true. Besides, I've seen with my own eyes the fine big statue of King Gradlon seated upon his horse afore the cathedral in Quimper. Every November, come rain, come shine, a minstrel climbs up to offer him wine from a goblet of pure gold, and afterwards he—"

"Wine for the statue?"

"That's right. It's to honour the king for bringing grape vines to the far western lands. First the minstrel ties a new white napkin around Gradlon's neck, and then he raises the golden goblet to the king's lips while a great choir sings a lament for the loss of Ys. Next, the minstrel respectfully wipes the king's moustache, before draining the goblet on Gradlon's behalf. Afterwards, as I started to say, he throws the goblet of pure gold into the crowd. And whoever catches it..." the witch makes a moue of regret. "Alas, I was always too small and too slow." She brightens. "It is said that when mighty Paris is swallowed by the Seine, the city of Ys will in that very same hour rise up from beneath the waves."

"What will become of the mermaid then?"

"Who knows? Who cares? She was wicked through and through. Of all sinners, the women are always the worst. Or so they say."

"So they say...."

"Speaking of wicked women, did you ever hear the tale of Azenor? It was a long time ago, mark you. A hundred years, maybe more. Azenor was the king of Brest's daughter and wife to the Count of Goelc, but she wasn't the wicked one. Oh, no. You see, the king took a new wife and this wicked stepmother was so jealous of Azenor's beauty that she accused the girl of being unchaste – and Azenor was pure as sea foam, let me tell you – causing her to be locked, alone, in a high tower with no door and a single window. You can see the tower to this day."

"In Brest?" It can't be so very far away. Maybe I can see the tower from my window.

The witch nods. "Even that wasn't enough for the evil stepmother. *La garce* wanted Azenor burned at the stake, but since the girl was with child, she was only nailed inside a wooden barrel and cast out to sea."

I laugh. Even to my ears it's a bitter sound. "To be locked in a high tower – what a terrible fate."

The witch narrows her eyes. "Yes, but poor Azenor had no hope of escape, no choice in the matter, whereas you...."

"But you know I will never leave this place until—"

"Enough of this foolishness," cries the witch. "For the thousandth time, no young man is going to come wandering up these stairs unbidden to ask for your hand, no matter what it says inside those foreign books of yours."

"This is nothing to do with any book. I was told—"

"A pack of nonsense by some fortune-teller – how is that any better? Those frauds say the first things that come into their heads after they've pocketed your silver."

"She wasn't a fraud. There were no coins. And I believe her." And because I can see the witch is working herself up to pour even more scorn on my fairy, I quickly ask: "You've told me about two wicked woman, but do you have no stories of wicked *men* in your homeland?"

She screws up her face. "I'll think on it."

"Why are you always writing?" demands the witch, as she unlaces my ribbon ties. "What are you setting down? All my bits of stories were passed down to me by my mother, my aunts, and my grandmothers and freely shared with you. I wouldn't like to think you were trapping them between the nib and the paper. That's a sure way of striking a tale dead." She thrusts forward a hand like a cramped seagull's claw. "Give me that petticoat, if you please, there's no need to let it drop to the floor."

"But Granny, there are those who claim that writing a story down is the one sure way of keeping it alive. Safe inside a book, they say, a tale can be passed hand to hand and thus shared with more people, far and wide. That way, goes the argument, at least they're not forgotten."

"No, no, no." The witch wrings her hands. "Stories need red blood running through them, not black gall ink. They change with the wind and the tide and the seasons of the earth. They bend without breaking before the madness of wars and the horrors of famine. That's the way of it. No tale is ever told the same way twice."

"At least in that we agree."

She reaches for the hairbrush. "Tales are never forgotten when they're passed around in the proper way, mouth to ear, borne on the living breath. As for a tale written down, well, it's fixed and finished, like Our Lord's Parables, or the Ten Commandments on Moses' stone tablets, or a name chiselled on a grave marker."

"Don't worry, Mamie. I'm not murdering your tales with my pen. I'm simply weaving words and ideas to make new stories. Nothing's trapped. Nothing's kept. If ever one gets finished, which rarely happens, I immediately give it its freedom by sending it out into the world."

"I see," said the witch, though her expression said otherwise. "Sit down, *ma chère*. Let me brush your beautiful hair." She was silent for a few moments. "Tales *can* be forgotten, it's true. When you asked me about the wicked men of my homeland, the faintest shadows of two old tales flitted across my mind. I've spent most of the afternoon trying to remember how they went. The first was about that same King Gradlonvawre of Ys I told you of earlier. It's said that a barbarian warrior queen from the North, beautiful but flame-haired and savage, asked the rich and powerful Gradlon to murder her cruel husband and take her for his bride. He agreed, and out of that ill-starred union was born the wanton Dahut. I can't recall the rest. Would you say Gradlonvawre was a wicked man?"

"I've heard similar things happened during the Affair of the Poisons in Paris. It was usually husbands that were done away with."

"And the other story came back to me when I heard of someone hunting for hares. Around here, they hang the creatures' bodies from hooks and catch the blood in a bowl. Where I come from it's a sin to slaughter a hare for fear of killing your granny." The witch makes a small secret sign with her little fingers. "Did you ever hear tell of *la gueule du loup*?"

"The wolf's maw – is this another wolf story?"

"In a way – *La gueule du loup* was a wicked Breton baron who had a secret room in his great castle where he hung young maidens up on hooks to watch them die. Or so they say. The baron's real name escapes me…but I remember that his hair and beard were said to be a strange, unnatural colour."

Chapter Four

The idea came to him during a lull in an otherwise heated debate between several members of the Académie française.

Charles, ensconced in seat twenty-three – his for life, at least none of his disparagers could rob him of that honour – between Louis de Verjus, Count of Crécy, a small man, ill-favoured and unnervingly polite, and the shadow of Jean de la Fontaine – for the man was absent again, really these days one never knew where he was or indeed where one was with him – Charles cast a jaundiced eye around the newly quieted chamber. On the other side of Verjus sat Pierre-Daniel Huet, Bishop of Avranches, another of those who revered ancient pronouncements over modern achievement. And beyond him, the industrious Jean-Paul Bignon, elected relatively recently and already working on new rules for this assembly. There was some talk of allowing honorary membership but really one could not imagine any such revisions being adopted by this collection of *intransigeants*. With that thought, Charles leaned forward, the better to observe François Charpentier who, being a clever man and a fellow Modernist, was also burdened with more than his share of detractors. His gaze travelled on round the chamber, lingered on Armand de Camboust, the duc de Coislin, in seat number twenty-five – he was a military man, reliably silent when it came to fine points of literature – and came back to la Fontaine's unoccupied seat.

Once Upon a Time in Paris

It was then that his thoughts turned to the fables. And hence, though in retrospect he was at a loss to explain it, to the newly rediscovered key. Afterwards, he hastened home from the Academy, for once not even stopping to take coffee and enjoy animated conversation in the nearby Café Procope.

During the next few days, Charles was so engrossed in his idea – and equally preoccupied with the return of Pierre, a decidedly unrepentant prodigal son – that he paid scant attention to the painter as that young man went about his preparations. The initial stages of a portrait were always tedious in the extreme. First the artist prowled around his subject, viewing him from every possible angle; then came measuring with callipers, the transferring of those measurements to the canvas, followed by a great deal of shuffling backwards to judge the accuracy of first strokes and scampering forward again to make adjustments…a small series of acts repeated *ad nauseam*.

The fifth sitting found Charles suffering from a minor digestive affliction. A surfeit of cardinal's leg, he was sure. And yet, since mutton usually agreed with him, it might have been his third helping of the rich pottage of tortoise that preceded it. This indisposition forced him to abandon his carefully arranged pose at frequent intervals. On returning this time, he observed that the portrait painter had removed his wig revealing a mass of unkempt hair, scraped back and secured with a length of grubby ribbon, thereby allowing glimpses of a single earring, the lowest quality imaginable, the type of thing with which – were it through the creature's nose and not made of silver – one might lead a bull to market.

Charles was forced to register his disapproval. "I would be much obliged, Monsieur, if you remained properly coiffured while in my presence." Without waiting for a response he shuffled himself into a comfortable position, placing his left hand firmly on the copy of *Le Labyrinthe de Versailles* – in this painting at least his work for the king would be immortalised – and, though no one could ever call him vain, surreptitiously raised his head a fraction so that his prodigious waterfall of chins might assume less prominence.

"Monsieur?" The young man smiled. "Formality never sat well with me, sir. When being addressed, I'll settle for plain Lew, if it's all the same to you."

"Louis," chided Charles, "named for our illustrious monarch, I presume."

"Just Lew, if you please. As for the other, I'm unable to wear a wig for long when I work. No, truly, it's impossible. I might burst into flame. My creativity is so intense that heat flows from every pore of my being." He laughed. "One might as well wear a wig while making love."

Charles stared frostily at him. A dozen tart rejoinders suggested themselves. But one had to be careful. To sit before any painter was to place oneself in a vulnerable position and of late there were a few…*unfortunate*…aspects of his appearance that he would prefer not to be captured on canvas for all eternity. "I have already conceded that you may work in your chemise," he said finally. "However I must insist upon the wig. Think back to our agreement. To be correctly presented *in every detail* was a condition of your appointment."

Lew inclined his head, hardly a bow, little more than a nod. "Then I regret—" He slowly gathered together his brushes.

"So be it." Charles pursed his lips. "There are countless other painters – an unfortunate decision on your part, since I shall require a great deal of additional work to be carried out shortly." He shrugged, gratified by the immediate change in the fellow's demeanour. "I have in mind an enormous commission."

The brushes spilled onto the floor. "What sort of commission?"

"It's a prestigious project, one entailing several months of well-remunerated employment – for a compliant artisan."

Charles, waiting for the import of his words to penetrate the other's skull, glanced down and noticed that his hands needed further attention. He beckoned to Poucet, hovering just inside the door with the tray of cosmetics. It took a skim of beeswax followed by a generous dusting of powder to conceal Charles' liver spots – the loathsome barnacles of advancing age – to his satisfaction. In the interim, Lew had jammed the wig back on his head.

"May we continue, sir?" His tone was agreeably deferential.

"We may." Charles squared his shoulders, raised his chin and faced the painter adopting a three-quarters pose, an innovation from Flanders, popularised by Botticelli, reputed to allow the personality of the sitter to project itself from the canvas.

He watched Lew from the corner of his eye as the work continued. Whatever the man's skills, he had no finesse, always scratching and scraping at himself, wiping his nose and brow on his cuffs, muttering, humming tunelessly or whistling between his teeth. After a time the fellow began to perspire profusely. First he tugged the chemise free of his nether garments; it sagged at the neck and fell in grimy folds around his hips. Soon afterwards, he rolled up his sleeves. Charles grimaced, repressing a shudder. Heavens, the fellow's arms and chest were like a field labourer's – sinewy and unspeakably hirsute. It bordered on indecent.

'*Les gens propres vont chez les baigneurs pour se faire dépiler*,' he was tempted to chide, for indeed, it was true: civilised people went regularly to the barber-bathers to have their bodily hair removed. And there was no shortage of these barbers in Paris. François Quentin was the most fashionable, and the most expensive, but of course La Vienne – as he preferred to be known – also provided other services, little *confortatifs*, including the aphrodisiac potions that had been of such service to the king in his many amours. Aside from that, the business could be dealt with at home by one's valet. Numerous recipes for depilatories circulated using turtles' or bats' blood, the urine of young bitches, distilled newborn puppies, excrement of cats, honey, resin, pitch, animal fats, even arsenic and quicklime.

The application of quicklime to his person was something Charles could never countenance. History was clear about its dangers. Little more than a century ago, in the reign of Henri III – perhaps seeking revenge for his majesty calling their so-called virgin queen a *putain publique* – the godless English navy had destroyed an entire French fleet by throwing the noxious substance in the crews' faces, thereby blinding them. To call Queen Elizabeth a public whore was perhaps an insult too far. Still, it was a mercy for France that Henri had rejected calls for a royal alliance with her, an overbearing old hag, a mannish harridan, almost bald, with legs said to be monstrously disfigured by swollen veins. With notably few exceptions, the English were a vile race, their womenfolk unspeakable, harpies in petticoats—

Lew coughed. "Perhaps, sir, we have done enough for today?" Charles started. He'd slumped in his seat. The book had slipped from his fingers and Poucet hurried to retrieve it, smoothing the crumpled pages.

"Yes, yes," he said irritably, easing himself from the chair and shuffling forward to inspect the portrait's progress. He was agreeably surprised: the pronounced thrust of his aquiline nose had been tamed, his jowls diminished, and the troublesome moles painted out, as had the ink-black hollows beneath his eyes. Through the magic of Lew's brushwork his entire appearance was stepped back in time by at least a decade. In truth, this was a far more sympathetic likeness than the one of him by Charles Le Brun, the king's own painter. One could almost have believed the young man felt some affection for him.

"That's a r-really nice p-picture," announced Poucet. "D-do you l-like it, s—" Charles waved him away.

Lew smiled. "I hope my efforts please you, sir."

"Very satisfactory, so far," said Charles, bending closer to peer at the roughly painted outlines suggesting his hands and book. "Make sure the volume's title is readable, if you please."

"I thought to pick the letters out in gold leaf."

"Indeed – an excellent notion."

"Sir," Lew pulled his wig more securely onto his head, holding it down for good measure, "about the other commission you mentioned…."

"Ah, yes." Charles continued to examine the canvas, noting the cunning blending of colours to create realistically youthful skin tones, the mesmerising gleam of the painted eyes, the way light and shadow had been juxtaposed to bring forth convincing folds in the small portion of velvet sleeve almost completed. It must be admitted, albeit unwillingly, that whatever Lew's shortcomings, he could undoubtedly turn out excellent work. Rumour had it that the young man came from a good family but had been dispossessed because of his scandalous behaviour. Nevertheless, he came well recommended: those of his acquaintances who'd used the artist's services swore by his dedication to whatever task he undertook.

Charles, surreptitiously glancing sideways, observed the fellow vigorously scratching a place unmentionable in polite society. He sighed. It meant little: sometimes it was the young aristocrats who exhibited the worst manners. Look at that business with the king and his brother hurling bowls of hot porridge at each other. Years ago now, but it had never been forgotten. Of course Louis set aside youthful excesses to become the greatest monarch France had ever known, and where he led his people followed, so it was entirely possible that, given time, this young oaf would redeem himself, maturing to become a renowned artist and a refined gentleman.

In the meantime, his services were exceptionally cheap. Perhaps, Charles thought, giving Lew a chance to prove his worth would be advantageous to both of them.

"Your portrait will be finished by the end of the month," prompted Lew. "After that I'll be free to contemplate another project." He moved a few steps closer. "And I'm doing my utmost to portray you honestly, sir – as an esteemed gentleman of great depths, a thinker, a writer and a poet, a luminary of the French literary scene."

Charles inflated his chest. "Very well," he said, the decision made. "I suppose you might at least see what's involved." Reaching for the newly rediscovered key, he found himself holding it by the heart within its bow, just as in happier times. "Follow me."

With Poucet trailing after them, Charles led the painter along the gloomy passages of the oldest part of the house, stopping before a door that hadn't been opened in years. He fumbled with the key, which grated and groaned, turning reluctantly in the lock. Finally, its hinges squealing in protest, the door swung ajar, only to jam immediately against the floor, whereupon Lew put his shoulder against the wood, forcing it fully open. The three men stepped over the threshold, entering what had once been known as the Red Drawing Room. In the dim light, its shrouded furniture pressed hard against the walls took on the appearance of a fright of ghosts. Charles waited in silence while the two younger men threw back the shutters to reveal a large space thick with dust and hung about with cobwebs.

"A good-sized room," commented Lew, looking from the boiserie-panelled walls to the gilded-wood chandeliers. He raised his voice to be heard above Poucet's sneezing fit. "Elegantly proportioned and easily refurbished."

Charles nodded, envisaging the place ablaze with light: the old-fashioned chandeliers would have to be replaced by crystal ones, preferably made of the new London glass-of-lead, which was considerably cheaper. Furniture must be purchased. The floor might need replacing. Such details would have to wait. He strode across the room, companions in tow, pausing to unfasten the wide double doors that led into the octagonal salon. A faint mustiness greeted them. Once this space served the house as a modest ballroom; these days it was full of nothing save dust and echoes.

Lew's eyes shone. "A space like this would need immense paintings."

Charles silenced him with an upraised hand. He shuffled towards the nearest stairs and climbed laboriously to the gallery where he clung to the balustrade, breathing heavily. The mustiness was more pronounced here. Mice had set up home in the *broccatello*-cushioned seats lining the walls. A few damp patches disfigured the vaulted ceiling. Crumbles of plaster littered the walkway, and he was almost sure a colony of bats hung along one of the stone ribs high above like so many crochets on a musical stave.

"You would need eight main paintings at ground level," said Lew, "with eight smaller ones at this, the window level." His gaze travelled upwards. "And possibly, for the sake of symmetry, eight more, but smaller yet again, above them."

"You misunderstand," Charles gasped, as soon as his ragged breaths allowed. "This room *is* the canvas."

Lew frowned. "But—"

"You will have seen Charles Le Brun's painted ceilings at Versailles? In particular those in the *Galerie des Glaces*—"

The painter looked away. "No. I must confess—"

"Not seen the Hall of Mirrors?" Charles sighed. The fellow was from the provinces. It was only to be expected. "Perhaps," he said, more kindly, recalling his earlier pleasure at the young man's work, "something might be arranged at a later date. However, Madame de Briou tells me you were trained in Italy." Charles paused momentarily, realising his mistake – the marriage had been set aside and Charlotte-Rose was Madame de Briou no more. Nevertheless, she continued to be notorious for her dogged pursuit of younger men, which was perhaps why Lew had winced at the mention of her name. "If that is so, you must be familiar with the *Cappella Sistina*."

"S-Sistine Chapel," put in Poucet, nodding sagely.

Charles sighed again and waved the valet away. Instead of leaving, the fool merely shuffled back a scant half dozen steps. Lew appeared not to have noticed the interruption.

"Of course – and with the work of Michelangelo," Lew's tone turned reverent. "Who is not?" His gaze travelled the length of the neglected room. "Do you mean me to reproduce some of *Il Divino's* themes here?" His mouth twisted. "To *copy* him?"

"Nothing like that," Charles replied, his tone brisk. "Listen carefully. You may not know that the Sistine Chapel's ceiling was previously decorated more simply – as were many chapels – with golden stars on an azure sky. Here, in homage to the king, I wish the stone vault ribs of the ceiling to be painted gold, radiating from a golden sunburst at the apex. There, do you see? And running down each side of the ribs there is to be a border of fleur-de-lys. The vault itself is to have stars superimposed on the intense blue that is His Majesty's favourite colour near the top, gradually fading to paler sky-blue lower down, perhaps to the bottom third, where the stars are to be replaced by representations of all the birds of the air."

"One would need a head for heights." Lew looked uncomfortable.

"It is said that Michelangelo himself struggled against vertigo," Charles said dismissively. "I wish the remainder of the room to be decorated with scenes from La Fontaine's fables, a theme I suggested for the fountains in the maze at Versailles. The sculptures there were provided by Étienne Le Hongre," Charles sniffed disdainfully, "of lead, painted with indifferent colours…the fountain of the wolf and the stork, another of the hare and the tortoise and, my favourite, the fountain of the rats' council, and many more. One's efforts are not always appreciated.

"But here the fables must come to life, represented in glorious jewel-like colours, interspersed with images from nature – flowers and butterflies and small creatures of the countryside." He looked up, already seeing the completed work in his mind's eye: hawks and owls, gaudily painted parakeets, swifts and swallows, turtle doves, all the humble birds of the field and hedgerows. "Not forgetting a swan or two, of course…for the king. No goose of any sort, however." To include geese would render the project useless. "No goose," he repeated, turning to face Lew, who was gazing abstractedly into the middle distance. "Have you any experience in this type of work?"

Lew blinked. "I've assisted with many such projects. And last summer I single-handedly painted a fresco of the Three Fates for my – for the dining room of a country estate in Normandy."

"This proposal must be considerably larger. Are you capable of executing work on such a scale?"

"Naturally, but first some repairs are necessary." Lew pointed to the discoloured plaster. "It looks as if the roof's been leaking."

"Indeed, yes."

"After that's done, the surfaces must be prepared."

Charles nodded. "It shall be attended to."

"I'd need help."

"You may engage other workers, subject to my usual strictures

– presentable costume, courteous deportment, and so on." He glared at the fellow, adding with great emphasis: "I'll tolerate no improper behaviour here."

"You need have no fears on that score," Lew said quickly. "Sir, it would give me the utmost pleasure to carry out your wishes. I'll devote myself to the task, but even so, it might take years."

"It must be done quickly. I'm planning an autumn ball, which means you would have no more than six months." Charles began descending the stairs as rapidly as he dared, for the cardinal's leg was again prompting him to revisit the latrines. "I look forward to seeing some initial designs."

The moment the old man disappeared from sight, Lew seized Poucet's hands and whirled him round in an impromptu gigue. "This is just the commission I've been praying for," he gasped, as they finally staggered, breathless, to a standstill. "My beautiful paintings will be seen by everyone who attends the ball. And Monsieur Perrault having held high office – Controller-General of his Majesty's Buildings and Gardens, I believe – *everyone* who attends the ball will be a *somebody*."

Poucet moved away, brushed down his livery, and smoothed his ruffled hair. "You'll d-do it then?"

"Of course – if it means my name being known throughout Paris. News of this may even reach the king's ear. Fame and fortune await me, my friend. I have much to thank your master for." Lew gazed at the discoloured walls. Bright colours, he thought, plenty of red, and as much gold as possible. "Prepare to see this room magically transformed. Oh, I'm going to enjoy the next few months."

"Yes," said the valet, "as l-long as you can p-put up with Monsieur P-Perrault."

"He's not that bad. There's a kind soul, I'm sure, behind that brusque façade of his." Remembering an earlier concern, Lew looked over his shoulder before whispering: "There is just one thing: is Monsieur Perrault of sound mind? He often nods off during our sittings. Sometimes he mutters and frowns as if he's holding an argument with himself. At home, an elderly neighbour who must be of an age with him, does exactly the same and I suspect he's fast approaching his dotage. Also," again he checked that they were alone, "you remember the day I brought my materials to the house? When I left, he was out in the street, jumping up and down after snowflakes like a babe in a pudding cap."

"That's n-nothing," said Poucet. "You should just hear some of the things I'm r-required to do. For a start, would you b-believe he sends me round the streets collecting up scraps of used p-paper?"

"You mean he's poor?" Lew asked, alarmed.

"Not at all, just strange – they say all the P-Perrault brothers were strange."

"In what way, *strange?*"

A light drumming began close by. Poucet held out his hand and looked up at the ceiling. "It must be r-raining. And you were r-right – there is a l-leak." He dried his palm on a dainty lace-trimmed kerchief. "Claude P-Perrault died of b-breathing in noxious fumes while cutting up a d-dead camel. P-Pierre P-Perrault was an embezzler who collected the king's taxes, used them to p-pay off his own d-debts, and then talked about nothing b-but water for the r-rest of his l-life. I heard N-Nicolas was a heretic, and as for Jean—" Poucet scratched his head. "I don't actually remember anything about Monsieur Jean P-Perrault. But *our* Monsieur P-Perrault, *Charles* P-Perrault, he's a monster."

"A monster? Dear me." Taking out his table knife, Lew rapped on the walls with its handle in several places; to his relief the plaster seemed sound. He smiled. "You really don't like him, do you?"

"I've g-got my reasons," Poucet said darkly.

Lew waited, but since the valet didn't elucidate tentatively broached the subject of more immediate family. "I've heard his wife died young…any children?"

"Huh," muttered Poucet.

"All right," said Lew, "forget I brought it up. The old lady nearly bit my head off when I asked her. In the circumstances it seemed a reasonable question."

"Yes, you'd think so."

"I don't need to know," added Lew, suddenly overwhelmed by curiosity and determined to winkle an answer out of his companion by fair means or foul. "After all, what's it to me?" He waited. "I'll stay an outsider, keeping myself to myself – even if I am going to be living here for near enough the rest of the year." Lew's patience began to ebb. "And if, during that time, I should happen upon an unknown face, in a corridor, say, or in the salon, or my work space, even in the kitchen, possibly the courtyard, I'll look away, say nothing, pretend whoever it might be is invisible—"

"There are two sons," announced Poucet.

"I see. Well, thank you for telling me."

"Another b-boy, little Charles, a sweet child, d-died many years ago of the smallpox, and—" Poucet stopped abruptly, and chewed on his fingers for a moment before continuing. "Of the two sons still living, the oldest, Charles-Samuel, is a p-prig. The younger one's called P-Pierre and he's n-nothing b-but trouble."

"I take it you don't like them any better than their father."

Poucet grimaced. "I d-don't have to. Anyway, you won't see much of either. Charles-Samuel's l-learning the l-law, l-lodges with some relative or other, and hardly comes near the place. P-Pierre stays out as l-long as he can find a t-tavern open – only comes home l-looking for money." He swung his foot, drawing two curves in the dust. "N-never p-play cards with him."

"A small family then," said Lew, "much like mine. I have one sister. My mother died when she was born and father never remarried." He paced out one of the walls, and wrote the rough measurement on his wrist. "So this is altogether a compact household – five servants, three family members—"

"And then there's the cripple," added Poucet, "an old soldier who's so terribly m-maimed and m-mutilated that he never shows himself."

"There – I told you Monsieur Perrault had a kind soul," said Lew. He wasn't surprised: his father maintained a few veterans of the king's interminable wars on the family estate. But they weren't hidden away, no matter how bad their injuries. He stretched and yawned. "I'm famished. Can you guide me back to the kitchen? Maybe Jacques will spare me a crust and a dab of butter. Besides, I need to beg a favour of him."

"I should go, too." Poucet started towards the outer door. "The m-master can get quite n-nasty if he suspects I'm off somewhere enjoying m-myself."

It was a sort of compliment, Lew supposed. He cast around for a matching pleasantry. "I look forward to the next time." And after a moment or two, added: "You know, my friend, your slight speech impediment almost disappears whenever it's just you and me talking together."

"Does it?" A few thin threads of colour crept up Poucet's sallow cheeks. "M-maybe that's b-because it feels as if I can trust you."

Lew squeezed the little man's shoulder but it felt so thin and bird-bone frail that he hastily withdrew his hand. They walked in silence for a while until, thinking back on how the day had unfolded, Lew had a sudden vision of the valet patting powder onto the old man's hands and face. He started to laugh. "We have more in common than I thought: at the moment we're both making a living from painting the same face."

Poucet shot him a shy smile. "My mother and I once lived alongside a troupe of travelling p-players. I learned m-many tricks."

"With your skills, you could leave and work for a mild-natured society lady, or perhaps even in a theatre, rather than staying here where you're so clearly unhappy."

"I will. But first there's something I need to—"

"What's that?" barked Norik, emerging from a side passage.

Poucet flinched. "A d-draught," he gabbled, "I n-need to m-make up a sleeping d-draught in case the m-master r-requires one tonight."

"And where do you think you're off to?" demanded Norik, watching the valet scuttle away. Lew smiled politely.

"I'm going to the kitchen, Madame." He was not surprised to find her following close at his heels and her disapproval settled over him like a miasma when Jacques handed him a hunk of bread and beef dripping without being asked. Lew had already decided to come straight to the point.

"Sir, would you allow me to use a corner of table to prepare some drawings for Monsieur Perrault? My lodgings are excessively cold and dark. They're a—" He cast about for a word that would describe their full awfulness without offending Norik, who was still standing in the doorway.

"*Trou de merde?*" supplied Jacques, who seemed to have no such scruples.

Lew winced. "Well, yes. And I fear trying to produce designs in a tavern would attract too much unwelcome attention. Any warm corner would do, sir. I could manage in the smallest of spaces." He waited while the cook considered this request – the cook having rolled out his pastry, and lined a vast coffin of a pie dish ready to be filled with tongue and numbles.

"You can do your drawing in here, young Leonardo, as long as it doesn't interfere with my work, which must come first. The master might like his pictures, but he likes his food more and I – a full-fledged cook, duly examined by my guild – am the one he relies on to meet that need."

"I'm very grateful," said Lew, hastily finishing the bread. "In return, would you like me to make a small sketch of you?"

"A picture of me?" Jacques gaped at him. "*Absolument pas!* No, no, I say no, absolutely not – my likeness might shrivel the paper."

In spite of his protests, the cook sat as directed, his expression solemn, clutching the rolling pin and a silver porringer before his chest in a way that suggested regal paraphernalia. Lew worked quickly, minimising – as was always his way – the worst ravages time and custom had worked on the huge man's features. At some point during the process, the clattering of wooden soles signalled Norik's approach; not a word was spoken, but she stood so close to Lew's shoulder that the tip of her large nose was clearly visible from the corner of his eye.

Once the sketch was finished, Jacques took it without a word and studied his likeness carefully before attaching it to the wall with a meat skewer. "*Morbleu!*" he exclaimed, smoothing his chin, turning his face this way and that, as if before a looking glass, "what a tragedy to have gone all these years without realising what a handsome fellow I was."

Blanche immediately ducked under the cook's arm and, a dripping rag still in her hand, stood on tiptoe for a better view of the drawing, but Escarlatta tossed back her hair and thrust out her bosom as she homed in on Lew. "Perhaps I might allow you to make a drawing of me one day, artist."

"I'll look forward to that," Lew said politely, aware of Norik's eye on him. "Now I really must set down a few ideas." He'd last heard *The Fables* read some time ago and he covered his eyes, conjuring up images that had presented themselves to him then:

a reckless grasshopper and some mean-spirited ants; Monsieur Reynard and the gullible crow; the frogs who prayed for a king and, ah – *The Hare and the Tortoise*. He'd begin there.

His entrance to the salon was greeted by a brief silence followed by a gentle ripple of applause – the delicate clapping of soft hands, the rhythmic tapping of folded fans against silk skirts. Gratified, Charles bowed low in response, but the babble and chatter had recommenced even before he managed to straighten his spine.

Edging a little further into the room, his nostrils flared with distaste as he was forced to pick his way through a litter of superfluous furniture – *lachinage* screens and tables, lacquered chests – each piece decorated with representations of cavorting Chinese creatures in slavish deference to the king's current obsession with all things Oriental. There were mirrors in profusion, some with chased gilt frames, yet others with borders of over-fed cupids. It was hardly possible to avoid perusing his reflection. In addition, every window was draped with gauzy fabric in those shades of pink that always looked faintly grubby, or trimmed with the deep lace that was supposed to encapsulate femininity.

Charles resolved to adopt a far more austere approach when refurbishing his Red Drawing Room. Simplicity was the key. Elegant and understated décor would set off the flamboyantly beautiful octagonal ballroom to perfection.

An excessively thin maid offered him *délicatesses de bouche* from a silver tray, while two little black boys dressed in ancient Moorish costume carried around salvers bearing tiny cups of coffee-flavoured milk. A dwarf and a chained monkey gibbered and grinned as they tormented the pair of lovebirds fluttering helplessly in their gilded cage.

The room was far too warm. Charles mopped his brow.

He could practically taste the argentine females caused to be thrown upwards so that, descending, it turned their hair the fashionable silver-white. The air – a thick stew of perfumes given off by costly pomades and powders, scent-drenched gloves, fans and handkerchiefs, the fragrant little cushions that half the women wore tucked into their bodices to correct imperfections, yet more rising from the potpourri dishes with their disgusting concoctions of salted herbs and fermenting petals – was almost impossible to breathe. At least this difficulty would soon be resolved. The king, once known as *le roi le plus doux fleurant* – the most sweetly flowered king – had inexplicably developed a sudden dislike of all perfumes. As in everything, and really one could not say it too often, where Louis led, the rest always followed.

Charles quickly determined that he was the only man present. True, François Timoléon – the abbé de Choisy – was here, today wearing an outrageously décolleté gown, but he hardly counted. Masculinity was surely as much about intention as physical form. Seeing that François was holding a spirited conversation with his niece, Marie-Jeanne L'Héritier de Villandon, Charles made his way towards them, stopping only to bend over the hand of the hostess, Madame de Caylus, a wretched woman with pretensions to literary talent.

"My dear Marie-Gabrielle," his eyes were on a level with the creature's torso and he suppressed a shudder, noting her bodice seams straining to accommodate an ever-increasing girth. "What a pleasure it is to find myself in such illustrious company."

"Dearest Charles," she cooed. "All here are honoured by your presence."

He raised her plump fingers to within a hair's breadth of his lips. "The honour is mine, most beautiful of women."

"So very gallant," Marie-Gabrielle simpered as he relinquished her hand. "We have an enormous treat in store. This afternoon, Marie-Catherine is to continue reading us one of her delightful *contes de fées*."

"A treat indeed," said Charles, squeezing the words between his gritted teeth. Marie-Catherine d'Aulnoy's tales bordered on the ridiculous, all frills and furbelows and excess – and yet, in spite of their manifold faults, immensely popular. He bowed again, excused himself, and blundered into a pair of pedestals decorated with fire-snorting dragons only to stumble immediately afterwards over a yapping of small dogs, the usual stump-legged products of some gutter *mésalliance*, pampered and spoiled but not above relieving themselves in corners.

Charles greeted his niece with the requisite dry pecks to the air an inch or so from her exceedingly pale cheeks, making a determined effort not to show his perpetually simmering resentment. She, being family, could have done more to help. "Marie-Jeanne, my dear, you look…*well*." There was no more to be said about her appearance: Marie-Jeanne was possessed of a lively wit wasted on a female *laide comme un pou*, veritably ugly as…. She'd never marry.

Now her small eyes sparkled. "Ah, dear Uncle Charles – you are the very person to advise us on the details of an ancient story. Who was it argued about whether men or women took more pleasure in the act of love?"

"It's from the writings of Hesiod," he replied tersely. Really, this stretched to the limits those unspoken rules governing suitable subjects for public conversation. "The story concerned Hera and Zeus. While Hera averred men had the most pleasure, Zeus claimed the opposite to be true. Unable to agree, they sought the opinion of Tiresias, a priest who, in his youth, had been transformed into a woman as punishment for clubbing to death a pair of copulating snakes. Later, thankfully, the transformation was reversed. Since—"

François eyed him reproachfully. "I become a woman for my own pleasure – and the pleasure it gives others to see me." He hitched up his skirts to display a heavily embroidered satin petticoat and large, pearl-encrusted mules. "As I see it, the punishment was turning poor Tiresias – like me, a priest – back into a man."

"Nevertheless," Charles continued testily, "having experienced being both male and female, Tiresias sided with Zeus, replying that if pleasure was divided into ten parts, nine of those would be enjoyed by women and only one by men. Whereupon," he grimaced, "whereupon in a predictably spiteful act by an old crone, Hera struck Tiresias blind."

"And was that the end of the story?" demanded Marie-Jeanne.

Charles shrugged. "He received the gift of prophecy."

"There's some hidden meaning there, I'm sure," she insisted.

"Perhaps." Charles made another dismissive gesture. "Let's brood no more on the classics, for are we not the *Modernes?* As I wrote in *The Century of Louis the Great*—"

"That's all very well," interrupted Marie-Jeanne, "but we still had to turn to the ancient writers for the answer to our question."

"How cross you both look." François giggled. He plumped up his bosom. "I have an idea for a new story. It's about a girl who believes she's a boy falling in love with another girl."

"I hardly think" began Marie-Jeanne, tightening her already thin lips. The giggles grew louder.

"Oh, you suspect it might be about your friend, poor Henriette-Julie de Castelnau? On that score you may put your mind at rest. This is no Sapphic romance. Anyway, it wasn't just her penchant for love affairs with the gentler sex that got Henriette-Julie banished to Loches." François shook his head in mock sadness. "Alas, in the eyes of the world, wild behaviour signifies strength in a boy, but frailty in a girl."

"But to be treated like a criminal for nothing more than high spirits? As if she was an enemy of the king? He might as well have imprisoned her in one of the iron cages built in that God-neglected place by Louis the Cunning." Marie-Jeanne folded her arms over her woefully flat chest. "Can you imagine a more terrible thing for such a gifted woman, uncle, than to be shut away from all society and learning...?"

"It's never stopped her writing," Charles responded, sourly. He pensively flicked a few dog hairs from his cuff. "Many of the comtesse de Murat's...*efforts*...have been aired in this very salon."

"*No one* would begrudge such a small compensation," declared his niece, "to a poor sequestered woman who—"

"*Sequestered?*" exclaimed Charles. Heavens above, did the silly woman not understand the full import of that word? "On the contrary, the comtesse de Murat's life in exile seems anything but sequestered or, indeed quiet." He mopped his brow. "Rumour has it that her activities continue to scandalise the entire area from Loches to Tours. How then can the term *sequestered* apply?" Marie-Jeanne said nothing but, too late, had the grace to look faintly abashed.

"Neither of you are paying the slightest attention to me," François said plaintively. "All right, forget the first idea, this one's even better. How about a ravishingly beautiful girl who thinks she's a boy falling in love with a very pretty boy who's been brought up as a girl?"

"Pray lower your voice." Charles glanced uneasily towards the nearest huddle of chatterers. "It would be prudent," he whispered, "to avoid writing anything that might be seen as an allusion to certain members of the royal court."

"The Duke of Orleans, you mean?" François smirked. "Oh la! Philippe wouldn't care, any more than he heeds the entire court whispering about his enthusiasm for the Italian vice. Don't forget, as children we played together. Why, even his mother called him *'my little girl'*. I tell you this – his collection of silken gowns is fifty times the size of mine. Be assured that if we turned the story into a play, he'd demand the female part."

"Nevertheless."

"Anyway, His Royal Highness wouldn't be interested in the boy once he found out she was in reality a girl, whereas in my story—"

Charles gasped. François was appallingly indiscreet. And it wasn't simply this relaying of court tittle-tattle. There was worse. As an abbé, he'd occasionally been entrusted with the education of young girls. Rumour had it that he, apparelled as a female, had dressed them all as little boys for the purposes of seduction. Still, surely no one who cared a fig for their reputation would have chosen to attend the Pope's inaugural ball in a scandalously low-cut woman's gown.

"In my story," François continued, "the two could fall in love and live happily ever after, despite not being entirely accepted by the world." A wistful note crept into his voice. After a moment's silence, he brightened. "It's not an impossible idea. After all, look at me. I was dressed as a girl until I was eighteen. Did I ever tell you about the time I ran away to Bordeaux…?"

"Yes," said Marie-Jeanne. She stifled a yawn, moving aside to allow a sturdily built servant to serve them with glasses of chilled violet syrup, little *poupelain* buns, and those tiny sweetmeats, flavoured with orange-blossom water, known as *pets de putain*, whore's farts.

"I became an actress. For five whole months I played ravishingly beautiful women in a large theatre. Everyone was deceived."

Charles nodded, wearily. "Indeed." This was what happened when a boy was born to an ageing mother. He chewed morosely on his remaining whore's farts. The intense sweetness set his teeth on edge. It was fresh air he needed, not sugar. More logs had been piled on the fire. Minute by minute, the temperature was rising and his glass of syrup, hastily gulped, hadn't helped in the least. Behind him, applause more enthusiastic than that which had greeted his arrival signalled the frightful d'Aulnoy rising to her feet and preparing to read more of her nonsense in a voice laughably unlike her own.

"You will remember," she trilled, "that after the departure of her monstrously deformed suitor, the horrid Migonnet, in his chariot of fire, we left our heroine shut up in a tower awaiting the return of her beloved husband."

Charles turned in time to catch the odious creature's gratified expression as a ripple of assenting murmurs greeted this gibberish. As one, the ladies of the salon leaned forward, their faces displaying eager expectancy. He ground his teeth and recalled the airing of an earlier part of the story, some convoluted nonsense about wicked fairies and a white cat. The clothes. The jewels. The mirrors. The styles of lighting. He'd nodded off once or twice during the endless descriptions. Undoubtedly today there'd be more of the same. Not one of these so-called *précieuses* understood the value of simplicity.

"Of course," d'Aulnoy continued, squinting round at her captivated audience, "her husband was equally impatient to see her and, since we are all equally impatient to hear about their reunion, let us continue." Charles shuddered as she ratcheted her voice half an octave higher. "Without more ado I tossed down the rope ladder, determined to run off with him; he climbed it nimbly and proffered me such tender words...."

François raised his voice. "Of course, I had many admirers – lovely boys, rich and handsome men." He smirked. One hand smoothed the fabric of his skirt, pressing it against an ample thigh. "To whom I granted small personal favours."

"Yes," said Marie-Jeanne. "You told us."

"And not one of them ever guessed that—"

"I really think, François," muttered Charles, in response to furious glares from those seated nearby, "that it behoves us to pay attention to this reading."

"Oh, that," the abbé sneered and made the sign of the cross at arm's length, as though over a grubby street urchin newly deceased. "It's nothing but *baliverne* – mere poppycock. Now this delightful story of mine—"

"Sounds no less an *absurdité*," snapped Marie-Jeanne.

"Ooh, a thousand pardons, I'm sure," François fanned the air vigorously. "What ails the pair of you today? Both with faces sour as varges. As dear Mama used to say – be careful the wind doesn't change or you'll stay like that forever."

Charles sighed, summoned the nearest of the little Moors and took one of his thimble-sized cups. The flavoured milk was cold. A skin wrinkled as old Norik's had formed on its surface. Nauseated, he looked for a table within reach whereon it might be discarded. Finding none, he settled for a lacquered chest; immediately, one of the dogs, a disagreeably liver-coloured member of the species with a tail twisted like that of a pig, jumped up to bring it crashing to the floor. Fortunately, the clatter was masked by the outburst of cries and whimpers, gasps and groans that greeted the demise of the heroine's husband – devoured by a dragon. Charles' lip curled. The room fell silent.

"In desperation at his fate and mine," breathed d'Aulnoy, clutching her bosom, "I flung myself into the jaws of that hideous monster."

The heat had become intolerable. Charles dabbed at his damp brow and looked longingly towards the firmly closed windows. He'd assumed the narrative must be nearing its end, but the heroine – whose name he could not for the life of him recall – was instead transformed into a cat. With another sigh, he settled himself into a chair as the reading ground on, mentally replaying the immensely superior tale of a cat he had in his possession – a real cat, retaining its arrogant feline nature, rather than some spellbound idiocy. *Le Maître Chat*, being resourceful and clever, had no need of enchantments, but left them to the doomed ogre. How was it done? Ah, yes – first the cat inveigled the ogre into proving that he really could transform his shape into that of a lion. That done, Master Puss slyly persuaded him to change himself into something infinitely more precarious.

> "I have further been told," said the cat, "that you can also transform yourself into the smallest of animals, for example, a rat or a mouse. But I can scarcely believe that. I must admit to you that I think that that would be quite impossible."
>
> "Impossible!" cried the ogre. "You shall see!" and *en même temps il se changea en une souris, qui se mit à courir sur le plancher. Le chat ne l'eut pas plus tôt aperçue qu'il se jeta dessus, et la mangea.*

"He ate the mouse up!" chuckled Charles. It was a masterstroke.

"Something else amuses you?" enquired a voice close to his ear. "You're full of secret musings today." Charles blinked and found François bending over him.

"Forgive me. I was thinking about a quite delightful story I've been composing morals for."

"A story? Pray God it isn't as long as this one." François narrowed his eyes in the direction of Marie-Catherine who, with a beatific smile, was now describing her heroine's matchless beauty as a prelude to the wedding. "Or as tedious."

"And so conventional," added Marie-Jeanne. "Marriage is certainly not the answer to everything. In my stories—"

Charles interrupted her. "One moment, niece, I believe this ordeal has almost run its course."

D'Aulnoy had now steepled her hands beneath her chin and adopted a faintly sorrowful expression. "Ah me," she said, scanning the salon to make sure that every eye was upon her. "This young prince was lucky indeed, *To find in a cat's disguise an august princess—*"

Charles eased himself from his chair. If she was remembered at all, which he doubted, history would not be kind to Marie-Catherine Le Jumel de Barneville, Baroness d'Aulnoy. She was little better than one of Boccaccio's maundering old hags, sitting late by the fire, making up farcical tales of hell, imps, ghosts, and the like. But etiquette decreed that all present should heap loud praise on each and every piece of work presented to the gathering – regardless of merit. Besides, he had no wish to hear more details of his troubled niece's bizarre literary strivings, littered as they were with sheep's bladders full of blood concealed in straw effigies, noble princes being dispatched into sewers, or robust heroines wielding axes and threatening to cleave skulls. Marie-Jeanne claimed to have learned certain of her tales at the knee of her nurse. It was unlikely. Charles remembered that woman as a garrulous old dame with a flask of spirits tucked into her bodice. He often wondered if his niece had suckled on that bottle; it might explain her peculiarities.

"I'll speak no more of the unworthy mother," shrilled Marie-Catherine, "who caused the White Cat so many sorrows

> By coveting the accursed fruits of another,
> Thereby ceding her daughter to the fairies' powers.
> Mothers, who have children full of charm,
> Despise such conduct, and keep them from all harm."

She bowed her head in false humility. "My dear friends, I thank you from the bottom of my heart for listening to my poor efforts."

Charles applauded with the rest, though his clapping was almost soundless. What utter *rubbish*, he thought, forcing himself to bow and smile in Marie-Catherine's direction, what *boniment*.

His thoughts turned to another of the stories kept under lock and key in his writing table. There was a dreadful mother in that tale, too – perhaps all mothers inherited a touch of the ogre – but the point was, if this absurd tale met with such approval what praise would rain down on the infinitely superior *La Belle au bois dormant*? Charles decided to read it again immediately on returning home. He'd make a fair copy – perhaps add an improving moral – and visit Jean Donneau de Visé at the *Nouveau Mercure galant* in the hope and expectation that it would be published in this month's edition and thus in time for a certain birthday…anonymously, of course. Such an action couldn't fail to please. The magazine was much favoured by the king. What greater honour could there be than to know that in all likelihood one's *conte de fées* had been savoured by Louis and the ladies of the court? On the other hand, get hold of a few more of these delightful tales and he'd have enough for a charming little illustrated volume with—

"One might as well be locked in an oubliette," murmured François.

"What? What?" Charles visibly jumped and stared at him, aghast. Had he spoken aloud? Or was it possible that the abbé was privy to his innermost thoughts? He drew himself up. "Your meaning, sir?"

Marie-Jeanne took it upon herself to answer. "It is as if you've forgotten we exist. We speak. You fail to answer. A conversation with a wall or a looking glass promises to be more rewarding. My dear uncle, are you ill or simply preoccupied?"

Charles rubbed his eyes and looked around. Apart from Madame de Caylus and the comtesse d'Aulnoy, who were engaged in mutual billing and cooing over each other's latest scribblings, the salon was almost empty. Most had dispersed to enjoy a musical entertainment in an adjoining room. Servants hovered in the doorway, waiting to set the place to rights, though one, already armed with a stick, was attempting to dislodge the monkey from its perch on a cornice board. The dwarf was busily scampering between the furniture, draining wine dregs from a score or more of glasses, and the two small black boys had tugged off their turbans and crawled beneath the largest table, where they sat surreptitiously gobbling the remnants of the refreshments – whore's farts, *dragées*, and butter simnels, together with a sugar-coated snout-smasher apiece, no doubt rewards straight from the kitchen for good behaviour.

"My apologies," he said, his tone deliberately contrite. "You're correct. I have been preoccupied with many things, including my desire to make a small collection of what might be termed *highly superior* fairytales, in addition to overseeing the details of some very exciting house refurbishments."

His niece came closer and lowered her voice. "I take it things haven't improved?"

Charles shook his head. "Alas, no."

"Pierre has much to answer for."

"I cannot lay all the blame on his young shoulders. However, the unfortunate circumstances continue." Charles brightened. "Nevertheless I am optimistic. I feel change on the wind." He beckoned to one of the servants and sent him in search of Poucet. "Marie-Jeanne, François, have the goodness to dine with me…shall we say Thursday? I can promise you excellent food and, more importantly, we will be free to discuss our literary ideas without interruption."

Having worked himself into a fury over his stag's antler jelly – which simply would not set – and convinced that he'd been palmed off with a mixture of chalk and ox bone, or worse, Jacques sallied forth to do battle with the cutler who'd supplied him with the grated horn. This afternoon the kitchen was full of acrid smoke. A March wind, come early, was amusing itself by blowing straight down the chimney, alternately whipping up the fire and threatening to dout it. From time to time ash fell, looking like small grey feathers, destroyed by a single breath. But at least the room was warm and, despite his smarting eyes, Lew took advantage of the cook's absence to continue working on his designs for the fables there. The proximity of a Comté cheese and some scallions was an added incentive: he'd lived too long with his arms crossed tightly over his hunger not to find that comforting.

But so far, his studies of rats were disappointing: they'd turned out mean-featured, wary and villainous. He'd unwittingly created a gang of pick-purses and cutthroats rather than the type of stout, self-important individuals prone to attend council meetings. Putting aside the page, Lew began again, this time calling to mind the autumn-sleek rodents that plagued his father's granaries, and produced a series of dignified rats, some solemn and serious, others anxious and earnest, all comfortably rotund.

After a time Blanche crept shivering from her pot-scouring in the scullery to warm her hands before the fire. "May I look?" she asked, timid as always. Lew turned the page and waited for her reaction. "In shape, they look very like Monsieur and his friends." Her laughter brought Escarlatta from the onerous task of grating lumps of sugar Jacques had hacked from the block earlier.

"What sort of artist makes pictures of rats?" she enquired sullenly. "You might as well draw cheese maggots or *les mouches à viande*."

Lew smiled. "Surely anything the Almighty created must be worth drawing, even maggots and blowflies."

"Would you draw a picture of me?" asked Blanche, without looking at him.

"Of *you?*" Escarlatta's tone was scathing. "Whatever for?"

"It would be a pleasure," said Lew, drawing up a stool for her. His pencil became a magic wand as – making Blanche's eyes a little larger, her lips slightly fuller, cheeks more rounded – he quickly transformed the young cinder-streaked drudge into a radiant beauty. "There you are, my little friend." All smiles and dimples, Blanche nodded her thanks and studied her likeness carefully before slipping it inside her bodice.

"He's made you far too pretty," declared Escarlatta. "Just like he made him," she pointed to the sketch of Jacques, "not nearly ugly enough."

"I think that picture of Jacques is very nice," said Blanche.

Escarlatta sniffed disdainfully. "You'd probably even make the cripple look like a Christian," she told Lew, "and they say he's the vilest creature the world has ever seen." She perched on the stool vacated by Blanche and looked expectantly at the artist.

"I doubt that's true," Lew said mildly, ignoring her unspoken request. There'd be no more work today. He carefully rolled up his studies, securing them with a length of kitchen twine.

"They say he has no legs and only one arm," reported Escarlatta.

"No," said Blanche, "I heard he had a great big hump on his back and was all over pox scars."

Lew raised his eyebrows. "So neither of you has ever seen him?"

"I wouldn't want to." Blanche shuddered.

"In that case, who tends him?" wondered Lew. "Is it Poucet?"

"What, little Spindle-shanks?" scoffed Escarlatta. "Not him – the fellow's so squeamish he can't stand to see a chicken's neck wrung. But—" She frowned. The two girls looked at each other and then at him.

"Madame Norik?" ventured Blanche.

"Then the unfortunate man's existence must be bleak indeed," said Lew. "I've never yet seen Norik smile or heard her utter a cheerful word."

Blanche grimaced. "Perhaps he's deaf as well as deformed."

"And probably blind, too," said Escarlatta, with a careless shrug, "if he's had the smallpox."

Somewhere a shutter slammed shut as the wind redoubled its efforts, roaring down the chimney, sending a fresh blast of smoke into the room. The air turned thick and foggy, redolent of last week's dinners. Ashes settled onto every surface. Working in the kitchen's fuggy warmth continued to be attractive, especially since Jacques frequently anticipated his hunger, but there were disadvantages. Lew coughed and spluttered and mopped his eyes.

"Why don't you ask the master to give you a better place to make your pictures?" asked Blanche.

"I should," agreed Lew, but knew it wasn't worth the risk of having Monsieur Perrault standing over him. Perhaps he'd try working in the ballroom – there must be a table of some sort under all those dustcovers – surely no one could object to that.

La Belle au Bois Dormant
Il était une fois un roi et une reine, qui étaient so grieved at being childless, so grieved that words can hardly express it. They visited all the healing waters in the world, swore vows, took pilgrimages, made acts of devotion, tried everything, but nothing worked. Yet finally the queen became pregnant and gave birth to a girl.

Charles carried on reading his copy of *The Beauty in the Sleeping Forest* – it was far longer than he'd remembered – corrected a handful of spelling errors, added words missing from the ragged margin, and then painstakingly copied the tale onto his very whitest and smoothest paper. When that task was completed to his satisfaction – the sufferings of the princess ended, the ogreish mother-in-law destroyed – he applied himself to writing a concluding *moralité*. A touch of gently acerbic wit coupled with his name practically guaranteed publication in the *Nouveau Mercure galant* – though he'd not yet made his mind up about submitting the story.

The lines came more easily than the ones he'd composed for *Le Maître Chat*, but doubts began to creep in as he sat looking over the finished result.

> *Attendre quelque temps pour avoir un époux,*
> *Riche, bien fait, galant et doux,*
> *La chose es assez naturelle,*
> *Mais l'attendre cent ans, et toujours en dormant,*
> *On ne trouve plus de femelle,*
> *Qui dormît si tranquillement.*

Could the lines 'To wait some time for a husband who is wealthy, good-looking, gallant and tender, is quite natural, but to wait a hundred years…' be construed as a criticism of the fairer sex? He hastily amended the second verse, changing the first four lines to read: 'The story seems to want us to understand that even where the pleasures of matrimony must be deferred, they are no less enjoyable for that, and nothing is lost by waiting.' Charles frowned, still not pleased with the result. He worked on the verse again, producing three more versions before he was finally satisfied.

> *La fable semble encor vouloir nous faire entendre,*
> *Que souvent de l'hymen les agréables nœuds,*
> *Pour étre différés, n'en sont pas moins heureux,*
> *Et qu'on ne perd rien pour attendre;*

Mais le sexe avec tant d'ardeur,
Aspire à la foi conjugale,
Que je n'ai pas la force ni le cœur,
De lui prêcher cette morale.

Assuredly, no exception could be taken to this. The last two lines he considered particularly apt, for though it was known how strongly he disapproved of women waiting for an impossibly perfect love match, writing 'I have neither the strength nor the heart to preach such a moral' signalled acceptance of young women's decisions in these matters.

Setting the tale aside, Charles' thoughts turned to Thursday's dinner. Although his niece was famously unappreciative of good food, François was something of a gourmand; this was an opportunity for the cook to prove his skills by producing something out of the ordinary. No doubt the news would delight him.

Unfortunately, Jacques was in a foul mood. It was not an unusual occurrence and though the cause was usually apparent – on such days his clothes and skin often reeked of Dutch *brandewijn* – he was adept at finding all manner of things to blame. This time it was the weather.

"It never stops bloody snowing or raining or blowing gale-force winds here in the north," he grumbled, jerking his chin towards the open door. "And today *il pleut comme vache qui pisse* – as you would know if you've ever had the misfortune to be near the back end of a pissing cow." Charles flinched at the fellow's vulgarity.

Norik clicked her tongue in disapproval. "Where my family come from, folk say *il pleut des grenouilles*."

"Raining frogs," Jacques looked unimpressed, "a fine supper for lean days if you can catch 'em."

"I believe," said Charles, "that the English describe it as *raining cats and dogs*."

"Where's the sense in that?" Norik asked tartly.

"Exactly so, Madame." Charles turned his attention back to the cook and found him engaged in the grizzly business of dressing larks, removing the gizzards and crushing their stomachs with the flat of a blade. It was on days like this that he felt the lack of a wife most keenly. Kitchens were no place for a gentleman of breeding. He averted his eyes. "There will be company for dinner on Thursday."

"Aye?" Jacques waited, one bloodied hand clutching the knife, looking anything but delighted.

"All that's required is a simple repast," Charles said, hurriedly revising his requirements. "Perhaps we might have pigeon bisque?"

"If there are any pigeons left," grunted Jacques, crushing the last of the larks' stomachs. "That damned cat sneaked into the dovecot again yesterday. *Hey, ho, a thief brings grief.* Feathers everywhere – courtyard was ankle-deep in them."

"Ah. Well, yes, we'll say the bisque *if possible* then. Maybe it could be followed by your excellent lamb dish, the one with bitter oranges and garlic? And perhaps, afterwards, *une boutonnée?*" Charles hesitated, for Jacques was glowering and tapping his foot. "On second thoughts, it's far better if I leave the choice of dishes to you." He suddenly recalled a passage from *The Beauty in the Sleeping Forest*, where the ogress had demanded her granddaughter cooked and served up accompanied by a spiced onion sauce. "There's just one thing I would ask however – serve nothing with *sauce Robert*, if you please." The request was not well received.

"And what's wrong with my sauce, pray?" Jacques glared at him. "You liked it well enough last time."

"Indeed yes, but I—"

"Isn't it enough that I must exist as you have decreed, kept a virtual prisoner in this benighted house by the unreasonable amount of work," Jacques tore off his apron and slapped it against the table repeatedly as if finishing off a freshly landed trout, "slaving away in a kitchen such as Charlemagne's cook might have endured and following ludicrous recipes from a book written by a puffed-up buffoon?" He stopped to draw breath. "Why must I also live with constant complaints and so rarely a word of praise?"

"I see nothing wrong with this kitchen," declared Charles, ignoring the rest, but uncomfortably aware of Jacques towering over him. From the corner of his eye, he measured the distance to the door, planning a hasty retreat should it be necessary. A small movement there caught his eye, possibly the flick of a drab skirt, as if one of the maids – he could not have told them apart to save his life – had stationed herself out of sight, eavesdropping on the conversation. He stepped backwards, hoping to catch her in the act, but she'd already gone. "Cooking food, though highly skilled, is surely a relatively straightforward operation, whatever situation it takes place in."

"Nothing wrong? *Nothing wrong* – abiding by all these damnable high-and-mighty Versailles rules and regulations in an ordinary house means everything here takes fifty times as long as it should. *I*," Jacques beat on his chest, "am a full-fledged cook, duly examined by my guild. Since there is no assistant cook, what help do I have? At the very least there should be properly trained kitchen boys to fetch and carry, to tend the fires and turn the spit. You burden me with two *escueleries*, no better than scullery sluts – and even those the old woman constantly steals away for other tasks."

Charles pulled at his chin. "It was made clear – *before* you came into my employ – that I deliberately keep few servants." He didn't add – and only those that were deemed capable of keeping their eyes averted and their mouths shut.

"Yes, yes," Jacques said testily, "the danger of snoopers getting their hands on government secrets…and the other thing. *Be they high or low, theirs not to know, tra-la.* I haven't forgotten. And how does that help me? As for my work being *straightforward*, no! No, I say! Never! I am an *artiste* not a common miller or a pig-sticker, or…or…a faggot-cutter."

"And your creations are much appreciated—"

"No," said Jacques. "They are not. Rather than being savoured, they are simply guzzled down, sir, guzzled down."

Charles drew himself up. "Now just a minute—"

"And let me tell you this – if I want to do something as simple as whisking egg whites, this fool," here Jacques thumped La Varenne's priceless cookery book, "advises the use of a feather! All well and fine if there are enough hands for the task, but not here, where I struggle unaided through the day's toil, only to rise exhausted on the morrow and begin again." He threw up his hands in despair. "Moreover, the kitchen is without a clock. Why is there no clock? What must I do to time my baking? Walk fifty times around the yard? Mumble a hundred Paternosters?"

"Very well," said Charles, "I will purchase a timepiece."

Jacques was in no mood to listen. "And another thing," he gestured disdainfully towards the book, "the fool has no idea of how to make proper pastry. Still, what can you expect when he thinks there are thirteen ounces of butter to the pound? As for milk – what's a practical man supposed to make of a recipe using a *chopine* for measure? A *chopine*, I ask you! It calls itself half of a pint, but request a *chopine* in some parts of Paris and you'd get near enough a full pint, while in others you would need three of their *chopines* to get an equal measure."

"It's certainly a challenge," murmured Charles, "and I'd understand…." He left the sentence hanging in the air. Jacques gave him a sharp look.

"A challenge that I continue to be equal to," he said quickly, "as long as the numbers are not too great."

"There will be two guests. A manageable number, I think you'll agree." Charles nodded. "However, I am drawing up plans for a ball later in the year."

"A ball in this house?" murmured Norik, catching his eye.

"Not as grand," Charles continued, "as many of those held in this city, but certainly one that will set society talking on account of its uniquely beautiful setting. You probably know that I've retained the young painter to carry out work on the octagonal salon. No doubt the results will enhance his reputation. And naturally the name of whoever is in charge of the cuisine will not go unnoticed."

"Oh." Something approaching a smile distorted Jacques' face. "Such an occasion will require a collation of the daintiest," He searched for the word, before finishing triumphantly, "the daintiest *comestibles*." All previous difficulties forgotten, he began listing aloud delectable morsels fit to hand around at a ball – gilded *tartes* containing *foie gras*, nipples of Venus, Little Princess pies, nun's bellies, snow-sugar biscuits, *fleurons* and *petits choux* fashioned from puff pastry, cakes with candied raspberries, crystallised violets and rose petals, new fillings devised for *feuillantines*....

"We'll discuss the arrangements at some future date," put in Charles, edging towards the entrance. "Certainly, you must have considerably more help on such an occasion, but for now, we'll continue as agreed. As I said, on Thursday there will only be three of us dining."

Charles paced his bedchamber, quite unable to sleep. His candle began to gutter, the flame becoming weak and lopsided in its death throes. There was little need to replace it: tonight the perfectly full moon illuminating the streets of Paris also brought a modicum of light to his room as it fingered through chinks in the shutters. He'd woken from a dream of a great grey goose skimming the roof, shedding feathers like snow. As each feather alighted on the ground, it had opened like a flower, its petals covered with cross-hatched writing that disappeared before he could read a word.

But now Charles was beset by other concerns, gripped by dark forebodings, formless as yet, but deeply disturbing. A second strange occurrence within his circle of acquaintances in the space of less than a week – could that be a coincidence? This time it was Madame de Caylus. He'd never particularly liked the woman and suspected the feeling was mutual, but – was it only yesterday? – they'd greeted each other civilly enough. Marie-Gabrielle had been in good health and high spirits, though he'd observed that she'd grown considerably larger than could be considered civilised. Tonight she lay near death's door, and brought there in such peculiar circumstances. Really, the way it happened would not have been out of place in the most farcical of the *contes de fées* in circulation.

For the twentieth time, Charles went over the details his niece had conveyed to him, trying to wring some sense from it. According to Madame de Caylus' maid – a woman considered reliable due to possessing extremely ill-disposed features – a *couturière* arrived unannounced with a vast array of garments to show Marie-Gabrielle. It was not an unusual occurrence. Competition was fierce. The numbers of these erstwhile seamstresses increased rapidly in Paris once they had their own guild.

Before she was sent to fetch refreshments, the maid caught glimpses of exquisite garments in a veritable rainbow of colours, silks, satins and velvet, some delicately embroidered, some trimmed with ribbons and lace. There were silk stockings from China, too, the latest style, hand-painted with the most charming little designs imaginable. More important than any of this was the *couturière*'s claim that she made corsets so cunning in design that they were guaranteed to take twenty years off any woman's figure, rendering her sylph-like and utterly feminine in an instant. It was natural, Charles supposed, that an over-large woman such as Marie-Gabrielle would want to verify such a claim. And just as natural that the *couturière* would want to prove what could be achieved – but not that she should exceed all reasonableness, pulling the laces so tight that Marie-Gabrielle could neither draw breath nor cry for help. Perhaps the *couturière* panicked. At any rate she and her wares had vanished by the time the maid returned to find her mistress blue in the face and almost beyond help.

He kneaded his temples. Was there a crime here? Perhaps it was only one of vanity on both sides. On the other hand, not only did peasants believe that misfortunes came in threes, but the ancients, too: *omne trium perfectum*. A third vicissitude might or might not befall them. Only time would tell. Charles climbed, reluctantly, back into his bed, wondering if he could recapture his dream.

Chapter Five

After his long absence, Reims comes back and hops along the windowledge waiting to be fed as if he'd never been away. But something's changed: today he ignores the bread, eats nothing, and instead carries off a sliver of cheese and some pieces of brioche.

"Your jackdaw's been a-courting," says the witch.

"What makes you say that?"

"I know these things. His little wife is getting ready to lay her eggs. She'll be having her cravings just like every other female, and it's her husband's duty to bring her whatever she wants. It's the same the world over. Why, even the headless mother of the old queen of England craved apples by the tree full when she was with child. And if the jackdaw wife doesn't get what she's yearning for, well then, her babies will be born with the mark of whatever it may be upon their foreheads."

"Old wives' tales," I scoff, and the witch agrees.

"Of course – who better to know these things?" She carries on with her obsessive polishing of objects that would far rather be left in peace. "Yes, you may laugh, *ma petite*, but whether it be a pinch of dirt or a haunch of venison, I've seen what happens when a pregnant woman's burning desire for something is ignored. A boy in my own village was born with a scarlet mark shaped like a lobster upon his shoulder."

I look down at myself. "My own mother must have craved—"

There was once a queen whose window overlooked the garden of an enchantress. The most beautiful flowers, fruit and vegetables grew there, almost as fine as those in the gardens of Versailles, but the queen had eyes only for a fine bed of lovage. So strong was her desire—

"No good ever comes of dwelling on what can't be changed," the witch says briskly – her quickest about-face yet. "You're as God made you."

"So must I blame God or my mother for my affliction?"

The witch narrows her eyes. "You'd better watch that tongue of yours, miss. Being so high up, we're near enough the heavens for a bolt of lightning to strike you down dead." The old hag shuffles around the room picking up this and moving that, achieving nothing at all as far as I can see. Finally, she puts more wood on the fire. "Let's hope those jackdaws haven't built their nest in the chimney or we'll have roasted chicks dropping onto the hearth by and by."

"What nasty things you say."

She shrugs. "It's true."

"It's no less nasty, whether true or not." I beam hate at her. "Go away, old woman. Leave me in peace."

"I will, by and by. I will." She peers at me with her little black-as-midnight eyes. The day they turn red will probably be my last. Now she gives a little shriek. "Oh, for the love of heaven don't pull such faces. You know what would happen should the wind change."

"Yes, you've said many, many times."

"What a tragedy if you ended up looking like our *Bugul Noz*," says the witch, gathering together her rags and beeswax. "He's the last of an elfin race that once lived alongside us. It's said that he's a kind and gentle creature, with not a malicious bone in him – unlike some I can name – but so repulsive-looking that he's forced to hide deep in the Breton forests where no human or wild creature can ever catch sight of his face. And there he must stay, all alone, until the end of the world."

"I'm sure he'd appreciate your company and conversation – at least for a short while."

"Yes, yes, you can't wait to see the back of me. Perhaps I'll come back. Perhaps I won't." She cackles. "If I don't, you'll be sorry."

"No, I won't." I return to the window, breaking up the rest of my brioche and waiting for Reims to reappear.

There was once a woman whose window overlooked the garden of an enchantress. The most beautiful flowers, fruit and vegetables grew there, almost as fine as those in the gardens of Versailles, but this woman had eyes only for the fine bed of livèche. So strong was her desire that she gave her husband no peace until he'd climbed over the wall and picked a large bunch of the lovage for her.

When the enchantress came home she went straight into the garden to gather vegetables and herbs for her pottage. She saw immediately that someone had been plucking leaves from her precious lovage plants and swore to make the thief sorry if she ever caught him there again. The woman's husband had already decided he would never go back to the enchantress' garden no matter what befell, but his wife's desire for the herb continued to be so strong that he became afraid their unborn child would be born with a lovage-shaped birthmark on its face. Night after night he climbed over the wall to steal more leaves. Finally, the enchantress caught him red-handed. He threw himself on her mercy, explaining that it was not greed or gluttony, but his wife's condition that had driven him to steal, and begged her not to turn him into a toad or a fish or a tarasque. The enchantress spared him on condition he handed over the baby, and such was the man's terror that he agreed.

When the baby was born, the enchantress took the little girl to her own house and named her Lovage.

I cease spinning the thread of my tale to wonder where I first heard the grandmother of this story. Since I have no memory of another teller, perhaps it's new to me, borne into my lonely chamber – as my good fairy might have claimed – by a benign wind from the south. Even now that wind may be circling my tower, lingering to see how much of myself I'll add before snatching it from my lips and carrying it away, east or west, northward, even southward again, wherever the mood takes it.

Lovage grew into the most beautiful child ever seen, but when she reached twelve years old, the enchantress locked her in a tower in the middle of the forest. Being a magical tower it had neither door nor stairs, only a window so high up that it was level with the treetops. Whenever the enchantress bawled up to her, "Lovage, Lovage, let down your hair," the girl unbraided her long plaits and let her hair hang out of the window. The enchantress ascended and descended this golden rope as nimbly as a sailor climbing a ship's mast.

One day, as Lovage was looking out of the window, a prince who'd been hunting in the forest caught sight of her and instantly fell in love. He could find no way into the tower, but every day returned in the hope of catching a glimpse of the girl's beautiful face. It so happened that on one of these visits he heard the enchantress shout "Lovage, Lovage, let down your hair," and watched as the old woman clambered upwards.

Once Upon a Time in Paris

> *The next evening the prince returned and called out: "Lovage, Lovage, let down your hair." And the minute the golden tresses were dropped through the window, the prince climbed up them. At first Lovage was alarmed to be confronted by a tall, splendidly apparelled young man, but little by little they became friends. When he asked her to be his wife she agreed and they decided that the prince would bring a rope on his next visit in order for her to escape. But the lovers were seen by a friend of the enchantress who lived in a cave nearby. The next time the enchantress came to the tower and cried 'Lovage—'*

Suddenly, all my certainty deserts me – of late it happens with increasing frequency – because it's clear that no matter how hard I tug at my hair, it will never grow long enough to reach the rocky wastes below. And even if it did, no tall, splendidly apparelled young man could possibly squeeze through this tiny window opening.

As for the way into my lonely tower, a magical veil renders it almost invisible. Even I walked past the place at least seven times seven times before noticing it and discovering the secret of what lay beyond.

How will he ever find me here?

What if the witch is right?

I throw myself on my couch and weep.

"Feverfew for your headache," says the witch, setting down the steaming bowl. "Drink it hot, *mon petit pigeon*. It always tastes worse as it cools. That's it, straight down – the pain will be nothing but a memory soon."

"Oh Granny, it's vile."

"The bitterness is what cures. That's it…all gone. And here is a sweet lozenge to take away the taste." She gives me a *manus Christi*, awarding herself one at the same time, and takes another item out her bottomless basket of things to be mended. "Tonight I have another Breton tale for you, one from my great-great-grandmother's store, given to her by a travelling tailor many and many a year ago. Would you like to hear it? Very well, I shall begin.

There was this fairy called Melusine, who was Fairy Queen of the forest of Brocéliande. One day, she met a man, Raymond of Poitiers, who was wandering through the trees, mad with grief because he'd accidentally killed his uncle during a boar hunt. Being very fair of face, Melusine cured him of his sorrow and they became betrothed. She made one condition – Raymond had to promise that he'd never enter her chamber on a Saturday. He agreed, and Melusine used her magical arts to bring him great wealth and prosperity. She built for him many castles and fortresses, including the one at Lusignan, as well as churches, towers and whole towns, and each was completed in a single night. She and Raymond had ten children, but—

"Dear, me, this bedsheet is so worn it must be turned edges to middle. That's too big a task for this tale, so I'll replace the trimming on your petticoat instead. Pass me the scissors, my dear." The witch hums to herself as she snips away the torn lace. "A shame to be so careless, miss – this is lace made by those Venetian settlers in Aurillac, the town built of black hellfire stone. It must have cost a pretty penny."

"Why have you stopped your story, Granny? Go on."

She ums and ahs and shoots sidelong glances at me before continuing—

They had ten children, but each child was flawed in some way. The eldest son had one red eye and one blue eye. The next had an ear several sizes larger than the other. Another had a lion's foot growing from his cheek. One child had but a single eye in his head. Yet another was hairy as a bear. The sixth son was known as Geoffrey Great Tooth, because he had a huge tooth like a goat's horn that jutted down over his chin. Another's back was humped. Yet another again had six fingers upon his right hand. The next had toes webbed like those of a duck, which is but a small imperfection when compared with that of the youngest who had the snout and tusks of a wild boar. In spite of these flaws, all the children were strong, wise and loved throughout the land.

The witch fixes me with her beady black eye and repeats herself in a voice heavy with emphasis.

In spite of these flaws, all the children were strong, wise and loved throughout the land. Now Melusine, being of fairy stock, stayed young and beautiful so that men still looked upon her with longing while Raymond soon bore the marks of his years and in time he grew suspicious of what went on in her chamber every Saturday. Forgetting his promise he spied on her through a crack in the door while she was bathing. He saw that his wife was alone and not with a lover. But he also saw that she had the body and tail of a serpent from the waist down. He said nothing about this until their son Geoffrey Great Tooth attacked a monastery and killed the monks, a grievous sin for which he was excommunicated. Then Raymond flew into a rage and accused her of contaminating his family's bloodline with her serpent nature, thereby revealing that he'd broken his promise. Uttering a great shriek, Melusine left the castle immediately and forever and Raymond was never happy again.

"So even the fairy Melusine had something terrible to hide—"

"And yet they say that the line of nobility which sprang from her will endure until the end of the world."

"Why didn't you tell me this story before?"

She won't look at me. "I've only just remembered it, *ma chère fille*. But I know it's true – and not just because it was passed on to me by my great-great-grandmother but because when I was a child they sold little spiced cakes stamped with the serpent woman's picture at the May fair in Lusignan. Maybe they still do. Melusines, they were called, though I never had the good fortune to taste one. The dear lady won't be forgotten in a hurry."

"But she and her children were all monsters."

"Perhaps." The witch spreads her hands and shrugs. "Better to have a flaw on the outside than one in the soul, I say. Don't be so hard on a little difference." A long silence follows. Perhaps my happy-ever-after won't be so happy if bearing such offspring is to be my fate. Finally she says: "There's a tale about a prince who looked like a pig. It might even be about Melusine's youngest. Whether it's to be trusted is quite another thing for I heard it from a rough woman outside a tavern. If I share it, perhaps some day soon you'll return the favour – as you keep promising – and tell me one of yours. Now, let me see—

> *There was this queen who fell asleep in her garden and three fairies happened to pass by. They each decided to give her a gift. The first fairy granted her freedom from ever being hurt by anyone and that her son would be more handsome than any other. The second fairy granted her freedom from ever being offended by anyone and that her son would possess virtue and charm. The third granted her wisdom but that the son would have the appearance and manners of a pig until*

Once Upon a Time in Paris

he had married three times. Time went by and time went by and the queen gave birth to a son in the shape of a pig. The king wanted to throw him into the sea until the queen persuaded him not to and they raised the pig like any other child. He learned to talk and walk upright, but still wallowed in the filth every chance he got. One day he told his parents that he wanted a wife. At first they refused, for what woman would agree to marry a pig? Finally the queen persuaded a poor widow to give her eldest daughter to be his wife in return for great riches. The girl let it be known that she would kill the disgusting creature on their wedding night. When he heard of this, the pig stabbed her with his hooves and she died. He then demanded to marry her sister, who also announced her intention of killing the revolting beast. She died as her sister had. The pig then married the youngest sister who treated him courteously and kindly in spite of his hideous appearance. Soon after their marriage the pig prince shared his secret with her – at night he took off his pigskin and came to her bed a handsome young man. Every morning he put the hide back on and went off to roll in the mire. Time went by and time went by and the youngest sister gave birth to a baby son with a perfect human form. Yes, a perfect human form. And it was at this time that she shared her secret with the queen who did not believe her at first. That very night the king and queen came to her chamber and found their handsome son asleep on the bed. The king immediately ordered that the pigskin lying on the floor should be destroyed so that the curse was broken. When the prince came to the throne he became known as King Pig and lived long and happily with his queen.

"There," says the witch, "my tale is done – but as for the

stitching and making-good, that will never cease until the skies fall and the seas run dry." She holds up the strip of frayed lace and runs it through her bony fingers, as if gauging how much is worth saving. "How's your head?"

"A little better."

"You bring these megrims upon yourself, my dear, with all this fruitless wishing and dreaming – not to mention the day and night scribbling. It's enough to make anyone weep. Why were you carrying on so, this time?"

"For fear that the good fairy was wrong," I mumble, "and that I'll be alone here forever." The witch purses her lips and takes out a roll of ribbon made from fine netting embroidered with sprays of flowers; it's fairy stuff, white as snow, fragile as gossamer. I watch as her needle quick-stitches it to the hem of my petticoat; woe betide me if it gets torn. "Aren't you going to say anything, Granny?"

"Why would I? The Good Lord gives us a limited amount of breaths. It's a sin to waste them repeating myself. I've told you what to do time without number." After a few moments, she clicks her tongue, throws down her work, and takes my hands in her bony old claws. "Listen to me, *ma chère*. If you want this prince of your dreams to find you, get out in the world and make it a little easier for him."

"But to do that I'd have to—"

"Want something badly enough, and you'll do whatever it takes," says the witch, pushing my hands away and searching about for her needle.

"But he wants me to marry—"

"Are you lacking in women's wit, girl?" She sighs and mutters. "First ask for the impossible – jewellery made of the sun, the moon, and the stars; gowns the colour of every leaf and flower that springs from the earth, mantles in every shade and mood of the ocean. Demand hats trimmed with the tail feathers of the phoenix and a flask of dew from the meadow at the end of the world. Ask questions that no man can answer." The witch laughs. "You can trust Granny to help you with that."

"But—" I shake my head. None of this will stop people ridiculing my appearance.

"But me no more buts," snaps the witch. "And don't ask me again for advice you've no intention of taking."

This afternoon the ogre seems remarkably cheerful for someone so obviously unwelcome. As usual, I sit at the window – *muet comme une carpe*, silent as stone, hardly moving a muscle – while he lays out his gifts and delivers his budget of news. He reports with relish that severe fines are to be imposed in England for swearing or blaspheming, and says London will raise huge revenues thereby: unlike the French, the English are not a God-fearing people.

His voice becomes more sober when he speaks of the losses in Catalonia – 500 honest Frenchmen killed or injured at the Battle of Sant Esteve d'en Bas, hundreds more despatched when survivors took cover in the convent at Olet – a shocking betrayal by people who'd so recently looked to the French king for protection. Backwards and forwards the ogre paces, throwing out his arms as he envisages fire and brimstone raining down upon rebellious Catalan peasants who'd dared to object to their village being razed to the ground. Today, my yawns are ignored. If I knew what the Catalan flag looked like, it would be worth flying one from my tower just to annoy him.

His pacing ceases when Reims misses his footing, flapping wildly before settling on the window ledge and tapping his beak against the glass. The ogre snorts and growls, dismisses my little friend as a thief, one of the Devil's own creatures, and moves on to his acquisition of a new bronze medal struck to commemorate the expedition to Brest.

I stop listening and stare into the distance until my vision blurs and my inner eye clears. There stretch endless plains where nobles hunt the pure white stag, forests where fat boars are caught and slaughtered, only to rise again on the morrow, and meadows studded with a thousand flowers where the silver unicorn and the gold lock horns in mock battle.... But what would happen if a girl was forced to marry an ogre?

> *A monstrous brute appeared before her, a great pig-bear reared up on its hind legs, with red eyes, a filthy, tangled coat and huge tusks that protruded from its mouth to curve over its snout.*

The ogre has moved on to gossip concerning the Mauresse de Moret. Now I listen more carefully, as she's another princess, also shut away because of her appearance – though in the abbey of Moret-sur-Loing rather than at the top of a lonely tower. The ogre dismisses her as a she-blackamoor, this novice who goes by the name Louise Marie-Thérèse in an effort to confirm her royal parentage. If it's true that she's preparing to take the veil, perhaps the tittle-tattle will finally cease.

Becoming a nun is surely better than marrying an ogre.

> *She trembled at the brute's monstrous appearance.*
> *"Do you think I am very ugly, beautiful maiden?"*
> *"Yes, ogre."*
> *"Will you marry me, sweet maiden?"*
> *"No, ogre, never."*
> *And the brute sighed and went away.*

And this ogre does, too – but only after making an announcement about his ogreish castle so unexpected that it startles me.

Once Upon a Time in Paris

The witch gives me no peace: thrice a day she demands one of my stories.

"A promise is a promise," she says. "Many and many is the tale you've had from me and I've waited a long time indeed for my debt to be repaid."

The only story I have makes me uneasy, arriving as it did almost completely formed. But tell it I must for we now spend much of our time together sitting in chilly silence, and it's clear I'll get no more tales from her until I do.

"All right," taking the page from its hiding place means finding a new one later, "as long as you don't interrupt."

"I'll be quiet as the grave," the witch assures me, "silent as a *maen hir* – yes, yes, mumchance as a standing stone."

There was once a wealthy merchant who lived in a splendid mansion not a stone's throw from the Place des Voges. This merchant had three daughters, all of them beautiful, but the youngest, whose name was Isabella, also possessed a sweet nature, while the other two were calculating, selfish and vain. A sad day came when the merchant lost his entire fortune following a great storm at sea. He and his daughters were forced to retire to their small country house and attempt to make a living there. For a whole year the merchant strove to till the soil and Isabella learned to keep house while her sisters lay on their beds bewailing their hard lot.

The witch sniggers meaningfully. I immediately fold the page in two.

"Go on," she cries. "Go on. A standing stone I said, and a standing stone I'll be. Not another sound. That's a promise."

Then news came that one of the merchant's ships had escaped destruction and sailed into port laden with goods. The eldest sisters were delighted with this news and, before he set off to deal with his affairs, begged their father to bring them jewels, ribbons, scarves, silk gowns, copies of the *Extraordinaire du Mercure galant* – but only if it contained fashion plates – and the newest Pandora dolls decked out in the very latest fashions. After promising to do his best, the merchant turned to his youngest daughter. "And what will I bring you, Bella?" And Bella, who had come to understand that *il ne faut pas vendre la peau de l'ours avant de l'avoir tué* – that is to say, it was wiser not to sell the bear's skin before killing it – asked only for a single rose, explaining that this was simply because none grew in their garden.

Sadly, more misfortune greeted the merchant on his return to the city. His rich cargo had been seized to pay off his debts leaving no money at all for gifts. He started for home with a heavy heart and was so preoccupied with sad thoughts that he lost his way while traversing a dense forest. As night fell it began to rain, and the further the merchant went, the heavier the rain became until he was soaked right through to his skin. At the same time, the howling of wolves grew ever closer. The poor man, convinced that he was about to meet his end, was about to commend himself to his Maker when he came upon an avenue of trees. A faint light gleamed in the distance and he hastened towards it, only to find a grand château with brightly lit windows. To his surprise, no one appeared either to welcome him or to ask his business there. Neither did anyone appear when he sought the stables. After calling out for a while the merchant unsaddled his horse and made it comfortable in a stall before approaching the house. The great doors, beautifully ornamented, opened as if by magic as he drew near. Inside, he found a roaring fire, and since no one *arrived to tell him otherwise, he took the liberty of removing his sodden cloak and warming himself at the flames. As soon as the chill had left his bones, he turned from the fire and to his astonishment found that a table had appeared, set with a delicious dinner. "Esteemed sir or madam, is this meal intended for me?" he enquired of the empty air. "If it is, I thank you for your kindness and generosity." As if in answer, a beautiful gilded box appeared and flew open revealing a golden knife, a spoon, and even a fork. The merchant ate heartily and when everything was finished cutlery, plates, and table disappeared. Almost immediately, another pair of doors opened and he saw a bedchamber beyond, with a comfortable bed, the sheets turned back as if by invisible hands. He was now very weary and needed no further invitation to sleep. In the morning he found his clothes newly laundered and delightfully perfumed beside a breakfast of hot chocolate and freshly baked white bread. Before leaving the house, the merchant once again expressed his gratitude to his unseen hosts.*

His path to the stables led through a beautiful garden in which roses of every colour imaginable covered arbours and bowers and trellises. Remembering his promise to Bella, the merchant reached up and plucked a few pure white blooms. At once, a terrible banging of doors and crashing as of metal was heard and a monstrous beast appeared before him, a great brute up on its hind legs, with red eyes, a filthy, tangled coat and huge tusks that protruded from its mouth to curve over its snout.

"What an ungrateful wretch you are," roared the brute. "I saved your life last night by granting you shelter. And you repay me by stealing my roses, which are the only things in

this world I care about." It took a step forward. "Now you must die."

The witch stares at me, wide-eyed and with parted lips. One hand clutches her bodice and her sewing basket has tumbled onto the floor.

The merchant fell to his knees, and begged for forgiveness, explaining that he'd gathered the roses as a gift for Bella, his youngest daughter. Finally the brutish ogre seemed to take pity and said the merchant could return to his home and give his daughter the roses, but only if he promised to return in seven days, and only if he swore not to tell Bella what had befallen him. The merchant sadly accepted the brute's conditions and went on his way.

On arriving home, he told his family only that they were no richer than when he started out on his journey. The two eldest sisters wailed and tore their hair and complained that they were reduced to wearing rags, but Bella brought him a simple meal and tried to comfort him. In the days that followed, his unhappiness was so evident that Bella pried the secret from him and declared that she would go in his place to face the monstrous brute. In spite of his protests, on the seventh day she said farewell to her sisters and insisted that her father set her before him on his horse. This time just as before, the great doors of the house opened as they approached, but closed as soon as Bella stepped over the threshold, leaving her father outside. A voice welcomed her and assured her that she had no reason to be afraid. Just as before, a table set with a fine meal appeared, but no sooner had Bella pulled up a chair than the foul ogre appeared. She trembled at its monstrous appearance but forced herself not to run away.

"Did you come willingly, Bella?"

"Yes, brute."

"May I stay while you eat?"

"Sir, this is your house. You must do as you wish."

"No, Bella," said the brute, "you are now the mistress of this château. Everything you see belongs to you. If you find my presence too disagreeable to be borne, I will leave immediately." It looked at her for a long time. "Do you think I am very ugly, Bella?"

"Yes, brute."

"Will you marry me, Bella?"

"No, brute, never." And the creature immediately dropped down onto all fours and, sighing mightily, padded mournfully away, its great claws click-clicking against the marble floors.

In the days that followed Bella explored the great house and found it contained everything her heart desired in the way of furniture, books, clothes and musical instruments. She was served by unseen and silent attendants but this did not concern her for she'd learned, when her father was a wealthy man, that it was the duty of servants to remain invisible. Each evening the brute came and sat with her as she ate and each evening he stayed a little longer, so animated was their conversation. After a time she began to notice his ugliness less and look forward to his company more. Every evening the brute asked her to marry him, and every evening Bella said no, after which the dejected creature left her with many sighs and backward glances.

There came a time when Bella became homesick and pleaded with the ogre to permit a visit to her father and sisters. The brute agreed on condition that she promised to return in one week and gave her an enchanted mirror that allowed Bella to show her family the château and its grounds, together with a magical ring that would bring her back in an instant if turned three times upon her finger.

The next morning Bella awoke to find herself in her old room in her father's house. He was overjoyed to see her alive and so were the elder sisters, for life had not been easy without Bella to tend to their needs. They eyed her fine clothes and jewellery and were hardly able to hide their jealousy. But when she brought out her enchanted mirror and showed them her luxurious new home, with its sumptuous furnishings and beautiful gardens, the two sisters almost choked on their envy. On hearing that Bella had promised to return seven days hence, the sisters plotted to make her stay with them a few more days, hoping this would enrage the brute so much that he'd tear her limb from limb. First they rubbed onions in their eyes and with tears pouring down their cheeks told Bella how much they'd missed her. They behaved so affectionately towards her that when the agreed time had expired she readily agreed to stay for another week. And at the end of that week she was persuaded to stay just a few days longer.

That evening, when Bella was alone in her room, she guiltily thought of the brute waiting for her return and looked in the enchanted mirror hoping to see him, for the truth was she missed his friendship and their lively conversations. To her horror she found that the glass had turned dark and clouded. All that could be seen of the brute was a still form lying under the bush from whence her father had plucked the white roses. Bella immediately turned the ring three times on her finger and in the blink of an eye found herself back in the château where everything, inside and out, was cold and grey as if touched by hoar frost. She ran into the garden and found the poor brute exactly as she'd seen him in the mirror. He was so stiff and still that Bella feared the worst but when her tears fell on his muzzle he roused himself a little.

"Ah, Bella, you forgot your promise and now my heart is broken, but at least I die happy having seen you once more."

"No, dear brute," said Bella, pressing her face to his tangled coat and weeping bitterly, "you must not die for I cannot exist without you. Only live and I will marry you and never leave your side again."

As soon as the words left her mouth the gardens and château were illuminated by a brilliant light and sweet music began to play. When Bella raised her head to ask the brute what this meant she found that he'd disappeared and a handsome young man crowned with gold had taken his place. She jumped up immediately.

"Dear Bella," said the prince, extending his hand, "how can I thank you?"

"No, no." Bella shook her head and backed away. "Where is my dear brute? What have you done with him?"

"You see him before you," said the young man. "My father rules over these lands. Many years ago a wicked fairy laid a curse upon me. It could only be broken when a beautiful maiden agreed to marry me despite my hideous appearance."

When he took Bella's hand, she thought she might weep again, this time for joy. They were married the very next day and lived in great happiness for many years.

"Now that," says the witch, wiping her eyes on a corner of apron, "was a long tale worth listening to – and waiting for – and it will be even better when you put down the paper and tell it straight from the heart." She sighs. "Most men don't look like any girl's idea of a prince. That much is true."

Even while she's speaking, I'm secretly nibbling the edges of the paper with my fingernails, nipping at letters, biting off whole words, tearing away entire sentences. It must be destroyed: this story, more than any other, might give the ogre ideas.

"The mother of your tale was surely my story of the pig prince," she continues, "although now I think on it the tusks remind me of Geoffrey Great Tooth." The witch screws up her face. "And I can hear bits of other tales woven into it – do you remember that ancient Breton tale I shared with you about the magician who accidentally turned himself into a golden ass, for instance? That's got roses in it, too. Yes, the only way the spell could be broken was by him eating every single rose in his sweetheart's garden, thorns and all." She cackled gently. "And he did. He did. Yes, he ate every single one, thorns and all."

"I remember, Granny." A few words scatter around my feet. "I'm sure you're right."

"And you know, *ma chère*, the same old wife – her name was Nonna Kerouak, a net-mender by trade and a fine teller of tales – who passed on the story about the golden ass, shared another one, too. It was about a husband who is such an ugly monster that he can visit his new wife – and she was *jolie comme un papillon*, let me tell you, yes, yes, pretty as a butterfly – only in complete darkness. She'd never clapped eyes on him. A strange courtship that must have been and how they came to be married Nonna didn't say. But what happened next, I ask myself? What happened next?"

"Isn't that an ancient Latin story?" I look towards my books. "I'm sure it is."

"No," the witch says, outraged. She shakes her head. "No, it is not – though it's possible that a Roman tin trader heard our tale in the once upon a time and took it home with him. But after all, what does it matter? Stories are great travellers. Who knows where they are born? All we know for sure is that they're hard to kill."

"What does it matter?" I agree, still secretly shredding the page.

"Ah, I have it. I remember it all. It was the mother's fault. Or the sister's…one or the other, yes. One night the bride secretly lights a candle in order to see her husband while he sleeps. Three drops of hot wax fall onto his cheek—"

There, it's done. Opening the window, I throw the fragments of my story high into the air. They float like feathers.

"Whatever did you want to do that for, girl?" cries the witch.

"What's the fuss about? As you say, my story's woven from many other tales from many other times and as many places. It came to me from nowhere and everywhere. And now that it's been sent back out into the world, everything is as it should be. Tell it my way or your way– change whatever you wish. Whoever catches those words on the wind may do as she pleases with them."

Chapter Six

The waning moon brought more heavy rain and news of a third extraordinary occurrence, this time involving not only another near death but also an appalling public spectacle. Thankfully, it only concerned a servant. Nevertheless the servant belonged to someone known to Charles, for she'd been the personal maid of Mademoiselle de La Force for nigh on fifteen years. Her name escaped him, it was of no consequence, but on this occasion there could be little doubt that poison was involved.

Charles hoped peasant superstition would prove correct and the news would mark an end to the small series of misfortunes. If not – an alarming thought – perhaps Paris was about to endure a replay of the Affair of the Poisons which only ended in 1682 after most of the main perpetrators had been executed, imprisoned, sent to the galleys, or exiled. *Most* of the perpetrators, he thought glumly, but clearly not *all*. He peered dubiously into his bowl of breakfast potage, wondering if he still had the bezoar stone surreptitiously purchased as an antidote to deadly potions at the height of the scandal.

People were poisoning each other right, left, and centre in those terrible days. Some did it for lust, others for rank or position, but most for money – hence the popularity of so-called inheritance powders. The Marquise de Brinvilliers, coveting the wealth of her father and brothers, did away with all three. A scoundrel by the name of Lottinet poisoned both daughters on the eve of their weddings in order to retain their dowries. And many women, anxious to be rich and merry widows, resorted to sprinkling their husbands' food with lethal powdered diamonds, or to serving the unfortunate men with what was euphemistically known as 'soup from the rue Saint-Denis', then – and probably still – the haunt of sorcerers with their arcane knowledge and gruesome practices. Grievously sinful though these crimes were, Charles supposed the perpetrators had their reasons, but he could see no reason for poisoning a nothing, *a nobody*, someone without wealth, position, or even, apparently, what passed for a paramour among servants, which left him with the grim realisation that the intended recipient had probably been her mistress, Charlotte-Rose.

Charles pushed the bowl away. It was no good; he couldn't sup another mouthful. The flavour was much the same as usual but, as anyone knew who'd been privy to the investigations carried out at the behest of the *Chambre de l'Arsenal*, there were poisons in existence that possessed neither noxious taste nor smell. Liquid arsenic, for example, was undetectable mixed with wine or water. He shuddered: it could, or so it was whispered, even be administered in an enema now that they'd become fashionable again.

What poison would make the maid's eyes roll up into her head and cause her to speak in tongues, kicking and flailing and gurgling, her clothes in unseemly disarray, while frothing at the mouth so copiously that onlookers cried out that she was possessed? Ergot? Mandrake? *Vitriol?* No doubt Nicolas de la Reynie with his network of *flies*, his paid informers, would get to the bottom of it; as the first Lieutenant General of Police he had his excellent reputation to preserve. Charles compressed his lips. The murderer would be a woman of course. Poisoning accorded with the deceit inherent in the frail female nature. They smiled at their enemies even as they extended the poisoned chalice.

Fear that a new outbreak of poisonings was underway so preyed upon Charles' mind that he determined to find his protective bezoar stone and keep it on his person at all times. To this end he brought the leather-bound chest of curios out from his commodious *garde-robe* and knelt on the floor beside it. The chest hadn't been touched for years. Its straps were in desperate need of beeswax, the buckles stiff and unwieldy. When he finally managed to work them undone, Charles glanced over his shoulder, then crossed himself before reaching out the first of the items – a *grimoire* carefully wrapped in fine linen – purchased at great cost and while using a false name. Its cover was of thick hide with the seal of Solomon etched upon the front; the pages were said to be virgin parchment, made from the cauls of newborn infants.

Convinced that the book contained a passage about the qualities of bezoars, Charles flicked past the pages on secrets of angels and demons—

> *I shall first declare what the Devils are, and how they may be distinguished by their differences, and what power they have over humane affaires…*

past the secrets of artificial fire—

> *a mixture of fire that will burn under water…*

to the section dealing with secrets of physick and surgery. Within the sections, there was little order and he began skimming the close-written recipes, remedies for those afflicted with quartan agues, tertian fevers, the bites of mad dogs or vipers, plague – calling for herbs and spices, gold and silver, for fragments of sapphire, rubies, emeralds and granite, elk's claw, monoceros horn, basilisk tears, bones from the heart of a stag – until he found what he was looking for.

Against poysons
That there is an effectual Stone against Poysons, there are many witnesses of great authority, and Physicians very antient and many. Julius Scaliger and Amatus Lusitanus boast that they have seen such a Stone; and they say that they have seen it given in a little Wine to many that were infected: for by the vertue of it, it will provoke so much sweat that you would think all the body to be melted by it. By this only the pestilent venom is driven forth. The Arabian Physicians call this stone Bezoard, and from this, medicaments to drive forth poyson are called Bezoardica.

This was immediately followed by three other remedies for treating those who'd been poisoned, which Charles deemed it prudent to read.

An antidote against poyson
One saith, that in the closets of the great King Mithridates was found a manuscript written in his own hand, a composition of an Antidote of two dried nuts, as many Figgs, and a score of leaves of rue beaten together with one grain of salt. He that takes this fasting needs fear no poyson that day.

An experiment of an antient physician of the King of England and it is a wonderful powder against venom and against all poyson
Take Pimpernel, root of Tormentil, Cinnamon, of each half an ounce; Lignum Aloes, Juniper berries, Ginger, of each one dram; sometimes there is added Carduus Benedictus, root of

Angelica, of each half a dram: make a fine powder of all these and keep it close in a box for use.

An antidote of King Nicodemus against poyson
Take Juniper berries two drams, earth of Lemnos two drams and six carrats; powder all these, and mingle them with Oyle or Honey, and lay them up for use; and when need is, with two cups of Honey and water, give the quantity of a walnut.

Charles closed the book, but not before his eye had travelled down the page to a method for making an enemy leprous, and another for eating away a man's flesh by the simple touch of a cloth dipped in a mixture of salted toad and horse dung.

He felt among the remaining bundles for the bezoar stone in its gilded holder, a cunningly wrought thing of two domed halves decorated with pierced and engraved scrollwork, each end surmounted by a gilt flower head. The lining was of plain silver. A girdle of the same material held the two parts together, making a spherical form that enclosed a *genuine* bezoar, not from a goat as was so often the case, but a stone guaranteed to have been taken from the stomach of a Persian unicorn. Although more than a century old, it was almost perfect. The only damage was a little roughness on one side where a grater had been applied. Prior to the purchase, Charles was assured that the minute amount of powder thereby produced, dissolved in pomegranate juice, had saved the life of Sultan Tahmāsp I when an attempt to poison him was made during the civil war over the regency.

Not finding the stone, Charles unwrapped some of the other items secreted in his chest. His favourite was a silver flask in the shape of a breviary – once owned by François Rabelais. There was also a magical mirror, very costly and as yet untried, by means of which, it was declared, a powerful demon could be summoned to foretell the future. His groping fingers found a small parcel of consecrated wafers he'd forgotten about, the twist of paper containing nine five-leaf clovers, much damaged, and a *pistole volante* – a magical coin, in this case a *double louis d'or* – that could be spent repeatedly because it immediately returned to the owner's pocket. This he kept in case of a reversal of fortune. One had to be careful. Look at the way his poor brother was plunged into bankruptcy through no fault of his own. And yet, like a phoenix, Pierre had raised himself from the ashes of disgrace and written *de l'Origine des fontaines*, thereby giving the modern world his invaluable theory relating to the earth's water cycle.

On peering into the chest again, Charles saw one bundle remained. Alas, it was not the bezoar holder.

Years ago – around the time of his election to the *Académie française* – he'd made the acquaintance of a Monsieur Pidoux, an inveterate gambler, who'd bought a stillborn baby, said to be no bigger than a thumb, from the sorceress La Bosse, believing such a potent charm would enable him to win a fortune at cards. It did not. Three months later, Pidoux was ruined and forced to sell the miniature corpse for a fraction of the price originally paid. Charles examined the wizened form carefully. To claim it was the size of a thumb was an exaggeration; it was however small enough to sit comfortably on his hand. Nevertheless, the idea of a thumb-sized child was appealingly reminiscent of old tales told about fairy folk.

His knees were hurting. He longed for a comfortable chair, but there was still no sign of his bezoar stone. It was not more than two *pouces* long – unlike the infant, it really was scarcely the length of his thumb – so easily missed. He would have to search through the linen wrappings again. To conclude that it had been stolen, when a priceless magical gold coin was left behind, raised more fears about the threat of poisoning that now seemed to be closing in, hanging over him as did the sword over Damocles.

Even with the library windows closed, Charles could hear a blackbird clacking its frantic alarm in the yard below. Leaning on his stick, he shuffled painfully across the room in time to see the kitchen cat, tail hoisted aloft, surveying the area for possible nestlings. He wondered whether such a wily animal could have provided unconscious inspiration during the composition of *Le Maître Chat*; if so it would deserve a better name than the Ratter. Perhaps a diminutive of Giovanni would be apt, since a flavour of Giovanni Francesco Straparola's story *Costantino Fortunato* clung to the body of the tale. He craned his neck for another look, but this particular cat had disappeared and the blackbird abruptly fell silent.

Charles hobbled back to his chair, cursing the gout that had woken him in the early hours with excruciating pain in both big toes and a sensation of ice-cold water being poured over his feet and ankles. The rest of the night had been spent tossing and turning, calling for pillows to be plumped, covers rearranged, and hot stones placed in the bed. Just before dawn, a hefty dose of poppy tincture brought a couple of hours' oblivion. This morning his feet were so red and swollen that he could only tolerate wearing his oldest, most disreputable-looking pair of shoes. He felt fit for nothing. And now he was supposed to examine this wretched painter's scribbles and scrawls. He'd been putting it off for days. Charles considered sending the ruffian away, but then changed his mind: tearing a strip off the young idiot might provide some small diversion.

As the clock struck the hour, Poucet ushered in Lew, who was clutching a shabby *portefeuille*. The valet looked bad enough, pale and drooping, with dark rings beneath his eyes, for all the world as if he'd been the one who'd spent the night in agony, but his companion – Charles glowered at the sight of the artist's dishevelled clothing and the wig worn askew. He said nothing, but continued to stare disdainfully at a ragged edge of chemise that Lew had neglected to tuck inside his breeches.

"I trust you've inspected the remedial work," he growled, waving aside the tatterdemalion's greeting. "Is everything there satisfactory?"

"I've tested several sections of wall." Lew set down his bundle, pushed his wig more securely onto his head and made some effort towards tidying his clothes. "The surface has dried – though naturally I must dampen it again to paint – and seems thoroughly sound. I don't foresee any problems."

"With so little time, I was expecting work to have begun."

"But you said—" Lew paused as if selecting his words with care. "Sir, I've been waiting for you to approve my ideas and you haven't…you wouldn't…that is to say, it hasn't been convenient for you to see me for—"

"Yes, yes," snarled Charles, drumming his fingers on the desk. "As a member of the Academy, I've been otherwise occupied with state business. Are you saying nothing's been achieved?"

"It has, it most certainly has. I haven't been idle." Lew began fumbling undone the knotted ties of his scruffy portfolio. "I've made stencils for the stars – graduated in size, of course – and for the borders of fleur-de-lys you stipulated, as well as some for insects and smaller birds. Such a method wouldn't be possible with the larger birds, of course, since each one will be different."

His patience exhausted, Lew ripped off the last of the ties, threw open the case and began covering the writing table with sheets of paper. Charles noted with disgust that some were spotted with drops of wine or coffee. A greasy smear ran down the edge of one. Another had a margin of grubby, ash-coloured fingerprints. "These are my designs for the back of the gallery – butterflies, moths and dragonflies. They'll be set against flowers and foliage. Summer blooms for the butterflies, as you see there, and those paler blossoms that open at dusk for the moths. And as here, water-loving plants for the dragonfly family." He hesitated. "Do you—"

"Yes, yes, so far, so good." Charles folded his arms over his chest. Clearly, despite his slovenly habits, Lew was possessed of a prodigious talent. The drawings were charming, quite exceptional. Employing the young man had been a stroke of genius on his part. And he'd been right to agree to this meeting: his spirits were lifted and the pain in his feet had inexplicably diminished.

"They're *w-wonderful*," breathed Poucet. "Wish I c-could d-draw l-like that."

Charles narrowed his eyes. "Nobody asked for your opinion."

"B-beg p-pardon, sir."

"As for the mural itself," continued Lew, "my plan is to make eight large composites of the fables set against a background of plants and fruiting trees. You mentioned that your favourite is the rats' council...."

"*Conseil tenu par les rats*," murmured Charles.

"Yes, though I know it better as *Belling the Cat*, but the story's the same. The point is, I think, to get over the fable's message." Lew, riffling through his work in search of the relevant sketch, squinted up at him. "Would you agree, sir, that the moral of this tale is that it's one thing to think up ambitious solutions to a problem and quite another to carry them out?"

"T-talk's cheap?" suggested Poucet, picking up a drawing of fragile moths hovering over a spray of honeysuckle. "Oh, this is l-lovely."

Charles sighed and snatched the sheet from the fool's hands. "Your definition is as good as any, young man. Aphra Behn, a *very* minor English poet, remarked of this fable: 'Good council's easily given, but the effect / Oft renders it uneasy to transact.' As for your alternative title, I believe there exists a painting by Pieter

Breughel of a man wearing full armour and with a knife clamped between his teeth as he attempts to hang a bell round his cat's neck...." He stopped abruptly, sensing rather than seeing the look that passed between the two younger men. "Yes, anyway, carry on. What's next?"

"This one is a depiction of *The Wolf and the Stork* – or as here, a crane – you'll see the wolf is clutching the crane's legs as she puts her long bill down his throat and I have drawn the other animals, the ones that refused to help him, looking on. Here – sorry, upside down – here we have *The Hare and the Tortoise*."

"Ah, Zeno's paradox," announced Charles.

"What?"

"It's not important." How, wondered Charles, was it possible to be so ignorant? "And the next?"

"*The Grasshopper and the Ant*." Lew moved the sheet dead centre of the desk. "I've used some colour on this one, to give you an idea of what I hope to achieve.

"*La cigale et la fourmi*." Charles' lips twitched as he pored over the sketch which showed the grasshopper with a gipsy-bright scarf thrown devil-may-care around its neck and a fiddle clutched against its chest, watching with disdain the efforts of a dozen weary ants to glean enough wheat to sustain them through the winter. "Good, good." Really, one could almost hear the distant strains of wild music.

"I wouldn't clothe the creatures," said Lew, "but I thought we might allow some of them a few stylish accessories." He continued to bring sheets from the portfolio, laying them on the desk with a sort of reverence. And no wonder, Charles thought, congratulating himself for the second time. Each drawing was as fresh and witty as the next. His visitors would be entranced by them. He visualised the refurbished salon: the stars above glowing in the light of a vast chandelier while the painted murals to either side, from which his guests would hardly be able to tear their eyes, would be illuminated by hundreds, maybe thousands, of candles. He closed his eyes, the better to enjoy the scene.

Lew gave a discreet cough. "And here's my interpretation of *The Frogs who Wanted a King*."

"Eh? What's that?" Charles straightened his back. "Ah, *Les grenouilles qui desirent un roi* – that was another of the fables personally selected by the king from my recommendations for the labyrinth of Versailles. It was *I* who advised him to include in the garden's design the thirty-nine fountains, each representing one of the fables. Have I told you about it? Excellent, excellent, then you will know that it's a hedge maze with hydraulic statues – the water gushing from the animals' mouths represents speech – what a magical sight that is! And what days those were! The moral of the fable is," he held up one hand, "be content, for fear of change bringing something worse. Oh, how we laughed, the king and I."

"Very impressive," murmured Lew, glancing sideways at Poucet. "I have, of course, seen your book, *Le Labyrinthe de Versailles*. Now—"

"Our fountains use almost as much water each day as the entire city of Paris. The *machine de Marly* – fourteen massive waterwheels, each one more than the height of six men – sets in motion over 200 pumps in order to bring this vast quantity of water uphill from the Seine."

"Indeed." The painter pushed his pencil drawing of the frogs a little nearer to Charles. "You'll observe that I'm considering using a heron rather than a water snake. Making the scene over, rather than under, the water provides an opportunity for depicting bulrushes, a water lily and kingcups." He frowned. "I'm still not sure...."

"W-what are you g-going to d-do with all these p-pictures when the b-ballroom's f-finished?" enquired Poucet. "B-because I would l-love to—"

"It cost nearly six million *livres*," added Charles, "but that wasn't the end of the spending. The truth is, hardly a day goes by without expensive problems, in spite of the sixty men employed to maintain it." He frowned. A fresh twinge assailed his right toe. "What was that? The drawings will be my property, Poucet, *mine*, an intrinsic part of the project, not souvenirs. They will come to me and I will do with them as I think fit." He glared first at his manservant and then at his artist. "Is that understood?"

"Y-yes, sir," muttered Poucet and looked away. Lew merely nodded and began dealing out the remaining drawings as if they were oversized playing cards.

"Here we have *The Lion and the Mouse*." He waited while Charles examined his picture of a mouse scampering over the sleeping lion, drawing his attention to the way a fine network of branches in the background prefigured the hunter's net. "There's *The Jay Dressed in Peacock Feathers*, and now *The Fox and the Crow*."

Poucet laughed. "That f-fox would be in t-trouble if the cheese was p-poisoned."

"Never make a jest of poison," snapped Charles. To Lew he said "A fine depiction. Are there more?" But he began to lose his concentration as sketch after sketch was laid in front of him. Both feet were now hurting so much that he surreptitiously kicked off his shoes beneath the desk. He knuckled his tired eyes. He stifled a yawn. His shoulders slumped. Soon, an occasional small noise to indicate interest was all he could manage, though Poucet continued to express loud admiration.

"And this," Lew exhaled loudly, as though in relief, "is my last design, *The Two Pigeons*. As you can see, they're perched inside a bower of flowering apple boughs arranged in a heart shape."

"Turtle doves," said Charles, also relieved that they'd reached the end. "I would prefer them to be turtle doves. Not absolutely correct perhaps, but those particular birds are symbols of undying affection."

"Of course," agreed Lew. "I'll make them doves, if that's what you want." He started to gather up the sheets of paper. "So, does my work meet with your approval?"

"The p-pictures are incredible," said Poucet. "And I c-can't w-wait to see the f-finished walls."

"Your drawings are...," Charles paused, searching for a word that would express his appreciation without turning the young man's head. Intense pain, as of several knives being simultaneously plunged into his feet, interrupted that thought process. Battling against the impulse to cry out, he settled for: "Your drawings are *satisfactory*. I'm sure they'll appeal to my...to my guests."

"Thank you, sir." Lew scratched his head, rubbed his nose, and shifted his weight from foot to foot. "Sir, about my fee—"

"Be assured that you'll be well recompensed. I'd prefer to leave that discussion for now." Charles winced, and turned to his manservant. "Fetch me some wine, Poucet, quick as you can, and another large dose of poppy tincture." He watched as Lew attempted to refasten the fraying ties of the portfolio. "When will you start transferring your designs to the walls?"

"At once. Well, perhaps as early as tomorrow. I've found some young men to—"

"*Gifted* young painters, I hope. Artists of promise?"

"Naturally. Initially, they'll provide the backgrounds under my supervision. Any that show the requisite skill can assist me with the mural itself." Lew hesitated. "Sir, I suggest the room should be sealed off while work's in progress. Since we must all put in very long hours to fulfil your wishes, it will be easier if we can paint in er *déshabillé* – loose, comfortable clothing – without offending you or any visitors."

"Very well." Charles grimaced. "As for living arrangements – *you* may share Poucet's bedchamber, but any others will have to sleep above the stable. Meals will be taken in the kitchen. Notify Jacques as to the numbers. Thank you for bringing your designs to me. I'll bid you a good day." He glanced meaningfully towards the door, but was dismayed when, instead of leaving, Lew hovered, the battered portfolio clutched against him like a dancing partner.

"About the other room, sir, your red drawing room, I was wondering – if it was to be decorated in a similar way – unless you've decided on some theme already, whether we might build the designs around your poems? I've heard *Grisélidis* and would certainly be able—"

"No," said Charles. "No."

"Oh." Lew hesitated, but only for a moment. "Or perhaps, because many are, I believe, your friends, we could use ideas from some of the ladies' most talked-about *contes de fées?*"

"Pah! Those foolish things? I think not. But—" Charles produced his first smile of the day as a delightful idea occurred to him. "But I have to hand one or two exceptional tales that might be suitable for such a treatment. One is about a cat – no, wait. Far better in every way, is the story of a beautiful young girl in an enchanted sleep, waiting to be rescued from a spellbound castle surrounded by an impenetrable hedge of roses."

Lew nodded enthusiastically. "It should be a splendid castle, like that one at the edge of the Chinon forest."

"The Château d'Ussé, a capital notion." Charles shifted uncomfortably as the pain in his feet redoubled. "We'll talk of this again." He dabbed at the sweat beads collecting above his upper lip. In addition to suffering agony from the disease of kings, he now seemed to be afflicted by a fever. "As you leave, tell that scoundrel Poucet to make haste with my tincture."

"I will, sir. Thank you, sir. I'm most obliged to you for your time." Lew managed a deep bow, but as he turned away the dilapidated portfolio finally gave up the ghost and every last one of his drawings slipped from between its covers to lie scattered on the floor. "*Merde! Merde! Merde!*" and then, in response to Charles' raised eyebrows: "Ah, I sincerely beg your pardon, sir."

Dropping to his knees, Lew began frantically gathering up the pages with such a lack of care that Charles feared the delicate renderings of moths and butterflies, cranes and pigeons, foxes and mice would be damaged beyond repair. He was about to intervene when his eyes were drawn to the sketch for *The Grasshopper and the Ant* with its splash of scarlet. Next to it, half-hidden by the toiling ants, lay a creased and mud-streaked sheet that he couldn't recall being shown. Being so befouled, perhaps even the down-at-heel artist had been too ashamed to lay it before him. Charles gingerly extended one stockinged foot, wincing as he attempted to draw the page nearer with his clenched toes. A moment later, Lew snatched it up and thrust it in with the rest.

"May I see that?"

"This? It's nothing, just a scrap of paper – looks like an old letter. Paper doesn't come cheap and I thought it might be useful for trying out colours or cleaning brushes."

"A letter?" Charles became conscious of his heart beating a little faster. "So you haven't read it?"

"Not me." Lew shook his head. "I shouldn't think it's possible. The writing's blurred from being out in the snow and rain." He handed the paper over, obviously reluctant to surrender his small acquisition. It was still damp, with a fly's wing and one of last year's skeleton leaves caught in the slick of mud. "I found it lying in the Place Maubert," he added quickly. "There was no way of knowing who it belonged to."

"Don't concern yourself with that," said Charles, wondering

why an artist should be visiting a site where so many printers had been executed. He decided against asking. "However, should you come across any other such...*letters*, bring them straight to me. This might be government business and you wouldn't want to be accused of spying." He was silent for several moments, waiting for the threat to sink in. "My dear fellow, as long as you're working under this roof, you've only to say if you need paper. Make out an order for what you need, as with all the other necessary materials. And as for cleaning rags, ask downstairs. I'll tell the old woman – Madame Norik – to provide you with some."

"You're very kind, sir." The artist's surprise showed in his face.

"And perhaps she'd better address the pressing problem of certain other rags at the same time." He shook his head at Lew's blank expression. "That will be all, young man, that will be all."

Finally alone, Charles smoothed out the page with trembling hands. While it was true that most of the words were blurred, with a little care it should still be possible to decipher them. He bent closer—

Il était une fois une petite fille de village, la plus jolie, qu'on eût su voir; sa mère en était folle, et sa mère-grand plus folle encore. This good woman made her a little red hood which suited her so well that from that time on everyone called her Little Red Hood.

One day, her mother, who'd been making galettes, said to her: "Go see how your grandmother fares, because I've been told she was sick, take her a galette and this little pot of fresh butter."

Little Red Hood set off at once to visit her grandmother, who lived in another village. While passing through a forest, she met Camarade Wolf—

He hastily covered the sheet as a shuffling by the door signalled the return of Poucet. "What now?"

"I've brought your d-draught, sir."

"Ah, yes." Charles reached for the goblet of wine, but flicked his fingers over the tincture for the pain had miraculously left him. "You might as well take that away. I no longer need it."

Beyond the library, a passage ran for what Lew reckoned must be almost the length of the house. It was well-lit, having six evenly spaced windows, with a sizable picture between each. Family portraits, he decided, examining the workmanship of each with a critical eye, and probably his employer's brothers – with the exception of the first picture in line, which might well be of the Perrault patriarch judging by that gentleman's severe features and outmoded costume. Resigned to a long wait for Poucet, he turned his attention to the view, such as it was – rain falling in torrents from a dark grey sky onto equally dark grey rooftops for as far as the eye could see – and struggled not to make comparisons with verdant Normandy, where the apple trees must already be in bud.

A few moments more and the valet came scuttling back upstairs. So preoccupied was Poucet with balancing a silver goblet and a glass – both brimming – on his tray that only the briefest roll of the eyes acknowledged Lew's presence. He re-emerged from the library almost immediately, scowling and muttering over the small glass, which was still full.

"Is something the matter?"

"Run here, go there," complained Poucet, "b-bring me something for this unbearable p-pain. I've been b-backwards and forwards to his b-bedside all night with him groaning and m-moaning enough for an entire b-battlefield and tipping p-poppy juice down his throat like water. And still he asks for m-more, so I m-make up a fresh b-batch. What does he d-do? He sends it away."

"At least now you've got a few minutes to yourself. By the way, I'll make sure you get some drawings. Choose those you like best. I'll set them aside and claim they've been destroyed. The old misery doesn't need every last one." Lew blinked, taken aback by the wide smile that completely transformed the little manservant's face. He waved aside the profuse thanks. "It's nothing. Look on it as recompense for having to share your room with me."

The smile faded. "What's that?"

"Hasn't he told you? I'm to share your bedchamber. A stroke of good luck – my assistants have to put up with the stable. Don't worry, I'm no snorer."

"G-good," Poucet said doubtfully, "b-because I'm a *very* l-light sleeper."

"And I sleep like a log. We'll get along fine." Poucet's face had reverted to his usual expression – one that Lew equated with a cowed dog. It wasn't difficult to work out the cause. "Is our lord and master often that cantankerous? It can't simply be his age. My only subjects for the last few months have been old men, but most of them were good-humoured, or at least philosophical. I admit he grew more amiable at the end." Lew stooped to pick up a handful of drawings that had again slipped from the disintegrating portfolio. "There's nothing wrong with his health, is there? I wouldn't like to start on this project and then not...I mean, if he—"

"I told you he had a b-bad night," Poucet said shortly. "G-gout – it w-won't k-kill him."

"Ah, that explains why he nodded off twice. I've no idea how many of my drawings he actually looked at. And even when he did, all I got from him was," Lew adopted a plum-in-the-mouth accent, "the drawings are *satisfactory*." He shrugged. "Well, it seems I'm to go ahead with them anyway."

"They're w-wonderful p-pictures," said Poucet. "Incredible."

After descending the main staircase, both men turned in the direction of the domestic quarters. There were a few more portraits here, though these seemed to be less well regarded than those of the Perrault men. Some were so dark with age that, however hard Lew peered, the subject matter was hardly distinguishable. Poucet didn't spare them a second glance.

"When the master's in a g-good mood ask him to show you his special p-paintings. They were meant to be p-part of a p-panelled ceiling in the old house – pictures of p-poetry, music, theatre, that sort of thing – and so b-beautiful they took your breath away. It was l-like seeing a vision of Heaven. There was going to be a great b-big one in the middle," here he drew a rectangle in mid-air, "with a round one on each side, like so, and then the b-border was planned with eight more p-paintings, oval in shape. I—" Poucet swallowed hard. His eyes turned frantic, darting here and there. The glass of poppy trembled and danced.

"Are you all right?" Lew couldn't see what had so alarmed him.

"Yes." The little manservant took a breath and steadied his tray. "But I d-don't understand why you're w-working here. I m-mean, with your t-talent surely you c-could be p-painting at Versailles."

Lew laughed. "The other day I said almost exactly the same thing about your skills. Perhaps we're meant to leave here together."

"Oh," said Poucet, blushing scarlet, "maybe. B-but why come here at all?"

"The thing is, my friend, I have to start somewhere. My father sees painting as a pleasant diversion much like my sister's embroidering of pretty flowers on linen. He asks that I give up this tomfoolery, for that's what he calls it, and concentrate on learning to run the...er...family business. No, I told him. A thousand times no. I can't do it. I *won't* do it. Who wants to be

Once Upon a Time in Paris

tied down to a place in that manner?" Lew looked away. "And it's because he seemed so shamed by my choice of livelihood that I – well, that doesn't matter. As Monsieur Perrault said, the decorated ballroom will attract attention – being so beautiful, how could it not? Thereafter my name will be on everyone's lips. That's all I want – recognition of my skills. Such fame will bring me important commissions…perhaps a little wealth, certainly great happiness. For that I'll put up with more or less anything. And in the end, father will be forced to—" They'd reached the very last picture when Lew stopped so suddenly that Poucet collided with him. "Who's that?"

The valet gave the portrait a cursory glance. "Could b-be Madame P-Perrault. They say she d-died young. It was m-many years ago."

"She's lovely." Lew laid his hand over his heart and continued to stare at the fair-haired young woman. "A lucky man to have such a wife."

"D-dead," Poucet said gloomily, "and b-buried." He pulled at Lew's sleeve. "I've g-got important things to arrange, b-but first I'd b-better show you where you're to sleep."

Scarcely had Lew finished eating when he became aware of Norik standing in the doorway silently beckoning him to follow her. From the expressions of Poucet and Blanche he understood that her summons should be obeyed on the instant. Clump, clump, clump, the old lady toiled up the staircase, groaning a little, and looking from behind like a slow-moving, rusty-black beetle. At the top she rested for a moment then, still without uttering a word, led him into a storeroom that was mostly cupboard and reached out a pile of linen.

"Here. Those should fit."

"These are for me?" Lew unfolded the topmost chemise and

looked at it, taken aback. "Thank you." The garments were much mended, but none the worse for that; these days, just having something clean to put on his back represented luxury, pure and simple. "That's very kind."

"Don't thank me. Thank the master. He can no longer bear to look upon your filthy rags and tatters. Just try to make yourself look respectable, young man. To have a ruffian living under one's roof gives the whole household a bad name." Norik held open the door. "Is there anything else? If not, away with you. I have things to do."

"As do I, Madame," he said defensively. "Yes, one more thing – Monsieur Perrault said I should ask you for paint rags."

Norik snorted. "Since it's already more holes than cloth, you can use what you're wearing."

"No." Lew's fingers flew beneath his outer clothes – unfortunately now lacking their fastenings – to the initials embroidered on the chest of his chemise. The old dame wasn't shy about moving closer to stare at them.

"A monogram – and neatly stitched." Her thin wheeze might have been laughter. "By your sweetheart, I don't doubt."

"My little sister," said Lew. "And I'll continue to treasure this garment, though ragged and worn out, for that very reason."

"Good linen in its time," she observed, watching him closely. "Your family can't be a poor one."

He thought it wiser not to answer.

"What did you say your father's occupation was?"

"Farmer." Lew unsuccessfully attempted to inch past her.

"A prosperous farmer indeed to afford fine embroidered linen and a thick woollen cloak for a son who doesn't work the fields alongside him."

"We have large orchards. He makes cider and raises the famous Normandy geese – white ganders, grey geese – great flocks of them." It was true, as far as it went. The thought of home reminded him of a small service he'd been meaning to offer. "Madame, about the unfortunate cripple who lives in seclusion here—" Lew stopped, for Norik's expression turned black as thunder. For all her small stature, she seemed to loom over him.

"Go! Get out of here."

"I simply thought," he persisted, "the poor fellow might occasionally appreciate another man's company and conversation. A few war veterans live on our...er...on our farm and I often—"

"This isn't the first time I've had to tell you to mind your own business." She looked past him. "The ill-fated lieutenant was practically butchered in battle by the Dutch, a thousand curses on them. He won't see any *outsider*, not even a priest. That's the end of the matter. Now go, and keep your nose out of what doesn't concern you before the master gets to hear of it."

"Fine," said Lew, escaping with his dignity in shreds. That's what you got for being amiable, for trying to repay the master's kindness. Damn the selfish old scold, the shrew, vixen, gorgon – and for that, damned if he wouldn't find out where the unfortunate officer was hidden away and visit him behind her back.

As was so often the case, his niece Marie-Jeanne arrived far earlier than good manners allowed. Already pressed for time after spending much of yet another afternoon attempting to persuade Pierre of the error of his ways, Charles was forced to cut short Poucet's cosmetic ministrations. This entailed limiting his application of patches to one – admittedly a particularly fine specimen of black velvet cut to resemble a swallow in flight – to disguise a troublesome aftermath of close-shaving situated near the corner of his mouth. He fingered the place gingerly, fearful that the hastily applied glue might fail him, leaving this imperfection exposed at a crucial moment during dinner.

Feeling grim and grey and badly presented in spite of his deliciously extravagant cravat – of heavy Venetian-style needle-lace tied with dove-grey silk ribbon – and his favourite coat of the moment, in sage green embroidered with coiling willow sprays, their tips highlighted in gold thread to match the buttons, Charles hobbled downstairs with a very bad grace. His head ached. A fresh attack of gout threatened. And it was still raining.

To make matters worse, it turned out that his niece wished to discuss the election of women to the *Académie française*; presumably she desired a change of the rules in order to be considered a candidate. Women in the academy – it was an appalling thought. His spirits sank still further. He looked at her glumly, noting that she'd chosen to wear a gown the deep dark green of a pine forest in winter, a shade that sucked every vestige of colour from her already sallow complexion. Her shoes weren't worth a second glance. Sensible and dull green, with no heels to speak of, they were the type of footwear an oyster-seller might wear. Charles wondered briefly why Marie-Jeanne's many literary associates never advised her to choose more flattering finery, before dismissing the thought. They were an ill-favoured crowd. It was probably a great relief to have someone even plainer to act as a foil.

Almost an hour of *ennui* elapsed before Poucet threw open the salon door to announce, in his usual lacklustre and stumbling manner: "F-François T-Timoléon, a-a-abbé de Choisy."

It was apparent that François, at least, had spent a considerable time on his toilette. His lilac gown was embellished with seed pearls; more strands of pearls adorned his wig, strung between clusters of tiny white porcelain butterflies. His perfume preceded him as he sashayed towards first Marie-Jeanne, then Charles, to bestow lavish kisses on the air. As they settled themselves, François used the opportunity to twitch his skirts a few inches above ankle level, displaying fine silk stockings and a pair of powder blue mules that Charles found entrancing though, alas, of far too large a size to be totally desirable. The two men talked of shoes – Marie-Jean exuding disdain – until Poucet reappeared to serve wine and small pastries.

"Ah, that reminds me," said Charles, helping himself to a savoury *feuillantine*, one of Jacques' own inventions, "our friend Charlotte-Rose will be joining us for dinner."

Marie-Jeanne smiled. "How delightful."

"Oh, does she have to?" grumbled François. "The conversation will be limited to a single theme for the entire meal, namely Mademoiselle Charlotte-Rose de La Force, her wit – *yawn* – her literary skills – *yawn* – her conquests – *yawn* – followed by second and third helpings of the same."

"Don't be so heartless," chided Marie-Jeanne. "You must have heard the news. Something frightful happened. A very dear member of her household was stricken by a terrible affliction and collapsed *in public* right in the middle of the rue Traversine while Charlotte-Rose was shopping for a new *mantua*. Imagine the anguish. Think of the inconvenience. Picture the embarrassment. Our poor friend is in distress and we must do our best to raise her spirits."

"Pah!" snorted François. "Charlotte-Rose distressed? I think not. She's the type that keeps a cut onion in her handkerchief to simulate tears."

"How heartless you are. We women feel these things very deeply." Marie-Jeanne sniffed. "Being a man, you wouldn't understand."

"And you, being the epitome of femininity, would, I suppose?" François said nastily. There was a long silence during which they glared at each other, necks extended like two fighting cocks.

Charles cleared his throat. "My friends, let's have no more

bickering. We're here to discuss this work you propose, François – your somewhat convoluted ideas for a story."

"Ah, yes." The abbé rose to his feet, shook out his skirts, and adopted a theatrical pose, hands open and thrust forward as if proffering a gift of great price. "I suggested, did I not, that a lovely young woman – who is actually a boy – meets a beautiful young man – who has been raised as a girl. They fall in love." He looked from one to the other. "A little time's elapsed since I first broached the plot. What do you think of it now?"

"What's the purpose of this *'story'?*" enquired Marie-Jeanne.

"Pleasure?" hazarded François, lifting his eyes to the ceiling. "Yes, sheer pleasure – just as I give pleasure with my beauty, so will my story give pleasure with its charming innocence."

"Define beauty," muttered Marie-Jeanne.

"Define innocence," added Charles, *sotto voce*, thinking of the abbé's reputation.

"Oh, la!" François fanned himself vigorously. "Find a purpose. Define this, define that. We aren't discussing a sermon. It's just a *story*. No need to start pulling it to pieces before a word's been written."

Marie-Jeanne sniffed. "I fail to see whom it would interest."

"Anyone who's interested in love, I imagine."

"But these two are—"

"Love," snapped François, "doesn't limit itself to bringing together wealthy princes and beautiful, virtuous princesses. Mankind wouldn't last long if it did. What about the ugly, but courteous and kind…or the squint-eyed, bow-legged, or just plain fat, but witty and clever? Yes, you see – you agree. So why not two people who, in the matter of gender, don't conform to the rules with regard to outward appearance? They suit each other. What else matters? And after all, everyone is interested in the dream of happy-ever-after, even though they know it can't possibly exist." He sat down, drained his glass and peered mournfully into its empty depths.

"More wine," roared Charles, embarrassed by Poucet's failure to look after his guests. He watched irritably as the manservant jumped visibly before shuffling forward with the air of a whipped hound, his hands trembling so much as he refilled the abbé's glass that a few drops were spilled into the folds of lilac silk. Luckily, they went unnoticed by the wearer. Charles clenched his fists. What a clumsy oaf Poucet was, to be sure, hardly able to get his words out, no finesse at all…and an inveterate daydreamer, too, though God alone knew what the fool had to dream about. If it wasn't for the fellow's undoubted skill at enhancing his appearance, he'd dismiss him and have done with it. Damned if he wouldn't frighten the halfwit, nonetheless. "Attend to your duties better," he growled as Poucet bent over his glass, "if you want to keep your position."

Poucet blanched. "Y-yes, sir. I will, sir. B-beg p-pardon, sir."

"See that you do." Charles sank back, reassured by the response. He turned to bring his superior narrative skills to bear on François' derisory proposal and was dismayed to find his companions once more at each other's throats.

"Nobody would take such a foolish idea seriously."

"Foolish? Ha! That's rich fare coming from someone who writes tales about strumpets called Loquatia and Lackadaisy."

Marie-Jeanne looked down her nose. "And far-fetched, too."

"Far-fetched?" François squawked indignantly. "My dear woman, for all intents and purposes, the duc d'Orleans was brought up as a girl – as was I. Yes, and what about Queen Christina of Sweden? *She* was practically raised as a boy. They called her the Girl-King – I believe her official title was King Christina."

"Yes," Marie-Jeanne said haughtily, "but everyone knew she was female."

"No, no," François protested, "they thought she was a boy at birth. She emerged covered in hair, like an ape, or so I've been told, with a howl loud and deep enough to wake the dead."

"Her mother was quite mad," put in Charles. "She kept her dead husband rotting in a box for years so that she could pay him daily visits."

"Protestants," said the abbé, gravely shaking his head. "They're all the same, alas. Nevertheless, King Christina wore men's shoes, never combed her hair, and had no interest in clothes or jewels whatsoever. And if that wasn't enough, she refused to marry and produce an heir. What's more, it's said she walked like a man, sat, rode and ate like a man, and swore like the roughest of soldiers."

"She killed Descartes," announced Marie-Jeanne.

"Enough!" Charles rapped on the floor with his cane, waving Poucet away when he came running. "Stop seeking historical precedent. As it stands, the idea has the makings of a tale. Perhaps even a long story. I've had a few thoughts that might be of interest." He paused. "Let the narrative begin in the aftermath of battle. The boy's father has been slain. The child is posthumous. The distraught widow prayed for a daughter, but the Fates denied her this wish. Nevertheless, being so anxious that her infant son would never meet the same end as his father, she decided to bring him up as a girl."

"Aha," said François, "very good. Yes, I like that."

"Which battle?" enquired Marie-Jeanne.

Charles pursed his lips. "Let the father of our beautiful child be killed in the Dutch Wars...let us say, to avoid being more precise, in a battle in Flanders."

"No, no, it should be during the Fronde," said François, "so that something exquisite emerges from the turmoil of our unfortunate civil war."

"Perhaps we could settle upon the Battle of Saint Denis?"

"That will do very well." François clasped his beringed hands. "And the beautiful boy's name?"

"Marianne," suggested Marie-Jeanne.

The abbé considered, and then nodded in agreement. "Excellent: the combined names of the blessed Virgin and her mother. Marianne. *La belle* Marianne. So that's settled. Now must come the fitting of iron stays to increase his hips and uplift his bosom. These details I don't need advice on, having experienced them myself. Did I ever tell you—"

"Hold fast," interrupted Marie-Jeanne. "It's not as easy as that. There are still things about your proposed story that don't make sense. All very well if you want people to ridicule your efforts, but—" She helped herself to the last of the pastries, licking her fingers afterwards in a manner which Charles found repulsive. "For example," she continued, "why does your little Marianne – in spite of being told he's a girl – not long to play the natural games of boys. Why no desire for *le chahut* – rough and tumble – or sword play, archery and fisticuffs?"

"Did I wish to do these things?" demanded François. "No, I did not. Look at me. Can you imagine me engaging in rough and tumble?" He smirked. "Well, I suppose it depends on what you mean by the phrase. But seriously, our little Marianne will be taught everything a young noblewoman should know – dancing, music, the harpsichord. It is how a child is brought up that determines his or her manners. Take it from me. I know."

"Yes," said Marie-Jeanne, with heavy emphasis, "but you're...*different*."

"You are as God made you," Charles said smoothly. He glared at Poucet, who rushed to refill the glasses.

François shrugged. "God likes his jokes. Nature makes errors. I should have been born a woman." He took a couple of small, quivering in-breaths, and then spread his fan so that it covered his face. Marie-Jeanne yawned and smoothed the flat front of her bodice.

Charles wished they would both depart. The headache was getting worse. His temples throbbed. Given the choice, he would crawl thankfully into his bed and stay there. "We have not decided on a name for your girl who believes she's a boy," he said, when the silence continued. François didn't answer. After a moment, he folded away the fan, sighed deeply, and dabbed at his eyes with a small lace-trimmed handkerchief. Marie-Jeanne's lip curled.

"Your explanation as to why a boy might be raised as a girl rings true, uncle, but really I'm at a loss to make sense of bringing a girl up as a boy." She darted a quick glance at François. "Well?"

"Don't ask me. My story was supposed to be light-hearted and happy. Now it's utterly spoiled and I've lost interest. *You* write the damned thing."

"I'm sure I'd do a better job than—"

"The nature of the tale," said Charles soothingly, "is such that it would benefit from being written by both a man and a woman...." He thought for a moment, and then added, "I'll give you a first line or two: *The Marquis de X, a gentleman from the so-and-so region, had been married to a beautiful heiress for only a few months when he was killed at the Battle of Saint Denis. His poor little widow was deeply affected by his death. Their love was still in its first bloom, and so on and so on.*"

Marie-Jeanne beamed. "I will happily co-author it with you, uncle."

"I meant myself and François," Charles retorted, "but you may be involved if you wish – with our friend's approval, and provided the experience is to be a mutually pleasant one."

"All of us?" Marie-Jeanne's expression turned sullen. "You mean, we three – in collaboration?"

"It would be a joke indeed if all three of us put our names to it," said François, his good humour instantly restored.

"Or none," suggested Charles. "I dare say *Le Mercure galant* would publish it anonymously – we could keep everyone guessing for years. Why don't we see if Jean Donneau de Visé will include a very short version in this month's issue in order to gauge his readers' reactions?" Having obtained their agreement, he added: "And if you concur, I may have the beginnings of a title – *Histoire de la Marquise-Marquis de* – somewhere or other." Although he hadn't heard any conveyance arriving, he saw Poucet was at the window, peering down into the courtyard. A moment later the manservant caught his eye before slipping out of the room.

"*The Story of the Marquise-Marquis of...*," mused François. "Ah, yes: so far, so good. But where in Paris shall our delicious little marquise live?"

"Why not match the mystery of the story's authorship?" suggested Marie-Jeanne, regaining her enthusiasm, "and select some nondescript place, somewhere almost anonymous in itself – Peuville, or Grandeville, or Banneville? Perhaps—" She was interrupted by a prolonged bout of suppressed coughing from beyond the door.

"If it is to remain a secret, we must talk more of this another time," said Charles, struggling to rise from his chair. "I believe my third guest has arrived."

"M-m-mademoiselle de C-Caumont de L-la F-Force," announced Poucet.

Charlotte-Rose was not her usual self, observed Charles as they went in to dinner. Some might consider the new persona an improvement: gone was the arch flirtatiousness; so, too, the incessant self-aggrandisement. But her cough – which had always reminded him of a riverboat's horn, though others claimed it reminiscent of the noise made by fog-stranded Alpine goats – seemed particularly sepulchral this evening and was ill-matched to her delicate finery. The ivory-coloured dress she wore was of tasteful simplicity, the central panel of her petticoat embroidered with tiny Chinese scenes in blue silk – bridges and sampans, pagodas, birds and trees – and trimmed with scarlet ribbons.

Judging by the brief glimpses he'd caught of her mules they matched the trimmings, being fashioned of bright scarlet leather, and with exceptionally high heels. Although he yearned for a better view, Charles hesitated to stare too intently at the shoes since every few moments Charlotte-Rose stooped to scratch her legs and ankles with increasing violence, acts thoroughly unbecoming of a lady of quality.

Marie-Jeanne was behaving oddly, too. She'd offered condolences for the unfortunate malady suffered by Charlotte-Rose's servant several times and seemed agitated by the lack of response. He began to wonder if his niece knew more about the incident than she'd divulged, or had perhaps been privy to some gossip which she'd not chosen to share. Charles remained convinced that poison was involved and his thoughts again turned to his protective bezoar stone, which seemed to have disappeared without trace. Since the chest in which he kept such treasures hadn't been opened in over a decade, it might have been stolen many years ago. Few people would have had the opportunity, certainly not Poucet who'd been with him under six months; besides, the fellow was so contemptibly ignorant, he would never have comprehended the stone's true value.

Charles settled himself at the head of the table, surreptitiously moving his chair as far away as possible from Charlotte-Rose, who was seated on his right. One could never be too careful when it came to fleas and lice. Saint Francis was welcome to his so-called *pearls of poverty* – tomorrow Norik must prevail upon the maidservants to sprinkle the rooms with horsemint and gorse water, and to lay sprays of butcher's broom on floors and beds alike.

"We were all so very sorry to hear about the *incident*," Marie-Jeanne repeated. "It must have been dread—"

Charlotte-Rose cut her short. "The episode was a *cauchemar*, I tell you, an absolute *nightmare*. And I endured it alone. Quite, quite alone. That is to say, the street was busy, every shop full of people, but nobody came forward to assist me as the woman turned into a fiend from Hell, twitching and prancing, screeching and gabbling, drooling...*scandaleux*." She shuddered and lowered her voice. "What old goat had the foolish creature been consorting with to deserve a visitation like that, I wonder? It was a punishment from God, for some unspeakable sin, I'm sure. I don't wish to think about it." Her hand disappeared beneath the table and the sound of frantic scraping could be heard. "Let us amuse ourselves. Make me laugh, François. Distract me with one of your risqué stories."

François attempted to look solemn. "Mademoiselle de La Force, you forget yourself. As an abbé, I'm the last person in the world to engage in such vulgarity."

"Stop playing the fool, François. You might be a priest, but you're still wearing powder, paint, and a gown that's very much *à la mode*. Anyway, I've heard your naughty stories before. Tell us the one about the three – or was it four – wishes?"

"Four, if you mean *The Four Wishes of Saint Martin*. No, absolutely not. Well, perhaps, with our host's permission, but first," François leaned back as the pigeon bisque was set in front of him, "I must do justice to this delectable broth." He seized his spoon. "It's almost impossible to eat daintily in this house. I swear, Charles, one day I shall kidnap your cook."

Charles raised his eyebrows. "Is this story similar to my own composition, *The Ludicrous Wishes?*"

"That was in verse," replied François, "and suitable for polite society. This story is not, being roughly told and, belonging to the common people, somewhat indelicate."

"I hope you don't mean it's indecent?"

"As do I," said Marie-Jeanne, drawing herself up.

"Oh, no." François pushed away his empty bowl. "If she'd wanted a filthy tale, there are much more highly spiced ones, for instance *Le Chevalier qui fist parler les* – well, perhaps I will draw a veil over what part of the female anatomy the knight made speak."

Charlotte-Rose started to laugh but was overcome by a prolonged coughing fit that left her struggling for breath. "Yes," she gasped, and leaned back, allowing Poucet to brush crumbs from the table with a peacock wing mounted on a silver handle, "we should hear that one, too."

"No, we should not," snapped Marie-Jeanne. "Really, uncle, must we be subjected to such unpleasantness posing as entertainment?"

Charles felt a fresh wave of dislike for his niece and her tight-lipped stance. Besides, Marie-Jeanne could have helped more. She could have done *something*. Instead, and this was unforgivable, she'd recently incorporated certain aspects of the tragedy into one of her farcical yarns. He cleared his throat. "Since Charlotte-Rose has requested it, let us hear the tale of the four wishes. It sounds harmless enough."

"Exactly so," François grinned at Marie-Jeanne's exaggerated sighs, "what harm can words possibly cause?"

"But no indecent terms," Charles cautioned.

The abbé smirked. "Very well then," he paused as if mentally reviewing the story, "I shall begin—

There was once a poor peasant in Normandy who was so

> *utterly devoted to Saint Martin that he invoked him for every act of his working day. Such piety was rewarded: one morning, Saint Martin himself appeared in the fields and granted the peasant four wishes. The man immediately abandoned his ploughing and ran home to tell his wife. Of course she begged him for one of the wishes. 'No,' he said, 'all women are stupid and vicious and you're no exception. You'd wish that I'd be turned into a pig, or an ox, or a mule.' His wife smiled and blew into his ear. 'Sweet husband, light of my life, joy of my nights, I promise you that I'd never wish your manly shape changed to anything else.' Thereupon, he gave her one of the wishes. 'I wish,' she bawled, 'that you be covered from head to toe in pillicocks, every one of them as hard as iron, so that everyone will know what a pillicock you are.' Hardly had she finished speaking when her wish came true. I'll spare you the descriptions dwelled on in fireside peasant retellings. Suffice it to say the pillicocks were of every size, shape and colour – and religious persuasion – covering every inch of his body, ears, brow, hands, knees, everywhere. There was even a pillicock upon his pillicock. Of course, the peasant was furious and in retaliation wished—"*

François looked around the table. "Did anyone hear that? It sounded like fabric ripping."

"It's probably nothing," said Charles, his eyes flicking sideways to where Charlotte-Rose appeared to be intent on shredding her stockings. He coughed meaningfully, but it had no effect.

There'd always been something odd about the woman. He recalled that she'd once allied herself to an itinerant musician who made his living by leading a troupe of dancing bears around the streets and into the courtyards of the better houses. Charlotte-Rose had dressed herself in a shaggy old bearskin. By shambling alongside the actual bears, she'd managed to gain access to the Briou boy after his family forbade their proposed union. If she'd been a pretty young girl disguising herself in an animal skin to, *say*, avoid an unwanted suitor, it might have made a good story, as in *Donkeyskin*, but she was not.

At that moment the *relevé* arrived. "Ah," he said, in a further effort to distract Charlotte-Rose from her frenzied scratching, "here we have Jacques' delicious roast lamb, garnished with bitter oranges newly brought from Andalusia."

"Shall I continue?" enquired François.

"Perhaps another time," said Marie-Jeanne. "Your tale turns my stomach."

"A story should never be left half-told," declared Charlotte-Rose. "Besides, we haven't got to the best bit." She ate a single morsel of lamb before setting down her cutlery. "*Délicieux*. Do please tell us the rest, François. Marie-Jeanne can always stop her ears if her sensibilities are offended."

"I think it best not to dwell on the sites and descriptions of the many uh..."

Here François paused for so long that the pause itself became comic—

"...pearly gates inflicted on this good wife by the second wish. Suffice it to say that she was covered with them from head to toe with the same generosity as her husband was covered with pillicocks. 'Now everyone will recognise you for the pearly gates you are,' he said. They looked at each other. 'Oh, husband, we have wasted two of the wishes. We can't stay like this. You'll have to use a third wish to get rid of these things. But don't worry, the last wish will bring us so much wealth

we'll still be able to live in comfort for the rest of our days.' So the husband used the third wish to get rid of all the pillicocks and pearly gates."

At this point, François turned his wholehearted enthusiasm on his food, ignoring Charlotte-Rose's loud demands for him to desist until the story's conclusion. Her face looked very flushed, but although a considerable quantity of wine had been poured Charles observed that her glass remained practically untouched. She was now clawing her thighs through the thickness of her skirts; most unseemly. He moved his chair an inch or two further away, glaring at the clatter Poucet made in clearing the plates.

"And so," said François, daintily dabbing his lips with his napkin. He patted his hair and checked his appearance in a tiny pocket mirror. "The story...now where were we?"

"Get on with it," urged Charlotte-Rose.

Charles was conscious of a faint drumming noise nearby. The others had heard it, too: the abbé looked at the ceiling, Poucet at the walls, but it was Marie-Jeanne who peered beneath the table and discovered Charlotte-Rose tapping her feet so fast she might have been dancing a *gigue*.

"My dear friend, what on earth's the matter with you?"

"My feet – they're a trifle hot."

"Are they painful?" enquired François. "Should we summon a physician?"

Charles shook his head. "She should go home at once."

"There's nothing wrong with me," croaked Charlotte-Rose. "Finish the damn story, can't you?"

François nodded, looking ill at ease. "I'll be brief. What the two peasants had failed to take into account was that such a wish would also deprive them of their original organs of generation. So there they were, neither man nor woman, since they were lacking in everything that makes them so. Think of that. How would life be? Hence the last wish had to be used to restore them to normal."

"Exactly as happened in *The Ludicrous Wishes*," said Charles. "There, as I'm sure you know, I had the simple husband wish for a fine *boudin* and the ambitious wife, already dreaming of gold and diamonds, fine clothes, a palace, railed at him for his stupidity. He retaliated by wishing that the black pudding was hanging from the end of her nose."

Marie-Jeanne took a very small sip of wine. "We all know your verse tale, uncle. A charming rustic story, elegantly narrated – but this disgusting peasant yarn of yours, François, which would be more at home in the very lowest of taverns, has nothing whatsoever to recommend it."

"Come now," murmured Charles, "let us not quarrel over—"

"And yet, Mademoiselle," said François, raising his voice, "it's precisely those simple peasant tales that you and your fine literary friends claim to draw upon when—"

"I've heard him tell it better," commented Charlotte-Rose, waving away Poucet and the cheese. "It's more amusing when he gives descriptions of the pr—"

"No *lady* would have repeated it," said Marie-Jeanne, "but then, he's no lady, *faux* or otherwise, no matter what airs he puts on or how frivolous and costly the gown upon his back"

François sneered. "There's more of the truly feminine in me than there ever was or ever will be in a dried-up stick like you."

"Pah!"

"I think of myself as truly a woman," François declaimed. "It is a source of great pleasure to me."

Marie-Jeanne groaned. "We've heard this speech before."

"And I have searched long and hard within myself to discover how I came by it. Indeed, I have prayed for an answer. As I understand things, it is an attribute of God to be loved and adored, and man, so far as his weak nature will permit, has the same longing. Since it is beauty which creates love, and beauty is generally woman's portion."

"Yes, but it's not just that, Madame l'Abbé," cooed Charlotte-Rose, glancing disdainfully at Marie-Jeanne's drab apparel, "you have such exquisite style, such a sense of what is becoming, that you are an inspiration to us all."

Her face was now as red as the ribbons on her bodice. Charles noted with alarm that her bulging eyes had become threaded with scarlet veins, while rivulets of perspiration ploughed furrows in the thick white paste applied to her face. Perhaps all this unpleasantness signalled the onset of some hitherto unknown ague. However, her scratching had not abated and it seemed the parasites must be travelling upwards, for now the ill-bred creature was tearing at her abdomen, snagging the delicate stitches of the silk-embroidered panel. He was suddenly reminded of a rabid dog he'd once seen creating alarm worthy of Pan himself among ladies shopping for fashion prints on the rue Saint-Jacques.

Charles forced his eyes away from Charlotte-Rose's clawing hands, fixing them instead on a small pool of spilled wine next to his cheese knife. "That's very true," he murmured, judging it prudent to agree with her.

"My dear, dear friends," murmured François, "I am overwhelmed by your kindness. It is wholly undeserved – though I must say that many others have remarked upon my good taste. Indeed, several ladies have sought me out to instruct their daughters in the womanly art of dressing well…a felicitous arrangement. Ah, such ripe young ladies. Did I ever tell you about the time—"

"Yes," snapped Marie-Jeanne.

"It is possible," said Charles, "that I may yet need your advice on appropriate womanly dress." He immediately wished the words unsaid. Three pairs of eyes widened. They locked onto his face. François laughed.

"My friend, it is a little late for you to be thinking of transforming yourself with corsets and hoops."

"He jests – and at your expense." Marie-Jeanne tossed her head. "Shall we talk of something else? Earlier this evening, my uncle and I were discussing the possibility of women being elected to the *Académie française*." She scowled at François' dismissive laugh.

"*La b-boutonnée*," murmured Poucet.

"Ah, the buttoned-up pie," said Charles, eagerly. "This is a new version, exclusive to the Perrault household, using sweet almonds and honey, the top, as you see, studded with cloves."

"Remarkable." Marie-Jeanne looked unimpressed. "As I was saying, we were discussing reforms to the Academy—"

"Charles," cut in François, putting up one shoulder as if to exclude her from the conversation completely, "you spoke of a small collection of stories when we last met. Prose, not verse – it seemed unlikely. Is my memory at fault?"

"Your manners are," snapped Marie-Jeanne. "Well, uncle?"

"At present," said Charles, making placatory gestures, "I'm writing the morals for a charming tale about a young maiden, lost in a very dark forest. The child is trying to find her grandmother's cottage when she falls in with an elegant fellow, a *bzou*—"

"Did you say a *werewolf*?" Charlotte-Rose interrupted, breathing hard and scraping at her chest. "O-ho, is this going to be an improper story?"

"It is not," he said very firmly. "The *bzou* kills the grandmother and dresses up in her clothes so that—"

"A cross-dressing wolf!" exclaimed François. "What in the name of Our Lord gave you such an idea?" He giggled. "And what, pray, does this naughty, naughty wolf have in mind for the equally naughty little girl?"

"He eats her."

"Eats?" François laughed. "Did you say *eats*? I take it that's a euphemism."

Charles scowled and said nothing.

"It doesn't sound like a moral tale to me," said Charlotte-Rose, rising and clinging to the back of her chair. "But it does sound like an *érotique* one and I should *very* much like to hear it." She took a few steps. "Forgive me, my feet...I must move around. You know, in the streets, when a trollop jettisons her maidenhead they say that *elle avoit vû le loup* – she's seen the wolf." She looked at their blank faces. "Surely you knew that?"

"In that case, you'd better dress her in a little red cloak," suggested François, nodding as Poucet bent to replenish his glass, "like a miniature Magdalene." He started as Charlotte-Rose moaned loudly and began rapidly moving her weight from one foot to the other. "What is it now?"

"My feet are on fire. They won't stay still. I feel as if my shoes were made of red-hot iron." She lifted the hem of her skirt revealing ankles so grossly swollen that bruised-purple flesh lapped over the top of her shoes.

"*Hydropisie*." Marie-Jeanne looked thoroughly alarmed. "The servant should be sent for a physician."

Charles' jaw dropped. The dropsy, if dropsy it was, was so pronounced that only brief glimpses of the fine scarlet shoes could now be seen – and what could be seen looked for all the world like small flames at the base of stout tree trunks. Her hands were swollen, too, huge and lumpy, the size and shape of *Jésus* sausages. Charlotte-Rose began walking backwards and forwards. Her moans grew louder. Her steps grew smaller. Her pace increased from a walk to a trot to a run, until she whirled and spun in a crazily graceless *passepied* dance that had her blundering into furniture and colliding with the walls. So must she have lumbered around, thought Charles, rising and backing away, within her bearskin all those years ago.

"Physician," squawked Marie-Jeanne, pulling at her uncle's arm. "Send the boy to summon a physician."

"It's all right," gasped Charlotte-Rose, sinking into a chair. "No physician. The discomfort has passed. I am perfectly well but feel the need to rest. Kindly have my conveyance brought round so that I may take my leave. Unfortunately, I must forego the rest of the evening's entertain—" She slowly slipped sideways and crashed onto the floor where she lay quite still, staring at the ceiling, her mouth a round O of surprise. Nobody spoke. Nobody moved. Then the clock whirred and struck the hour.

"Poucet," prompted Charles, "help Mademoiselle to her feet."

The manservant darted across the room, but stopped abruptly as Charlotte-Rose heaved herself into a sitting position and waved him away. With a sense of relief Charles observed that her high colour was already fading and the need to scrape at her flesh had correspondingly diminished.

"François," she beckoned the abbé to come forward, "I need your good offices. Something evil is at work. My beautiful new shoes are transformed into scarpines and I fear this costly gown has been sprinkled with noxious powders. Is this the act of a jealous rival? Have I been poisoned or bewitched? Take me home. Let us pray together."

Those sitting around the kitchen table followed Poucet's account with interest, sniggering at the abbé's tale and repeating the best bits to each other – though Lew, grinning with the rest, suspected the original had been far more salty than the version served up here – and laughing outright both at the comical sufferings of the fine lady visitor and the obvious discomfiture of their master. When, stumbling over the words in his haste, Poucet reached the end and reported Mademoiselle Charlotte-Rose's fear of poison or bewitchment, Jacques brought his fist down hard on the wooden surface.

"They'd better not bring suspicions about poisoning into my kitchen. Anyone who tries that will regret it. They'll wish they'd never been born. I'll pull their lying tongues out, chop them small, and make—"

"She d-didn't say anything a-a-bout the f-food," said Poucet anxiously, "except that the lamb was delicious."

Jacques subsided. "A good thing, too – nothing prepared by these skilled hands would cause such antics. I know nothing about magic and even less about poisoning." He glared around the table. "I am a full-fledged cook – an honourable position, though not as well-respected as I should like – and anyone who doesn't believe me can enquire of my guild."

"I do believe you," said Lew, methodically clearing the leftovers from upstairs, every third mouthful followed by a large swallow of wine. "How could food tasting this good cause harm?" He eyed the empty breadbasket so hungrily that Jacques hacked another section from the huge wheaten loaf and tossed it on top of the crumbs. The kitchen maids looked at each and giggled.

"Why do you eat so much?" asked Blanche.

"It's because he's a *rustre*, a country bumpkin." Escarlatta smirked. "Maybe he's half man, half hog."

"No, seriously," Blanche leaned her chin on her fist, watching Lew as he furiously chased the last traces of gravy around his plate, "how can you still be hungry when all you do is draw pictures?"

Lew grinned. "Don't be deceived, fair Mesdemoiselles. Wielding a brush is hard work. I pour with sweat. My body aches.

My eyes grow dim. And speaking as a country bumpkin, I can tell you that at the end of a painting session I'm as exhausted as any lusty peasant ploughing his furrows." He winked at Blanche, who giggled. "The results of my work may look prettier than a field of turned clods, but painting is still hard labour."

"Not as hard," retorted Escarlatta, "as scrubbing pans and doorsteps."

"Or carrying firewood," agreed Blanche.

"Enough of your whining," roared Jacques. "I, for one, would rather look at his drawing of me than a thousand of your scrubbed pans or doorsteps. Clear this mess away, you flibbertigibbets." He frowned at Lew who'd risen and was helping Blanche to carry away the plates.

"Tell me, Blanche," Lew whispered, once they were out of general earshot, "where can I find the cripple's quarters?"

"Why?" The maid stared at him, astonished. "What for?"

"It would be a kindness to speak with the poor man."

"Maybe you're right, but I can't help you. Parts of this house are unused and closed off, thank the heavens, or the cleaning would never end. Being so monstrous to look upon, he's probably kept out of sight somewhere in there."

"What's going on here?" A grim-faced Escarlatta was suddenly standing behind them, arms akimbo. "Why are you two whispering together?"

"Lew wants to befriend the hunchback."

"Whatever for?" demanded Escarlatta.

He shrugged. "Out of Christian charity – his must be a lonely life. Which is his door?"

"Take my advice, painter, and stop asking questions. The maid Blanche replaced was sent away on account of her curiosity. We servants soon learn to look after number one. You should too."

Lew returned to the kitchen, none the wiser, to find Poucet

crouched before the fire and Jacques shuffling cards. The cook stared hard at him, his expression verging on contemptuous.

"It's a bad habit, chasing after maids, young Leonardo."

"I never would," protested Lew. "I was asking where I might find the cripple. They claim not to know. What about you?"

"How the hell should I know? The poor mangled unfortunate eats little and bothers me not at all." He slapped down the pack. "Now, who's for cards?"

"Which game do you favour?" Lew, glancing in Poucet's direction, saw the little man frantically shaking his head, which caused him to watch the cook's deft shuffling of the pack even more carefully. Clumsy sleight of hand didn't unduly worry him – Lew prided himself on being able to out-cheat a man like Jacques any day of the week – but he was unwilling to admit he'd hardly a *sou* to his name. "And what's the stake?"

Jacques shot him a sidelong look. "Playing for money's been forbidden under this roof." He squared up the pack. "Basset? Hoca? Or a few hands of piquet if you prefer. Perhaps ombre, if young Poucet will play."

"N-no, I d-don't like card games."

"Piquet then?" Jacques removed cards two to six from each suit, set them aside, and shuffled again. "By your leave, I'll be the younger." He dealt them each twelve cards.

Ignoring Poucet's frown, Lew nodded and drew his stool closer, raising his voice to be heard above the clattering of pans in the space adjoining the kitchen. "So how can we make this more rewarding?" After some haggling it was arranged that Jacques would stake several batches of his almond *gaufrettes* against Lew producing for him a pack of playing cards, the normal hearts, tiles, clovers and pikes to be replaced by certain kitchen implements, and the royalty by various renowned cooks.

Jacques was a wily opponent and far too large to be accused of cheating. An hour or so later, when two more pitchers of wine had been downed, and Poucet had long departed, Lew conceded defeat. "I'm for bed." He stretched and yawned. "Tomorrow I begin an artistic endeavour that will ensure my name is known first in Paris, then throughout France, and after that the whole of Europe, and England too."

"We're all entitled to our dreams," growled Jacques. "And when hens grow teeth I'll be cooking for the king himself."

Clutching his lighted chamber stick, Lew climbed unsteadily up the back stairs, lurching along the narrow passage – which seemed to delight in maliciously bouncing him from wall to wall for its entire length – leading to his new sleeping quarters. The door creaked wearily. His head grazed the beams. The candle flickered wildly and a loose floorboard sprang up to trip him. "It's only me," he whispered after finally exhausting his fund of expletives. And as an afterthought added: "Where can I find the wretched cripple, my friend?" But Poucet only curled himself into a tighter ball.

Though unlucky at cards, Lew considered himself to be very fortunate as he eased his body onto the hard straw mattress beside Poucet. Already his skills had earned him a bed, two good meals a day, and fresh linen for the morning. He lay awake for a while, staring into the darkness and listening to the murderous fantasies of his companion – who didn't stutter in the least while talking in his sleep.

Chapter Seven

From early morning right up to that moment when the daylight thickens into dusk, my jackdaw, Reims, comes and goes, too exhausted by provisioning his young family to bother with learning to speak. "Bring your wife to see me," I urge. "Bring your brood of children." His silver eyes glint as he seizes whatever is put out for him and flies off, contemptuous of my idle wish for company. The ogre hasn't visited for days. Good. I hate him. It would be so easy to creep behind him next time he leaves: one small push between his nasty shoulder blades and down he'd tumble, thump, thump against every stone step, down and round and down again. But there's no getting rid of the witch.

"Mind yourself, miss – I need to open the window and shake out your bedding. Just look at those black clouds! A cold wind, too. Hard to believe it's spring down below." The witch continues to mutter and fuss for a while until her mood changes and she breaks into song.

> P'edon war bont an Naoned, di ge don lan li ra,
> P'edon war bont an Naoned, di ge don lan la
> An deiz all o kanañ di ge don lan li ra
> An deiz all o kanañ di ge don lan la....

The witch's voice isn't a pretty one. At the best of times it resembles – I swear – the harsh call of a carrion crow sighting a freshly sown battlefield, but it's worse today for now she's waging war on the furniture again, pushing and shoving and turning as she croaks, only to replace everything exactly as she found it. Why anyone prizes such pointless industriousness is beyond me. You've only got to look at the story of Mary and Martha to see what Our Lord thought of it. But I'll keep such views to myself: a witch is a witch when all is said and done.

I once scribbled down a tale about the two daughters of a widower, one hardworking, always cheerful, forever looking for something to keep her pretty little hands busy, and the other branded coarse and sluttish because she couldn't see the point of eternally fussing over things that must all be done again on the morrow. My tale concluded in a way that would surely have pleased the witch: flowers and precious stones dropping daintily from the lips of the energetic girl, serpents and toads spewing forth from those of the idle and forthright one. I regret that ending now. Perhaps the story should be rewritten.

"*Me gwelet ur plac'h yaouank,*" rasps the witch. "*Hed ar stêr o ouelañ—*"

There's only one way to stop her singing: "What's your song about, Granny?"

"There was this young girl weeping on the bridge in Nantes. A young man passing by asks what ails her. The girl says she's dropped her gold ring into the sea. He dives in once to look for it. He dives in twice. But the third time he drowns." The witch sighs and attacks the big carved chair with her polishing cloth. "It's a true story."

"True or not, it's very sad." I set out paper and ink. My quill's blunt and it takes me several moments to locate the knife. The witch lets out an enraged squawk and pounces.

"Don't drop your dirty feather shavings all over my clean floor."

"Haven't you finished yet?"

"Everything must be spick-and-span." She eases her back and groans a little. "I'm certain sure you'll have a visitor later."

"I've no wish to see him."

When he does come to my tower, the ogre has nothing new to say.

And, as usual, I say nothing at all to him.

Today, he's brought daffodils. Their fragrance fills the air, but I won't look at them any more than I'll spare a glance for the aigrettes dripping with diamond *briolettes* that his ogreish hands have laid on my writing table. They'll be swept into the chest with his other gifts – for what use do I have for hair ornaments only suitable for grand occasions? One of my childhood dreams was of the day I'd be old enough to attend my first ball, to see the magnificent clothes and elegant dance steps; the handsome prince, his beautiful princess. But I never could: one look at me and everyone would burst out laughing.

After the ogre's gone, I stand at my window all forlorn and look towards the ocean, where – so says the witch – leviathans eternally churn salt water to make the tides, bishop fish preach to the shoals, and sea pigs till the rich earth beneath the waves. In my mind's eye I see fishermen wearing kokers – their big salt-rimed sea boots – hauling in nets lively with quicksilver harvests of *la plie*, barbels, sea eels and lampreys, *les marsouins*, dolphin, herrings and burbot.

And beyond them lie at anchor tall ships such as once carried *les filles du roi*, the king's daughters, to New France – tens of Marguerittes, Georgettes and Nicoles, dozen upon dozen of marriageable young women named Fleurance, Antoinette or Catherine, scores of Mathurines and Genevièves, in addition to all those others christened Françoise, Étiennette, Marie-Rose.... I know every one of those girls and they didn't sail to Quebec in search of adventure. They didn't go for the new clothing, although it was most assuredly welcome. Neither did they go for the *poitrine espoir*, the bridal chest – even if it was well stocked with riches in the form of one hundred sewing needles and a thousand pins, a spool of white thread, a pair of scissors, two knives, a comb, one pair each of stockings and gloves, and the same of shoe ribbons, one taffeta handkerchief, a bonnet, four lace braids, and a headdress, plus two *livres* in silver. Nor did they make that hard and perilous journey for the pair of chickens and pigs, an ox, a cow, and two barrels of salted meat promised to every newlywed. Not even for the generous pensions that came with the birth of children.

They went because they could choose their own husbands. They went because in New France they could say *no*.

"Beautiful," says the witch holding up the aigrettes so that each diamond sparkles and flashes in the candlelight. "These must have cost a pretty penny. What a pity never to wear them. Think how they'll look on a head piled high with golden curls." She tries holding one against my hair, but I push her hand away.

"Take them, since you like them so much."

The witch cackles. "What grand parties will I ever be invited to?"

"What grand parties could I ever attend, looking as I do?"

"Listen to me, my girl, you make too much of—"

I look down at myself. "You only say that because you're used to the sight."

There was once an ugly princess, truly the ugliest, the most laughably ugly princess, seen since the world began....

"But anyone seeing me for the first time—"

"Would look no further than your sweet face," the witch says briskly.

"You don't know what you're talking about, old woman." I

clench my fists. "Were you there when I was teased, tormented, and called cruel names? Did you see them point and laugh?"

"No need to shout, miss. I'm standing right next to you." She replaces the silly bits of jewellery, lining them up with such pernickety care that I feel like sweeping the whole lot onto the floor. "Any fool can see nothing will change your mind." Her little witch eyes gleam on discovering the ogre's candied fruits and sugared nuts. "Here you are and here you'll stay. Let's hope you don't die waiting."

"Don't say that. As soon as my true love finds me, we'll leave this place together." The witch mumbles something and shakes her head. "What was that?"

"I said, *têtu comme une mule*, and so you are – no good pulling that face – stubborn as a mule. Any girl with anything about her would get out of this tower, by fair means or foul, and go in search of him instead of sitting and stewing in her own misery. But why waste my breath? You've heard it all before time without number." She places the candied fruit between us. "There, perhaps they'll sweeten your mood."

"I don't want his horrible sweetmeats. Take them away." And so she does – but not before selecting the largest fruit, moreover the only *reine-claude* in the box, and eating it in front of me. Greengages are my favourite as she well knows. We don't speak for a very long time.

Even when the diamonds are shovelled into the carved wooden chest, which is now brim-full of the ogre's unwelcome gifts, their costly sparkle still seems to hang in the air before my writing table, reminding me that the ogre is rich and doesn't care what he spends. No matter what the witch says, I fear asking for the impossible would help me not one whit when it comes to his marriage plans, so – should I ever be forced to accede to his demands – all that would be left to me is the business of asking questions no man can answer. Does she mean a riddle?

"Granny, what's greater than God and more evil than the devil?"

"That's a question for a priest, *ma petite colombe.*"

"No, listen, it's a riddle. There's more. The poor have it, the rich need it and if you eat it you'll die." The witch shakes her head. "It's not difficult, Mamie. The answer is – *Nothing.*" I search around for another. "How about this – All about, but cannot be seen. At night they come without being fetched, but by day they are lost without being stolen. What are they?"

"You're too clever for me, my little dove."

"*The stars.*"

"Well, well, fancy that."

"What always runs but never walks, often murmurs, but never talks, has a bed but never sleeps, and has a mouth but never eats?"

"Let me think about it."

"All right, Mamie." I wait for a few moments, but it's soon obvious that she's more interested in finishing her pile of sewing. "You're not even trying. The answer is: *A river.*"

"Ah, yes – easy to solve it now you've told me." I've proved nothing: a witch is not clever, simply sly, whereas the ogre is both sly and clever. I'm sure he'd know the answer to any riddle. After a while, she folds the mended linen and looks up at me. "Clever I'm not" – perhaps she really can hear what I'm thinking – "but I've just called to mind an old tale about the King of Riddles."

"I'd like to hear it."

"Come then." First the witch pats the stool at her knee, and then she smoothes my hair. "I hope soon you'll share another of your stories with me. Now—

There was this king of a faraway place – do not ask me his name for the passing years have swallowed it whole – and the queen, his wife, gave him a son. Then she died. Soon afterwards, as men will, the king married again. The new queen also gave birth to a son. Time went by and time went by; the two boys grew up tall and strong and handsome. But the queen grew restless for the king was old and, being the younger, her son would not be the one to succeed him. She ordered the cook to put poison in the heir's wine, but the younger son overheard and warned his brother. When the elder son didn't die, the queen gnashed her teeth and commanded the cook to use stronger poison. But again the younger brother overheard and the same thing happened. This time the heir poured the poisoned wine into a flask and kept it. And he said to his brother, 'If I stay here the queen will murder me sooner or later. It is better I leave now and make my own way in the world.' His brother said he would go with him. They saddled their horses and left that very night. They'd not gone far when the elder brother started wondering whether leaving was the wise thing to do. And they'd not gone much further again when he started doubting whether there really had been poison in his wine. So he put a few drops in his horse's ear and the horse dropped down dead. After that—"

"Poison in an *ear*, Mamie?"

"That was the way of it. Hush, don't fray the thread—

After that they rode on the one horse for a few leagues until the elder started doubting that poison had killed his horse for it had been an old beast, all skin and bone, coughs and complaints. So he poured a few drops from the flask in the ear of the other horse and it too dropped down dead. Since it was midwinter and night was upon them, the two brothers flayed the horse and used its hide to keep them from freezing. In the morning they saw twelve fine big ravens come down to feast on the horse's carcass. And the ravens straightway fell down, stone-dead. Well, the brothers took the ravens and went to the nearest town where they asked a baker to make twelve pies from the birds. And when the pies were baked, they travelled on until they came to a forest. Here four-and-twenty black-hearted brigands came out of the trees wanting their purses. But the brothers had only food so the brigands took that. And after eating the pies they fell down dead as dead could be. So the brothers stripped the brigands of all their silver and gold and went on their way.

Before long they came to the castle of the King of Riddles. Now this king had a beautiful daughter with twelve handmaidens almost, but not quite, as beautiful as she was. And this princess would only marry the man who asked her father a question he could not answer. Any man that asked a question the father answered aright was put to death. So the elder brother told the younger to pretend he was his page. And this was the question he put to the king: One killed two, and two killed twelve, and twelve killed four-and-twenty, yet two escaped. As was the custom, the two brothers were maintained as honoured guests until the king could guess the answer.

Time went by and time went by. Still the king could not guess the answer. And there came a day when one of the twelve beautiful maidens came secretly to the page's chamber and tried every wile she possessed to get the answer to the elder brother's question. He would not tell her – but he kept her fine zibellino—"

Once Upon a Time in Paris

"What's a—"

"A *zibellino* is a fur tippet such as fine ladies wore in days gone by, made from the pelt of a sable with its head and legs left on. I daresay if you weren't so fine it might be made of a polecat or weasel," the witch frowned thoughtfully, "but then, ermine is only stoat fur and that's worn by the highest in the land. Hush your questions, girl. Let me finish – that's twice you've yanked on the thread. Do it again and the tale will escape and run away into a mousehole.

> *Day after day, each in turn of the princess's handmaidens came to him privately and tried, in every way a woman could, to persuade the page to tell her the answer. The younger brother would not tell, but one and all he kept their zibellini. And when the last handmaiden came he told her that no one had the answer save his master who even at that moment sat in the Great Hall with the king. So finally the princess herself, all arrayed in her very finest robes, approached the elder brother. She asked him for the answer and after a very long stretch of persuasion he told her – but he kept her zibellino, which was made from a rare white sable, fitted by the jeweller with golden paws, its skull covered in gold leaf and encrusted with precious stones.*
>
> *The next day the King of Riddles summoned the elder brother and gave him the answer to his riddle. At the same time he gave him a choice in the manner of his death – to have his head struck off or to be cast adrift in a skin boat without a paddle. At that the elder brother stood up in the crowded Great Hall and said: 'I have something that must be told before making a decision. My page and I were hunting in a deep dark forest. My page fired at a vixen and she fell before*

him, but he took off her fur and let her go. And so he did to eleven more vixens and they all fell to him and he took their furs and let them go. And at the last came a fine glossy vixen and it was my turn to fire, so I took the fur off her and let her go.' And here he laid the thirteen zibellini at the king's feet.

The king looked long and hard at the elder brother for by this account he realised that the young man knew he had not guessed the riddle but had been told the answer. And being at bottom an honourable man the king gave him his daughter to marry. As for the younger brother, he went back home with his brother's blessing to claim their father's throne."

"Yes, Granny, it's a good story, but how does it help me find a question no man can answer?"

The witch gives me a strange look. "Perhaps the question you need is one that no man *will* answer. There's an ancient tale about that very thing. But now is not the time."

And no amount of cajoling can get it out of her. So I stand at my window and whistle for Reims, mostly because it always annoys her.

"*Une femme qui siffle et une poule qui crie porte malheur dans la maison,*" chants the witch.

"What was that, old woman?"

"A whistling woman and a crowing hen are neither fit for God or men," she says, mumbling over the words. And so she should because it wasn't what she said the first time.

I'm busy with a new story about another forsaken girl, a beautiful one, gentle, kind, but tormented and teased beyond endurance, reduced to terrible misery and loneliness. In spite of this situation, I'll triumph. She'll marry the finest prince in the land –

and all those who persecuted her will shrivel up and die of envy. Finally the witch agrees to tell me her ancient tale in return for the first few paragraphs.

We strike the bargain, but there's a glint in her eye that tells me she's holding something back. I don't trust her. Why would I? She's a witch. Out comes the inevitable mending. And, ah yes, here comes the patting of the stool at her feet.

"Well," she says, "now let me see—

There was this elvish knight, handsome as could be and a sweet talker above all others. One midsummer night he stood on a hill near the enchanted Forest of Brocéliande and blew upon his horn, which was a magical one so that any woman who heard it was filled with longing for him. It happened that the miller's young daughter heard the sound and she wished aloud that the toothsome elf lay in her arms. Before she could take another breath, the elvish knight stood at the foot of her bed. First he tells the maiden that she's far too young to be a wife, but the miller's daughter says that isn't so as her younger sister is already married. So he sets her a task. She must make him a shirt of the finest batiste without cutting the cloth and without using needle or thread. And after the shirt is finished and done, it must be washed in the nearby dry well where dew never gathers nor rain ever fell. Well, perhaps by then the elvish knight's magic was wearing off, for the maiden ups and says to him that she has a task he must carry out first. Her father owns a strip of land that lies between the salt sea and the shore sand. The elvish knight is to plough it with his magical horn, spread it with a cartload of lime pulled by a wren and sow it all over with a single ear of wheat. When he has reaped it with a sickle of leather, tied it up with a peacock's feather, and winnowed it in a cockle shell, he must bring his harvest to her father's mill for grinding, and then he may have his shirt. Until then she'll remain a maid."

"That is not what you promised," I say indignantly. "It was supposed to be the story about a question that no man can – or will – answer."

"It's about asking for the impossible," she retorts, all hunched up like an owl, and with her bony claws grasping at the air. "And that was part of it."

I don't mean to stamp my foot, but there it is, done. "Since we're talking about impossible tasks, old woman, here's one for you: unsay your tale! For I'll not let you hear mine."

Neither of us speaks for a while. The hateful old hag sits and finishes the candied fruit. In spite of the sucking and slurping, I pretend not to notice.

"Very well," she says, and I swear there's a red tinge to her eyes, "I'll share my tale with you. And afterwards you will berate me again, for I doubt you'll care for all of it.

There was this king and, thinking to hunt, he rode into that same forest, the forest of Brocéliande, which you will know by now is an enchanted place that often stays dark in the day and is bright by night, ice-cold in summer, and bakehouse-hot in winter. Moreover it is not always in the place where it was yesterday or will be tomorrow, and sometimes disappears altogether. Hardly had the king got into the deep of the forest when twilight fell, though it was still morning. There was neither sight nor sound of his companions, not even of his hounds, and the king soon discovered he was lost. He stopped at a spring to drink. It was then that a gigantic knight emerged from the dark trees – which moved aside to let him pass – mounted upon a huge black stallion and clad in black armour from head to toe. Thirteen black hounds followed, all with red ears and scarlet eyes. The king found himself rooted to the spot, unable to move, unable to speak, only to listen. And what the black knight told the king was this: since he was a powerful magician as well as a mighty warrior, he would take everything the king possessed, his castle, his lands, his horses, his hounds, his cattle, sheep, and geese, everything, even his outward appearance unless… unless he could return hither in three nights and a day with the answer to a question. And the question, he went on, fixing the king with his black, black eye, was this: 'What is it that women most desire?' With that a small wind shivered the leaves and the knight disappeared as though he were woodsmoke. The king's movement was restored forthwith and the way out of the forest opened up before him. As he made his way home, he asked the question of every woman from the humblest goose girl to the miller's wife, from the women pounding laundry at the river's edge to the bailiff's lady. A good dinner, a pretty gown, a comfortable bed, a new husband – each of them had a different answer. He asked the ladies of the court. Some said beauty, others wealth, yet others said it was to be his wife – but none of them could agree. So after three nights and a day, the king returned to the forest with a heavy heart and tried to find the spring, which was not where he expected it to be. But then he saw a figure sitting under a great yew tree and hurried forward thinking to ask directions. The closer he got, the more he quailed. The figure was a woman dressed all in green velvet, the sleeves trimmed with silver and gold. She was the ugliest creature he'd ever set eyes upon, as gnarled and twisted as a *willow. Her head was bald on its dome and covered with sores, while greasy white hair hung down over her ears. Instead of a nose, a pig's snout was spread across her face, and her yellow teeth were the same size as those of the king's horse. One eye was large and grey, the other small, clouded, and red-rimmed. Her eyebrows were like un-pleached hedges covered with hoar frost."*

The witch stops. I'm almost sure she's smiling. "Go on," I urge, for surely we were getting to the nub of the story, "go on please, Mamie."

Her hands were as knobbed and bent as the roots of an ancient oak, her knees were swollen, her legs leathery as old saddles. As for her feet, they were as broad as a field, as long as a cow's tail, and as flat as floorboards. Such a sight the king had never seen before. In one hand she clutched a staff hewn from blackthorn, carved all over with magical symbols. The king stopped at a distance and kept his eyes on her stick as he asked for directions to the spring. He did not think for one moment to ask her for an answer to the question.

'Why so careworn, my lord king?' asked the hideous creature, and he felt bound to tell her. At that she laughed. 'I can answer that question,' said she, 'but in return you must grant me one wish.' The king said he would grant her anything. She laughed again. 'Anything – whatever that wish may be?' And the king swore on his life that she would have whatever her heart desired. And the woman laughed for a third time before whispering the answer to the black knight's question in his ear. 'Now for my wish,' she said, and laid her hand upon his arm. The king nodded and said again that whatever she

wanted was hers for the asking. 'I would be your wife,' she answered. At that the king nearly fainted. He shook his head and attempted to back away, but her hand was still on his arm. 'A king never breaks his word,' she reminded him. At that the king was overcome by shame. He apologised and promised to return the next day with his retinue and take her back to his castle for the wedding. Releasing his arm, she pointed him in the direction of the spring.

The black knight was waiting for him. And his dark hands reached out as if to steal everything that the king possessed and everything that he was. When the king repeated what the terrible old hag had told him – that what women want most is sovereignty over their own lives – the black knight's rage was terrible to behold; a great wind rose and the forest trembled. Stronger it grew, stripping leaves from branches, tearing saplings from the ground, finally growing so strong that trees themselves were bowed down like people at prayer. Then the black knight was gone and the king returned home, sick at heart, horrified at what he'd promised. Nonetheless, he announced his forthcoming marriage to his court and next day returned to the forest as he'd promised, dressed in his finest robes, accompanied by a company of knights, together with a richly decorated carriage pulled by two dappled grey horses. His knights could hardly believe their eyes when they saw their future queen. They shuffled their feet and nudged each other and exchanged horrified glances. But the king kissed the monstrous hag's knobbly hand and led her to the carriage. At the castle the entire court stood in silence as the king led his stumbling, shambling bride into the Great Hall. After the wedding came a feast. No one ate. After the feast came the dancing. No one had the heart to dance. But at last the king reluctantly led his limping lurching loathly lady around the hall in a stately measure, moving extra slowly so as not to leave her behind and taking great care not to stand on her enormous feet. At midnight the bride and groom retired. The king sat with his head in his hands, grieving over the prospect of being wed to such a hideous creature. There was such silence in the bridal chamber that eventually he forced himself to turn around and saw before him the fairest maiden he'd ever set eyes on, with long golden hair, a slender figure, and skin as pale and smooth as apple blossom. 'I am your wife, my lord king,' she said. 'By marrying me you have released me from the first half of a spell. Now I must return to that hideous shape for half of each day, unless you can answer my question. Tell me: would you rather have me beautiful by day and hideous by night, or hideous in the daytime and beautiful when we are alone together?'

The king thought about her question for a very long time. To be ugly by day meant that the whole court would mock her, but at least she would lie in his arms as a beautiful woman. To be as lovely by day as she was in that present moment would make of her a charming companion beloved by everyone, but in their private hours she would lie beside him as he'd first seen her in the forest. 'I am unable to answer your question, dear wife,' he said finally, 'the decision must be yours. Choose whatever you think best.' At that the queen clapped her hands and laughed for joy. 'That is the right answer to my question, husband. You have given me what every woman desires – sovereignty over my life – and thus have broken the spell.

"There," said the witch, "my tale is done. That was the last. My store is now empty. I can see from your face it didn't please you overmuch." She cackles, quietly, an old hen having just laid her final egg. You were warned, *ma petite*. I said you wouldn't care for all of it." Oh, how I hate her.

"I liked the tale well enough, and the question. It's the extra bits you put in – that was just spiteful."

"Do you think so?"

"I *know* so." The witch seems unconcerned and yet I could push her down that staircase far more easily than I could dispatch the ogre. Crunch. Crack. Splinter. Snap. She'd arrive at the bottom with every one of her little bird bones broken in a thousand places.

"And now," she says, all false innocence, "you promised me a few lines of your new story."

"Very well, then." I take out my hastily penned page. It's not much and for that I'm thankful—

There was once a learned and well-respected lord whose dear wife died, leaving him with a daughter who was gentle and kind-hearted, as well as being beautiful. After a time, the lord took a second wife, a proud and haughty woman with two daughters who took after her in every way. The wedding was hardly over before the stepmother showed her true qualities. She couldn't abide the child and didn't trouble to hide it, forcing her to do all the rough household chores and sleep in an attic on a pile of straw. After the girl had finished her work she used to sit in the corner of the fireplace among the cinders. For this reason the stepmother and her eldest daughter called her Cucendron.

"*Cucendron?*" exclaimed the witch. "Cinder-arse – what sort of name is that for a girl?"

"I've heard unfortunate girls are often called worse. Anyway, that's all I've written."

"It calls to mind something I once heard—"

"Another tale from Brittany, no doubt," I say tartly, wanting – but at the same time not wanting – to hear it.

She looks at me askance. "It's where the best tales were born."

"Go on."

The witch hums and haws for a while before beginning. "It was about a highborn maid called Gwennolaïk, whose mother, father and sisters had all died, one after the other, leaving her at the mercy of a wicked stepmother."

"How does the rest of it go?"

"Can't remember," claims the nasty old hag, pinching folds into her apron. "As I've already told you, my cupboard is bare, the wool all spun, every last bit of a yarn woven."

I don't believe her; not for a minute. "What about the end? Didn't Gwennolaïk's prince come? Surely you must recall what became of her."

"It was her foster brother, but he came too late," the witch says lugubriously, "for the stepmother had already married her to the village lunatic. And though her foster brother galloped like a trade wind from Nantes on his great white stallion, carrying a gold ring for her finger, Gwennolaïk had died of sorrow." Her mouth shuts like a trap.

"A miserable tale," I say, and pretend not to mind. Cucendron's story is also a sad one, but her prince will come. "My story will end happily, I promise you. Now please go away. I want to think."

Chapter Eight

Lew woke late, to find Poucet had already risen. He dressed quickly and went outside to run cold water over his hands and face before going in search of anything that might serve as breakfast. At the kitchen door he was met by a high-pitched shriek and flattened himself against the wall, angling himself carefully, so that he might watch whatever was going on without being seen. At first, Lew's view was blocked by a stranger's back, a slender man sporting a very fine burgundy coat trimmed with gold lace; moments later, the fellow lunged forward, precipitating another shriek.

"*Ta gueule*, woman!" roared Jacques. "Shut your trap! That squealing is enough to turn the milk."

"There's the cause," retorted Escarlatta, red in the face and brandishing a ladle. "The dirty young dog won't keep his hands to himself."

Jacques shrugged. "He's the master's son. What do you expect me to do?"

"Do something, anything, you *poltron*. Send him packing. *Très bien*, if you, a giant of a fellow, are too much of a lily-livered coward to stand up for me." Escarlatta swung the ladle. A dull thump was swiftly followed by a muffled yelp. "Perhaps that'll teach you to keep your hands to yourself, Master Pierre. If it doesn't, I'll be up those stairs right away complaining to your father."

"Only a bit of fun," said Pierre, rubbing his shoulder. He turned, allowing Lew his first glimpse of Monsieur Perrault's youngest son, a handsome young fellow sporting the worst black eye he'd ever seen together with an alarmingly bruised nose and cheekbone. "Don't be such a misery, Escarlatta. Anyway, who says my father would believe you?"

"He'd believe *me*," said Jacques. "Especially when I tell him you're interfering with preparations for his lunch. Behave yourself. How can I bring my expertise to bear on this piece of veal if I have to keep checking to see what your hands are up to?" He looked up as Lew sidled into the room. "Ah, good morning to you, Leonardo – though it's nearer noon than daybreak, but I suppose we must make allowances for a fellow with your skills."

"So you're the portrait painter," said Pierre.

"Lew le Sauvage." Lew inclined his head.

"Daresay you're after a bite to eat, Leonardo." The cook handed him a bowl containing the usual broth poured over bread before turning his attention back to Pierre. "What are you hanging around my kitchen for anyway, Master Pierre? At this time of day you're usually out gallivanting with your friends."

"No money," said Pierre, gingerly fingering his nose. "Allowance stopped."

"And why bother," snapped Escarlatta, "when he can make so much mischief here at no cost whatsoever?" She muttered something beneath her breath to Blanche, who nodded and continued picking stones from a bowl of lentils.

Pierre laughed. "It seems I'm a disgrace to the family's good name. Dear Mama will be turning in her grave. *Grand-père* Perrault would have taken a horsewhip to me. And so on and so forth. I'm bored witless – the only entertainment my father can offer is a book – Lord save me from becoming like him. That's why I've been trying to persuade Jacques to set up a few card games later."

"I've said it before, I'll say it again – no gambling permitted in this kitchen." Jacques threw a chunk of amber into the mortar. He gestured towards the upper floors with his pestle, but surreptitiously winked at Lew. "I've had orders from on high. *Winning* rhymes with *sinning*. You'll never see a deck of cards in here, or a tumbler of gaming dice, upon my word, no."

Pierre grimaced. "What about you, Lew?"

"He won't play either – not if he knows what's good for him," said Jacques, raising his voice above the thump and grind as the pestle reduced the golden resin to powder, "your father's word being law, and all that."

"No good counting on me," said Lew, having caught a particularly meaningful look from the cook. "Thing is, Pierre, your father's honoured me with this very large commission." He set down his scraped bowl, resisting the urge to lick it. "And once I really get into my work, I hardly notice the time. Days and nights roll into one. No time for entertainment. I barely stop to eat or sleep."

"Shame," grumbled Pierre. He paced the kitchen, fiddling with utensils, until his eye was caught by the drawing of Jacques. "Well, you are a handsome devil, Jacques, truly a handsome devil!" He looked at Lew. "My compliments, sir – thought you were another of Pa's old fogey artists, but I believe I've underestimated you. Would you do a picture of me?" Pierre gestured at his face. "I mean, later, when the bruises have faded."

"It would be a pleasure," Lew said smoothly. Regardless of his present disgrace, Pierre was obviously the apple of the old man's eye; making a friend of him would be prudent. "In fact, now that your father's portrait is more or less finished, why don't I make drawings of all the other members of the Perrault family? You, Pierre, naturally; your brother, Charles-Samuel, when next he calls, and...." He paused, daring himself to try again, "...and I believe there's also another relative living in seclusion here, sadly a—" He stopped, suddenly aware that Pierre was avoiding his eye and shifting his weight from foot to foot. The two maids hastily left the room. Jacques coughed and let his eyes slide sideways to where Norik stood, her mouth tight with anger. Lew swallowed hard. "And you, Madame. Are you not as good as family? It would be an honour to produce a small sketch."

"*Non.*" The word hurtled towards him with the force of a sling stone. He was about to make himself scarce when Pierre seized the old lady by the shoulders and backed her towards a stool.

"Sit there, Madame Norik," he cried, "and let Lew capture your exquisite loveliness. Yes, yes, you must! I insist – and I'm sure Pa would, too."

"A pleasure," mumbled Lew, making space among the bunched herbs to rest his paper. "Perhaps a small smile, Madame?" he suggested in response to her furious expression. And, that failing, added: "No, I'm certain you're right – a certain air of haughtiness befits your important role here," whereupon the fury was replaced by a look of deep suspicion.

Norik's face, which he carefully examined from every angle before beginning, was an interesting one, despite – perhaps because of – the telltale signs of a hard life. His instinct was to capture that austere story in its entirety, but months of painting aged clients had taught him some valuable lessons about the enduring nature of vanity. He worked quickly, capturing her strong jaw while underplaying the *Polichinelle* nose, emphasising her shrewd eyes but doing away with the network of lines etched around her once-shapely lips. A border of lace was added to Norik's collar; a few rosebuds to her austere head-covering.

"I hope my sketch meets with your approval." Lew bowed as he handed it over. "Age hasn't extinguished your beauty, Madame. The bones never lie." This had long been his standard compliment for an elderly woman and usually elicited, at the very least, a pleasant response, but Norik clutched the paper and left the room in silence, with only the merest of glances in his direction.

Lew shrugged. And someone stifled a laugh. He was pleased to observe that the laughter was not mockery but awe. Pierre and Jacques had been standing at his shoulder throughout, silently watching him bring depth to the initial outline of Norik's face – boldly contouring with the softer side of the graphite stick, sometimes stippling or blending lines with his fingertips to create softer shadows and hollows.

"They lie who say magic is dead," said Jacques. "Like me, you're a born craftsman. At your touch the very paper takes on life. A genius takes knife or brush, and glorifies duck, lamb, or thrush."

Pierre nodded. "You're damn good, Lew. I've many friends who'd pay good money for such a likeness of themselves."

Lew bowed modestly. "Send them to me." Such sketches were almost effortless. A little extra money was always welcome. Besides, pleasing the sons might well bring larger commissions from their parents. "I'm anxious to get my work known."

"And I'm anxious to cook *déjeuner*," growled Jacques, "so away with you now, Master Pierre." As soon as he heard the boy's footsteps on the stairs, the cook caught hold of Lew's arm. "Don't trust that ne'er-do-well any further than you can throw him. He's a cheat, a liar and a sneak. Never lend him money. And never take him into your confidence – he'll immediately run squawking to his pa, hoping to be rewarded with a few pieces of silver to spend in the nearest tavern."

A visit to the Pont-aux-Maul was long overdue and, although Charles didn't relish the prospect, the arrangements he'd made with Déchets were dependent on him opening his purse for the fellow at reasonably regular intervals. One had to be careful: in that area it was not advisable to appear well-heeled. He instructed Poucet to bring out his plainest woollen coat, a faded blue-grey in colour, without any ornamentation, and so old that the fabric was on the edge of becoming threadbare at the elbows.

Poucet frowned as he helped him on with it. "It s-seems a l-little t-tight across the sh-shoulders."

"Yes, yes," snapped Charles. "Do you really think I'm not aware of the fact?"

"B-beg p-pardon, sir."

"Shabbiness is an advantage where we're going, as is a poor fit. Now find me a cravat – something suitably drab – and a dark ribbon." Charles glowered at his reflection. Unsatisfactory though his appearance was, he was unlikely to be seen by anyone that mattered between a horse butchery and a glue factory on the banks of the Bièvre. The thought of the foul river made him queasy. "And I'd better carry my most strongly perfumed gloves."

It was a fine morning and Charles decided to walk, partly because he'd been advised that exercise would be beneficial to his health, but also because it was hardly possible for a carriage to move once it turned into the narrow rue Mouffetard. Besides, who knew what jettisoned treasure he might discover between this house and his destination?

After instructing Poucet to keep close and watch out for pickpockets, he led the way along the rue des Fossés-Saint-Marcel, stopping only when the pale gleam of something lodged against a guard stone caught his eye.

"J-just an empty e-eggshell, sir, a p-pigeon's…. D-do you—"

"For goodness' sake, put it down!" Charles marched straight across the Place de Fourci without finding anything, and into the rue Contrescarpe where he directed Poucet to investigate a twist of grey in the gutter – it turned out to be a scrap of lace ruffle – and to retrieve a crumple of paper from a darkened doorway –

this proved to be the final few bars of a musical score. "Take them away. What on earth would I want with such rubbish?"

From there it was no distance at all into what must surely be one of the most noisome streets in Paris. The *Mouffe*: the great stink. Charles braced himself.

"This is a very ancient highway," he murmured to Poucet, as if defending the place. "One could follow its course due south to Italy." But the *sot* only stared at him open-mouthed.

Clutching his cane more tightly, Charles fixed his thoughts on reaching the church of Saint-Médard at the street's far end. Nothing would be found here. The crowds were so dense that moving quickly was out of the question and to step from the pavement was to risk being trampled by horses goaded to the point of madness by shrieks and cries, in addition to over-use of the whip. Anything that could have a price slapped on it was sold here – rabbit skins, pottery, discarded finery, rush candles, human hair, feathers, spoons. It was hardly possible to hear one's own thoughts above the bawling of sellers hawking services or wares – from the cobbler squatting on the pavement with a hobbing foot between his knees to the rat-catchers swinging their poles of gibbeted vermin. An endless succession of women elbowed between the close-packed bodies, carrying bunches of herbs and cresses, or with trays of food – fresh bread, pastries, cheese, even leftovers from the banquets of the more fortunate – suspended from their shoulders. The stench of the river and the cemetery slunk at their heels and a sour taste rose in Charles' mouth for he'd always imagined such offerings could not help but be tainted by dung or the dead. It was not yet eight o'clock, but he observed that wine peddlers, with barrels strapped to their backs and drinking horns chained to their belts, were already doing brisk business.

Beggars circled like flies: old soldiers, blind or *sans* limbs, the hunchbacked and the lame, skeletal mothers holding up sickly infants. Worse were the near-naked urchins running alongside, clutching at Charles' sleeves, diving for his pockets, tugging at his coattails, laughing in Poucet's face as he attempted to drive them off. Charles threw down a few coins and tried to quicken his pace. But the swarm only grew larger, its demands more shrill until, all patience and compassion spent, Charles laid about him with his cane. He glanced nervously over his shoulder, but Poucet was still close at his heels – and vigilant moreover, his eyes constantly peering from left to right. The fellow might have his faults but at least he was conscientious, which was more than could be said for many servants.

Charles moved aside for an aged oyster seller, bent almost double by the dripping wicker basket hoisted behind her, and then stumbled on, past the mean drinking houses he feared Pierre frequented: here, *Les Deux Colombes*, a pretty name for a dark, low-ceilinged hole, and there, *Les Trois Déesses*, inhabited by beckoning slatterns with grotesquely painted faces that one could hardly imagine being less like goddesses. He flicked a quick sideways glance at *Les Poings d'or*, and kept walking, unwilling to catch the eye of its pugilistic owner, who leaned against the doorframe exhibiting fists red and raw as pounded meat rather than golden as his signboard suggested.

A few yards more and Charles was forced to raise his scented gloves to his nostrils as the stench of the Bièvre rose to meet them. At the same time he became aware of discordant sounds in the distance – a rapid drumbeat punctuated by the clash of cymbals – soaring above the shouts of the sellers and the trundling of wheels. The racket originated from a building immediately opposite the church, but owed nothing to Christian worship. And, although firmly resolved to keep his eyes fixed forward, Charles found he was compelled to glance at the workplace of the infamous Saint-Médard tooth-puller, a huge man, of a size with Jacques he was sure, ferociously ugly, and whose bulging arm muscles rivalled those of any farrier. Blackened molars threaded on strings were draped across his shop front like the nightmare necklaces of some Dutch ogress; above hung a gruesome representation of Saint Apollonia – the patron saint of toothache sufferers – having every tooth smashed from her head by barbarians seeking to deprive the martyr of her faith.

"Keep up!" bawled Charles, noticing Poucet slowing down to stare as the drumbeats grew louder and faster. Muffled screams followed by a final clash of the cymbals marked the successful extraction of a sufferer's rotten stump and – since today no storyteller was present to hold their attention – those who'd gathered to watch this entertainment began to drift away.

Charles was grateful that his few remaining teeth were sound. Rotting fangs weren't simply an affliction of the poor. During conversations an increasing number of his acquaintances were forced discreetly to raise their hands – or fans – to cover appallingly discoloured or missing teeth. And, though it was never mentioned, the stench of decay from the king's teeth could have been used as a battle weapon. His entire court had given heartfelt thanks when he'd finally agreed to have them pulled. Now Louis hadn't a tooth in his head – although he'd been born with two already present.

With the bridge in sight, the crowd started to thin. The threat of pickpockets lessened but other dangers lurked in the Passage Moret and it was in this insalubrious place that Monsieur Déchets' premises were situated. After being jostled to within an inch of the filthy river on his last visit, Charles had sworn never to come here again unless accompanied. Jacques would have been the most sensible choice, but that would have meant holding up lunch. He took the gloves from his face and gestured with his cane.

"This way. Follow me."

"You're n-not g-going along there?" Poucet stared in dismay at the slippery cobbles, the lowering buildings, and the murky red-brown water streaked with pinkish scum. "Sir—"

"Stay close." Charles kept as far from the river's edge as possible, looking neither to left nor right until his nose told him they were approaching the glue factory. Here the walkway was partially blocked by barrels piled high with picked bones, among which the quick flick of rats' tails was clearly visible. Hordes of black beetles scuttled around the building's open doorway, which exuded hot, greasy out-breaths in time with the massive bellows beneath the furnaces. Beyond the barrels lurked Déchets' ramshackle establishment. Glancing back, Charles saw that Poucet's face had taken on a faintly green tinge. "Wait for me out here."

Inside, he found the proprietor reclining on his throne, a fine, old-fashioned ebony and damask chair which, now lacking one leg, depended on a cross-section of tree trunk for support. In front of him stretched a venerable oak table so long that it might have served time in an ancient refectory. The remainder of the floor space was covered by mounds of fabric, mostly ragged garments and household linens, being sorted by two wretched-looking women. Déchets seemed to be fast asleep, judging by his stentorian snores, and yet his eyes remained wide open. To doze during the day wasn't surprising, thought Charles, since the fellow spent every night scouring the city streets for any discarded objects that might turn a *sou*, but it was well known that only alchemists and sorcerers slept without closing their eyes. Would a man possessing magical powers really stoop to earn his bread by such humble means? Déchets usually called himself a dealer in antiquities…at other times a *chiffonnier*, but most of his income seemed to come from collecting rags, which were sold to the paper-makers. No matter. It was the paper itself that Charles was interested in. He coughed gently.

"What?" barked Déchets, sitting bolt upright. He blinked, rubbed his eyes and sprang to his feet. "Ah, papers," he said, pointing at Charles' chest, "*billets-doux*, court documents, proclamations, certificates, deeds, charters, letters, contracts, records and reports. I have many. Most, as you requested, recovered from the area directly surrounding the Montagne Sainte-Geneviève." Reaching for a worn leather bag, he brought out a thick wad of paper, handing it over with a flourish.

It had long been apparent that Déchets was unable to read. The sheets were of many sizes and in various states of filth and decrepitude – pages torn from books, a milliner's bill, back copies of the *Nouveau Mercure galant* and what appeared to be a schoolboy's rote-copying of a Latin text. Charles flicked through the pile quickly, shaking his head with disappointment. He was about to double-check when a roar from Déchets made him drop the collection onto the table.

"What are you after? Get out! There's no work here."

"I w-was j-just—"

Déchets produced a cudgel. "Clear off you—"

"He's with me," said Charles, glaring at Poucet. "I told you to wait outside."

"B-but—"

Charles glared. "Wait outside as instructed." He waited until Poucet left before returning the sheaf of papers to Déchets, who squinted up at him.

"Have we found what Monsieur desires to recover?"

"Alas, no," said Charles, taking out his purse, "but please keep looking. Perhaps we'll have better luck next time."

Suddenly weary and unwilling to face again the hustle and din of the Mouffetard, Charles beckoned Poucet to follow him along the rue de l'Arbalète intending to make his way home by means of the longer, but infinitely more peaceful rue des Postes. There was room there to walk two abreast and Poucet soon fell into step beside him.

"S-sir, w-why d-do you keep on wanting b-bits of old p-paper...?"

Charles reasoned a half-truth might stop unbridled speculation among his servants later. "I'm constantly seeking something – a missing document – that was thrown away by mistake."

"One of your p-poems?"

"Er, yes, er, an important poem, exactly so – and although you continue to look for them whenever you're bidden, since Déchets makes his living by collecting rubbish from the streets of Paris it seems sensible to call on him from time to time."

"Them? D-do you m-mean," asked Poucet, his face creased with anxiety, "that m-more than one d-d-doc...?"

"Document," Charles frowned. "Yes, there have been many."

"All a-at one t-time or...?"

Charles sighed. "Unfortunately, it's happened on several occasions."

"It w-wasn't me, s-sir." Poucet wrung his hands. "It really w-wasn't. I'd n-never throw out y-your—"

"Nobody's blaming you," Charles said irritably. "I think a jug of chocolate would be refreshing when we return home, Poucet. Perhaps you might ask Jacques for some orange zest to flavour it, and—" Charles stopped abruptly, his eye caught by something grey-white fluttering along the pavement. Strips of paper, not just one: at least four, and all moving in different directions. "After them, man!" he shouted, throwing himself at the nearest fragment. "For the love of God, don't let them get away."

Moments later, Poucet returned, breathing hard and with grazed knuckles. He gingerly handed over three pieces of paper that appeared to be from sheets torn top to bottom. "D-did we g-get all of it?"

"There doesn't seem to be any more." Charles rubbed one bruised elbow and peered into the nearest courtyards. "I won't know for certain until they're fitted back together."

"B-but that's no p-poem. W-what is it? W-what d-does the writing say?"

"You don't need to know that." Charles folded the strips and slipped them into his pocket. "Thank you for retrieving these. I believe Norik will provide salve for your wounds." Poucet made a small dismissive gesture.

"B-but where d-did the p-paper come from?"

"A mystery indeed," murmured Charles, looking anywhere but at his valet, "yes, a mystery indeed."

Charles smoothed the strips of paper and lined them up on his writing desk, using the inkwell, his sander, and the empty chocolate pot to hold down their curling edges. It was, as he'd hoped, another stray tale. This time, the writing – though by the same hand – was not only smaller than before, but cross-hatched, meaning it might take the rest of the day to decipher the text and make a fair copy. Not that he resented the use of his time; he was grateful for the opportunity.

"Another saved," Charles muttered as, guided by the title, he turned the strips about until the sentences were reasonably well matched, "but how many more have been lost to the world?" He allowed himself a small sigh of regret, and then brightened: if this story proved to be complete, it would be the fifth in his possession. The first paragraph made him smile.

La Barbe-Bleue
Il était une fois un homme qui avait de belles maisons à la ville et à la campagne, gold and silver plate, des meubles en broderie, et des carrosses tout dorés; but unfortunately this

> *man had a blue beard: it made him so ugly and terrible that there wasn't a woman or girl who didn't flee from his presence.*
> *One of his neighbours, a lady of quality, had two perfectly beautiful daughters. He asked to marry one, leaving her the choice of which one she would give him. Neither was at all willing....*

The smile faded as he read on. Bluebeard had already been married several times and nobody knew what had become of his wives. It disappeared altogether by the time the young wife, all a-tremble, stood before the forbidden door. Charles moistened his dry lips and pressed on, almost trembling with her.

> *D'abord elle ne vit rien, parce que the shutters were closed; after a few moments she began to see that the floor was covered with dried blood, and that the blood mirrored the bodies of several dead women hanging from the walls (they were all the women Bluebeard had married and murdered one after the other). She thought she would die of terror, and in that moment the key to the room which she had withdrawn from the lock fell from her hand.*

"An ogre," Charles murmured, "the husband is an ogre." He turned the paper to read of the mounting terror that followed Bluebeard's discovery of his wife's disobedience—

> *She threw herself at the feet of her husband, weeping and asking for forgiveness, with every sign of real repentance for not having obeyed him. She would have melted a stone, so beautiful and distressed was she, but Bluebeard had a heart even harder than stone.*
> *'You must die, Madame,' he told her, 'et tout à l'heure.'*

Once Upon a Time in Paris

'Puisqu'il faut mourir,' she replied, looking at him with eyes full of tears—

until he reached the satisfactory arrival of her brothers, when—

Ils lui passèrent leur épée au travers du corps et le laissèrent mort.

"They thrust their swords through his body and left him dead," he said aloud, "and rightly so, rightly so." It occurred to Charles that such a bloodthirsty story would be well received by his niece. But of one thing he was sure, being very familiar with her style and her various scripts: Marie-Jeanne L'Héritier had played no part in *Bluebeard*'s composition. Since there was no one else to hazard a guess, for now the authorship of all the tales must remain a mystery to the world.

Charles made a point of standing with his back to the window as his youngest son sidled into the library, obviously intent on keeping as much distance as possible between them. "Come in, Pierre. Sit down." He indicated a chair facing him, where the light would be full on the young scoundrel's face, only to regret it as Pierre unwillingly crept forward thereby revealing the full extent of his bruises. In an instant, Charles' carefully stoked anger subsided, his disappointment in the boy replaced by fatherly concern.

"I'll call Poucet." He started for the door. "We must summon a physician."

"No need, sir." He touched his nose. "Madame Norik has applied salve. She assures me there's nothing more to be done."

"What about your eye?" Charles blenched. "Is your vision…?"

"I can see perfectly well, sir."

"Where did this happen?" Now for the falsehoods, thought Charles, sinking wearily onto a seat by his writing table, now for stories so unbelievable they might as well be fairytales. "Presumably you were set upon." And what this time – the gigantic one-eyed blackamoor again, a clan of bellicose Irish settlers from Brittany, a drunken demon priest, or perhaps a return of the horde of midgets who'd hunted Pierre and his cronies – *taïaut! taïaut!* – through the back streets of Paris astride savage dogs, intent on stealing their clothes and hair. "Out with it."

"Yes, sir." Pierre looked at his hands. "Well, sir, I was walking from the Tuileries Gardens past the Louvre with a small group of friends – and of course we stopped to admire Uncle Claude's splendid colonnade—"

"Perhaps safer to view his architectural models next time," Charles said, struggling to keep his impatience under control. "As you may remember, they're in two wooden cases in the storeroom." He sighed. "Go on."

"Yes, sir." Pierre shifted uncomfortably. "Well, sir, after that we crossed over the Tournelle Bridge, deep in quiet conversation, pausing only to view the river, thinking to make our way peacefully back along rue—"

"Don't give me a step-by-step account of your journey home," thundered Charles. "Who attacked you?"

"A gang of ferociously drunk sailors, sir, ten at least, and—"

"Where?" barked Charles, wishing for a large pinch of salt.

Pierre hung his head. "Outside the *Maison de la Pomme de Pin*, sir."

"*Bon Dieu.*" Charles' eyes bulged. It was bad enough for his fool of a son to scrap and brawl in seedy taverns – places he'd been repeatedly forbidden to enter – but to take such behaviour to *la Pomme de Pin* really was beyond the pale. In truth, the Pinecone was equally insalubrious – a den frequented by loose women and students, a place of flying chairs and bottles, where stolen goods were traded. However, and here was the thing, not only was it a drinking hole at some time frequented by Racine and La Fontaine, but also by Nicolas Boileau-Despréaux – Boileau, his arch-enemy. In fact, he was almost sure Boileau had commented on the adulterated wine sold there in his *Le Repas ridicule* – frankly, the satirical poem was a poor rehash of work by Horace – but the point was, if Boileau and his cronies came across his inebriated son, Pierre Perrault, throwing punches and rolling in the gutter, then life would become even more unbearable.

"Pa?" Pierre's voice emerged tinged with alarm. "Are you unwell?"

"You'll be the death of me," snapped Charles, raising his head from his hands. "Never go near that place again. Do you understand?"

"I won't, sir, I swear."

"Let us hope so." Charles sighed again, knowing the worthlessness of his youngest son's promises. The boy's brother, Charles-Samuel, though distant in manner, was a model son any father would be proud to own. Pierre, different as chalk is from cheese, had been wild and noisy from the very beginning: a beautiful infant, a charming *bambin*, but sometimes even his childhood mischief had teetered on the edge of sheer wickedness. I should have been firmer, thought Charles. Instead of which I humoured him, continually overlooked his shortcomings, paid his debts and – God help me – even rewarded his bad behaviour with a small property to safeguard his financial future. My father suggested thrashing him. I balked at that. Maybe he was right, after all. Maybe that would have prevented Pierre from precipitating the chain of events that had brought such pain to the family.

Pierre attempted to rise. "May I go, sir?"

"No, Pierre, you may not." Charles straightened his back and adopted a severe expression. "You have too much time on your hands. Idleness is a curse that invariably leads young men into trouble. Clearly you aren't fitted for a life of study. We must therefore seek a worthwhile position for you."

The boy's demeanour brightened. "What about the army?"

"Not the army," Charles said quickly. "You're presentable, well spoken, and have a neat hand, Pierre – when you apply yourself. I feel you might do well at court. There is," he hesitated, "that is to say – one of my colleagues has apprised me of a *possible* opening as Junior Secretary to Mademoiselle. By Mademoiselle, I mean Élisabeth Charlotte d'Orléans," he added irritably, in the face of Pierre's blank stare, "the king's niece, a *petite-fille de France*. Would such a position appeal?"

"Court life sounds diverting – dancing, hunting parties, banquets."

"I refer," Charles' tone turned cold, "to the work."

"Oh," said Pierre, "the work." He sighed. "I suppose so. Yes."

"Very well, in that case we'll pave the way by making Mademoiselle a presentation."

"Excellent." Pierre eyed the door. "Something costly, I suppose."

"Very little more than the last one, but the cost is immaterial."

"Last one?" Pierre looked around the room for a moment before realisation dawned. "Of course – that poem about some prince who married a long-suffering shepherdess."

"My verse tale – *Grisélidis* – indeed, yes, I dedicated it to Mademoiselle." Charles remembered the dedication had taken almost as long to compose as the verse tale itself.

> *En vous offrant, jeune et sage beauté,*
> this model of patience,
> I never flattered myself that you would imitate it in every way:
> that would be too conscientious.

Although a delightful young woman, it was unlikely that Élisabeth Charlotte would ever meekly suffer in silence as had the unfortunate *Grisélidis*. As a child she'd been described as a hoyden, wild and rough as a boy. Now, she was exceedingly outspoken, much like her mother. "And her Royal Highness expressed great pleasure in receiving it. As I'm sure she will on being presented with yours."

"Mine?" Pierre's one good eye widened with horror. "But I could never write a story."

"I have come by some excellent *contes de fées* which, bound into a small book and signed by you, will serve our purpose." A stroke of genius on his part, Charles thought, thereby killing two birds with one stone, as the saying went.

"But…but *women* write fairytales." Pierre looked at him aghast. "What will my friends think? And…and anyway, everyone will know they're yours."

"No, no," Charles assured him, "these are quite different to anything I've ever written."

"But…but…. No, I couldn't, I can't—" Pierre's voice emerged as a squawk, "everyone acquainted with me knows I couldn't write a story to save my life."

"Come now, Pierre, these are simple stories, the sort of thing you might have heard from that nurse of yours, years ago."

"Mother Goose tales she called them." Pierre's face turned crimson. His hand flew to his mouth as if to stop more words escaping. After a moment he mumbled: "Sorry, sir, I didn't mean to offend."

"Hmm," said Charles, "no offence taken." With so much on his conscience, well might his son's hands shake and beads of perspiration spring from his brow. Nevertheless, as a title, *Contes de ma mère l'Oye* was not a bad one – a story in itself, though others might never realise it.

"But still, what if people ask me about them? What if...?"

"Make a mystery of it, my boy. Don't admit or deny anything. Look wise and stay silent. That way nobody will ever know for sure." Charles looked up. "What is it, Poucet?"

"Sir, the a-a-abbé de Choisy—"

"Ah," Charles clapped his hands together, glad of an excuse to bring the discussion to an end. "Don't keep a visitor waiting. Show him in, man, show him in. And, Poucet, bring refreshments."

The swish of skirts could clearly be heard in the corridor. A faint scent, something floral, jasmine perhaps, wafted into the room.

"Oh, God," muttered Pierre, and fled.

"Dearest friend," cooed François, today resplendent in a gown of figured blue silk covered with huge creeping, crawling flowers in a design totally asymmetrical and which, though unquestionably fashionable, Charles found vaguely unsettling. "I wanted you to be the first to enjoy an extract from the full version of *The Story of the Marquise-Marquis of*...wherever we decide it shall be. I feel the description of Marianne's education is better left to those who know nothing about beauty and everything about rote learning. I have instructed your niece accordingly. Let me read you a few lines about *la belle* Marianne's toilette. But first," he lowered his voice, "has anything about this new rash of poisonings reached your ears? Several of our joint acquaintances – and a few old friends – have been struck down, and really it can only be *empoisonnement*. No deaths, as yet, but severe discomfort and prolonged misery. It's a trifle worrying after that dreadful business with Charlotte-Rose."

"She's recovered, I presume?"

"Yes, yes. A worrying time, though, especially when you consider," François moved closer, "all that took place fifteen years ago."

"You mean the Affair of the Poisons?" Once again, Charles wished for his bezoar stone.

François nodded. "All France trembled then. Could it happen again?"

"If it does, every poisoner will burn. However...." Whatever he'd meant to say the noise of Poucet approaching with a tray drove it from Charles' mind. What was the matter with the fool? How was it possible to make such a din? Every piece of china was juddering and clattering. Any moment now it would all be on the floor. "For Heaven's sake put it down, you clumsy oaf," he snapped.

"B-b-beg p-p-pardon, sir."

"Just go."

"Anyway," said the abbé, eying the bowl of *fleurons*, "have the goodness to tell me what you think of this—

The beautiful Marianne pored over her books until noon and declared the rest of the day would be spent preparing for the pleasures of the evening. 'After devoting the entire morning to the improvement of my mind,' she said, 'it's only right that I should devote the entire afternoon to my pretty face and my whole dear little body.' But in fact she did not commence dressing until past four in the afternoon. Her visitors had assembled by then and took the greatest pleasure in watching her make her toilette."

Charles continued to listen, nodding sagaciously at intervals, until his thoughts returned to the tales. Tomorrow, after giving a final polish to the morals and writing the dedication, he'd put the collection into the hands of his copyist. Afterwards, he'd have the manuscript bound in red morocco with Mademoiselle's coat of arms gilt-stamped upon the cover. It must be a thing of beauty, with a frontispiece and vignettes – ah, another small task for the talented Lew – and moreover, a book of small size, one that would easily sit upon a lady's hands.

> *"Her maids dressed her hair, but she always added some striking ornament to her coiffure. Her fair hair fell in curls upon her white shoulders. Her eyes were dazzling. Countless pretty remarks emerged from the most beautiful mouth in the world. Those who looked on were rapt in adoration. With perfect grace, she hung upon her ears clusters of pearls, rubies, or diamonds. She added beauty spots that were so tiny they would never have been noticed on those with complexions less fine than hers."*

François stopped reading. "Really, the smell of those *fleurons* is wickedly tempting." He scooped up a handful of the crisp little puff pastry knots. "What do you think of the work, thus far?"

"Most enjoyable," said Charles, wondering if the over-large abbé had once thought of his guise in the self-congratulatory terms described, "and insightful. How interesting it will be when Marie-Jeanne adds her contribution. And I mine, of course," he added hastily.

"Good," responded François, turning the page. "Now, luckily I have brought a little more with me."

Starting was always the problem, whether it was the first line or the first brushstroke and Lew had been alternately shuffling his drawings and staring at the walls for a considerable time when Poucet joined him.

"You haven't d-done m-much."

"I'm thinking."

"B-better not let him catch you d-doing that. He'll w-want to see something happening in here."

"Something *is* happening," Lew said shortly. "I'm thinking and planning." He was silent for another few moments before laying the drawings aside. "I haven't seen you all morning, my friend – been hard at work?"

Poucet nodded. "First off, I went d-down to some *atelier* on the b-banks of the B-Bièvre with the master."

"Bet it stank to high heaven by the Pont-aux-Tripes now that the weather's turning warmer. The workshops, tanneries and abattoirs crammed along the riverbanks are foul places – especially those by Guts' Bridge. And that river's the vilest thing under the sun. As the poem goes – Is it mud or water? Is it sweat or ink? Or a chamber pot for pigs?"

"It w-was all of that and smelled even worse." Poucet grimaced. "And since we came b-back, I've been p-patching up young P-Pierre's face. You should see the state of it."

"I did – he was in the kitchen earlier, teasing Escarlatta." While he was talking, Lew picked up a pencil and made a quick sketch of the valet. "Don't think I've ever seen such a black eye." He frowned at the paper, turned it over, and started again. "And as for his nose…. The young idiot must have had a long conversation with someone's fist to end up looking like that."

"Some of the b-bruises could be powdered over, b-but there was no way of disguising that eye."

"Oh, well," muttered Lew, hardly listening. What was the matter with him? His hand seemed to be moving independently of both his will and his sight. He took out a fresh sheet of paper and tried again. Sighing loudly, he turned the paper over.

"The master won't half carry on."

"Damn it all!" roared Lew, screwing up his fourth attempt at capturing the valet's bland features.

"I'll go," said Poucet, scuttling towards the door.

"No, wait, I wasn't cursing you." Lew caught up with the valet halfway across the Red Drawing Room. "Listen, please – I wasn't cursing you," he repeated.

"D-don't worry. I'm used to it."

"I was cursing myself."

Poucet grinned. "That's surely the act of a m-madman."

"No doubt about that, my friend." Lew went to throw his arm round the valet's shoulder, but the thought of his failed drawing made him think better of it. "Give this space a few days' grace," he suggested. "My assistants will be starting work almost immediately. If I crack the whip hard enough, by then there might be something worth seeing."

For once, Lew ignored Poucet, who'd flattened himself against the door to watch, apparently entranced, as the painting of sky and stars on the upper dome finally came to an end. He was far too engrossed with his own panel of the fresco to spare time for pointless chitchat; besides, the valet came to check on progress several times a day and seemed content to stare for hours at a time, whenever his duties permitted it. As soon as the assistants filed off in the direction of the kitchen for their evening meal, Poucet scuttled forward and began to fuss over Lew's appearance.

"Look at the state of you, all covered in p-paint – and not just your clothes, it's in your hair, on your nose, ears. Oh, and your poor hands! They're so red you could have b-been in a b-battle."

"So I have – with a grasshopper and some ants." Lew pointed to the almost completed section. "You see – *The Grasshopper and the Ant.*"

"I've been w-watching you work." Poucet stepped closer and Lew stood beside him, attempting to view his day's work with fresh eyes. He'd surrounded the improvident grasshopper with ears of ripe wheat set off by scarlet poppies; beneath them the industrious ants toiled – among wild heartsease flowers with their trefoil seed pods – as they painstakingly built up their winter store. The poppy buds, Lew decided, needed more attention.

"I'm sure the m-master will like this."

"I hope so."

"B-by the way," murmured Poucet, "you'd better p-put it b-back."

"What's that?" Lew looked at him, startled.

"That p-picture, you know which one I mean – the p-pretty girl that caught your eye, the master's young wife. If I've n-noticed it's m-missing, others will too."

"Don't worry; it'll be back before anyone has the chance. I only borrowed it to make a quick copy."

"Why?"

"Don't know really," for Lew couldn't explain the compulsion that had repeatedly forced him back to admire the portrait. "It seems important."

Poucet peered at the grasshopper's violin. "You p-prefer b-blonde hair to dark, then?"

"Perhaps only because it's so different to mine." Lew wondered if that was really true. The few women in his life had mostly been raven-haired, and though one beautiful wanton had boasted wild tresses of a rich, deep copper, there'd never before been one with golden hair. And she, being dead, was unattainable. Nevertheless, he couldn't get her face out of his mind. "Yes, I suppose I do."

"Oh."

"No, it's more than the hair. The lady pictured has such a sweet smile, such a gentle look in her big blue eyes…the curve of those lips, that perfect chin…." Lew sighed. "It feels as if someone looking like that could never utter a word in anger. Where will I meet a woman so lovely?"

"Oh."

"I don't even know her name, but having seen her, how could I settle for less?"

"Oh."

"What about you, Poucet? Are you drawn to gentle blondes or bold brunettes?"

"Neither." Poucet turned away. "No, when it comes to women, it isn't their appearance I find important."

"Then you're a wiser fellow than I am." Lew added another splash of scarlet to an unfurling poppy bud and stood back to consider the effect. "They do say *choisissez votre femme par l'oreille bien plus que par les yeux* –" he smiled and repeated the old saw: "*Choose a wife by your ear rather than the eyes* – but perhaps you mean something else. I'm sure my lady, who as you pointed out, is long dead and buried, possessed the voice of an angel. Now, was it just my portrait pilfering that you were waiting to discuss?"

"No, but it d-does concern *a* p-portrait – the master is hosting a meeting for his literary friends and of course he wants the new p-picture on display. He's fussing over the gold lettering on his b-book."

"Damn," muttered Lew, annoyed at his own forgetfulness. "I've been so caught up with this room. Well, finishing the lettering's an hour's work, no more. Tell him it'll be done in the morning."

"He'll probably expect you to p-put in an appearance, too."

"What, at his meeting? Not me. I know nothing about books."

"Nevertheless...." Poucet spread his hands.

Lew sighed. "If I must, then I must." Although he resented the time, it would be as well to appear alongside Monsieur Perrault's portrait.

"If you let me have your coat, I'll clean the cloth and find some buttons for it."

"That's very kind of you."

"And now," said Poucet, attempting to take the brush from his hand, "you must stop work and eat."

"Soon – not yet." Not for the first time, Lew flinched from the valet's touch. "Leave something before the fire for me. I have to finish this panel before I can rest."

Lean days never thwarted Jacques' creativity. Today, luncheon had been so satisfying that one could almost forget how far into Lent they'd travelled. A frog's leg pottage had been served – a delicious bouillon of pea purée with saffron, fresh Normandy butter and chopped parsley, nicely garnished with the legs themselves *en cerises*, that is to say each dipped into batter and fried in hot butter, with the bone of one end left bare, to be gripped like a cherry stalk. Charles also enjoyed some eel saveloy, followed by grilled sea otter garnished with candied cockscombs, and creamed asparagus, the latter being a little insipid on account of being forced. Afterwards there was a *tourte* filled with damascene raisins…which sufficed.

Replete, Charles intended to spend the rest of the afternoon putting the final touches to those passages from his *Les hommes illustres qui ont paru en France pendant ce siècle* that he judged ready for their first public reading. He decided to commence with his description of Cardinal Richelieu and, finally satisfied with what he'd written, addressed the tapestry over his fireplace with the utmost gravity.

"Armand-Jean du Plessis, Cardinal-Duke of Richelieu." He paused, cleared his throat, and continued in suitable ringing tones. "Armand-Jean du Plessis, son of François du Plessis, Lord of Richelieu, Knight of the King's Orders, Steward of the Household, was born in the Castle of Richelieu on the fifth day of September, 1585. He showed so much vivacity of wit and solidity of judgement in his studies, that his future grandeur was very early presaged. It would seem he himself had a presentiment of it, being heard to say several times to those of his own age, when they pressed him to join with them in the sports of youth, that he was destined for business which would not permit him to waste any time."

Charles frowned as the noise of coarse singing, almost immediately drowned by a burst of raucous laughter, drifted up from somewhere below. He huffed a little, re-found his place in the text, and raised his voice above the discordant sounds. "He was so careful to employ it to good purpose that at twenty-two years of age he was consecrated Bishop of Luçon...." His voice tailed away as another bout of tuneless braying rose, from the street perhaps, immediately followed by hoots of laughter.

Once again, he returned to his reading. Setting aside, for the moment, his history of Cardinal Richelieu, he next selected the life of Henry de Sponde, Bishop of Pamiers as a suitable literary offering to put before his guests. And once again, he addressed the tapestry: "Henry de Sponde was born at Mauleon in Bearn, the 6th of January 1568," he declaimed, "and had the honour of having for godfather Henry de Bourbon, who was afterwards Henry the Great.

"His father was secretary to Joan d'Albret, Queen of Navarre, and made profession of the pretended reformed religion, as did the most part of the Bearnois at that time. As soon as the young Sponde had finished his studies, and his philosophy, which he did in Greek, he left France to go travelling. He followed into England William Salust de Bartas, so famous for his poem of the Creation of the World, and then the king of Navarre's ambassador, where in a little time he learned the language of the country and had familiar conferences with King James. He waited also at London upon Queen Elizabeth. A queen of an extraordinary merit," here Charles grimaced, "and much above her sex, who showed she made great account of his parts."

The afternoon had steadily grown warmer; somewhere a window was thrown open just as the unseen singer's voice, cracking on a high note, was greeted by a fresh salvo of laughter. Whoever it was, he sang *comme une casserole* – no, no, worse than a *cracked* cooking pot. What had been irritating was suddenly unbearable. Summoning Poucet, Charles roared: "Go outside. Find whatever fool workmen are making that din and send them packing."

"B-begging your p-pardon, s-sir...."

"What now?"

"It s-sounds l-like it's c-c-c—"

Charles banged his fist against the writing table. "Spit it out, man. I haven't got all day."

"C-c-coming from d-d-down—"

Anticipating the rest of Poucet's spluttering, Charles hauled himself upright, seized his cane, and stamped towards the main staircase with the tongue-tied valet trailing behind him. He should have known it was something to do with that damn ruffian of an artist. Talented he might be, but the oaf was also ill-bred, ill-presented, and with no consideration whatsoever. He'd a good mind to—

The chanting grew louder and the laughter more raucous as they crossed the Red Drawing Room.

"...under her skirt," bellowed the singer, "and got a surprise, fa-la-lah—"

Poucet tugged at his sleeve "It s-sounds l-like a s-song."

"I'm not deaf," snarled Charles, yanking himself free. "Run ahead and open the door."

"M-m-monsieur Ch-Charles P-P—" announced Poucet.

Charles pushed him aside. "Idiot!"

The noise stopped abruptly. It was impossible to tell which of the assistants had been responsible for the caterwauling, for they were all smirking. Every eye was now fixed on Charles, from the pair high up on the scaffolding, to those belonging to the imps sitting cross-legged on platforms and working on the lower levels. "What was the meaning of that outrageous noise? Where's the fellow in charge? Where's what's-his-name…Lew?"

"I'm here. Is there a problem?" Lew slowly descended the gallery stairs, wiping his hands on a rag. Rivulets of perspiration – tinted grey, blue and ochre from the paint he was applying to the walls – ran from his face and neck onto his partially bared chest.

Close to, the smell of stale sweat was intolerable. Charles stepped back, disconcerted by the artist's haggard appearance, the dark rings beneath his eyes. He also noted that far more work had been completed than anticipated since his last inspection. Already the domed ceiling was spectacular, far more beautiful than he could ever have imagined: at its centre gleamed the golden sunburst, the stone ribs radiating out from it gilded and bordered by fleur-de-lys. As he'd directed, below the stars the spaces between were already partially filled by representations of birds in flight, some completed, others simply rough outlines, but still recognisable.

Charles made a determined effort to curb his anger. At this stage of the project, being too harsh with the fellow would achieve nothing. "The noise," he said severely. "The noise is the problem. I won't tolerate loud singing, particularly not of bawdy ditties. I'm engaged in writing an important book."

"I beg your pardon, sir." Lew mopped his brow, neck and chest with the rag. "I hear nothing while working. I retreat to a place beyond any sensation save the purely visual."

"Hmm," said Charles. "I'll forgive your carelessness this once, but don't let it happen again." He lowered his voice. "Young man, the responsibility for this undertaking is yours. After all, *you* are the artist and it's *your* name that will go down in history. It is most important to establish your position here. In future, set an example – dismiss any troublemakers immediately. Do you understand me?"

"*Oui.*" Lew inclined his head, and then yawned widely without taking the trouble to cover his mouth. "Yes, I understand."

"You d-don't half l-look t-tired," muttered Poucet. "You n-never came to b-b-bed l-last night or the n-night b-before—"

"Haven't shut my eyes for three days," admitted Lew. "Don't notice time passing when I get into something like this."

"M-maybe you sh-sh—"

"Kindly keep your opinions to yourself," snapped Charles, emphasising his displeasure with a light tap on the valet's head. To Lew he said "Make sure you get adequate rest, young man. Exhaustion will predispose you to illness which might hold up the work. Now I'll leave you to your task and return to mine." He leaned on his stick for a moment longer, turning slowly to take in the domed ceiling in its entirety. "So far the results are highly satisfact—" He stiffened. The cane stabbed the air. "And what, pray, is *that*?" Poucet and Lew followed the direction of Charles' furious stare.

"A young s-swan?" hazarded Poucet, nervously edging away.

"It's a goose, you imbecile," yelled Charles, longing to close his hands around the simpleton's neck, "a grey goose. And what did I tell you about geese, young man? Huh? Huh? What did I tell you? No goose of any sort, I said. *No* goose. Those were my express orders. Swans, yes, I specifically said there should be swans to honour the king, but *no* geese."

"Oh," said Lew, but Charles saw the artist was no longer looking at the goose. Instead he was staring at his fool of a manservant's face with such incredulity that it was necessary to thump his cane hard against the floor to regain his attention.

"Get rid of that thing, I say. Do you hear me? Get rid of it. Paint over the damn creature – immediately."

The next morning Charles unwillingly descended to the kitchen,

Poucet in tow, to discuss the provision of refreshments at his fast-approaching literary gathering. Although the most recent attack of gout had abated, he made a play of needing his walking stick in order to have some slight means of self-protection. Since the arrival of Lew's crew of painting assistants Jacques had become increasingly bad-tempered, lashing out at all and sundry, using whatever kitchen utensil came to hand, and garnishing his usual profanities with physical threats.

Today he was quiet, but surly and uncooperative. "I'm already overburdened. So," the cook snatched an enterprising bluebottle from the air and crushed it in his palm, "when it comes to extra work the answer is no. I can't. *I won't.*"

"But it's imperative that I provide a pleasurable experience for my guests," protested Charles, "or what will they say of us? Come now, Jacques, I'm relying on you to provide your usual delicious fare. A few *mignardises*, let us say."

Jacques shrugged and continued chopping up a large piece of beef. "Do you know how long petits fours take to make?" *Bang.* "They're bloody fiddly things." *Bang.* "Here I am, worked to death, and yet you expect me to toil single-handedly for the rest of this week creating delicacies so that folk won't speak ill of you behind your back." His chopping became frenzied. "No, I say no, a thousand times no." He concluded by striking the back of his cleaver on the wooden board with such violence that Poucet visibly jumped. "No, it can't be done. It *won't* be done. I am a full-fledged cook, duly examined by my guild. If push comes to shove, I can soon find work elsewhere." He took down a stack of pans and rattled them vigorously and at great length for no apparent reason before replacing them. Poucet covered his ears and attempted to run from the room but found the way blocked by his master's cane. "After all," Jacques growled, "what do I get out of these events?"

Charles bit hard down on his rage. "You're well recompensed."

The cook held up a stout forefinger. "Aye, there's money in it, but you know full well that I have another remarkable talent beside my sublime cooking skills."

"Oh," Charles said, and dark forebodings settled on him, "your poetry."

"My poetry," agreed Jacques, drawing the word out. "And it's at least as good as the long-winded stuff written by many others I could name."

"Of course," Charles said soothingly, remembering the appalling Rabelaisian doggerel spouted by Jacques on the one occasion he'd agreed to listen.

"Will any other poets be giving the company the pleasure of hearing their new work?" Jacques again raised his cleaver. "Your nod indicates *yes*, but will I be allowed to air mine? No."

"Unfortunately," gabbled Charles, "on this occasion the programme has already been drawn up, leaving no time for an additional poet to present his work."

"A short poem," insisted Jacques, "will take but a few moments to recite, whereas refreshments for your event would take me many hours to prepare." He glowered. "But I believe there are establishments in Paris – for those not too particular about quality – that will deliver *some sort* of comestibles directly to your door...."

"No, no," said Charles, "their services won't be required."

"So...?" Jacques waited, cleaver still clutched in his upraised hand.

"Very well, on this occasion you may recite *one* short poem – but as you say, for a few moments only, right at the end." Charles resisted the urge to shudder. With any luck his guests, already preparing to leave, would look upon it as an amusing joke. "As for the subject matter—"

"Nothing unsuitable," finished the cook, now wearing a grin the size of a quartered melon. He set down the cleaver. "And to show my gratitude, I shall set my mind to inventing new delicacies – *pets de poètes*, true lovers' knots, *les bouffées de cardinaux*, sugarpaste quills, *des ailes de fées* or, wait, far better would be little cakes surmounted by those fairies' wings – and perhaps even some little black nuns."

The sense of foreboding increased as Charles returned to his library. Certain of his friends, François in particular, would find the appearance of a *poète naïf* – fresh from the kitchen chimney corner, reeking of onions – vastly amusing. Others might view presentation of a member of the lower orders to a literary event as the culmination of his *moderne* stance. He was laying himself open to the risk of ridicule, even though Jacques would hold forth for a few moments, no more, and few would even bother to listen. Every instinct warned Charles that he should have stood by his initial decision.

There were very good reasons for excluding the cook. He was not always an agreeable man. Allow the fellow unlimited access to alcohol, cross him in some trifling way, and there was no knowing what damage he was capable of.

As for his looks – that bulbous red nose and orange-peel skin, the greasy kitchen wig worn to hide his great bald head fringed with fox-coloured hair, the odour, his very height and *girth* – some might find them alarming. Charles grimaced. Since he didn't wish to lose Jacques and his excellent culinary skills, nothing could be done. Whatever the man's physical shortcomings, once *properly* bewigged and dressed in suitable attire – and hopefully further transformed by Poucet's magical touch – even a lurching hulk like Jacques could probably acquire a civilised veneer, albeit temporary.

Yet another death, thought Charles, and this time it had taken several days for the news to reach him. To be fair, Jean de La Fontaine had never been a friend, even though they'd occupied adjoining seats in the academy and shared an adoration of Marie Anne Mancini in their younger days. The man had been in poor health for years so his demise was not wholly unexpected. No poison was involved. Besides, seventy-three was a good age and he'd left a magnificent, if sometimes licentious, legacy.

Of course, Jean had his weaknesses. Most men did. He was almost as careless of his appearance as Lew – did that denote genius? Surely not, thought Charles, for he was meticulously careful about his own. Add to that La Fontaine's rudeness in company, his adultery, neglect of his family, and the fact that, being such a fearful spendthrift, management of his wife's property had to be legally removed from his hands. Be that as it may, La Fontaine recognised his own shortcomings for not only was he wearing a hair shirt at the time of his death, but he'd also composed his own self-deprecating epitaph—

> Jean departed exactly as he'd come,
> Having consumed both capital and income
> With scant regard for storing or saving.
> The trick of spending time he knew,
> Dividing it in portions two,
> One for sleep, the other for idling.

Although he could not mourn too deeply for Jean de La Fontaine, his beautifully decorated ballroom, while serving to heal past wounds within the family, would also stand as a memorial to the man and his work. And perhaps, Charles thought – with a well-worded invitation – the king might be moved to view its splendour and thereby restore him to favour, but not yet, alas, not yet.

His main drawing room, furnished with costly simplicity a decade previously, still exhibited, Charles firmly believed, exceptionally good taste. Its large windows were hung with sumptuous brocade draperies. Displayed in shallow alcoves on the opposite wall were marble busts, his father's legacy, of various lesser known Roman Emperors – Pertinax, Avidius Cassius, Galba, Commodus, Aulus Vitellius, Lucius Pescennius Niger – all of them leaders killed by their own men, and presently in urgent need of cleaning. A single painting, of a good size, but so darkened by age that it was impossible to distinguish more than one raised arm and the terror-flared nostrils of a horse, bore the title *The Battle of Veillane*. The new portrait would be exhibited a little to the left – or possibly to the right – of the central window. His most precious works of art – those purchased for his proposed *Cabinet des Beaux-Arts* at the old house in rue Neuve des Bons Enfants – still occupied their own small room adjacent to the library and, as usual, might be privately viewed after the event, by those Charles deemed worthy.

There were no rugs or carpets in this salon, which he considered a great advantage since certain of his visitors refused to be parted from their disgustingly undisciplined dogs. Instead it benefited from a floor of the latest design, formed of polished oak blocks arranged in a herringbone pattern and set in bitumen as hot and dangerous as that once poured through murder holes in the barbaric past. Laying such a floor followed the example set at Versailles, although in that case the *parquet de menuiserie* was laid to replace marble after the continual washing and scrubbing this had required eventually resulted in wet rot of the supporting joists.

A large orange tree in a *chinoiserie* pot – Charles' only concession to the prevailing passion for all things Oriental – purchased at considerable expense, had been set before each window. Not only were these studded with fruit, but they were also smothered in newly-opened flowers, a felicitous state he was almost sure the royal gardeners rarely achieved. The air was thus delightfully fragranced without the need for bowls of decaying petals and half-rotted wood shavings with which he'd observed others attempting to dispel stale odours.

He consulted his pocket watch. There was almost an hour before any guests would start to arrive, plenty of time for a final rehearsal of his work. Everything seemed to be going smoothly: Jacques and Norik were setting out a quite remarkable array of delicacies on numerous trays, the scullery maids had been instructed to scrape the grime from their hands and necks before donning the snow-white collars and aprons that would render them fit to serve above stairs. All that remained was to close the doors into the oldest part of the house, blocking off access to the rooms undergoing transformation, an action designed to keep curious guests from entering as much as ensuring none of the uncouth assistants emerged to trespass on this private event.

Charles reached his chamber somewhat out of breath, and was forced to sit for a while before striking a pose in front of his looking-glass and rereading an extract from his preface. "All ages have afforded great men, but all ages have not been equally fruitful of them." He read on to the final paragraph: "With regard to the public, as commendations are not what they love the most of any thing in the world; and as those I give are very short of that fine and delicate turn which might make them please, I am disposed to take as a favour the least good reception the world shall please to give to what is mine in this work." His smile of satisfaction faded. The usual creative doubts surfaced. A text read aloud to an audience had a different impact to that which was declaimed privately. Would his presentation hold an audience's attention? In this his niece might have helped him – for all her physical shortcomings Marie-Jeanne was an invaluable critic – but she'd sent her apologies, claiming indisposition; so, too, had François. Their collaboration wasn't proving a happy one. He suspected they were avoiding each other.

At first Charles was gratified by the sheer volume of applause, but with so many more people than anticipated packed into the space – the majority had thanked him politely for his invitation, but he certainly hadn't requested their presence – and with the general noise correspondingly high, he found it difficult to gauge how well his introduction to *Les hommes illustres qui ont paru en France pendant ce siècle* had been received. Many of those clapping appeared to do so for no reason other than to keep up with their neighbours. A few kind words were tossed his way…much, he thought despondently, as titbits were thrown to a dog or bear after the acceptable performance of some clever party trick. The fact was they were more interested in each other than in his literary work.

He was unhappily aware that control of the occasion was in danger of slipping away from him. Never before had the combined voices within a salon sounded so strident. Never, in his memory, had an audience been so openly inattentive. In retrospect, perhaps it would have been wiser to offer cordials or Italian waters rather than allow Jacques to bring whatever he thought fit from the wine cellar. No doubt the cook's intention was to reduce everyone to a state wherein they'd be appreciative of his bad verse. Naturally, the guests were as delighted by this largesse as they were by the dainty refreshments, falling upon both with great enthusiasm, and losing their critical faculties together with an ability to conduct serious conversation in the process.

With two presentations of his work still to come, Charles was too anxious to eat or drink. He moved among the tightly packed throng, lending half an ear to other literary contributions, vouchsafing a little gracious conversation here, and bestowing occasional compliments there. He was pleased to see his new portrait being admired but noted with fury that his trees had been denuded of fruit and that a great sow of a woman – her name escaped him – was wearing an entire branch of orange blossom in her hair. On his second circuit of the room, he came across Poucet secretly nibbling on a *petite tartelette* and glared at him so furiously that the valet crushed the pastry in his hand, letting it fall to the ground. Instantly, two brindled curs leaped forward to claim it, snapping and snarling at each other's jaws long after any trace of the mushroom filling had been devoured.

Such was his unease that to his dismay Charles found himself unable to recall the names of all those present. Furthermore, his eyesight was not what it had been in his youth. Wasn't that woman in apricot silk Sophie-Adèle de Belleroche? He hadn't seen her in fifteen years and certainly couldn't recall inviting her. And the monstrously fat woman in cherry red could almost be Viviane-Marie Fleuriot, a frequent visitor both before and after his wife died, but why would she be here now? Instead of addressing either, he made a beeline for two guests he had no trouble in recognising: shy little Madame Beffort, an inveterate plagiarist, and Madame de Caylus, finally recovered from her disastrously tight lacing but, alas, still no slimmer. Today her stout form was encased in a dappled puce gown unpleasantly reminiscent of sausage skin. Charles greeted both ladies effusively.

"Susanne, how utterly charming you look." He noted, however, that her apparel was an inferior copy of that worn by Catherine Bernard on a previous occasion. Evidently, Madame Beffort possessed as few original ideas about dress as she did when it came to writing. "Dove-grey is such a becoming colour. Though with such a perfect complexion, I imagine most shades become you."

Susanne turned pink and fluttered her fan. "You're too kind, sir."

"I see you have no refreshments. Can I get you—" When she shook her head, claiming to have partaken sufficient already, Charles turned his attention to Madame de Caylus. "My dear Marie-Gabrielle," he murmured, bowing over her chubby hand, "my humble dwelling is honoured by your presence."

"Always so gallant," she purred. "I enjoyed your reading immensely, Charles."

"It was *une bagatelle*, Madame, a mere trifle."

"Will you be sharing more with us?"

After assuring her that his brief life of Cardinal Richelieu would follow in due course, Charles made his escape, pushing through the crowds until he discovered Mademoiselle de La Force accompanied by a partially veiled old hag.

"Charlotte-Rose, how good of you to join us now that you're fully recovered." He peered questioningly at her companion.

"Ah, Charles, how could I *not* come? With so many delightfully elegant invitations issued, this reunion has become one of the most talked-about events of the spring." Charles frowned at that, but feared questioning her on the subject of his own invitations would make him look ridiculous. She gestured to the shapeless form at her side. "You'll remember Mademoiselle Barbazan, I'm sure. Like the rest of us, Marguerite's keen to hear your new work."

"Enchanted," lied Charles, absolutely certain he hadn't invited the Barbazan, a dreadful creature from the old days he'd thought long dead. And by the state of her she might as well be: one could so easily imagine a smell of the grave hung in the air. He made no move to raise her wrinkled claw to his lips. The very idea repulsed him. Once regarded as a great beauty – like so many others she'd fleetingly caught the old king's eye – now, even through a merciful shroud of lace, she resembled one of Notre Dame's less well-preserved gargoyles. Noticing that Charlotte-Rose was carrying Marguerite's lute, Charles steeled himself to ask: "Will you grace us with some music this evening, Mademoiselle Barbazan?" Pray heaven she wasn't intending to sing. Such decrepit crones should be neither seen nor heard.

"And I know," continued Charlotte-Rose, after they'd waited in vain for a coherent reply from the old woman, "how pleased you'll be to see Antoine."

Charles looked around, and then down to where Antoine Galland crouched on the parquet, his eye to a hairline crack between the wooden blocks. "Indeed, I am." Although this was yet another uninvited guest, at least he counted Antoine among his friends, in spite of having reservations about his title of Antiquary to the King. However Charles was taken aback by the scale of the man's inebriation. He affected grave concern. "Is our friend indisposed?"

"If he is, then it's only from a surfeit of pastries while attempting to drink your cellar dry." Charlotte-Rose made a moue of distaste and pushed at the crouching body with one elegantly shod foot. "Get up, *ivrogne*."

Charles nodded sagely. The insult was well deserved: although amusing, Antoine was indeed a *souse*, an habitual drunkard, and in danger of going down in history as such despite his involvement with the prestigious *Bibliothèque orientale*. Rumour had it that his claim to be working on a translation of traditional tales from the Levant was much exaggerated – in short, it was said he'd been inventing salacious stories and claiming them to be of Arabian origin.

"Get up," repeated Charlotte-Rose, emphasising her words with a discreet kick. This time Antoine complied, pulling himself upwards, hand over hand, by means of Charles' coat. Once on his feet, he clung on, swaying gently.

"Is that you, Charles?"

"My dear friend, Antoine," said Charles, with as much warmth as he could muster. Friendship aside, it was never wise to offend anyone who'd found favour with Louis.

"Are you aware that there are small beings living under your floor?"

"Indeed?" Charles attempted to free himself of the buffoon's clutching hands.

"I believe them to be a family of travelling jinn from Baghdad."

"Astonishing – and what must we do to be rid of them?"

"Shout *Hadeed! Hadeed!* seven times seven times. Iron is a metal they dread."

"Invaluable advice," said Charles, stepping away so swiftly that Antoine was forced to loose his hold. "Pray excuse me. I believe Monsieur Dupâquier has finished reciting his poem, which means it's time for me to begin my second reading." He retreated as quickly as the press of bodies allowed.

"*Hadeed, ya meshoom!*" Antoine yelled after him. "Iron, thou unlucky one!"

Charles affected not to hear. On reaching his lectern, he rapped on the wood to attract attention. The noise hardly abated, but eventually a handful of women turned their chairs to form a semi-circle facing him, and others began pulling up seats behind them. It was left to Marie-Gabrielle to clap her hands and call for silence.

Without further introduction, he cleared his throat and commenced reading. "Armand Jean du Plessis, son of François du Plessis, Lord of Richelieu, Knight of the King's Orders, Steward of the Household, was born in the Castle of Richelieu on the fifth day of September, 1585. He showed so much vivacity of wit and solidity of judgement in his studies, that his future grandeur was very early presaged." Charles was gratified to see those seated immediately in front of him nodding their heads attentively and, his confidence restored, began making small hand gestures to underline salient points.

On reaching 1622 and the cardinal's appointment to First Minister, he looked up from the page and was surprised to find that members of his audience were still nodding, some with extreme violence. Moreover, Charlotte-Rose appeared to be blowing bubbles. And she was not the only one. Many others, as far back as he could see, had froth-covered lips, or lines of saliva trickling down their chins. Maybe it represented an adverse reaction to his work. Perhaps this was a bad dream. Alarmed, he returned to his text, for waking or sleeping to stop mid-disquisition would be to accept defeat.

"Seeing himself at the head of affairs, he proposed two things principally, to pull down the heretics and humble the House of Austria. For the one he induced the king to undertake the siege of Rochelle, which was attacking heresy in its strength, in the very place where it thought itself insurmountable. This place was defended by the sea, by a strong garrison, and by its inhabitants, to whom the zeal of their religion gave strength and courage which seemed invincible."

Charles risked another glance at those listening. His eyes widened: those ladies nearest to him were leaning forward as drool poured from their mouths in such quantity that they might have been rock crevices from which foaming mountain springs issued. For the most part, those standing further back were bent double and in much the same state. Even the dogs—

A terrible thought struck him: was it possible they'd all been poisoned? He was almost sure Poucet's gossip concerning Madame Bédier's demise had contained a mention of foam on the lips – but of course her ills were self-inflicted, the result of gluttony. And hadn't liquid reportedly streamed from Charlotte-Rose's maid during that sinful creature's frenzied ordeal?

With an effort, Charles pulled himself together. Trembling in the face of such ungrounded thoughts was not appropriate for an educated man – poisonings were increasingly rare since the king had put so many checks and safeguards in place. It was far more likely that he'd overtaxed his brain and the out-flowing of saliva was an illusion. Therefore he would continue reading normally. "England furnished them with continual replenishments of men and provisions, and there appeared a great deal of temerity in the siege of that place. However, Cardinal Richelieu, to whom the greatness and difficulty of enterprises was encouraging, found means to reduce it…." His voice petered out, almost drowned by the sound of liquid splashing onto his beautiful parquet floor. This was no illusion. He beckoned to Poucet. "What's the matter with them?"

"What d-do you m-mean?" asked the valet, after a cursory glance.

"They're dribbling bucketsful, damn you."

Poucet looked again. "Oh. Ugh." He backed away, his face a mask of horror. "That's sp-spit p-pouring out. What's the m-matter w-with them?"

"Imbecile! Blockhead!" Charles seized the valet's arm, tempted to box his ears. "That's what I asked you."

"I d-don't know b-but I'm g-going outside. It m-might b-be c-catching."

"You will *not* leave this building or it will be the worse for you. You will stay here and we will continue as planned." He smoothed out his manuscript. "On second thoughts, fetch me my stoutest stick."

"P-p-perhaps," whispered Poucet, on his return, "you've offended s-some local s-sorcerer."

Charles grunted and, with a slight quiver in his voice, went on with his reading. By the time he reached the end of Richelieu's life – "what honour has not this great man done to France, he who had no other view but the glory of his prince and country?" – a matter of ten minutes, surely no more, those afflicted had stopped drooling and, carefully avoiding looking at one another, were attempting to disguise the damp fronts of their clothing. A smattering of applause followed his perfunctory bow and the obligatory thanks to them for being an appreciative audience, but all semblance of attention disappeared as the kitchen maids brought in several more trays of food, which were cleared in an instant.

"Gluttons," said Charlotte-Rose, wiping crumbs from her chin. She peered into her décolletage, extracted a small piece of crust and ate it greedily. "But who can blame them? Your refreshments are astonishingly delicious, really quite addictive."

Charles looked at her in dismay, observing that the cosmetics on the lower part of her face had been completely washed away by the disagreeable occurrences of the last quarter of an hour. The exposed skin was hardly fit to be seen. "Are you in good health, Charlotte-Rose?"

"D-drunk," muttered Poucet. Charles cuffed him.

"I am a little dizzy," she replied, craning her neck to look behind him, "but exceedingly hungry. Will more refreshments follow?"

"And you," he asked of Marie-Gabrielle, who was swaying gently, "are you well?"

"Dear Cardinal Richelieu. I shall visit his white marble tomb at the very earliest opportunity." She beamed at him, her face illuminated as in a painting of one beatified. "Oh, what joy – I am transfixed by happiness."

Poucet leaned in close. "She's d-dead d-drunk, too."

"Hush," snarled Charles, nonetheless suspecting his simple-minded valet had hit upon the truth. It was not only Marie-Gabrielle's apparent euphoria that alarmed him – all around them his guests were reeling and squawking in the manner of beggars celebrating the discovery of a silver *écu*. Several were clinging to each other, weeping with merriment. There was something very wrong here and unless he took immediate steps to restore order he'd be the laughingstock of Paris.

"Tell Jacques to water the wine," he whispered to Poucet. "Bring in as many pots of coffee and chocolate as can be mustered. Advise him some jugs of syrups and cordials wouldn't go amiss. And get him to send up more food, anything, even bread and cheese if there's nothing else." With any luck such solid fare would counteract the excess alcohol in their systems. The manservant scurried away.

Charles glumly inspected his floor. At least the trains of so many long skirts were mopping up most of the puddles, but it would need several coats of polish to restore it to Versailles' standards. He observed the kitchen maids reappear, looking the worse for wear following the previous scrum, but nevertheless laden with veritable mountains of food. Uttering loud whoops of pleasure, the company fell on them like seagulls alighting on a newly ploughed field. Within seconds the trays were empty.

After this process had been repeated several times – he judged it wise to overlook the maids' shrieking of increasingly vulgar profanities – a sudden quiet descended on the room. Charles breathed a sigh of relief and regarded the crowd with satisfaction. His strategy had worked. Some guests stood motionless, wearing expressions of quiet introspection. Others were engaged in closely examining minutiae – the stamens of an orange flower, a loose thread hanging from a neighbour's gown, a rogue moth's antennae, the pale half-moons of their own nails or the intimate details of the marble busts, their nostrils, ear lobes, or eyebrow ridges – or had even focused their attention on folds in the curtains. Many sank onto the floor. A few lay stretched out, admiring the ceiling with its ornate plasterwork, a pattern of fleurs-de-lys and roses, while several more had curled into foetal positions, apparently dozing. One elderly dowager was sucking her thumb.

They seemed to him like people under an enchantment, asleep and yet not asleep. Charles walked, unnoticed, among those still standing, spoke to some, touched others, but received no response. His guests resembled nothing more than statues carved from living flesh and granted a little movement. Or possibly, he thought, the automata of Greek mythology – but, no, his analogy was not sound, for now he recalled that Talos, the giant wader through the waters, was cast in bronze, while the guard dogs of Alcinous, grandson of Poseidon, were fashioned of gold and silver. Pindar, in his seventh Olympic ode, also spoke of animated figures, but those were carved from marble. There were many tales of cunning automata from the Orient, too—

"Are they g-going to d-die?" whispered Poucet, wringing his small white hands. "Has s-someone c-cursed them?"

Charles permitted himself a very small smile. Some comfort was to be found in his great learning. To return to the ancient Greeks, it appeared to be Dionysus, rather than a black-hearted sorcerer, who was responsible for turning his guests into living statues. "No," he said firmly, his words intended to reassure himself as much as the nervous valet. "They have drunk too deep and are now recovering."

Already, a few of his visitors were stirring, looking about them with expressions of bewilderment as they came to their senses. He judged this to be the perfect moment to reassert his authority. The room was quiet, the atmosphere serene, and Charles could not imagine anything better suited to reminding these people of their responsibilities as guests than the sound of his voice reading to them. He returned to the lectern. "I give you," he announced, "Jean-Baptiste Colbert, Minister and Secretary of State."

A few heads turned. Eyes blinked like those of owls caught in bright sunshine. The supine dowager's struggles to rise put him in mind of an upended turtle.

"Cardinal Mazarin, when he lay dying, told the king that he was infinitely bounden to his majesty, but that in giving him Monsieur Colbert to serve him in his place he believed he should make return of all the favours he had received from him. The cardinal knew perfectly well what he said having seen after what manner Monsieur Colbert had fixed his affairs."

Charles continued reading, occasionally surveying the satisfactorily quiet salon. He'd almost arrived at Colbert's end when Jacques, having shed his lard-stiffened kitchen carapace, made a grand entrance in attire so hopelessly outdated, so singularly inappropriate – slashed doublet, massive lace collar, voluminous petticoat breeches – that it took immense willpower to read the final paragraph using the serious tone it deserved. It was with some relief that Charles reached the conclusion: "The three daughters married the Dukes Chevreuse, Beauvillier, and Mortemar." He folded the pages, slipped them into a pocket, and bowed.

This time there was no reaction whatsoever.

Blank faces, wherever he looked. No one clapped. No one spoke.

Charles knuckled his temples. Was his composition inadequate? Were they waiting for more? Never in his life could he remember such a lack of response. Comforting himself with the possibility that the room's acoustics were at fault, he made his way – unnoticed, un-greeted – through his indifferent audience to where Jacques stood leaning against the door frame.

"There you are, Jacques, and very fine you look, if I may say so."

He forced himself to ignore the strong odour of burnt fat. "Tell me, could you hear everything from here?"

"Aye," the cook brushed a few coarse red hairs from his sleeve, "only the best for such an occasion." Then, realising more was required, added: "Every word. Clear as a bell. But—" the contortions of Jacques' face indicated the intensity of his vain struggle to find fitting words. "But—"

"Out with it, man," Charles said, growing impatient. "You're beginning to sound like my spluttering half-wit valet."

"You underestimate Poucet." Jacques scowled. "He's no half-wit. Lad's got a big heart in that small frame of his. Aye, and as for his loyalty...."

"Yes, yes, I dare say. Clear as a bell, you said, *but*— What follows that 'but'?"

Jacques shifted uncomfortably. "Your pardon, sir – it seemed to me that nobody was listening."

Charles turned on his heel and stalked away. If only François was here, or even Marie-Jeanne, his niece; either would have given his work the respect it deserved. At least the worst was over. He elbowed his way through the crowd, still at a loss to know why so many people were here, unable to explain the business of the 'delightfully elegant invitations', and struggling to think of a polite way to make the unwelcome horde leave.

"Are you aware that there are small beings living under your floor?" breathed a voice at his shoulder.

"Yes, Antoine," Charles squeezed his reply through rigid lips, "you told me earlier. Just now I'm a little preoccupied with other matters...."

"I believe them to be jinn from Baghdad. As you can see, I'm rapidly shrinking. When I am small enough to join them, we shall be able to converse. I hope thereby to collect more Arabian tales for inclusion in *One Thousand and One Nights*."

"Shrinking?"

"Yes, we're both shrinking. Hadn't you noticed? I shall expedite the process." Antoine extended his arms and began to spin rapidly, like a child at play. "I may even fly."

Charles moved away before the lunatic became so giddy that he latched onto the nearest stationery object to steady himself. He was about to find Charlotte-Rose and reproach her for bringing him, uninvited, when, to his alarm, he noticed that Antoine wasn't the only person engaged in a curious physical activity. Was he bewitched…or were they? Some were executing gigantic leaps backwards and forwards over the length of the room, while others appeared to believe they were playing energetic games of *jeu de paulme* with imaginary paddle bats and non-existent balls. This was a nightmare. It must be.

And yet Charles knew it was not.

To his left, women jumped on the spot, like frogs contained in a glass vessel. On his right, Madame Beffort, having apparently shed all inhibitions along with her outer clothing, was moving her arms and legs in a dreadful parody of the *belle danse*. A group near the windows, its numbers rapidly increasing – encouraged by Marguerite Barbazan's haphazard and cacophonic plucking of lute strings – hopped and gyrated in frenzied abandon, some individuals tearing at their hair and clothes. Charles stared aghast, reminded of old stories of the Dancing Plague. It had lasted for a month in Strasbourg. He'd never get rid of these people.

Then his eye fell upon Charlotte-Rose who had gathered every one of the marble busts into the skirts of her dress and, in spite of their considerable weight, was walking briskly around the walls – shoving aside anyone who stood in her path – repeating a garbled version of the *paternoster* as she went. At this moment, Charles felt inclined to do the same. He grimaced as his senses were again assailed by the stench of *la cuisine*, and knew without turning that his choleric cook approached, his ingrained skin bearing an unwritten record of every ingredient handled and every meal ever produced.

"When may I recite my verse?"

Charles ground his teeth. "I suggest you wait for the audience to become calm."

"But the room gets more like a feast-day tavern by the minute," complained Jacques. "And what are they all laughing about?"

"Laughing?" Charles slowly turned on him. "Laughing, you say?" His mouth worked. His eyes bulged. His mouth shut like a trap.

Everything finally became clear. This was a hoax, a huge joke at his expense, probably orchestrated by Boileau – though he'd never suspected the man possessed a sense of humour – no, on second thoughts more likely Jean de La Bruyère, that notorious deflater of egos – though why should anyone think his ego needed deflating, if he had one at all? Or possibly Jean Racine, a fellow who wallowed in tragedy, and what could be more tragic than this? But then, it could just as easily be any of the foolish women producing their ridiculous essays and tedious stories, naturally jealous of his superior prose and sharply honed poetry. Or his niece – for no woman is totally trustworthy – or even François, who had taken on that female untrustworthiness along with the corsets and silk petticoats.

Charles struck his forehead with the flat of his hand.

He should have known. He should have guessed.

From that very first moment, when liquid appeared to pour from his guests' mouths, he should have remembered the Labyrinth of Versailles and the hydraulic statues with water gushing from the animals' mouths to represent speech. True, he had brought his work for the king, the part he'd played in setting up the fine fountains, to the attention of everyone he met –

perhaps he had mentioned it more frequently than was strictly polite, he was proud of his involvement in the project – but was that any reason to mock him, here, in his own house? And now that he came to think of it, all this *faux* somnolence, this pretence of standing or sitting or lying down dream-fasted and abstracted, what was that but an exaggerated expression of the ennui one felt when hearing a story too frequently told?

As for the leaping and jumping, the wild dancing and spinning, he was at a loss to explain it…unless it was the equivalent of the rustic *charivari* and intended as a comment on some impropriety in his verse tales, the disobedient and ungrateful daughter in *Donkeyskin*, perhaps, or the impertinent way the lowly, discarded wife is permitted to speak back to the prince, her husband, in *Grisélidis*.

"W-what's h-happening?" wailed Poucet, white-faced and trembling from head to toe. "Is it a c-curse?"

"And when may I read my poem?" enquired Jacques, flourishing a sheet of paper torn from a book. Charles craned his neck, almost sure that the book in question was La Varenne's.

"*Ta gueule*," he snarled, "shut up! Just shut up!" And would have said more were it not for Marie-Gabrielle groaning and falling flat on the floor. As if at a signal, dozens more followed suit. This wasn't part of any hoax, Charles was sure. He watched, frozen with horror, as his guests fell, right, left and centre, as though they were oversized skittles in a game of *quilles*, struck down by an invisible ball. "Poison," breathed Charles and promptly crossed himself in spite of Poucet, who clung to his arm, sobbing hysterically. He looked accusingly at Jacques. "They've all been poisoned."

The cook's jaw dropped. His face took on a greenish tinge. "*Merde! Un millier de merdes!* Hear this, my good sir: poisoned they might be, but I swear it's nothing to do with me."

Lew bounded into the salon, rehearsing apologies; he'd been

ordered to attend on Monsieur Perrault an hour or more ago but, intent on finishing that section depicting *The Frogs Who Wanted a King*, had lost all sense of time. Stopping only to scrub from his hands the brash yellows of iris and kingcups, the drab olive green of the frogs, he'd come at a run, expecting a sharp reprimand, only to be met by an extraordinary sight. The salon was in total disarray. There was his employer, clinging to a lectern, apparently in a state of shock, and next to him Jacques – inexplicably clad in fancy-dress costume – surrounded by two score or more guests lying flat out on the floor, the clothing of some dripping wet. As for poor little Poucet, he was leaning against the wall a few paces away, his frail body convulsed by sobs.

"What's happened here?" Lew demanded of his employer. Receiving no reply, he looked questioningly at the cook.

"He says they've been poisoned," growled Jacques, brandishing a sheet of paper, "but I say they're all plastered, pickled, well and truly drunk. Look around. See for yourself."

"My enemies have succeeded at last," muttered Charles, leaning his forehead against the lectern. "Now the name of Perrault will become the standing joke of Paris."

"How's that?" asked Lew, impatient at this exhibition of self-pity. "Since when did the drunken behaviour of a man's guests tarnish his reputation? If it was me, I'd get Jacques here to turf the lot of them out into the street." Catching sight of his portrait of the academician lying facedown in a tangle of window drapes, he hastened between the recumbent bodies to replace it on its easel. Nearby lay a clutch of marble busts – chipped and battered, some lacking noses and ears – scattered like a clutch of eggs tipped from the broken nest of a roc, and a small tree, wrenched from its pot, clawing the air with upended roots. The scene looked like the aftermath of a brawl, but one in which nobody seemed to have been wounded. Unless, perhaps, Poucet—

"My friend, are you hurt?" Lew patted the valet's shoulders, attempting to comfort him. "Has someone attacked you?" Poucet kept his face turned away, continually dabbing his eyes and nose, while his entire body juddered at each ragged in-breath. "What have they done to you? Let me see."

Intent on persuading Poucet to reveal his injuries, Lew was almost knocked off balance when the little man broke free with a muffled wail, and ran. He hesitated for a moment, torn between duty to his employer and care for his friend, before reasoning that Jacques was a better protector than he could ever be and following Poucet. On the stairs Lew hesitated again, for the tail ends of sounds from above sounded less like misery and more like—

He increased his pace, arriving at their shared room gasping for breath.

"What do you want?" demanded Poucet, blocking the doorway.

"Since you were laughing – not weeping as I supposed – the first thing is to know what you found so funny."

"Who wouldn't find it funny?" Poucet asked, without any trace of a stammer. "You saw them all." He still hadn't stepped aside. "Come back later, can't you?"

"And the second is to know what you're hiding." Lew pushed past him, noting the loose floorboard levered up to reveal a small collection of phials; a pipkin and a loosely wrapped package sat nearby, presumably waiting to be secreted with the rest. Easing the lid from the earthenware pot, he sniffed cautiously at its malodorous contents. "What's this stuff?"

"Don't touch that whatever you do!" Poucet snatched the pipkin from his hand and hastily replaced the lid. "It's just a remedy. For me – I get megrims."

"Plants, twigs, herbs, and what about these…they're toadstools, surely?"

Once Upon a Time in Paris

"What's that to you?" demanded Poucet. "Norik's right – you're always nosing in things that don't concern you." He tried covering the open space with his feet, but Lew was already on his knees peering into the dark cavity. "Get your ugly great hands out of there. Mind your own business. Those things are mine."

"What's this?" asked Lew, tugging undone the cloth bundle.

"Put that down!" cried Poucet, his face ghastly in the candlelight as a pair of women's shoes tumbled onto the boards. "Give it here, damn you," he snarled as Lew shook out the dress.

"So this is yours, too?"

"*Un bâtard fouineur* – yes, that's what you are, nothing but a nosey bastard."

"I should have guessed," Lew said. In fact, some part of him already had. That day when he'd attempted to make a sketch of Poucet – four times his hand had presented him with a woman's features and four times he'd denied the evidence of his own eyes. Now he squirmed, recalling how he'd stripped off his garments and thrown himself stark naked onto this very bed beside her.

Poucet's mood abruptly changed. "Don't tell anyone. I can't lose my position here. Please don't tell the master."

Since leaving home, Lew had seen enough abject poverty at close hand to believe a masquerade such as this could be solely about obtaining work. He was about to pledge his silence – after all, whether Monsieur Perrault's valet was male or female didn't affect him in the least – when another image presented itself, the murderous expression that had flickered across Poucet's face during the old man's rant about geese in the ballroom. A moment, no more, and it had disappeared, so out of place, so unexpected, that he might have imagined it. But Lew knew he hadn't. There was more to this than straightforward deception. "Those unfortunate people downstairs.... What have you done, my friend? What have you done?"

Poucet's mouth twisted. "Nothing they won't recover from – more's the pity." One small hand reached out to clutch Lew's sleeve. "You say I'm your friend. Promise not to speak out against me."

"If you want my silence, you'd better—"

"I'll tell you everything. There's not one innocent among them. They deserve to suffer far more than humiliation and a few days of blinding headache apiece. When you've heard me out, I'm sure you'll agree."

"Go on," said Lew. What a peculiar household this was, to be sure: a giant and a dwarf below stairs, together with the red maid and the white – and now this, a servant who transformed appearances as if by magic, but was not at all what he claimed to be.

"All right, but first I'll have to…." Poucet jerked his head towards the stairs. "The master's incapable of putting himself to bed. If I don't go, he'll know something's amiss."

Chapter Nine

This morning – and I had not thought such a thing possible – the witch looks even more hideous than usual. Those wrinkles have become deep valleys, bottomless chasms. That puckered mouth seems determined to swallow what little is left of her lips. As for her eyes, they've sunk back into her skull and, alarmingly, their rims are now quite definitely tinged ruby-red. I'm almost sure – though I dare not stare – that her nose and chin are within my little finger's breadth of meeting each other. The nasty creature's mood matches her appearance: she shuffles here and she shuffles there, moaning, groaning, griping and complaining, all the while making threats about my untidiness. I try ignoring her, but then Reims alights on the window ledge and utters his very first word.

"Did you hear him? *Chacun*, he said, *chacun* – everyone." Although it's still a far cry from *they lived happily ever after*, one must begin somewhere. I crumble stale bread for the bird and he tilts his powdered-grey head judiciously, appraising his breakfast first with one silver eye, and then the other. It seems Reims is now accustomed to better fare. Finding my offering unacceptable, he departs. "What did he mean by it?"

"All I heard was *Tchak-tchak*," the witch says sourly, "that being the noise made by every other jackdaw in creation."

"*Chacun*. He must be telling me something."

"Nothing but foolish chatter," she grumbles. "They say swans will sing again when jackdaws fall silent."

"How very gloomy you are today, Granny."

"I dare say I am. Life is hard. One can only endure so much."

"What ails you?"

"Apart from being taken advantage of?" The witch grouses about me under her breath while continuing with the usual business of moving things here, there, and back again for no reason save to persecute a few stray feathers and a speck or two of dust. Finally she tucks away her polishing rag and straightens. "Nought but old age, I dare say – it comes to us all."

"Sit down then, Mamie. Stop fussing, and rest for a while." I bring the little wooden box of *calissons* from its hiding place and place it on her knee. She sets it aside, a very bad sign: these almond-shaped sweetmeats are one of our favourites, being made of candied melon and marzipan, each topped by a sugar crust flavoured with orange-flower water. It is whispered that at Christmas these are given instead of consecrated bread in certain sinful places.

Nothing more is said for a while. I gather together my strewn clothes and toss them onto the bed. I replace my books on the shelf, fling the bread crusts out of the window and even scrape up a great pile of crumbs. None of this seems to impress the witch. Her eyes are fixed on some distant place and her mouth works as if in silent conversation with ghosts. Suddenly she reaches out and pats my hand.

"It will soon be time for me to return to the land of my birth, *ma chère*."

The witch has used this threat before. Today it's different: she's not screeching and throwing her arms out for a start. "Do you mean," I can hardly force the words through my teeth, "to leave me here – alone, and at his mercy?"

She doesn't answer – another bad sign. "The sea calls me. I miss its salt tang and the sound of waves grinding pebbles against the shore. I miss the call of fishermen, the slap of wet sails. I miss my native tongue. And I long to hear again the seal folk singing of the coast as it was long ages ago when the world was new." The witch gives me a sidelong look. "Besides, night after night I dream of an apple branch in bud—"

"Your wind-raked seashore is no place for tender apple trees to thrive," I say, hoping for a smile, but she clicks her tongue with annoyance.

"We've shared enough tales of my homeland for you to know what such a dream means. I'm being called to the Land of the Ever Young, the place of song." Her voice turns softer, *"Deuit ganinme da gompezenn al Levenez, O! Mar goufec'h e teufec'h' vit atao!"* When she looks up at me, her eyes seem full of light. "It means, *Come with me to the plains of joy. Oh! If you knew you would stay forever!"* The witch sighs. "Maybe not yet, but my time is coming."

"But not yet," I say quickly. "Not yet." For while it's true that I hate the witch, at the same time – and this is a curious thing – somewhere deep down I harbour a feeling, let us call it *a fondness*, for her. Perhaps that's why I feel compelled to take her bony little hands in mine and gently chafe them.

She peers at me. "No one should meet the end of their life in such a lonely place as this...."

"Don't talk of such things, Mamie. You're not going to die for many years yet."

"Ma chère demoiselle, I was talking about you."

This again; I'm tired of repeating myself. "Go if you must, Granny. Forget about me." I let her hands fall. "Lonely or not, I'll continue to wait here."

"Since it seems your unhappy enchantment is also mine, I must wait with you," sighs the witch. Then she gazes at the box of *calissons* until I fetch my quill knife and lever off the lid.

Even great nobles find the works of confectioners worthy of

discussion, but perhaps it's to sweeten our sadness that we talk of other delicacies: *cotignac*, the delicious quince paste that must be eaten with tiny silver spoons; *sept-en-gueule*, those lovely ribbon-tied bunches of candied pears so tiny that seven will fit into the mouth in one delicious bite; crystallized fruits, and flowers…musk pastilles, and sugared almonds.

"They say that every Valentine's Day, the Duke of Lorraine gave a casket of sugared almonds to a poor young girl from Verdun, chosen by lot." And then I remember that a hundred years ago King Henry sat down to a great feast where everything on the table was spun from sugar: "Everything – plates, knives, *forks*, tablecloth, napkins, statues, decorations, even the bread – imagine! Over a thousand beautiful things spun from *sucre*, Granny, for just one meal." It sounds so enchanting that I wonder about using such an idea in my story about poor little Cinderbottom's rise to happiness. After all, if statues and tablecloths can be produced from a sugar-loaf with a few flicks of an ordinary kitchen spoon, what could not be achieved with a fairy's magical one?

Chapter Ten

On his return to the bedchamber, Poucet produced a pocketful of candle stubs, several of which were speedily lit. "How can you see to draw pictures in this light? Please stop, *mon cher ami*. You'll ruin your eyes."

"My vision's fine. No need to start fussing over me." Lew set aside his finished copy of Madame Perrault's portrait and stood the original near the door. "I'll replace that later." The night air began to bite. He wrapped his cloak around himself, uncomfortably aware of Poucet perching on the very end of the bed, as far away from him as was possible. "Don't worry, my friend, I'll be sleeping downstairs from now on." His words were acknowledged with the slightest of nods. "What's Monsieur Perrault's mood?"

"Ill done by," Poucet's tone was terse. "Down in the mouth. But by the morning he'll be breathing fire, looking for someone else to blame."

"Someone else?" Lew raised an eyebrow and the servant shrugged.

"At the moment it's Jacques. Last place he'd look would be in my direction. To the master, I'm just a tongue-tied fool, hardly capable of anything beyond patting powder over his blemishes. Unless...." Poucet's constantly twisting hands took on the appearance of two small animals endlessly circling as they sought comfort from each other. "Unless you give me away, that is. *Are* you going to give me away? Don't just shake your head, Lew. I need to know my secret is safe."

"If you mean that you're not a man, yes."

"So promise me you won't tell anyone."

"I promise."

"Swear you'll tell no one, not ever."

"Come now, I've already given you my word not to tell anyone else." Lew sighed. "Listen, I swear on my little sister's head. Is that better?"

"What's her name?"

"She's called Fleurance. More to the point, what's your—"

"It's a pretty name. Is she...? Yes, I know, you want my story, but where to start? Perhaps...no...." Poucet took a deep breath. "All right – well, after the shock of my father dying so horribly," here the valet's face contorted, "from so-called cures bought of a quacksalver at the Michaelmas fair, my little brother was stillborn. Maman, having no other means of support, brought me and her ample breast milk to Paris. Wet-nurses are always in demand here. They say no *lady* feeds her own babe, which—"

"But first *your* name," prompted Lew. "What's your true name?"

"Oh," Poucet grimaced, "my name. It's Judith. Judith Goubert. But please don't use it here – when it comes to names, can't we just go on as before?"

"I think we must," agreed Lew, reflecting that it would be as well to keep in mind the biblical Judith, a woman possessed of ruthless cunning. And, if he remembered correctly, one who prayed that God would make her an unsurpassed liar.

"We came to the Perrault family," went on Poucet, "towards the end of 1677. Not at this house, you understand, but the old one, a huge great place in rue Neuve des Bons Enfants – close to the Palais-Royal – very grand, very showy, elegant visitors day and night. It's gone now. There's a big round *place* where it stood, with a statue of the king in the centre. Anyway—"

"What does this have to do," Lew gestured towards the still partially dislodged section of floorboard, "with those baneful...?"

"They're not *baneful*," Poucet said indignantly. "Nothing there is *deadly* poisonous. Those bits of things plucked from the wild, they're the remedies of the poor and the powerless. I never meant to kill anyone. It wasn't my fault the greedy old ox gorged herself on the apples – yes, yes, I'll tell you about that if you wish, and everything else. Give me a chance, will you? Listen, I just wanted to make them all suffer, to give them a foretaste of," the candles flickered and dimmed, then sprang back to life – "Hell," Poucet finished, "because that's where I hope they're all going."

"But I still don't understand why you're here, pretending—"

"It's m-my story," said Poucet, "so you'll have to put up with me telling it my way. Or I can stop, if you p-prefer."

"No, no." So Poucet was here to mete out punishment for some real or imagined slight. At this rate, Lew decided, getting to the whole truth was likely to take all night. He stifled a yawn. "No. I'm listening. Go on." Beneath him, the close-packed straw creaked and rustled as he sought a more comfortable position. As he did so, a goblin shadow shifted into the space between bed and wall. From old habit Lew raised his hands, laying one over the other to form the silhouette of a hog's head; one crooked thumb provided an ear; wriggling two fingers a mere crack apart produced its wicked little eye and, with care, it was possible to open and close the snouty jaws in a semblance of speech that was always guaranteed to reduce Fleurance to helpless laughter. "Go on – please."

"Pierre wasn't born until the following spring, so there were the two boys, hardly more than babies, Charles-Samuel, Charles, and," here Poucet hesitated for so long that Lew imagined something was being left unsaid, "and so I had a friend because Monsieur Perrault smiled on us playing together and listening to my mother's stories. He even let me learn to read with—"

"So that's where you learned. I did wonder. And you see I was right," Lew said feeling a little smug, "about a kind heart lurking under that curmudgeonly manner." He frowned. "But surely he wasn't teaching his baby sons their letters?"

Poucet's mouth opened...and then closed again. "Being very young myself, I can't remember exactly *when* things happened. And before you ask, I don't remember Madame Perrault clearly either. In later years, Maman described her as lonely: her family lived at Troyes, getting on for a hundred leagues away. Anyway, by the following October the smallpox had taken her, and little Charles, too. Not Pierre, though for, as a girl my mother had been a milkmaid and the Holy Mother protects babies suckled by such women."

"U-huh," murmured Lew to prove he was still awake and listening. Another long silence followed. His companion must be finding this account painful – unless he was taking his time over spinning an intricate web of lies – either way chivvying him would have no effect. *Her*, thought Lew, but found it was still impossible to think of Poucet as anything but a manservant.

He wanted to ask about the beautiful young wife's death – wasn't Monsieur Perrault utterly consumed by grief? Faced with such a blow, how could one go on living? But then Lew remembered his mother's death – Papa had married for love, and the barely muffled sounds of his heartbreak would stay with him forever – and realised, perhaps for the first time, how he and Fleurance must have anchored their father to life during those dark days. And the bereft husband, in return, had transferred all his affection to his children. So must it have been with the Perrault family.

Lew gave the smallest of sighs. A man could not have asked for a kinder or more loving father than his own – what sort of son turned and walked away, so intent on fulfilling his selfish ambitions that even the family name must be left behind? He shifted uncomfortably. His shadow writhed with him before collapsing into an outline reminiscent of a loathsome toad, while Poucet's remained motionless, hawkishly hunched and brooding.

The silence continued. Resigned to patience, Lew entertained himself by surreptitiously reproducing another shadow beast, this time the silhouette of a deer's head he'd devised to amuse his little sister: left hand bent at the wrist, ear finger dropped to make the gaping mouth, while the right hand – how did it go now? Ah, yes, the pointer and middle fingers raised to form antlers, the physick finger crooked very slightly so that the resulting chink became an eye – and there it was, straight from the deep dark forest. As for Fleurance, before he'd left her repertoire had expanded to include a rabbit, a goat and, of course, the goose. But time marched on. Perhaps she'd already outgrown such things, leaving childhood behind to become a young lady alongside their papa and their noble grandfather, whose hair might by now have turned completely white.

These were painful thoughts, especially when three days on the road would see him back in Normandy. With a great effort of will, Lew set aside his longing and loneliness; rethinking the course of his life must wait on the completion of the magical ballroom. In the meantime – antidote to selfishness – he'd redouble his efforts to befriend the poor maimed *ancien combattant* hidden away in this vast old building.

A small wind from nowhere crept under the eaves to finger his cheek. One of the candles guttered and died.

"I'd better tell you about my mother next," announced Poucet. "When you know what happened to us, you'll understand why I hate these people."

"Very well."

"Maman wasn't a witch or a sorceress, whatever they said about her afterwards, but give her a pack of cards and she could read them like the pages of a book being newly written right there before her eyes. And who do you think came to her, begging for a glimpse of the future?" Poucet's eyes gleamed in the rapidly dimming light. "Was it the butcher's wife, the baker's daughter, the cat-fur seller's moll?" Lew had no idea how to answer this question. As it turned out, there was no need. "Oh no," continued Poucet, "it was those so-called *précieuses*, those hoity-toity literary friends of the master. First their maids came, tittering and nudging each other, then the mistresses themselves, trip-trap, trip-trap, down the back stairs to wile away an hour in the kitchen corner. We'd watch through a gap in the door, biting our knuckles against fits of the giggles at those wrinkly old ladies still dreaming of winning the love of a great prince."

"We?" breathed Lew, but Poucet spoke over him.

"I can't read the cards myself, though it's not for want of trying. From what I've seen you also need a silver tongue and a knack for spinning tales. My mother, God rest her soul, had that knack in full. 'Listen carefully,' she'd tell them after they'd shuffled and cut, 'this story is about you, but by the end you may decide you want to be someone else.' Maman always laid the cards out in the shape of a cross before examining them, stroking their surfaces with her fingertips for several moments in complete silence as she considered their aspects and positions, their relationships with each other. Then it began: 'Ah look, there she is – the five of hearts, that's a fine lady thinking about leaving the safety of her comfortable home and venturing into the darkness of the forest – embarking on an adventure of the heart, perhaps – but here, see, following close behind, beware the knave of pikes, flitting from tree to tree, keeping in the shadows, intent on no good.' Sometimes mother tapped on a card with crossed fingers and we'd know it was the ten of pikes, the card of grief, bringing unwelcome news, or even the queen of pikes, the cruel black widow, who represented a jealous rival. We soon lost interest though – unless, as sometimes happened, there was a great deal of weeping and snuffling and pleading with Maman to look again, which was as good as theatre for us." Poucet's hands recommenced their terrible twisting and wringing. "My mother would never read my fortune from the cards. Nor her own, evidently, or she would have known what was coming."

Another candle stub gave up its ghost. Somewhere a dog howled.

"Go on," said Lew, fearing another long silence. "What happened to her…to you both?" Poucet rose and coaxed flames from a few more candle stubs.

"How much do you recall about the Affair of the Poisons?"

"Not much." Lew had been little more than a boy when the scandal came to an end in the early '80s, though he could remember a few of his father's acerbic comments. "I was told the king unwisely relaxed ancient laws banning the sale of dangerous chemicals. From then on anyone could mix up poisons at home – and some did in order to murder unwanted relatives for their money."

"That's true enough, but after they'd rounded up the poisoners – a few from among the highest in the land – they came for those accused of witchcraft, for fallen priests rumoured to offer black masses for a price, and for those women that held séances, or sold love potions, or provided certain remedies governed by the moon for unfortunate maids. And finally the Eye – surely you must have heard of him, I mean Gabriel Nicolas de la Reynie, the Lieutenant General of Police – turned his pitiless gaze on the humble fortune-tellers of Paris."

"Oh," said Lew, finally sensing where this tale was leading. "And did he…?"

"Two things proved my mother's undoing. First, maybe because it grieved her so deeply, she unwisely confided in me her concern about baby Pierre – while still at her breast she foresaw a short life and a violent end for him. Nobody else was supposed to hear, but this ugly great widow woman who'd been hanging around for months hinting that the Perrault children needed a new mother – and badgering Maman to find marriage in her card readings – must have been listening. I thought we'd be turned out in the street right then, but the Perrault children were thriving and sober nurses are hard to find. Besides, the master...." Poucet paused, frowning. "Well, the upshot was, we stayed. In fact my mother gradually took over more of the household duties. The woman was furious. Bédier, that was her name, Madame Bédier, and I'm sure she was the one who sowed seeds of hatred in other visitors to the house. Yes, we stayed but it grew more dangerous as the weeks passed and the whispers of *sorcière* grew." Poucet jumped as the night air was ripped apart by banshee shrieking and wailing that could only be produced by a coven of cats. "Oh, it's only the Ratter holding court."

"Don't stop," urged Lew.

"Our candles are almost exhausted. The rest must wait."

"But I have to know what—"

"My story's a terrible one, Lew. It can't be recounted in the darkness."

"You said there were two things. Just quickly tell me the other and I'll go."

"Another fine lady came, on her maid's recommendation, to have her fortune told. She was the last, as it happened. Her name was Mademoiselle de La Force."

"Oh, *her*," said Lew with feeling, remembering a predatory hag, aptly named, who professed not to understand a courteous *no* to her unmistakeable advances. After finishing the small portrait of her, he'd pocketed his fee and made a hurried departure. "A somewhat domineering woman, as I recall."

"But brought to her knees twice by me," Poucet's voice was laden with malice. "Anyway, to return to that afternoon, almost fourteen years ago, Maman was reluctant: she sensed trouble before the first card fell, and it got worse. A marriage set aside by the king himself, no less, and a gloomy end, hidden away from the world. No amount of shuffling and dealing could change the outcome." Poucet plucked at the bedcovers. "And then the woman turned really nasty – you'd have thought my mother was creating this future and inflicting it on her out of spite. We never believed Mademoiselle de La Force acted alone – suddenly pious and self-righteous, they were all in on it – but it was her personal maid who gleefully carried the letter of denunciation to Nicolas de la Reynie."

"The Chief of Police," murmured Lew.

Poucet nodded. "They were to come for us the very next day. What would happen next was common knowledge: torture followed by burning at the stake; that or disappearing, never to be seen again. We fled that night with little more than the clothes we stood up in, glad still to have our lives and a chance of freedom."

"Thus averting a terrible injustice – *l'échapper belle* – and you survived."

"As you say, we escaped by the skin of our teeth. There's more, of course: our misfortunes didn't end there."

"But now you've had your revenge. Is that the end of it?" enquired Lew. And when Poucet merely shrugged, added: "Does that mean you're planning more reprisals? What of Monsieur Perrault?"

"What about him?"

"Is he to be punished?"

"Not yet," Poucet said darkly.

"Did he play a part in your mother's troubles?"

"I suspect his wrongdoing may concern someone else."

"Does that mean you're not sure?"

"Not yet," Poucet repeated.

"I hope," Lew said, "that you weren't planning to harm Monsieur Perrault. He can be *grincheux* all right – *really* grumpy and crotchety, nasty even – but I've known him show unexpected kindness, too." Ignoring Poucet's squawk of derision, he added emphatically: "My future depends on his patronage. Since you're my friend, promise me that you won't cause him any more distress." A long pause ensued.

"Not if *you* don't want me to, though I fear his crimes may involve a far worse betrayal than those of his cronies. But even if I'm right, even if he's committed the blackest, the most loathsome of sins," here one pale hand rose from the gloom and was placed over Poucet's heart, "for your sake, Lew, and your sake alone, I won't harm him in any way."

"Pleased to hear."

"From this moment on, my dear friend," Poucet's voice had grown tremulous with emotion, "because you wish it, no hurt or harm or humiliation will befall the old man. Henceforth, I'll care for him as if he were my own flesh and blood."

Lew inclined his head. "Then, as true friends must, we have each other's best interests at heart. I'll bid you good night in the hope that you'll tell me more of your adventures tomorrow."

"Oh," said Poucet, sitting up, "are you going?"

"As I said earlier, from now on I'll sleep in the ballroom."

"No. Please. You really d-don't need to."

"Anything else would be ungentlemanly." Lew stood, gathering his cloak more tightly around him, and shielding his candle from any stray draught. At the door he stopped undecided, for only a knuckle of wax remained. It seemed unlikely that such a feeble flame would last long enough to light him down those narrow stairs and through the rambling house. He looked back into the dimly lit chamber. "Don't you agree?"

Once Upon a Time in Paris

Many years had passed since Charles last experienced the blood-boiling urge to strike down his fellow-man. A rare occurrence: he was not a violent man. With effort he recalled – aged eight, and newly enrolled at the College of Beauvais – squaring up to a fellow-scholar who'd jeered at his poor reading skills. And some three decades later he'd squeezed, with deadly intent, the throat of a Jesuit for speaking disparagingly of his brother Nicolas after he'd refused to repudiate his Jansenist views. Furthermore, he'd broken a stout cane across the head and shoulders of an artisan suspected of bringing smallpox to the old house in 1678. Since then, almost seventeen years had come and gone. Time should have extinguished fires that so easily blazed into bloodlust. Yet here he was on the point of thrashing into the grave this stuttering, stumbling idiot, truly the most irritating creature in Christendom, who seemed unable to comprehend that today was not a day like any other.

"No, I say, *no!*" Charles pushed away Poucet's hands, so that face powder spilled over his breeches and onto the floor. The fool immediately came at him clutching brushes and cloths. "Leave me alone, damn you. Get out."

"Y-yes, sir, r-right away, sir," the wretch backed off, hands shaking, lips trembling, eyes blinking away tears. "B-b-before I go, sir, what else m-may I p-p-put out for you to w-wear?"

"Damn it, who cares?" growled Charles, who had no intention of ever leaving the house again. "Give me whatever old rag comes to hand and be done with it." The halfwit scuttled away, stifling sobs, and returned carrying a handsome, but rarely worn, *justaucorps* of indigo *Gros de Naples* with silver galloon passementerie ornamenting the fronts and cuffs, as well as the low-slung pockets. Charles narrowed his eyes. The valet flinched. "Oh, for the love of God…." This was no time for foppish finery.

To make matters worse, the blockhead had selected a more recently purchased silk waistcoat – lavishly embroidered with flowers in various shades of blue – for wearing beneath it. "Imbecile!" barked Charles. "You think this a day of fêtes, blockhead? Huh? Huh? You think there's something to celebrate?"

"I'd say the worse the d-day p-p-promises to b-b-be," gabbled Poucet, carefully keeping his distance, "the b-b-better a gentleman should p-p-present himself to the world."

Charles looked sharply at the little valet, for this selfsame admonishment had been levelled at him before, though he couldn't remember by whom – or indeed the where and the when of it. No matter. The observation had a ring of truth. "My appearance will soon be of no consequence," he muttered, while permitting Poucet to button the waistcoat. "As news of yesterday's fiasco spreads – and it will spread like Greek fire – I shall be shamed like a cur in the gutter. Give the beldams of Paris time and they'll be writing versions of what happened into their wretched stories."

"If I m-might v-venture to speak," began Poucet, holding up the *justaucorps* while Charles forced his arms into the sleeves. Like so many of his garments, it was a fraction too tight. His tailor must be skimping on the costly fabrics. "You weren't the one p-p-prancing and d-dancing, sir, no, nor d-dribbling and b-babbling nonsense, or r-rolling upon the floor. They were d-dead d-drunk, all of them, sir, while you remained d-dignified. It was your g-guests who shamed themselves."

Charles grunted. "I fear the world won't see it that way."

Poucet had the temerity to laugh. "Sir, the recounting of last night's p-pantomime here would b-be g-good as g-gold or silver coin to the servants of your g-guests and their n-neighbours. With such a tale I'll be w-welcomed into every kitchen, laundry and stable in the d-district. I could drop hints or whisper n-names. I can p-paint the scene even b-blacker than it was in reality. I'll insinuate shocking improprieties that no one could ever disprove. Word would soon travel upwards – kitchen wench to seamstress to lady's maid, stable b-boy to footman to gentleman's valet – and from thence to those ears that matter." Poucet discreetly unfastened the bottom two buttons of Charles' waistcoat and smoothed the strained fabric. "If you would p-permit me, that is."

Once again, Charles looked hard at his valet – this time in astonishment – unable to recall the fellow making such a long speech during the entire period he'd been employed, nor one containing so much good sense and so little spluttering. Was this the celebrated wisdom of the court jester? "Why would you put yourself to so much trouble?"

"Sir, n-nothing is too much trouble if it p-protects your reputation."

A glimmer of hope presented itself, like a patch of azure sky promising fair weather in spite of black storm clouds. "You're a good fellow, Poucet, permission granted. Indeed, I would be indebted to you." Charles eyed himself in the looking glass, noting that the dark blue coat had been an excellent choice on his part. This was no time for such an elegantly garbed man to hide from society. He straightened his back and decided to strike with the iron while it was still red hot. "Furthermore, as the host, I believe it is incumbent upon me to call at the establishments of those afflicted and enquire after their health."

"You m-might also," suggested Poucet, while knotting Charles' most lavishly lace-trimmed cravat, "m-mention your guests' extraordinary b-behaviour to those of your acquaintances who found themselves unable to attend." He flicked imaginary dust from his master's shoulders. "The esteemed abbé de Choisy, for one. And also your niece, Mademoiselle L'Héritier de Villandon, and p-p-perhaps there are other p-p-p—"

A small sigh of irritation, instantly regretted, escaped Charles. Poucet's hands dropped to his sides. He stared at his feet.

"P-p-pray forgive my stumbling speech."

"You misinterpret my impatience," Charles lied. "It was not directed at you. No, no, I merely sighed at the prospect of questioning the other servants about yesterday evening."

He hastily cast about for something to restore Poucet's wellbeing, for the poor tongue-tied little man had offered to perform a service far beyond what was expected of him. Clearly the fellow held him in high esteem, perhaps even felt affection for him. "Young man, have you heard of Notker, the monk of Saint Gall?" The valet squinted from under his lashes and Charles held his gaze. "If you have not – no matter, no matter, few have. This will interest you. In addition to being a venerable monk and teacher, this Notker was also a renowned musician, an author and a poet. Indeed, it is from his work, *Gesta Caroli magni* – amusing and witty tales, though perhaps lacking in absolute veracity – that we learn of the virtues of Charlemagne. This monk was also known as Notcerus Balbulus, that is to say Notker the Stammerer." He paused. "They say of him that though he was halting of tongue, he was possessed of a formidable intellect."

"Oh."

"Never allow anyone to insinuate that your small imperfection denotes dull-wittedness."

"No."

"Notker was beatified a century and a half ago. His help can be invoked against afflictions like yours."

"Oh."

"Miracles happen every day." Charles forced a smile. "A cure is not impossible."

A muscle below Poucet's eye twitched. "Yes, sir, thank you, sir."

"And now, young man," for it could be put off no longer,

"assemble the rest of the servants outside the library. I'd better interview Jacques first."

Charles continued to write for several minutes after Jacques entered the room. In fact he was simply ornamenting his signature with flourishes and curlicues, but only laid down his quill when the shuffling of the cook's feet and the clearing of his throat became unbearable. "Well, my man," he adopted his sternest expression, "what are we to make of yesterday's goings-on?"

"If you refer to the outlandish behaviour of your guests, sir," Jacques said sullenly, "they all seemed well sauced to me – drunk as sailors on their first night ashore. Of course, I know nothing about drinking habits in fashionable society."

Charles cleared his throat. During the long sleepless night, those strange occurrences bedevilling his acquaintances – enchanted apples, tightly laced corsets, wailing in tongues, crazed itching and burning feet, things inevitably resulting in the spread of tales wholly humiliating to the sufferer – had seemed to circle him, gradually growing closer. Clearly he'd been expected to eat and drink with his guests yesterday: only nervous anticipation regarding his readings had spared him. He must get to the bottom of this. "I fear something worse than inebriation may have been at work."

He stopped short as a great huffing and snorting filled the room. Jacques' eyes bulged. Fiery curls sprang from beneath his loathsome wig and he seemed to double in size. One large foot began pawing the ground in a manner that reminded Charles of Spanish bullfighting stories brought to the royal court with Maria Theresa. Gilgamesh, he thought, and Enkidu. His fingers walked slowly across the writing table until they rested on the open quill knife. A final snort issued from Jacques, but when he spoke his voice, though loud, sounded calm enough.

"Begging your pardon, sir, but the accusation levelled at me last night was yet another insult in a long line of insults I've endured in this establishment. It cut me to the quick, sir," here the cook thumped his chest repeatedly with one kitchen-scarred fist, "to the quick, I say. Morning, noon and night, I've served you well and never once spoken of certain delicate secrets entrusted to me. To lay such a charge at my door lacks both rhyme and reason. Why would a man such as I dabble in poison? It would end my career. One more step and I'll be a master cook." His mouth twisted. "After all that time suffering as only an underpaid, underfed, over-beaten apprentice can, I endured even more years labouring as an assistant cook, cursed and put upon but always striving to become what I am now – a fully fledged cook, certified by my guild, an adept in the culinary art of disguisement. I ask you again, sir – why oh why would a man such as I stoop to dabble in poison?"

"Who else could it have been?" demanded Charles, unable to keep the desperation from his voice. "You, Jacques, had sole responsibility for the refreshments. As for your question, there's no knowing the mind and motives of a poisoner."

"But I didn't poison anything or anybody," cried the cook. "As I keep saying, there was no reason. Bring me the Good Book and watch me swear on it. "

"And as *I* said, who else could it have been?"

Jacques scowled. "If I don't get an apology, I'll leave this place, take my skills to foreign lands and find work with some heathen prince."

"Perhaps not, for bad news travels fast, and is often much embroidered during its journey." Charles turned to Poucet. "Summon the females." In shuffled the two maid servants, subdued and with their eyes cast down, followed by Norik wearing a particularly fierce expression. "Now, my good women, you all witnessed yesterday's unfortunate events." He peered at

Once Upon a Time in Paris

the tow-haired scullion. "What did you make of it," he bent towards Poucet, who supplied her name, "Blanche?"

The girl bobbed a rough curtsey. "They were all bewitched, sir," she volunteered, her voice hardly audible.

"Bewitched, you say." Charles directed his gaze at her companion. "And what about you...?"

"Escarlatta," whispered the voice close to his ear.

"And you, Escarlatta – what do you think?"

"She's right. I know witchcraft when I see it." Escarlatta tossed her head. "All that prancing and dancing – if there wasn't an enchantment laid on them they must have taken a magical potion."

"Potion or poison," said Charles, "the distinction escapes me. In any case, it must have been one or the other and I'm wondering which of you added it to the comestibles." He flinched as both maidservants repeatedly shrieked denials over the deep bass of the cook's furious rebuttal. "That's enough! *Silence*, I say. Jacques produced the food. You two served it. Who else had the opportunity?"

"What about him?" demanded Escarlatta, pointing at the valet. "He gets everywhere – that little weasel's always sneaking about the place."

"Poucet was never out of my sight."

"If you p-please, sir...."

Charles frowned. "Not now, Poucet."

"B-but...."

"I said *not now*." Charles next addressed Norik. "Naturally no suspicion falls upon you, Madame. However, I'd value your opinion."

The old woman pursed her lips. "We all tasted the refreshments served to your guests. Jacques very kindly invited us to try his new creations."

"Only a few imperfect samples," the cook said hastily.

"With no adverse results?" enquired Charles, suddenly less sure of the culprit's identity. Norik shook her head.

"None whatsoever – of course, I can't speak for the wine."

"I tried the wine," said Jacques, averting his eyes, "but only to ascertain its quality. I assure you there were no ill effects."

"Did you find your breakfast potage satisfactory, Monsieur?" demanded Norik. Charles look at her, surprised.

"It was...adequate."

"And no doubt – as on every other day – you anticipate an excellent lunch?"

Charles smoothed his chin. "Yes, of course, but—" They'd spoken of the first asparagus of the year, and afterwards a squab *tourte*, with feather-light puff pastry – which Jacques could turn his hand to very well – enclosing not only the young dove flesh, but truffles, mushrooms and morels, artichoke hearts and chard ribs, sweetbreads of veal, and cockscombs, the whole bound together – eggs no longer being forbidden – with a dozen or more yolks. His mouth watered at the prospect. His stomach rumbled. To finish, there was to have been a large platter of *poupelains* filled with raspberry preserve and *crème pâtisserie*, well doused with rosewater before being sprinkled with powdered sugar. On the other hand, if his own cook was a poisoner....

"And also expect to enjoy, as usual and without any qualms, dinner prepared by Jacques. Common sense suggests that a cook has ample opportunities to do away with his master." She shrugged. "Either you trust him, or you don't."

"Ah," said Charles, "I take your point, Madame." Though he didn't relish the prospect, it seemed he might be forced to apologise to his giant of a cook. Eating humble pie, as the uncouth English put it. The fellow was already straightening up and inflating his chest. "But somebody must have contaminated the victuals." Close his eyes and he was confronted by vile images: flesh-and-blood fountainheads spouting jets of saliva; living gargoyles with water endlessly streaming from their gaping mouths.

"Sir, p-please," Poucet tugged urgently at Charles' sleeve. "There w-was someone else w-working here yesterday."

Charles frowned at him. "You surely don't mean the artist?"

"Oh, no!" cried the valet, looking profoundly shocked. "Not Lew – he wouldn't hurt a fly – no, no, I m-mean the girl."

"Oh, *her*," said Escarlatta. "But she was only a drudge who came in for a couple of hours to wash pots and clean up."

"No good asking me, Monsieur." Norik tightened her mouth. "I wasn't consulted."

"Who was she?" enquired Charles, rising from his chair in order to ease his aching back. "What was her name?" He stood over the younger maid. "Come now, her name?"

Blanche turned pale. "I don't remember, sir."

"So she wasn't a friend or relative?"

"No, sir – I never saw her before, sir."

"Nor me," put in Escarlatta, without being asked. "Her name was Barbe or Bathe or some such. Every day a dozen like her come to the kitchen door begging for crusts. Usually I send them off with a flea in their ear." She commenced rolling up her sleeves as if reliving previous experiences. "But yesterday I knew Jacques would be in need of a scullion – because me and Blanche here had to go upstairs and offer round refreshments – so I brought her inside. Just an hour or two's work, I told her. She jumped at the chance."

Jacques shed his indignation and turned defensive. "Left to manage entirely alone, I was grateful for an extra pair of hands."

"And this girl brought nothing with her?" Charles paced the room's length, turned on his heel and walked back to the writing table. "No phials or bottles? No toad skin? No bunches of simples?"

"Could have d-done," said Poucet.

"No, she was empty-handed and her gown was nothing but patched rags," said Norik. "Thin as a cobweb – hardly decent, if the truth's told. The girl had no pockets, nor shoes upon her feet, not even a scarf round her hair. There was nowhere she could have kept such things hidden from me. What with all the bits of household silver around, I keep my eyes open, let me tell you."

"P-perhaps she was a w-witch," suggested Poucet, "conjuring n-noxious ingredients from thin air. Or m-maybe she left something outside the d-door."

"I kept her good and busy," said Jacques. "As far as I know, she didn't move from the back kitchen, not even when she ate. The wench did her work, and after I'd inspected it, she took her coins and went off into the night. And then I," the cook bared his teeth, "prepared to read my well wrought poem. To those assembled upstairs – as was promised me."

"My apologies, Jacques," murmured Charles, hoping that would cover everything. "Perhaps another occasion will present itself."

After dismissing his domestic servants, and sending the invaluable Poucet to stutter an embellished account of yesterday's events to anyone in the area who would listen, Charles sat with his head in his hands wondering when the next blow would fall, and on whom. It was now clear that the poisoner had found a way of being invited into his home disguised as a beggar, just as she'd inveigled herself into the presence of the Bédier woman, and into Madame de Caylus' residence posing as a *couturière*. The evildoer would probably return. And he still hadn't found his protective bezoar stone.

Late afternoon, when the last of his assistants had departed, Lew heard footsteps crossing the Red Drawing Room. He went back to his work, convinced it must be Poucet, but it was Pierre who stuck his head round the door.

"My father isn't here, is he? Good. He's got a head full of bees, continually bothering me about reading stuff and practising a fair hand – anyway, enough of that. I've brought you a new client." He slid into the ballroom, closely followed by a sturdily built young man with ruddy cheeks, curly black hair and an open face, who stood looking about him, openly admiring the decorated walls and ceiling. "This is *mon ami*, Guillaume Caulle, who's also a neighbour. I told him about your incredible skills and here he is. Will you make a sketch of him? For some reason he's anxious to have his ugly phiz immortalised."

"At least I'm not pig-ugly like you," retorted Guillaume, elbowing him in the ribs. "Ugly as sin, that's Pierre Perrault – ask anyone."

"Even that's not as bad as being *laid comme les sept péchés capitaux*. Ugly as the seven deadly sins trumps plain ugly any day." Pierre aimed a kick at his companion's ankle before repeating his request.

Lew hesitated, reluctant to refuse but anxious to get back to his partially completed panel before it dried out. "Very well, I can spare a few minutes." The task was an easy one, though he thought the finished result a trifle bland. Nevertheless, Guillaume seemed delighted, departing immediately so that he might show the pencil drawing to his parents, and especially to his five brothers.

"A large family of boys," commented Lew. "Are they all alike?"

"As are peas in a pod – and there's a younger sister, too, as fair as they're dark, but she's a shy little mouse."

"It's a fine thing to have a sister. I really miss mine." Lew was about to say more, but stopped on catching sight of Pierre's wan expression. "Is something wrong?"

The boy shook his head. "No – absolutely not. Look, my bruises have faded. In a few days, I'll be back asking you to make a picture of me." He stepped closer. "Fancy a game or two of cards this evening?"

"Jacques is still adamant that no games of chance will be played in the kitchen," said Lew, carefully bending the truth to fit, "and since it's my belief that your father won't tolerate them anywhere under his roof, I can't risk it." His workspace was definitely not being turned into a gambling den. "Besides, I'll be working well into the night for the next week or two."

"You'll never get a woman if you carry on like that." Pierre nudged him and grinned. "Thanks for drawing my ill-favoured friend. I'll get the money out of him and pay you later. That's all right, isn't it?"

Lew readily agreed, quite sure he'd never see a *sou*, and decided not to mention it to Jacques. He could almost hear the cook growling, "I warned you about that young fool," as he dealt a series of vicious blows to whatever was unfortunate enough to have found its way onto the chopping board.

Poucet finally turned up, weighed down by a pile of bedding. "First things first – I've brought you some blankets, *mon ami*."

Lew darted a quick look over his shoulder. "That's very kind, though my cloak's been keeping me warm." More interruptions were the last thing he needed. Finishing the miniature paintings – illustrations for a small book, apparently – requested by Monsieur Perrault, had taken far longer than expected. Pierre was quickly dealt with, but idle chatter might go on for hours and he needed to make up for lost time.

"You're going to need them all," Poucet assured him. "Paris stays bitterly cold until August. The constant black clouds part for a few moments and people start celebrating the arrival of spring. What a joke. The northern sun has no warmth in it. Even at midday, I'm chilled to the bone here."

"A blazing fire would be nice," agreed Lew, blowing on his fingers, "but I've managed in far colder places."

"You d-don't have to sleep down here, you know." Poucet came very close, leaning forward as if to watch each brushstroke. "There's no need."

Lew moved aside on pretext of needing a different colour. "Don't worry about me. The benches are comfortable enough." He quickly changed the subject. "Been busy? It's not often I don't see you for an entire day."

"You missed me then?" Poucet's face brightened. "Busy? Yes, I've been out and about, flitting between kitchens and stables, spreading gossip – richly spiced with gluttony, drunkenness, lewdness and lecherousness – about the unaccountable way the guests carried on at Monsieur Perrault's respectable literary gathering. I spoke of his horror, his dismay, and his disbelief."

"And were you believed?"

"Of course – people love such news, the smuttier the better, especially when it's about their elders and betters." The little valet twitched. "What was that funny look for? Yes, all right, we both know how the mischief came about. What's done is done. But last night I promised to look after the master's well-being. That's what I've spent my day on – first buttering him up, then safeguarding his name and reputation." Poucet laid one hand on Lew's arm. "I only did it because you wanted me to."

"Didn't anyone ask," Lew stepped back, as if to consider his work, "why such peculiar things should have happened under Monsieur Perrault's roof?"

"I said they arrived in that state – yes, all of them." Poucet shrugged. "Any description of past events is a mixture of truth and lies. Only the proportions vary. And even then it depends on how much listeners are prepared to believe. Take it from me, *mon cher*, most of the put-upon underlings I spoke to were disposed to believe every word that came out of my mouth."

Lew shot the valet a warning look. "Let's hope nothing else untoward happens here."

"Nothing else will. I've done with all that." Poucet produced a cloth-wrapped bundle. "Jacques says you haven't eaten this evening. I've brought food. Look – bread, wine, meat, some cheese, a pastry. Won't you stop?"

"I'm starving," admitted Lew, breaking off a hunk of bread as he made for the gallery where the once beautiful brocade seats were now splattered with paint in addition to being mouse-nibbled. He watched with some amusement as Poucet fastidiously turned over one of the cushions, pummelling it so vigorously that the fabric split and a cloud of feathers drifted downwards. "Go on with your story. You and your mother fled Paris empty-handed. What happened next?"

"We went south, making for Spain, scared stiff, keeping our heads down. Days became weeks. Nobody came after us, but that was no reason to stop. Weeks turned into months. We walked until our feet were blistered and sore, kept going until our soles were tough as leather. We begged rides on carts, tramped with pilgrims making for Santiago de Compostela, plodded in the wake of cattle drovers herding their charges to large towns, trudged some more. Then we fell in with the Poquelin Theatre Company, a small troupe of travelling p-performers – French and Spanish – heading for their winter home beyond the Pyrenees."

"That was where you picked up your skills with cosmetics," said Lew, remembering an earlier conversation. "A stroke of luck, as it turned out."

"In more ways than one," agreed the valet, "by then we'd almost gone through our silver...."

"Ah, so you weren't completely empty-handed when you left Paris."

Poucet looked confused. "Strange, I never before wondered where that money came from. Not Maman's card readings, that's for sure. If she charged anything, and mostly she didn't, it would only be a token *obole*, not much better than nothing, being equivalent to a quarter *sous*. My mother wouldn't have – no, she was no thief, but…."

"Someone warned her when she was about to be arrested," Lew mumbled through a mouthful of food. "Could that person have given her money?"

"Suppose I'll never know," said Poucet, brushing away stray feathers. "Anyway, to get back to our flight, the performers were kind, mending our boots, sharing whatever food they had. We were soon put to work. My mother cooked meals and mended costumes. I helped Maria – she was Monsieur Poquelin's wife – grind powders and mix cosmetics. It wasn't long before she taught me how to apply them. She taught me about disguises, too – adopt a stutter, palsy, or a dragging leg, and that's what people see, not the person behind it. The trouble is, use it for too long and you start to b-b-believe it really is part of you. Yes, I learned many tricks of the trade from her, but a great deal more about vanity from the rest of the company."

"Vanity is what creates demand for both your skills and mine." Lew chased the last few crumbs, drained the wine, and wondered whether encouraging vainglory was the best use of his life.

"Yes, but the troupe's biggest vanity was fancying itself a travelling version of the Comédie-Française. Its plays – lumbering great things, poking fun at the bourgeoisie and the upper classes – were written by Monsieur Poquelin himself. He claimed to be related to Molière – they shared the surname – and thought a great deal of himself, issuing orders right and left, bellowing at everyone if the takings weren't up to scratch." Poucet sighed. "Nevertheless, they were happy days."

"But you said yours was a terrible story."

"It is. Only listen. Winter came early that year. We'd reached Sauveterre-de-Béarn, right down by the mountains, planning to give a performance or two there before crossing into Spain. Disaster struck. Thunder. Lightning. Hail stones big as pullet eggs. Followed by icy rain so heavy it might have been sloshed over us from gigantic buckets. No wonder, said Maria, the area was called the *pisse-pot* of France. We were never dry. Our skin turned grey and wrinkled as the hands of washerwomen. Our clothes sprouted mould. Water streamed in at the heels of our shoes and out through the toes. There was no chance of putting on a play, however much Monsieur Poquelin stamped and roared and waved his fists at the heavens. Finally, the decision was taken to press on towards Pamplona. Two days later the old horse died. Shortly after that, climbing out of Saint-Jean-Pied-de-Port, taking turns to pull the wagon, we struggled to find the route through dense cloud that descended like a curse and never lifted, even at midday. Everything turned on us. Even the Patous – those great white mountain dogs – abandoned their sheep to snap at our heels." Poucet gulped. "Then an old adversary began stalking us. In spite of the cold Monsieur Poquelin started sweating and steaming from a violent fever. It was followed by a rash nobody wanted to recognise."

"Smallpox?" Lew shuddered.

"It caught up with us as we descended into Spain by way of the Roncevaux Pass. By then Monsieur Poquelin was raging and terrified, shouting that this was the place where his namesake, Roland, had died during Charlemagne's retreat. Soon others were showing the signs."

Lew flexed his fingers, torn between the need to pick up his brushes and the desire to hear more of Poucet's story. "And did they all....?"

"Only Maria escaped, Lew – her face already bore the scars of *la variole* and you don't get smallpox twice – and my mother and me, since we were under the protection of the Holy Mother in that respect. The monks at Roncesvalles took us in – and buried our companions," Poucet leaned forward, lips almost brushing his ear, and whispered, "but not before we'd lightened them of their few worldly goods. They wore their riches about them, a gold ring here, rosary chains there, while Monsieur Poquelin, who'd been fleecing them all for years, had a store of coins sewn into his cloak hem that even his wife knew nothing about."

Lew sprang to his feet, repelled by the valet's warm breath on his cheek. "And afterwards you continued safely to Pamplona – excellent." His companion's face fell.

"D-don't you want to hear any more? B-but I thought you wanted to know everything about me."

"My apologies," said Lew, taking the stairs two at a time. "It'll have to wait. If that section of wall dries out...."

Poucet skipped after him. "I can tell the rest of my story while you p-paint."

"No, it doesn't work like that. I wouldn't be able to concentrate with someone talking to me."

"Well, in that case, come to our chamber when you finish."

"No, I shall be painting for hours yet."

"B-but I don't m-mind how late you—"

"Listen to me, my little friend." Lew placed his hands on Poucet's shoulders. "It's not *our* bedchamber. It's *yours*. And I won't ever enter that room again – *Judith* – for fear of being misunderstood." He was careful not to specify by whom. "Hell and damnation," he swore, his gaze sliding past her. "Some of those cushion feathers have stuck to the wet paint. What a bloody mess."

"I'm really sorry. I should n-never have b-beaten—"

"Never mind, they'll soon scrape off." Such a nuisance, his beautiful smouldering red fox, ruined, and it had taken much effort to capture the sly gleam in Monsieur Reynard's eye as he attempted to beguile the gullible crow. The only remedy was to begin again, immediately. It was with a sense of relief that he realised Poucet had already slunk away.

Lew worked on until his vision blurred and he could work no more. Throwing down a pile of cushions he rolled himself in blankets and immediately tumbled into a deep dreamless sleep. A small noise woke him at dawn and he sat up to see a pale shape, a phantom, gliding across the room. After rubbing his eyes, it was clear that this was no ghost; it was Poucet.

"What do you want?" he whispered. "I'm trying to sleep."

"I haven't finished my story. If you won't come to me, I must come to you."

"Oh, dear God," moaned Lew, "not now, my friend."

"Please listen. I want you to know everything about me, the things I've done."

"It'll have to wait." Lew pulled the blankets over his head. "I need more shut-eye. Leave me alone."

"Then I'll just sit here," said Poucet, perching on the very edge of the pile of cushions. "You can't object to that, surely?" A silence, during which Lew drifted in and out of consciousness, was followed by speech that seemed to be coming from a far distance, oddly muffled, as if heard underwater, much of it making little sense. "Maria taught me everything…bad plants…plants that hate mankind…powdered mad bean pods for itching…slobber weed to bring on drooling…man or beast…certain roots to cause swellings or turn the brain…sickness…fungus…insanity…death."

"Uh-huh." For a few blissful moments, Lew had imagined himself at home, striding through the orchards with a couple of the family's dogs at his heels. The mention of insanity and death wrenched him into the here and now. He unravelled his blanket cocoon, propping himself on an elbow. "What was that?"

"*I said*, you've probably been wondering how I managed to take revenge on so many of my mother's persecutors in one fell swoop. It was me that sent out all the invitations, written in my best hand."

"No, I mean the bit about madness and death."

Poucet smiled. "You must have dropped off for a minute. I was telling you about the uses of *la crapaudin* – that beautiful white-spotted, bright red toadstool found under pine trees in the forest. Some call it *le tue-mouche*, the fly killer. Yes, fly agaric, that's the one. They say it's conceived when a lightning bolt hits Mother Earth, just as all truffles are born from thunder. Maria says this fungus serves instead of wine in the cold northern lands of eternal ice and snow. Men take it to visit the Otherworld. It brings visions and madness and sometimes death."

The small hairs on the back of Lew's neck prickled. "That's what I saw upstairs, in your hiding place beneath the floorboard."

"It grows everywhere, even under the trees around Versailles, near monasteries and convents, even in churchyards. Mine came from the forest of Fontainebleau."

"If anyone should find out…."

"How could they, unless you tell them?"

Lew shook his head. "You should know me better than that. Nevertheless, there are those who'd be quick to shout witchcraft – especially if they found out about your mother. Women have been burned for less. You should leave this place, my friend. After all, you've achieved what you came for."

"Not yet, I haven't. There's still something that must be done." Poucet thought for a moment. "But I do yearn for my adoptive home. You'd like it, Lew. In spite of poverty, there's such happiness there. People smile, really smile. They never smile here in Paris – just squeeze the corners of their mouths while looking down their noses at you. Listen, it really will be spring there. We have a house, with a garden. By now, our pomegranate bushes will be flowering – bursts of scarlet against dazzling white walls. And as it gets warmer, the local people carry their *calderos* into the orchards to cook rice in the open air, simmering it with water voles, beans, saffron, and eels or, if times are even harder than is normal, with snails. I can't wait to be back there. As soon as this is finished with…." Poucet laid one small white hand upon Lew's. "I'd go right now if you would come with me."

"I can't." Lew shook off the hand on pretext of folding away the blankets. "I have this room to finish. Besides, I already have a home."

"Perhaps we could go there together instead," the valet said softly, "if that would please you." And, after waiting in vain for a response: "Is there anything I can do for you, anything at all?"

"Nothing," snapped Lew, then immediately tried to soften his brusque rejection. "Since you ask, there is one thing preying on my mind. This poor old invalid Monsieur Perrault gives shelter to, the maimed soldier that's deemed too grotesque for anyone to look upon. I'd be very grateful if you could help me discover where they've shut him away. No one will tell me anything. Norik greeted my questions with such hostility that I dare not ask again. But find him we must, for I promised myself to befriend him."

Poucet's eyebrows shot up. "Still worrying about that? Why?"

"Simple Christian charity – that's how my father raised me. Besides, I've had a few strokes of good luck recently, and—"

"I hope you count meeting me as one of them."

"Of course," Lew said woodenly. "The thing is, when good fortune smiles on me, I always try to pass some of the benefit on."

"I'm looking for someone myself," said the valet, "in Paris or somewhere nearby. I've been searching for months. I fear this person may be dead but I'm not ready to give up hope. Listen, I'll do what I can if you'll return the favour and help me after you've finished here. Agreed?"

"Agreed." Lew threw open the doors to the Red Drawing Room, letting pale early morning sunshine lap across the floor to illuminate the paintings. He yawned. His eyes felt raw and scratchy. And he feared Poucet – *Judith* – would return tonight and every night unless he was downright nasty. Life here would be unbearable if that happened, even without taking into account the cache of unholy ingredients in the attic. It might be worth having a quick look round later: there must be some quiet corner in this huge house where he could sleep undisturbed. "Time to think about work," he announced. "Your master will be stirring and my assistants should be here soon."

Charles stopped short on entering the library, outraged to find Marie-Jeanne sitting at his writing table openly reading the collection of tales, which had been left concealed beneath a linen cloth. He scowled – even a niece shouldn't take such liberties with a man's private papers – and stamped across the room, thumping his cane hard against the floor at each step to emphasise his displeasure. This was not a propitious start to the week. Pray heaven that it didn't turn out like the last one.

Being thick-skinned by nature, Marie-Jeanne continued turning over the pages as Charles approached. "These stories are exquisite; so fresh and lively. I've read every one, and particularly enjoyed *Bluebeard*. What a villain – a coward, too – and such a deeply satisfactory ending. Run through with swords. And, as it says here, *sa femme demeura maîtresse de tous ses biens* – his ill-used wife became mistress of all his property. Quite right, too." She looked down. "And this tale of *Little Red Hood* indicates a plucky writer, one willing to dispense with the traditional ending.

Even *La Belle au Bois Dormant*, which is, I suppose, a love story, stops short of being mawkish. Whoever wrote them? Uncle, I'm intrigued. Pray share the name of this new luminary of our literary scene?"

Charles pointedly picked up her glass and placed it on the little tray provided. "Would it surprise you to learn they were penned by Pierre?"

"Pierre? Pierre who?"

"My son," he said irritably, "your cousin – Pierre Perrault d'Armancourt."

Marie-Jeanne laughed. "That's exceedingly funny, my dear uncle." She looked at him expectantly. "Do tell. It's not like you to make a joke of such matters. Come now, the authorship of stories as accomplished as these can't remain a secret for long."

Charles huffed impatiently. He pulled forward another chair and stood waiting in the hope that she'd allow him to be seated at his own writing table. Predictably, Marie-Jeanne didn't take the hint. "I suppose I'd better sit here then. The author is Pierre, I assure you."

"For goodness' sake.... It's inconceivable that a *boy* wrote these tales, and particularly not my wild young carouser of a cousin. Oh, yes. I've heard about his escapades. Hasn't everyone?"

"Perhaps," Charles said carefully, "you don't know him as well as you think."

Marie-Jeanne produced a condescending smile. "Perhaps *you* don't know him as well as you think. It's rumoured that Pierre had a hand in suspending those frightful effigies of Gabriel Nicolas de la Reynie and his police chiefs from the walls of Philippe Auguste. The young rogues chose the exact spot from which they used to throw pickpockets and deserters. Apparently it was a protest against the closing of a," she hesitated over the words, "a bawdy house."

Charles stared fixedly at his niece. "I think not."

"I also heard my cousin was one of the young reprobates who painted lewd extracts from the poems of Claude le Petit on buildings around the Place de Grève last year. You must remember the shocking event. It occurred on the first day of September, the thirty-second anniversary of that depraved poet's execution – no coincidence, I'm sure. The miscreants defaced other places with snippets from le Petit's work, too – of which the only one fit to be repeated was that daubed on the Pont Neuf: *The world is full of fools, and he who would not see it should live alone and smash his mirror.*"

Charles said nothing. He watched as his niece shuffled the stories, moving *The Beauty in the Sleeping Forest* to the top of the pile.

"For a rascal like Pierre to have written such a tale as this would confirm anyone's belief in miracles. I'm sure you didn't compose them. It's not your style at all. You tread carefully, while these fairly trip along – I was never absolutely convinced about the authorship of those verse tales to be honest – although I sense your hand when it comes to the morals. So if not Pierre, and not Charles Perrault, then who?"

Charles finally found his tongue. "Accept that it's Pierre, my dear niece. Not all authors are models of exemplary behaviour. Consider Rabelais."

"Ah, so you're practising the same technique as you recommended for our story of the little Marquise-Marquis! Keep everyone guessing, is that it? We'll have to see how long that lasts. And by the way," Marie-Jeanne tapped the first page of *La Belle au Bois Dormant*, "there is a contradiction in this tale. Your mysterious author tells us," she searched for the place, "ah, here it is—

After fifteen or sixteen years, the king and queen being gone to one of their country estates, it happened that the young princess, exploring the castle one day, and climbing the stairs from room to room, came to the top of a tower...."

"Yes, yes," growled Charles, trying in vain to disguise his irritation, "I've read the story a considerable number of times. Where's the contradiction in that?"

"It's in this," his niece said severely, "she takes the spindle, pricks her hand, falls down in a faint – and forthwith her father comes upstairs to investigate, whereupon he recalls the fairy's prophecy. How then can he be far away at his country estate?"

"A trifle: I don't believe it spoils the tale." He snatched up the sheaf of pages and moved them to a chest beneath the window, weighting down the collection with one of his heaviest tomes.

"Spoil it – no, not at all." Marie-Jeanne hesitated. "But there's also the matter of the royal family's place of residence – sometimes it's described as a palace, while further down the page it's a castle, but as you say, it doesn't ruin the tale – except, perhaps, in the case of real pedants."

"Exactly," Charles said dryly.

"Additionally...." She caught his eye and appeared to think better of further criticisms. "As I said, these are exquisitely told stories. Which reminds me – there's another pretty tale being passed between the servants at the moment, a romance, I believe, though I've yet to hear it in its entirety. They fall silent at my approach. I'm sure some of the lower orders think one is out to steal a personal possession when the likes of us want to carry off their words and commit them to paper. This one seems to be about a spellbound prince – a gross, pig-faced beast – who can only be released from the curse if someone will love him in spite of his appearance. This falls to a merchant's beautiful daughter, but I've yet to catch the end. Ah, well, if not me then someone else will write it down, sooner or later."

"Didn't you want to talk about our collaboration?" enquired Charles, hoping she'd leave before dinner was announced.

"Ah, yes." Marie-Jeanne's demeanour changed. Two closely written sheets of notes appeared and were meticulously lined up with the edge of the writing table. "François, not being gifted with an outstanding intellect, has suggested I write those sections dealing with Marianne's education, while he concentrates on descriptions of frills and falderals and other inconsequentials. Let me read you a passage—

She was taught everything a young noblewoman needs to know – dancing, drawing, and the appreciation of great art works. Marianne showed a great aptitude for music and learned to play, not only the harpsichord, but also the viol and the lute. Her tutors had only to demonstrate a thing once for her to grasp the subject in its entirety. Since Marianne possessed such a quick mind, her mother arranged for her to be taught foreign languages, history, philosophy and the classics.

The question, is my dear uncle, how much detail relating to these subjects is necessary to balance the reams of frivolity François has in mind concerning the where and the how and the why of beauty spots, earrings, necklaces, rings, pearls, rubies, sapphires, diamonds, *coifs*—"

"Exactly so," put in Charles, and was ignored. Far be it from him to point out that François' intellect was in no way inferior to hers. He'd been a member of the Academy for eight years; recently they'd begun working on the *Dictionary* together. On the letter N as it happened. N for *narcissisme, nausée, néfaste*…but also, he thought, suddenly heartened, of *nulle*, that delicious bright yellow custard made of egg yolks beaten with sugar.

He spent the rest of her tirade – for that was exactly what it was – in pleasurable anticipation of dinner: capon with oysters and tiny onions stuck all over with cloves. Jacques, who was still trying to make amends for something he clearly hadn't been involved in, had also promised a Lady Lucia cake, a delectably rich sponge, which was to be served with strawberries – it was as well not to ask how these had been acquired. Only the hothouses of Versailles produced *des fraises* out of season. The king adored them dipped in wine, though Charles preferred them with cream, a taste said to be reserved for women.

"…and the hairstyles, the cornets, the *fontanges* – whether the *souris*, the Burgundy, the *effronté*, the *commode* or the heartbreaker version – in addition to scarves, gloves, ribbons, lace—"

"Precisely."

"And that's before he starts on clothing," Marie-Jeanne concluded glumly. "For the sake of my sanity, I am in the process of writing a more realistic tale about a young woman who is forced by circumstance to dress as a man and become a warrior." She folded her papers. "Uncle, is this collaboration really viable?"

"I'm sure it is," Charles said soothingly, though he had his doubts. He'd been quite sickened by a newly composed extract read to him by the abbé after they'd finished picking over the incomprehensible behaviour at his recent salon. The passage described vanity of the worst kind.

> *Although she had many suitors, she cared not a fig for them, being concerned only for herself and her own beauty. She would hear of nothing else and thought herself the most beautiful girl in the world, and relied on her mirror to confirm the truth of it at all hours of the day and night.*

There had been a great deal more of the same. He'd thought at first that it was written in jest; apparently not. "My dear, the curious blend of sober and frivolous will intrigue every reader as much as the confusion over gender. Add to that the mystery appertaining to the authors."

"And we've come full circle," Marie-Jeanne said triumphantly. "Those wonderful little stories – you're not seriously going to continue your joke regarding authorship when the time comes to send them out into the world?"

"It's already done," Charles said solemnly, enjoying his niece's palpable discomfiture. "A finely bound, nicely illustrated copy has been presented to Mademoiselle."

Marie-Jeanne's eyes widened. "Presented to Mademoiselle? You mean to the king's niece, to Élisabeth Charlotte d'Orleans? But the work wasn't ascribed to Pierre, surely?"

He smiled. "Indeed, yes, and to him will no doubt be granted the *privilege* – thereby conferring on him an exclusive licence to publish the book."

"I'm shocked. Pierre is a.... Well, even within the family he has a great deal to answer for – Oh!" She stared hard at Charles. "Oh, I see." Her mouth worked. "Now I understand. That's absolutely disgraceful. I will write to her. Yes, I'll write to her immediately."

Chapter Eleven

It seems the English king is to introduce a tax on daylight to punish his subjects for clipping bits off every coin in the kingdom. Presumably the ogre is trying to be funny this morning. I stare straight ahead, while he ponderously explains that since households will pay according to the number of windows in each dwelling, there are already plans afoot to brick up all but the most essential casements. A barbaric toll, worse even than their hearth tax: for me, life couldn't be endured without the cloudscapes, landscapes, and seascapes that are both seen and distorted – and reinvented, too – through this long narrow sheet of glass with its familiar bull's eyes and ripples, its bubbles and warps.

The ogre announces that Mignard le Romain, the court artist who stepped into Charles Le Brun's shoes, is at death's door. It seems he's painted everyone that matters: Molière, Descartes, Jacques Bossuet, the Duchess of La Vallière, Madame de Montespan, the Marquise de Sévigné, even Madame de Maintenon. I yawn. It always annoys him. What interest could I have in the lives and deaths of artists, men who only care for perfect beauty? What would they make of me?

Then I remember that Louise de La Vallière has one leg shorter than the other; her shoes are specially made with uneven heels to enable her to walk rather than lurch. Meditating on the possibilities suggested by this little nugget means I can ignore his ogreish pronouncements on a recently published memoir.

Mémoires de la cour d'Angleterre is dismissed as a complete fabrication. I give half an ear to mention of Madame d'Aulnoy, its author, but only because she was forced to marry an old man while still a young girl, a fate I narrowly avoided.

Next I must listen to him murdering the plot of a play – *Love for Love* – that has just opened in London. At least the comedy contains some true affection, ending happily for poor Valentine and Angelica in spite of long waiting, incredible complications and utter foolishness. But why is he telling me this? Does he really imagine…?

And now he produces another gift, teasing it out from layers of pale blue silk until he lays across my lap a diamond necklace in a style he says is all the rage at court. What's that to me? There's more, but who can believe an ogre's promises? After a few moments, I move my knees so that the gewgaw slides from my skirt onto the floor. In the long silence that follows the ogre begins that horrible snuffling again – sniff, sniff, sniff, he mops his nasty ogre face – and finally the hateful creature goes away.

With the window thrown open, it's still chilly in spite of the sunshine and I fetch my patched and faded coverlet to wrap around me. But it's no good. I can't settle. The ogre's snuffling and sniffing and mopping has stayed behind to torment me. I find myself pinching and plucking at the little counterpane, screwing it up and stretching it out again, wringing it into knots so tight that finally the worn fabric splits in a dozen places and feathers erupt onto the floor.

Now look what he's made me do! And it was all I had left of my good fairy.

I throw it after him.

It must be obvious that I need comforting, and yet the witch pretends not to notice. My request for a tale is turned down flat.

She's not even swayed by the offer of candied chestnuts, though her eyes gleam and the tip of her witch tongue sneaks out to moisten her witch lips.

"I told you, *ma petite*, my story-telling days are over. The cupboard is bare. The spring has run dry. The magic *buoch frech* – that's a spotted cow between you and me – will yield no more milk. The—"

"I don't believe you, Granny."

How can it be true of an old woman who's a veritable ledger, though unwritten, of her people's history? Just mention her homeland and its heroes – Nominoë, the Breton *Tad ar Vro*, for instance, or Morvan Lez-Breiz, called the *prop* of Brittany – and usually there's no stopping her telling of tales. Alas, this time it's too late to prove my point: she's seen the look in my eye.

"What I say is right enough, my dear, and testing me will do you no good. I'm as empty as a plundered grave. The years have sucked out my tales along with my marrow." The witch drapes the diamond necklace around her scrawny neck, humming softly as she peers at her reflection in my little hand mirror. "Ah, how different the course of my young life would have been, adorned with jewels like these. Even now, they would change it forever."

"Keep the thing," I say carelessly. "Sell it. Throw it away. I don't want it. I don't want *anything* from him."

"That's foolish talk." The witch wraps the precious stones in the blue silk and places them gently in the chest. "And you'll change your mind sooner rather than later."

"I won't. How dare you say that?"

"No need to raise your voice, miss. I'm standing less than an arm's length away."

"After all he's done…. In spite of all he wants to do…."

"Stop your shrieking, girl – I was talking about the necklace," the witch says, rather too calmly for my liking. "A diamond necklace like that would be just the thing to wear for a very special occasion. A grand reception, say, or a wedding if there was ever to be one."

"Huh." It's time to turn my back on her and concentrate on the view, staring into the distance until my eyes swim out of focus. Now I can see a hundred leagues in every direction, right to the wild eastern mountains, their slopes as riddled with holes as the local cheese. Many of those caves and grottos are said to be full of gold and gemstones guarded by a serpent, a fire-breathing dragon – some call her the Grandmother – who leaves her treasure just once every seven years when she goes down to the river to drink. I choose to believe this is a true tale so, if she was brave enough and quick enough, a girl could obtain all the rings and necklaces she could ever desire without being dependent on any man for bribes or rewards.

"Are you asleep on your feet over there?" demands the witch.

"No, Granny."

"Then you must be daydreaming again. When you've finished, it would be nice to hear some more of your story about – what was her name – Cinder-bum, Cinder-arse?" The witch cackles to herself like a pot coming to the boil. "Or was it Cinder-britches?"

"Cinder-*ella*. I've decided she is to be called Cinderella."

But the witch isn't listening. She's found something new to fuss and nag about. "What am I to do with this terrible patched and mended cover of yours? Goodness only knows how it came to be sprawled at the bottom of the stairs with half its insides spilling out. Feathers everywhere – one might almost think the Bird Mother had visited us." She tut-tuts and grumbles. Her bony fingers tug at the threadbare fabric creating new frays and weaknesses, demonstrating its decrepitude. "I'll save the stuffing. The rest can go out for the rag-pickers."

"You can't do that." I seize one edge, but the witch hangs on for dear life. "It might be old and ragged, but it's worth far more to me than that stupid necklace you liked so much."

"Don't talk such foolishness. It was bad enough before, practically beyond repair. Now there's next to nothing left of the poor tattered thing." She darts an old-fashioned look at me. "Someone must have well and truly lost their temper with it."

"Give it to me." I pull harder. "Let go!" There's a dull ripping sound, a dying groan of protest from the little coverlet that, though it was already ancient when I came by it, has comforted me for many years.

"It's your own fault," says the hard-hearted witch. "Still, there's no need to carry on like that – plenty of other bedcovers in the world."

"I don't want other...." It was all I had left of how things were *before*. The thought brings on a fresh flood of tears.

"*Pardieu!*" She throws up her hands in despair. "If the wretched thing is so very precious we'd better make a new cover for it. Stop that useless wailing, girl, and busy your hands. You shall help me pin and sew – for I know you can do it, even though you think such things are beneath you. And while we work you can share your tale of Cinder-whatever-you-called-her." The witch delves in her basket of mending stuffs and brings out some lengths of fine linen, of a pale apricot colour, with stitch marks which suggest it might be an old-fashioned gown, carefully unpicked. "But before we start, you must go down and pick up every spilled feather."

"No, I...." Years have passed since I went anywhere near those stairs. The thought terrifies me. It just can't be done. "No."

"You can't expect me to do it."

"But—"

"All the way down," the witch says firmly, without bothering to look up from her sorting. "And pick up every last feather. If you want the coverlet saved, that's what you must do."

Clutching my candlestick, I stand on the small landing peering downwards. The narrow steps are of stone, of which only three are visible; the rest have been eaten alive by a curiously thick and sooty darkness.

"Every last one," calls the witch. "And don't be all day about it."

The stone is cold. Its chill bites through my thin soles. It nips at my toes. One step, two – down I go, pushing the darkness before me as the stairs coil back on themselves. Near the top, the walls are blotched with lichen, patches of yellow and grey that look like wizened faces, snouts and gaping jaws of beasts that never were. Lower down, numbers have been carved into the hard grey granite. There are step-asides, too – passing places – one contains what looks like a latrine, the others with windows as tall and narrow as mine, but boarded over as if anticipating the ogre's daylight tax.

I don't remember any of this.

But now the feathers begin to appear: soft pale drifts of down; clusters of breast plumage in homely colours, buff and brown, grey and white, some plain, others speckled or stippled, tipped and striped; a few stiff wing feathers with scratchy shafts. I snatch what I can, holding out my skirt to accommodate them, kicking the rest deeper into the shadows. The witch won't notice if a few are missing.

And I've reached the bottom step.

In front of me looms the tower's great metal-banded door with its massive hinges and a stone-seated cubbyhole on the left-hand side where once a guard dozed away his watch. Unlike the staircase, I remember this tower entrance very well, for there is no easily discernible means of opening that door from the inside. Once an exploring child has covered her ears against the echoing boom of it closing behind her, she might well believe she'd never get out again.

"It's a steep climb," the witch says dryly, as I empty the feathers onto the floor. "And such a heavy load. No wonder you're out of breath." But it wasn't the steep incline that winded me, rather my burst of speed, from fear of the ogre suddenly opening the door and dragging me off to his lair. She eyes my pile of offerings. "I see you left behind more than you picked up."

In my absence she's tacked my poor coverlet together and covered the invalid with muslin bandages, forming little pockets into which we stuff the escaped feathers. It's my job to pin the tops of these pockets closed, the witch's to stitch them. My best isn't good enough: in no time at all she's grouching and scolding.

"The pins are supposed to go in the cloth, not your finger, you silly girl."

"Sorry, Mamie."

"Quick! Get some water. You've left blood spots everywhere."

"Shall I…?"

"You've done quite enough," grumbles the witch, moving the pins out of reach. "We'll get on a lot quicker if I sew and you tell your story."

I begin reading before she can change her mind. "It's called *Cinderella and the Little Fur Slipper*—

> *There was once a well respected lord whose wife died, leaving him with a daughter who was gentle and kind-hearted, as well as being beautiful. After a time, the lord took a second wife, a proud and haughty woman with two daughters who took after her in every way. The wedding was hardly over before the stepmother showed her true qualities. She couldn't abide the child and didn't trouble to hide it, forcing her to do all the rough household chores and sleep in an attic on a pile of straw. After the girl had finished her work she used to sit in the corner of the fireplace keeping warm among the cinders.*

Once Upon a Time in Paris

For this reason the stepmother and her eldest daughter jeered at her appearance, calling her Cinderbottom. But the youngest daughter, who was not as coarse as the others, changed it to Cinderella. In spite of her bad clothes and unkempt hair, Cinderella was still a hundred times more beautiful than her stepsisters.

One day news came that the king was to hold a ball in honour of his son's birthday. Everyone of rank was invited, including the stepmother and her daughters. From that moment on nothing mattered but what they would wear, how their hair should be dressed, and what jewellery might be borrowed to dazzle the prince. Finally the evening of the ball arrived.

After her stepsisters and their mother left in a blaze of excitement, Cinderella crept into the chimney corner and sat among the cinders weeping. It was here that her godmother, who was also a good fairy, found her and asked what was wrong. When the girl admitted how much she longed to go to the ball, to see the ladies in their beautiful gowns and watch the dancing – and maybe even catch a glimpse of the prince, who was said to be very handsome – her godmother only smiled and waved her wand. Cinderella's rags were instantly transformed into the most exquisite outfit imaginable, cut entirely from cloth of gold set with precious gems and trimmed with gold lace. A diamond necklace adorned her neck, while her hair was dressed in the very latest style and adorned with diamond aigrettes. And on her feet...."

"Yes?" said the witch, hand frozen mid-stitch. "Well go on."

"And for her feet the fairy godmother gave her the prettiest pair of dancing slippers, made of fur, pure white ermine

trimmed with swansdown. A carriage was magically summoned, but as the lackey helped Cinderella inside it, the godmother warned her that she must leave the palace by the final stroke of midnight. The magic would last no longer and immediately everything would become as it was.

Such was Cinderella's beauty that the entire assembly fell silent as she entered the great hall of the palace. Even the king found it impossible to take his eyes off her. As for the prince, he would dance with no one else. Not a soul could work out who she was, even the stepsisters failed to recognise her, but they all agreed that she must be some great princess.

Cinderella enjoyed herself so much, and was so pleased by the handsome prince's attention – for him it was love at first sight and he never stopped whispering the sweetest things to her – she completely forgot that this happiness must all come to an end at the stroke of twelve. Suddenly she heard the great palace clock begin its chime for midnight. Before it had struck three times she'd torn herself from the prince's arms. As it struck for the sixth time she was already running from the hall. By the time it reached nine, she was out on the palace steps. But in her hurry to find her carriage before the last stroke, one of her little fur slippers fell off and there was no time to go back for it. The clock had struck midnight. The carriage disappeared. And Cinderella found herself clothed in rags once more.

The prince, who'd followed her from the ballroom, questioned the guards at the palace gate, but none of them had seen a beautiful princess departing, in fact the only girl they'd noticed had been a ragged scullery maid. The prince sadly picked up the discarded slipper and looked at nothing else for the remainder of the ball.

A few days later a proclamation was issued: the prince would marry the girl whose foot the slipper would fit. Every girl at court, from duchesses to ladies-in-waiting lined up to try it. After that had proved unsuccessful, a courtier carried the slipper to all those houses owned by people of quality. Eventually it came to the house where the stepsisters lived. Neither of them could jam their feet into the little slipper. Eventually Cinderella begged for the chance to try. At that the entire household began laughing and jeering and making rude noises. 'You!' they cried. 'How can you possibly get the slipper to fit? Oh, quack, quack! Shall we bring you a sharp knife? Honkety-honk. Would you like a ssssssaw? Whatever were you thinking?' At that Cinderella—"

My witch sets the coverlet aside and fixes me with her eye. "Go on," she says, but more gently this time. "Don't stop there, *ma petite tourterelle*, my little turtledove. Don't stop there."

But stop I must for it was only magic that made poor Cinderella really beautiful by taking away her sad afflictions for a few short hours. Now there is only the tower for the ugly sister. "There's no more. That's as far as I've got."

"Then you must set to and finish it," the witch says briskly. "And you must finish it as you'd wish it to turn out in real life. What are these tales for if it isn't for you to sneak inside and look out through fresh eyes to discover a cure for your situation?"

Chapter Twelve

So far, barricading the door with disused furniture had served well enough: each night Lew caught a few hours of sleep in the ballroom, watched over by his paintings and undisturbed by the increasingly solicitous Poucet. Nevertheless, he still hankered after a small space of his own, one detached from the workspace, a quiet retreat where he might – without interruption – also consider his future. The narrow staircase leading to the bedchamber previously shared with the valet forked near the top, continuing upwards to a much larger space where the housemaids retired at night. Were all of the rooms there given over to the women, he asked Jacques, as casually as a man in need of solitude could manage? But the irascible cook was nursing a violent headache, which he claimed was due to overwork – a small flask of cure-all tucked into the pocket of his apron – and was in no mood for conversation.

"How the hell would I know, Leonardo?" he growled, honing an already lethally sharp knife held dangerously close to his throat. Lew, who could hardly bear to watch, fixed his eyes on the huge salmon gaping forlornly from the chopping board. Jacques stopped, took a nip of his remedy and brightened somewhat. "Would you dare go up there?"

"Well...." Lew thought of Escarlatta and decided not. He scraped out his *pottage* bowl, waiting for Jacques' nod of acquiescence before spooning another ladleful of the broth over some roughly crumbled bread. "So where are your quarters?" he began, wondering if there might be a disused corner there.

The cook cleared his throat meaningfully. In one fluid movement the knife was laid next to the salmon, the flask concealed. "Ah, there you are, Master Pierre. What can I help you with this bright and cheerful morning?"

"Is there anything here to drink?" Pierre kept his head down so that his voice was muffled.

"Some very pleasant cordials to hand, young master."

"Perhaps something stronger?"

Jacques looked at Lew and grimaced. "Now, Master Pierre, no young gentleman should be looking to a glass for answers at this time of the day."

"No young gentleman," Pierre retorted, "ever had to put up with such a father as mine. Give me a drink, will you?"

"Tell you what, Pierre," suggested Lew, recognising sheer misery when he saw it, "why don't I make that drawing of you now? Come, let's sit together. We've put it off for too long. And perhaps Jacques would be kind enough to make some chocolate."

"No chocolate for me. That's women's stuff. As for my likeness," Pierre raised his head, "do you judge this a good time?"

"Dear oh dear," muttered the cook, wincing before the boy's split and swollen lip, his bruised jaw and scraped nose, "you've been scrapping again. Who was it this time?"

"Guillaume Caulle."

Lew recognised the name. "Your friend, the one I sketched?"

"No friend of mine." The boy gulped. "Father put my name to that dratted book and now I have not a friend left in the world. They're all laughing at me. *Nom d'un chien*! Fairytales...about fairies – no man writes those. Word soon gets around. Mademoiselle's lady-in-waiting told the *marchande de mode* who told the *coiffeur* who told everyone else. It was the laundry woman who told Madame Caulle, who told Guillaume. And he – all doubled-up laughing – made short work of spreading the news. I'll challenge him to a duel the minute I get my hands on a decent weapon. I'll kill him by-and-by, see if I don't."

"Now, now, Master Pierre," Jacques' tone was commiserating, "in my experience these things blow over, given time."

"No," retorted Pierre, "this won't. I will kill him. Just wait and see." He scowled. "I'm nearly seventeen. Why won't the old man let me join the army and be done with it?"

Jacques turned the salmon over and began the slippery task of descaling. "That's a question I can't answer, young master."

"I can," said Lew. "It's because he's your father, and he cares about you."

"Does he now?" Pierre shot him a look of undisguised contempt. "Since you're not going to give me a drink, Jacques, I might as well try elsewhere."

"What book's this?" asked the cook, after Pierre left, slamming the door and causing a great gust of smoke to fill the kitchen. Lew shrugged.

"No good asking me. Ah, wait – I did some miniature illustrations for Monsieur Perrault." He thought about it. "There were cupids, I remember, but I don't recall fairies. One picture was of a man about to behead his wife. Another was of a cat walking on its hind legs and wearing boots. A strange collection, I thought." He laughed. "And two were of young ladies reclining in their beds. But that can't be what's upset the boy. I'll ask Poucet about it later and let you know." Palming a last hunk of bread, Lew started back towards his workplace.

The house was extraordinarily quiet. Monsieur Perrault had left for the Academy, the women were occupied elsewhere, even the ever-attentive Poucet must be off on his own business – while Lew's assistants had been stick-and-carrot persuaded to focus their entire attention on whatever leaf or flower or border they'd been set to finish. It was, however, as well to check on them at frequent intervals; being young, they were easily distracted. To that end Lew increased his pace. Turning down the poorly lit passage, which he'd been assured was the most ancient part of the building – a sombre place to his mind, crammed full of old regrets and unspent grievances – he was within sight of the Red Drawing Room when something small, odd, out of place, perhaps glimpsed from the very corner of his eye, stopped him in his tracks.

Lew slowly retraced his steps: nothing left lying on the floor, nothing new adorning the walls, nothing as far as he could see – and there was little enough of remark here – out of place in anyway. He shrugged, dismissing what must have been pure fancy. Then he saw the bowl.

It sat on a small table, a dark, crudely made, rustic table, at the end of a short passage, hardly longer than an alcove, really no more than twice a man's length. The bowl itself measured a hand's span across, of silver and ornate, with a skilfully chased outer rim in the form of a laurel wreath, the inside decorated with cherubs linked by loops of drapery and flowers, a mass of orange peel partially obscuring the design. The fruit was freshly eaten, a tang of tart citrus oil still hung on the air, but it was inconceivable to Lew that anyone in their right mind would stand in this gloomy place to enjoy oranges.

Not that it mattered to him.

What mattered at this moment was his depiction of *The Jay Dressed in Peacock Feathers.* He lengthened his stride, visualising the shimmering tail feathers of peacocks and the green, blue and turquoise pigments needed to capture them. In order to catch the light, all those subtle brown shades in the eyes of the feathers must be replaced by gold and—

Lew experienced a moment of terror as the ground trembled

beneath him. The floorboards shook, sending small shockwaves through his boots and into his toes. His first thought was of thunder; the second that he'd been struck down with deafness, for where was the angry growl and rumble? Then he caught the familiar *clack-clack* of Norik's sabots and spun around to see the old lady walking away from him, carrying the silver bowl.

"Madame," he called, "did you feel that?" When she didn't stop, Lew ran to catch up with her. "Madame, surely you felt the floor shaking?"

"The floor shaking – what sort of nonsense is that?" She leaned towards him. Her nose twitched. "Are you drunk, painter?"

"It was like silent thunder," he insisted, "but beneath the floor. An earthquake, perhaps – like the one last year in the Kingdom of Naples." It was said that thousands had died between one beat of the heart and the next. And that castles, cathedrals, churches and monasteries crumbled instantly into the dust which marks the end of all human endeavour. Lew crossed himself. "But smaller, of course."

"Pfft! Earthquake, indeed – what's more likely is that one of your young ruffians dropped something heavy." With that, Norik continued on her way, the sound of her clogs creating small echoes that ran back the way she had come.

Lew worked for an hour or more, hardly able to bring himself to relive the experience. He'd returned to the ballroom to find nothing amiss, nothing dropped or broken, his assistants concentrating on their various tasks, still motivated by this morning's promise of an interim payment. His main concern for the afternoon was the degree of shabbiness he should allot to the natural feathers of the upstart jay; the idea was to create a strong contrast with its borrowed plumage without making it look dingy. He stood back and examined the almost completed section, the words of La Fontaine's verse running through his head—

> *A peacock moulted: soon a jay was seen*
> *Bedecked with Argus tail of gold and green,*
> *High strutting, with elated crest,*
> *As much a peacock as the rest.*
> *His trick was recognised and bruited,*
> *His person jeered at, hissed, and hooted.*
> *The peacock gentry flocked together,*
> *And plucked the fool of every feather.*
> *Nay worse, when back he sneaked to join his race,*
> *They slammed their portals in his face.*

Portals, thought Lew, doorways. One moment the passage had been empty, the next filled with the sound of Norik's noisy footsteps. How had she come to be there? There were those who pointed to a connection between thunderclaps and the mysterious appearances and disappearances of witches…but though he could not like the old woman, that wasn't a charge he'd make against her. She'd come through a door like any other Christian – and picked up the bowl, indicating that the door must be in the alcove itself. Somehow he'd missed it. Finding that entrance, Lew was convinced, would lead him straight to the battle-ravaged old soldier.

As the weather grew warmer, many families abandoned the city for the less malodorous surroundings of their country houses, so at least on this occasion Madame de Caylus' salon was less crowded. Unfortunately, it was still crammed with superfluous items of furniture. Charles squeezed between and round and past and through, in terror of sending something priceless crashing to the floor, noting that her huge collection of Oriental pieces had been joined by several new items since his last visit. Most were of the type that used to be termed curiosities but which, now attracting higher prices, had become known as antiquities: a pair of lions in yellow-pink marble, each the size of a small child, lay in wait to trip the unwary, a portable altar decorated with anguished saints rocked uneasily on a flimsy side table, and a fantastically carved folding chair that would never, even in his youth, have accommodated his girth, kept company with half a dozen helms from more barbaric times. There were also several of the latest japanned *commodes*; he resisted an urge to pull open their drawers and riffle through the contents.

Etiquette had demanded his attendance; it did not specify how long he must stay. And perhaps if he could find a quiet corner....

"Ah, Charles," today Madame de Caylus greeted him quietly and avoided meeting his eyes, "how very good of you to come."

"My dear Marie-Gabrielle, to be in your presence is always a pleasure." Though still in the dark about what had caused her strange behaviour – and that of the rest of the largely uninvited throng – at his own gathering he was determined to be, and seen to be, magnanimous.

"Dear Charles, how very kind you are. May I offer you a sherbet. Well, perhaps later." With a flick of her plump fingers she dismissed the maid who'd scurried across the salon with iced glasses displayed on a tray of rose petals. "And you arrive at an opportune time. Sadly, Madame d'Aulnoy is unable to be with us, but she's permitted a reading from one of her new *contes de fées*. Forgive me, the title momentarily escapes me. It's the story of an unfortunate little princess changed into a monkey."

"Oh," said Charles. "Somewhat similar to the tale she gave us last time I was here, though that concerned a princess transformed into a white cat."

Marie-Gabrielle frowned. "I believe so. What a coincidence. But, listen to this – afterwards our own dear Suzanne is to read for us."

He flinched. "You mean Madame Beffort?"

"I do indeed. Are you familiar with her work?"

Charles struggled to keep his expression impassive. "I am." After excusing himself on the pretext of needing to rest an aching knee, he found a chair partially concealed by a screen decorated with pagodas, grotesquely squat temple lions, trees shaped liked clouds and vice versa. It was the perfect spot for quiet introspection. Marie-Gabrielle's fawning announcement woke him.

"Madame Beffort tells me that this story was wafted from the heavens to her pen on the back of a delightful spring zephyr."

Charles frowned, sat up and peered around the screen. Suzanne Beffort, attired in a gown of watered brown silk – its colour and pattern strongly reminiscent of the cross-section of a felled tree – her hair augmented by a cloud of netting with butterflies attached, faced her audience with an expression akin to that of a Christian facing the lions of ancient Rome. Was she, Charles wondered, being factual or fanciful in speaking of a story delivered into her hands by a breeze? One could hardly ask. He moved back – but not before François Timoléon had caught his eye – and waited stoically for the reading to begin.

"Once there was a beautiful queen who found herself with child. All day she entertained in her beautiful apartment full of costly antiquities bought at the Saint-Germain fair. At night her beautifully draped windows overlooked the beautiful garden of an old enchantress. The most beautiful fruit and vegetables grew there. They were almost as beautiful as those growing in the beautiful gardens of Versailles. The queen cared nothing for these. She could see a beautiful bed

of roquette and greatly desired some. The woman gave her husband no peace until he climbed over the wall and plucked a large bunch for her. When the—"

"Dear Lord, preserve us," muttered François, sinking into a chair beside him. "What's this but a plodding tale filched from a scullion, gracelessly retold by an ungainly frump in an ugly gown?"

"One can only salute her courage." Charles stretched his neck to one side in an attempt to ease his cravat, which Poucet was lately in the habit of knotting too tightly. "Most would not dare present such risible nonsense as literature."

"—her beautiful garden stealing roquette. She was very angry and swore to punish the thief if she caught him there again. The woman's desire for the beautiful roquette did not cease. Again and again the husband was forced to return for more. The old enchantress finally caught him. She threatened to change him into a frog. She spared him in exchange for the queen's child. When the beautiful baby was born the enchantress took her away. She named her Roquette and brought her up as her own."

"I've endured enough," François said, without troubling to lower his voice. "It was never my intention to stay longer than an hour and this wooden performance only strengthens my resolve." He drew a tiny hand mirror from his bosom and scrutinised the patch, cut to resemble a swan, placed *just so* on his cheekbone. "Charles, in spite of your niece's best efforts, our collaboration marches on apace. I believe it's time to bring all the parts together in order to evaluate the whole. Last time we spoke on the subject you were considering composing an introduction. And have you settled upon a suitable *moralité?*"

"One moment," Charles leaned forward, alerted by a single word in the Beffort creature's narrative.

"*—forest. It was a magic tower. There were no doors. There were no stairs. There was one window very high up. Roquette could not get out. The only way the old enchantress could get into the tower was by climbing up Roquette's beautiful long hair. One day a prince saw the old enchantress climbing up the girl's hair. After she'd gone he decided he would look in the tower. The prince climbed up and found the beautiful girl. He fell in love with her. But the old enchantress found out. Next time, as the prince climbed up, she cut off Roquette's beautiful hair. The prince fell down onto the rocks and lay as if dead. Roquette threw herself after him. Luckily a kind-hearted fairy was passing by. She restored them to life and—*"

"Heard enough?" demanded François.

"*—for many years afterwards. They had many beautiful children. The old enchantress was cast into a pit of serpents.*"

The end of the tale brought enthusiastic applause, which Charles judged to be prompted by relief rather than acclaim.

"I believe so." Whether borne to Madame Beffort's quill on a wind real or fancied, this tale was not even a poor relation of the ones he'd been so assiduously collecting. Charles turned his head from left to right several times and wondered about asking the abbé to discreetly re-knot his cravat, which was now causing him almost unbearable discomfort. Instead he worked one finger inside the silk, running it around his neck in the hope of stretching the fabric. "As for evaluating our collaborative work, we'll need to liaise with my niece to find a suitable time."

"She's here," said the abbé, stifling an obviously feigned yawn, "somewhere." He rose, carefully smoothing down his skirts. "Shall we…?"

"Wait!" A servant had appeared offering *pâtisseries salées*, delicate pastries shaped like water lilies and containing rillettes garnished with juniper berries. Charles' nose twitched. He clutched his throat. "François, for the love of God, first loosen my cravat for me before I choke."

Marie-Jeanne was not enthusiastic about investing more time in the Marquise-Marquis. "Uncle, I still have concerns relating to the constant attention lavished on perfection of face and form."

"But that's exactly what the story hinges upon," said the abbé. "It's a tale of enchanted perfection." He fanned his cheeks. "Or it was until you threatened to spoil the whole thing by making them go to their wedding attired in head-to-toe black, as if in mourning. If black it must be, then the velvet has to be covered with precious stones, and I insist upon scarlet ribbons."

Marie-Jeanne sniffed. "The black stays. As for me, I wonder if all such ceremonies shouldn't be accompanied by the tolling of a death bell. For the woman, marriage always signifies loss and therefore should involve mourning."

"What loss is that?" Charles looked at her, puzzled, for in his experience new brides gained financial security and greatly elevated social positions, which was precisely why he'd been so keen—

"I refer to the married woman's loss of dominion over her own life," said Marie-Jeanne in a tone suggesting this was self-evident. "And the abandonment of whatever potential she hitherto possessed."

The two men looked at each other.

"I see the lovebirds are no more," said the abbé, indicating the gilded cage, now empty save for a wilting plant. "And wasn't there a tame monkey here at one time?"

"Apparently, as it grew older, the beast's behaviour went beyond the pale." Charles' attention was fixed on a large blue-on-ivory porcelain vase, almost certainly from the enterprising Chicaneau family's pottery in Saint-Cloud. To his eye, it was the equal of expensively imported Chinese ware.

"Well?" demanded Marie-Jeanne, twitching with impatience.

"What you say *may* contain a grain of truth," agreed François. "But even so, most ladies long with great fervour for their wedding day."

Charles concurred. "It is the one day – often the only day – on which even those of the most humble origins become the centre of attraction. I refer to the bride's place in the ceremonial procession to and from church."

"As at her burial," Marie-Jeanne said tartly.

Once again, the two men looked at each other.

"I remember there being a dwarf here, too," said Charles, "a truly dreadful creature; a drunkard."

"Ah," cried the abbé, appraising a blushing young maid carrying a salver laden with little cups of berries, "we're being tempted with fresh country delights today, I see."

"Strawberries." Charles beckoned and selected the most generous of the servings.

"I've always thought straw a prickly and uncomfortable bed for such delectable offerings," said François, stroking the girl's hand. "What is your name, my dear?"

"If you please, Madame, it's Gabrielle," said she, blushing some more and pushing back the soft brown hair, which was making a determined effort to escape from her cap.

"Another cup of strawberries, miss," requested Charles. He looked at his niece. "Is no one else partaking?"

"No, for something sickens me," said Marie-Jeanne.

"What lovely hair you have, Gabrielle." François curled a tendril round his large forefinger. The maid managed an awkward little bob.

"Thank you, Madame."

"You remind me of a pretty girl called Grise I knew many years ago in Bourges. Now, as I'm sure you know, the angel Gabriel is the holder of the lily, signifying purity." The abbé patted the girl's flank. "You are pure, I trust, my dear?"

"Leave the poor girl alone, François," snapped Marie-Jeanne, at which Gabrielle looked from one to the other, frowned in bewilderment, and fled.

The abbé sighed. "Life produces yet another *rabat-joie*."

"I'm no killjoy." She appealed to her uncle. "Can it be right for a priest to torment such a child?"

Charles produced vaguely soothing noises. "My dear, let us focus on our little marquise's story."

Marie-Jeanne unrolled the sheets of paper she'd been clutching. "You'll notice," she shuffled through the pages, "that I've incorporated mention of *Sleeping Beauty*, the tale you claim was written by young Pierre. See – here, where Mademoiselle d'Aletref asks if the little marquise has read the story. 'Have I read it?' cried the little marquise. 'I've read it four times, but I was astonished when the name of the author was revealed. It's a boy of seventeen, no less, and one with the voice of a gentle nursemaid!'"

"I would rather that was not included," said Charles.

"Which story is this?" enquired the abbé.

"I'm thinking of adding the following: 'If written by a youth, I could understand the relish with which the matter of the flesh-eating ogress is addressed, but what boy could write with such poignant understanding of love?'"

"Pierre was always a sensitive child," Charles said vaguely. He winced at his niece's bray of laughter.

"He was *not*. Pierre pulled the wings from flies. He tied burning sticks to the tails of cats. And you can't deny the trouble he caused by tormenting – enough said on that score, I suppose. But to return to our collaboration, perhaps," she suggested, "we should weave into the text the notion of an *author* who is a girl posing as a boy?"

François moved to stand between them. "Perhaps one of you would have the goodness to explain—"

"I have been keeping a secret," Charles said mysteriously, hoping it would distract the pair from a subject he had no desire to discuss further, "which I would now like to share with you."

Marie-Jeanne gathered up her pages. "Go on."

"Pray don't keep us in suspense, Charles," cooed François. "It's too naughty of you."

"It relates to the house refurbishments I mentioned earlier in the year." He paused. "I have engaged an artist for a unique project. He's young, a little wild, but perhaps not without promise."

"Is he handsome?" asked François, peeping coyly over his fan.

Charles considered. "I might describe his face as pleasing if he paid more attention to his *toilette*."

"Never mind his looks," said Marie-Jeanne. "Tell us about the project."

"You may recall the octagonal ballroom within my house, unused since – well, you both know the story. My artist is even now turning it into a jewel among rooms, covering every wall with scenes from the fables. It's a space I'd envisaged being used for its original purpose – as a place of celebration and hope for the future. I certainly offered it to her as such. That was my sole purpose in commissioning the work."

"And she refused?"

"Alas, niece, yes – it seems that pleasure is permanently denied me. My offer has been spurned. I don't wish to speak more of it."

"You should have let me intervene in your troubles at the beginning," said François, adding a heartfelt sigh. "I still can, you know. After all, I've dealt with many troublesome cases of a similar nature."

"Thank you, but no." Charles quailed at the thought of such a dangerous arrangement. "I fear nothing can be done. But I find there's some comfort to be found in viewing the work as a glorious monument to Jean La Fontaine and I'd enjoy showing you what's been achieved. We can peruse our little marquise's story afterwards."

The walls within the alcove were panelled, as was the entire main passage, in well polished oak with simple raised mouldings. There was no sign of any door. And yet there must be one. Only a fool, Lew told himself, could believe Norik suddenly materialised from some otherworldly place, the fairy realms or the Land of Cockaigne. He dropped to his knees and, shielding his candle with one hand, worked inch by inch along the base of the panels.

It was the feather that finally solved the puzzle – a breast feather from a humble farmyard fowl, trapped beneath a section of panelling. Only the tip of the vane protruded, no wider than a single curved brushstroke of brown, and so similar in colour to the surrounding wood that Lew forgave himself for not noticing it immediately. Tapping the wall above it produced a hollow sound. Pre-armed with certainty, he pushed and pummelled until an oak pin fell at his feet and the panel swung outwards, letting in a rush of murderously cold air that immediately extinguished the candle, holding up further exploration while he coaxed a flame from his tinderbox.

Behind the opening loomed a gap in a thick wall – very thick, Lew gauged its breadth was considerably more than two *pied du roi*, almost a double ell – of dressed stone blocks. He stepped through it onto a cobbled walkway where a few more poultry feathers were being blown gently backwards and forwards. Facing him was another wall of equally substantial stone blocks, into which was set a stout door with iron bars nailed to its surface both vertically and horizontally forming a grid of squares; in addition, the centre of each square was studded with a huge knob-headed nail, making it appear impregnable.

Lew turned to the left, following the walkway past a narrow, unglazed window through which he caught a glimpse of stars. The rest lay in darkness, but noises from the countryside surrounding Paris were clearly audible: a cow bellowing for her calf; dogs warning off prowlers; the occasional squeal of a disgruntled pig, beneath the querulous calls of owls. He could go no further: the way was blocked by tumbled stones marking the site of an ancient staircase, now impassable, while taking the other direction brought him to an iron grille.

As for the door itself, despite being a barrier created in expectation of trouble, it was fastened by a simple bolt, recessed so that it could be operated from both sides. He placed his hand upon the wood convinced that the crippled soldier inhabited the space behind it. The man's injuries must look terrible indeed for him to be hidden away here, almost like a beast in an outhouse. Lew was tempted to go inside, but it was late and he was weary; besides, it would be impolite to disturb even the loneliest of strangers at such an hour.

He retraced his steps, securing the panelling with its wooden fastener, and returned to his workspace craving sleep. Poucet was waiting for him.

"I looked everywhere. Where were you?"

"Exploring and, I hope, unravelling a mystery." Lew described Norik's sudden appearance in the passage – leaving out the earthquake which he must have imagined – and keeping the precise whereabouts of the concealed entrance vague. "A massive iron-clad door," he continued, "and I suspect they keep the cripple there. I'll see for myself tomorrow."

Poucet seized the edge of his jacket. "Be careful. All this secrecy doesn't feel right. Listen, my guess is there's a dangerous madman caged behind that door. Some soldiers come back from battles raving, you know, full of bloodlust, like men possessed. Or...." The valet looked thoughtful. "*Pardieu*, what a fool I've been." He was silent long enough for Lew to yawn six times, before adding: "Tomorrow, you say? Promise you won't go without me."

Lew yawned again. He rubbed his eyes. "What about you?" he asked politely.

"Nothing as interesting, my friend – after lunch I was sent to rake the city for letters of state or poems or bills of sale or whatever else he claims to have lost – sheets of paper with writing on, is what it amounts to. Now that's madness all right. But it was a fine afternoon, good to be out and about and I made the most of it. Ever been to Montreuil? They grow peaches there for the kings and queens of Europe. Today the trees were coming into blossom against the walls. We could go together next time."

"Perhaps when the fruit ripens," suggested Lew.

"And since then I've spent hours altering His Fatness's clothes...by that I mean letting them out. He increased his girth over the winter and it shows no sign of decreasing. I'm constantly reattaching buttons and re-stitching seams."

"I'll see you tomorrow then," Lew said firmly.

"Oh." Poucet's face reverted to its mournful, beaten-dog expression. "You want me to go?"

"I need to sleep."

"Let me stay. We can sleep side-by-side, as before. No? Then I'll just sit quietly and watch over you. P-please – you won't even know I'm here."

"That would not be seemly, you being a young woman."

"And there was me thinking you'd forgotten that," Poucet muttered in a voice suffused with bitterness.

"I hadn't forgotten, *Judith*. Share a sleeping space with me and it would be you the world judged harshly."

"And if I say I don't care what the world thinks of me?" Poucet shrugged. "Besides, who would ever know?"

"Sooner or later, someone would find out." Lew hesitated, reluctant to spell out his uninterest in anything more than companionship. "They always do. Don't forget, all the rest of it might come to light at the same time."

She rested her forehead against his chest. "I'd take that chance."

"No really," insisted Lew, briskly moving to hold open the door. "Apart from anything else, this task will never be completed unless I have time completely on my own, to think, to dream the shapes and colours." Poucet left, head down and without uttering another word. Lew waited until the crestfallen valet reached the end of the passage before dragging pieces of furniture from beneath their shrouds and, as on the previous nights, barricading the room against a further visit.

Morning brought a minor calamity: two of Lew's assistants – and even worse, the most competent ones – had decamped during the night. Perhaps making such generous interim payments was a mistake. On questioning the remaining pair past their reluctance he learned they'd gone south, probably to Rome, where there was usually plenty of work. Neither Agrippa nor Jean-Baptiste would volunteer any further information. Sensing their envy, Lew spent some time elaborating on the excellent letters of recommendation they'd receive on the project's completion; more to the point, he took it upon himself to increase their rate of pay.

Nevertheless, the atmosphere remained strained and it hadn't improved by the time Monsieur Perrault arrived – Poucet following close behind, pale-faced, with downcast eyes – for one of his increasingly sporadic inspections. The old fellow seemed more morose than grouchy today, his few words punctuated by sighs. Lew still hadn't painted out the goose he had taken such exception too, didn't intend to, and was prepared to defend vigorously his inclusion of geese in a skyscape supposed to feature 'all the birds of the air'. But Monsieur Perrault said nothing, though must have seen it as he turned on his heels, head back, taking in the dome in its entirety. Next, he progressed slowly around the room, Lew accompanying him, examining each of the fable composites, saying little in response to the artist's explanations but occasionally nodding sagely or moving closer to peer at some detail in the roughly chalked guides. Finally he straightened and gave a particularly deep sigh.

"You know Jean de La Fontaine has died, of course?"

"No, sir, I hadn't heard."

A harrumph of disbelief greeted this confession. "Well, well, that's life, I suppose. Even the most illustrious author must recognise that death always has the last word." The old man kneaded his temples and sighed again. "If used for nothing else, this room will be a fitting memorial to the poor man. Having got this far, I suppose it might as well be finished."

"I-uh, yes," muttered Lew, shocked by this lack of enthusiasm. He glanced at Poucet, but the valet continued to stare at the floor. "Is the work no longer satisfactory, sir?"

"Satisfactory?" Monsieur Perrault paused as if giving the adjective close consideration, and Lew, hanging on his words, couldn't help but notice his drawn expression. He smiled tentatively; the gesture wasn't returned but at least the old man seemed to rally a little. "It's more than satisfactory, young man." His hand rested on Lew's shoulder for a moment. "The room promises to be magnificent. It's unfortunate that...." Another sigh followed. "But there it is – such a shame, alas, such a shame." He consulted his watch. "And now there will be more disruption. Come, Poucet, prepare some chocolate – my niece and the abbé are expected."

The valet trudged after him, still without looking up. Lew hauled him back by his coat. "What's going on?"

"What's that supposed to mean?"

"He looks unwell, out of sorts…as if he'd eaten something that didn't agree with him." Lew regretted the thinly veiled accusation the moment it left his lips.

"What's that supposed to mean?" Poucet repeated. "Why this suspicion – and hostility? I made a promise, remember?"

"Forgive me, I didn't mean anything by it. His lack of enthusiasm for all this—" Lew cast a despairing glance at the beautiful room, the jewel-like murals. "He was so keen, and now it's 'it might as well be finished'. What's changed?"

Poucet gave a careless shrug. "How should I know? Something or somebody has put him in a sour mood. It wasn't me. As for eating foodstuffs that didn't agree with him, maybe he has, but that's nothing to do with me either. The man's a greedy pig. A whole family could live for a day on what he stows away at a single meal." The valet glanced at Lew's assistants, judged they were too far away to hear the conversation, but whispered anyway. "What have I done to deserve this, Lew? For your sake, I've been looking after the master as would a…," Poucet almost choked on the words, "…a daughter. He's nothing to me, but his well-being is important to your career. That's why I do it – for you. I'm not asking for anything back, Lew, just hoping that one day you'll return my feelings."

"You're a valued friend," began Lew, fearing nothing he could say would make this right. Poucet flinched as if he'd been struck and made for the door. "These things can't be rushed," the artist added, wincing at his own duplicity, "especially not when things under this roof are so complicated. Perhaps when we leave here—"

"In that case, I can wait." Poucet kept walking. "Oh, yes, I know everything there is to know about waiting."

Lew was surprised to receive a second visit from Monsieur Perrault during the course of the morning. This time he arrived accompanied by two women, one of them a plain little creature who, with her bright eyes, dowdy plumage and lively manner reminded him of a wren; the other was large, slow-moving and showily dressed.

"Mademoiselle L'Héritier de Villandon and, er, Madame de Sancy," announced Perrault, "this is the young man whose work we've been discussing, Monsieur le Sauvage, my artist."

Since his hands were covered in paint, Lew's response was limited to small bows and murmured civilities. He watched as the ladies toured the room, exclaiming as they identified each of the fables depicted, pointing out to each other the sun and stars, the fleur-de-lys, the multitude of birds, while Perrault plodded after them, hands clasped behind his back, preoccupied with – or so it seemed to Lew – his own melancholy thoughts.

Finally, Madame de Sancy approached, with an arch smile and vigorous flutterings of her fan. "These murals are quite, quite delightful. You're very gifted, my dear young man, and your portrait of Charles could not but fail to please. Perhaps, when your work here comes to an end, you would consent to paint me."

"It would be an honour, Madame," said Lew, wondering about a certain heaviness in the lady's jawline, and there was something about the throat, "though I can't give you any idea of when that might be."

She nodded. "Now that Charles has let us in on his secret – for you know he hadn't breathed a word about you or this wonderful undertaking until today – I hope to be allowed back, both for my own pleasure and to keep an eye on your progress." Madame de Sancy turned to her companion. "What about you, Marie-Jeanne – will you also engage Monsieur le Sauvage to paint your portrait?"

Marie-Jeanne's nose twitched. "A portrait is not something I've ever considered."

"I'm sure he'd make you look divine," cooed Madame de Sancy.

"I've no interest," Marie-Jeanne said severely, "in falsity, or being made to look any different to how God made me."

"Oh, la, what a very unusual woman you are, to be sure!"

"But I am at least, a w—"

"Not in your soul, my dear, not in your soul."

"Lunch," said Charles, shepherding the bickering pair before him. "I believe we are to enjoy a fine goat-kid pie…a kid not yet of this world in a raised pie, with agaric, morels and truffles, capon livers, hard-boiled egg yolks."

"I am not over-fond…" protested Marie-Jeanne.

"Of anything," suggested Madame de Sancy.

The old man raised his voice. "There will be the first green peas of the season, too – and only a day later than those served to His Majesty at Versailles – *petits pois à l'anglais*, each pea delicately enrobed with butter and sprinkled with salt. For cheese, we have some Munster from the Benedictine monastery in the valley there, and a whole Saint-Nectaire – the rye cheese, do you know it? No? Then you are in for a treat. And to finish, some delicious sugar-glazed *poupelains* – my favourite."

Hungry though Lew was, forgoing his own lunch gave him a chance of undisturbed exploration. This time, after stepping into the chill space behind the panelling, he strode across the cobbled walkway and slipped back the bolt. The door opened soundlessly.

The space beyond was so grimly shadowed that Lew reached for one of the tumbled stones nearby, propping the door open to provide more light. Where he'd expected rooms, a cell, even a cage, there was only a stone staircase coiling back on itself into more intense darkness. Curiously, the base of the stairwell was covered with more of the feathers he'd seen outside – a tiny breeze kept them in constant motion – and a small trail, like a clew, pointing the way up, step by step, towards the unknown.

Lew paused, steeling himself to follow...and yet at the same time deferring action by casting his mind back, so strongly was he reminded of the barn at home where the old mothers gathered at Christmas to pluck the freshly slaughtered geese. Those were women to be wary of: the work needed strong hands. The speed with which they worked was impressive, especially since they sorted as they went – tail and wing feathers placed into one barrel, small feathers into another, the precious goose down stuffed into sacks. In spite of their care, each beldam sat surrounded by a pile of plumage; it lapped at their ankles, swelling by the minute, rising up their gnarled legs to warm their knees. The aged women gossiped as they worked, slandering all and sundry, besmirching names right, left and centre, with only a very short measure of praise reserved for the saintly few. Their cackles sounded as if they'd been ripped from the throats of the dead creatures draped across their knees along with their feathers.

And the stories spilling from these ancient ones' toothless mouths ranged from ribald to tragic...stories of old lechers, young lovers, the ruses of young wives saddled with dotard husbands, the fortitude of those who triumphed against all odds, the misfortunes of helpless infants. No wonder they called such yarns Mother Goose tales – which of course was what he'd inscribed, at Monsieur Perrault's request, copying the letters with infinite care, on the remaining illustration for his small book: two little girls, one dark, one fair, and a boy, plus the kitchen cat, listening to tales told by their nurse at the fireside.

Lew looked again at the staircase. His spine prickled. He was struck by the conviction that whatever he found here would change his life forever. But that, surely, was only a conceit, a fancy – an excuse. He was afraid. What was there to be afraid of?

The daylight below was soon swallowed by the curve of the stairs. Above, a little light sneaked through chinks in boarded-over arrow loops.

On reaching the top, he stepped onto a landing furnished with a small carpet. Two leather bombards rimmed with silver – one was full of water – stood beside a hide-covered dowry chest with the initials MG picked out in brass-headed nails. A mirror and candle sconces were affixed to the wall above it, the candles as yet unlit, while the remaining walls were draped with embroidered hangings, making the grim dark space almost pleasant. Lew was unsurprised. He'd never doubted that Monsieur Perrault would treat his charge well or care for every need – barring companionship.

Of the three doors leading off, one was ajar. It was apparent that a window must stand open within that room: the breeze playing with feathers at the base of the steps had started life here; even now it was rolling puffs of soft downy plumage towards the stairwell. He stood for a few moments longer, ears straining for sounds of madness, for whimpers, snarls, guttural moans, frenzied muttering, even, perhaps the rattle and clank of chains. Carefully arranging his features, determined not to show shock or repulsion at whatever sight greeted him, Lew finally pushed open the door.

The room was empty.

No madman. No invalid.

Nobody here but a ghost – he'd fallen in love with a dead woman, who'd now come back to haunt him.

As in the painting, she had golden hair, though now it hung loose, tumbling in soft waves to her waist. Her blue gown was old-fashioned. A carelessly knotted lacework shawl covered her shoulders. Lew had never seen a prettier sight. He continued to stare, expecting her to gradually fade and disappear from human sight as would a rainbow burned away by the glare of the sun. Minutes passed and still the beautiful apparition lingered, staring back, wide-eyed and unmoving – until suddenly she sat down, carefully arranging her skirts around her feet.

Lew's heart leapt in his chest. The enchantment passed. This was no phantom. He wanted to apologise for intruding, for staring, to introduce himself, to explain, but the words stuck in his throat and all he could manage was a deep bow accompanied by the hoarsest of croaks: "Your servant, Mademoiselle."

"*Est-ce vous, mon prince?*" she asked softly. "*Vous vous êtes bien fait attendre.*"

"What?" He felt himself gaping and blushed, mortified.

"I said, is it you, my prince? You have kept me waiting a long, long time."

"I uh, my lady, I am no prince," Lew looked at his paint-splashed hands, his pigment-engrained nails, at his worn boots encrusted with drips and splatters, "simply a humble artist."

"You've found me, I've waited for this day since I was a child."

Once again, Lew found himself tongue-tied and staring. He resorted to simple courtesies. "Allow me to introduce myself, Mademoiselle. My name is Louis – though I much prefer to be called Lew – and my home is near Coutances, in Normandy, a beautiful place, through perhaps a Parisian would find it dull and provincial." He took one small step towards her. "Might I be permitted to know your name?"

"It's Marie-Madeleine."

"Marie-Madeleine—" Lew was finding it impossible to marshal

his thoughts. Her name brought to his mind delicate colours of wild roses on hedgerows and tasted sweet on the lips. And because there were a thousand questions that it would be ill-mannered to ask, he was grateful when Marie-Madeleine forestalled them by pointing to a chair littered with papers.

"Please sit with me. Let us talk for a while." Lew, busy gathering the sheets into a neat pile, expected her to ask about his work. Instead she said: "Tell me more about your home. Is it near the ocean?"

"We have a fine cathedral – Notre-Dame de Coutances," he began, and then remembered she'd asked about the sea. "It's a little more than two leagues from my home to the coast – a short and pleasant carriage drive during the summer months. But ten leagues more would take you within sight of the Abbey of Mont-Saint-Michel." His eyes didn't leave her face while describing his first sight of the island, floating on sea mist like a far-off vision of Heaven. It had been a journey requiring faith, he explained. The path across the bay was uncovered only when the sea retreated; hide tide came in at the speed of a galloping horse with waves the height of a tall building, sweeping away saints and sinners alike. "It's said the Archangel Michael commanded Aubert, Bishop of Avranches, to build there," he continued, watching the light play on her hair, "and when he didn't, Michael took his flaming sword and burned a hole in the bishop's skull." Marie-Madeleine's eyes were more grey than blue. Lew was about to tell her about the great bull pawing the ground where the new abbey was to stand, but then recalled that she'd asked about his home and, that being so close to his heart, he launched into a description of the Normandy countryside, the pretty timber-framed houses, the grand manors with their land and lakes, the orchards, the—

Somewhere, far away, a clock began striking the hour.

By now, his panel might have dried out making the addition of more detail difficult if not impossible. "I must go," he said jumping to his feet. "I've work left unfinished." Lew blushed again, realising that Marie-Madeleine hadn't uttered a word since he began talking. "Forgive my bad manners in monopolising the conversation, Mademoiselle. In spite of that, I hope you'll permit me visit you again."

"You're going so soon?" She started to rise, looked down, and immediately sank back, rearranging her skirts.

"There are things I must attend to. I wish it could be otherwise."

"But you'll return? You won't forget about me?"

"Forgetting you, Mademoiselle," Lew assured her, placing one hand on his heart, "would be utterly impossible." They looked at each other for a moment without speaking. The air between them seemed to crackle and hum. He took a step forward, knowing that his presentiment had been correct, and that this day marked a turning point in his life. "Mademoiselle…Marie-Madeleine…it's my dearest hope that we—"

His stumbling words were interrupted by squawks and a wild fluttering of wings from the window ledge. A glossy black bird, a jackdaw, had alighted there and was now pacing backwards and forwards, glaring into the room first with one quicksilver eye, then turning its bewigged head to stare with the other.

"Yes," said Marie-Madeleine.

"You mean—"

"Call on me tomorrow, sir," she said, suddenly formal. "There's a tale I'd like you to hear."

Not a wraith, not a fantasy, but even as he ran down the staircase, scattering feathers with every step, Lew wasn't entirely convinced that Marie-Madeleine could be a flesh-and-blood creature. A young woman so slender and fair of face might be a nymph or a *fée*, stepped out of some ancient story – but who was to say that the old tales weren't true and that she couldn't be won by a mortal? It was a puzzle he'd start to unpick tomorrow, mainly by encouraging her to talk about herself.

On reaching the ground, Lew kicked away the stone block holding open the door, and was forced to cover his ears against the resounding boom that set the walls quivering. Now he knew where Norik had been, and who she was shielding. A dozen other questions sprang into his mind.

And were driven out by what greeted him as he entered the ballroom: not only had Poucet completely rearranged the worktable but he was now engaged in carefully cleaning every last one of his brushes. Lew cursed under his breath. "Please, please, never do that again. Everything's where it is for a reason."

The valet's shoulders slumped. "Oh."

"And I know it's kindly meant, but I like my brushes exactly as they are."

"Oh."

"After all I don't meddle with your cosmetics." Lew fought to control his irritation. Today of all days, an argument was the last thing he wanted. "After all, if I did you might send your master out into society looking like an over-painted character from the *commedia dell'arte* – Pantaloon, perhaps, or the clown. Imagine that."

Poucet produced a watery smile. "Columbine would be better."

"That might be more of a challenge." With his materials back in order, Lew tied on the voluminous, and very ragged, cast-off apron donated by Jacques.

"You missed l-lunch again. Thanks to me, you're in luck – there's some food under a cover, b-beside the fire."

"I haven't got time now." He was setting a bad enough example to his assistants without disappearing for a second time.

"You still haven't told me where you went." Poucet's mouth trembled as Lew told him. "We talked about the danger only yesterday and you p-promised not to go alone."

"Did I? Sorry."

"Well, did you find your horribly maimed b-battle survivor?"

"No." Lew pushed past the valet, anxious to gauge the dryness of the wall he'd been working on. It was still damp: his luck had held. "No, my friend, I found the girl in the portrait."

"B-but she's dead," protested Poucet. "I told you – Madame P-Perrault died years ago."

Lew smiled. "I found someone cast in the same image and very much alive."

"What are you saying? This isn't a matter for jest." Poucet grabbed his arm and held on despite Lew's efforts to shake free. "Tell me."

"I'm saying she looks exactly like her." Lew lowered his voice, conscious that Jean-Baptiste and Agrippa were craning their necks to see what was going on. "That's plain enough, isn't it? Perhaps you'll come with me next time. Let's talk later. Right now I must—"

"Her n-name, d-damn you!" shouted Poucet.

"Oh – it's Marie-Madeleine. Please let go of my arm. I must—"

"Then m-my search is also at an end. It was M-Marie-Madeleine P-Perrault I came here to find."

"Perrault," Lew repeated, feeling remarkably stupid. "She's his daughter—"

"Of course she's his daughter. The image of his wife, you said. What's the matter with you? But why is she imprisoned?"

"I don't think she is. The door wasn't locked. Now, I really have to—"

"If she's as p-pretty as you say, why would she hide herself away? Unless...." The colour drained from Poucet's face. "Listen—"

"*Pour l'amour de Dieu*, Poucet," roared Lew, "whatever it is will have to wait until later." Once again, he caught his assistants

Once Upon a Time in Paris

straining their ears to catch more of the conversation, and who could blame them? A moment later, ashamed of bawling at a woman, he softened his voice. "Can't you see how much work I've got to do here? Let me be. I need to concentrate."

"Fine," snapped the valet. "Go ahead, if that's more important. These days you're always telling me to clear off, so I might as well. B-but here's something to think about before I go – *peau d'âne*. P-perhaps that'll make you feel differently."

"What donkey's skin?" Lew muttered at Poucet's departing back. Dismissing the valet's nonsense, he focused on his depiction of *The Wolf and the Stork*. As in the preliminary sketch, he'd substituted a crane, considering its slate-grey plumage and darkly reptilian legs an improvement on that of the predominantly white stork. Such a pity his bird's head must be concealed in the wolf's throat, thus hiding its striped markings – and more particularly the dramatic red skullcap – but straying further from the fable would be unwise. Why think about a donkey's skin? It made no sense at all. And, Lew closed his eyes and smiled at the beautiful image secreted there, he had far better things to think about now, even apart from completing this project.

This time Lew bounded eagerly up the steps, pausing to tap on the door – though it was half-open as before – and then regretted it since he'd put considerable effort into scrubbing the paint from his hands, leaving the knuckles almost raw. "Mademoiselle," he called, nursing his fingers. "Marie-Madeleine, it's me."

"Come along in. Show yourself."

His spirits plummeted. This was unlikely to be the pleasant interlude he'd planned, for the voice was not Marie-Madeleine's. It was neither sweet, nor soft, but reminiscent of corncrakes nesting in the summer hay meadows at home – and he had a very good idea of who it might belong to. His scouring had been in vain: all expectation of taking Marie-Madeleine's little hand and raising it to his lips perished with the speaker's first syllable. Swallowing his disappointment, Lew gave a final brush to his coat front and stepped into the room...

...which was dominated by a fearsome, black-clad figure sitting hunched against the light. As Lew's eyes adjusted, he saw the beldam perched – gimlet-eyed, with nose and jaw reminiscent of a nutcracker – on a high-backed, ancient chair, the wood of its heavy frame carved with all manner of birds and beasts emerging from, and disappearing back into, sinuous foliage. Not sitting, he thought, but enthroned, in spite of her antiquated widow's weeds – though the sovereignty implied therein had little to do with kings or bishops, hinting instead at otherworldly powers. A ridiculous idea: he shook his head in an attempt to do away with it, much as a dog might try to rid itself of a troublesome flea lodged in its ear, but the idea of a malevolent *fée* persisted. And yet, there was Marie-Madeleine, skirt tucked under her feet, seated on a stool at the crone's knee, smiling gently at him and seemingly unperturbed by her proximity to such a vision of hideousness. A piece of sewing – a bedcover perhaps, for as he watched a few feathers escaped – lay across both women's laps, and even while she stared ferociously at him, the old woman never stopped her stitching. Lew tore his eyes from the ceaseless stab of the needle, the tireless yank on the thread. "Madame, Mademoiselle—"

"And this is your idea of a prince?" the beldam demanded of the girl. "This is the one you've spent all this time dreaming about?" Lew smiled, for hadn't he been dreaming of Marie-Madeleine also? "What either of you have to smile about," stab, yank, stab, "I really don't know. This wretch turned up at the door penniless, the rags on his back more holes than cloth, not a button to his name and hungry as a wolf."

"In the old stories, the prince often comes disguised, Granny."

"I have never claimed," began Lew, shifting uneasily.

Norik snorted. "Angels, too, so the Bible tells us, but this young rogue, being neither the one nor the other, is as welcome as frost in May or snow at harvest. He's nothing but a—"

"Granny!" protested Marie-Madeleine.

"If you're asking me to hold my tongue, save your breath, my girl. Don't be swayed by his good looks – such as they are, and they aren't much – this fellow's beneath you. He's a *rustre*, no more, no less."

Lew gasped. "You're branding me a yokel?"

"Hush now, Mamie, I don't care how humble his background is."

"Mademoiselle, it's hardly—"

"Oh, you would care, miss, I assure you, once all the pretty words were spent and the honeymoon hand-holding was over with. You'd have forever and a day to care about it with nothing to eat but stone-and-nettle soup, nothing to cover yourself with save *hardes et nippes* – yes, rags and tatters – and nothing to sleep on but a hard straw pallet. Ah, that's what it means to be poor. And that's exactly how it would be, for this fine fellow comes from the very roots of the land." Stab, yank, stab, went the old woman's needle, but her black eyes were firmly fixed on Lew's face. "According to him, he's a lowly turnip-puller's son."

"Pardon me, Madame," said Lew, as calmly as he knew how when confronted by such provocation, "but that's *not* what I told you."

"Take no notice, Lew," advised Marie-Madeleine, with a small dismissive gesture. "It rained in the night. Damp weather makes her bones ache, her few teeth rattle, and turns her blood to vinegar. She doesn't mean it."

The old woman glared, first at the girl, then at Lew. "You said your sire was a farmer. Now that's a walk of life covering all manner of hand-to-mouth poverty." Norik ceased her stitching. She leaned forward, one withered hand resting on the girl's shoulder. "Farmer, peasant, one's as much in the muck as the other's in the mire. *Ma chère fille* is not suited to such an existence. Be off, painter. Take your handsome face and soft voice elsewhere. There's nothing for you here."

"Granny—" This time a warning note could be detected in Marie-Madeleine's voice.

"Let me assure you, Madame," Lew said stiffly, "that, although he often describes himself as a farmer because of his intense interest in cultivation – like André Le Nôtre, esteemed gardener to kings, and a friend from his youth – my father is a gentleman, the descendant of a noble family with large country estates between Coutances and Saint-Lô." He unclenched his jaw muscles. "As for myself—"

"Ah, I thought we'd get the truth out of you sooner or later."

The beldam cackled, reminding Lew of a foreign play he'd once dozed through: three witches and a Scottish warrior who would be king. He watched sourly as she stroked Marie-Madeleine's golden hair. The girl's arm now lay across the old woman's bony flanks; she sat quietly, not meeting his gaze, almost as though her thoughts were elsewhere. Or perhaps, since she'd also listened and observed but said so little at their first meeting, quietude was a facet of her personality. Not so the hag. Indeed, it hardly seemed possible to staunch her flow of insults. Loath though Lew was to leave without directly exchanging more than half a dozen words with Marie-Madeleine, completing another panel would be infinitely more rewarding than standing here being harangued by a cantankerous old crone who must surely be diminishing his prospects with every word she uttered. He looked at the door. "Perhaps I should return at some more convenient time."

"Before you go," Norik pursed her lips and picked up her needle, "perhaps now is a *convenient time* to tell us your true name." She squinted at her stitched seam, tugging at the fabric to make it lie more evenly. "*Petra eo da anv?* Huh? What is your name? It isn't le Sauvage – of that I'm certain."

"That, Madame, is my concern not yours."

"That's as may be, young man, but since he who goes around cloaked in a false name is trustworthy as a wolf in a sheep pen," she stabbed viciously at the cloth, yanked the thread, stabbed again, "I say, better you leave now and don't return at all."

Lew winced. "Let me assure you, Madame, that nothing dishonourable is involved. My father frowns upon my choice of profession. Since he expects failure, I adopted the name *le Sauvage* to spare him embarrassment, but live in hope that my forthcoming success will change his mind. For now, I prefer—"

He stopped, for somewhere during that short speech his artist's eye had eclipsed his day-to-day vision. The two figures before him had been transformed into a curious *pietà* – and the thought was surely not blasphemous, for rarely had he seen love and pity expressed so strongly as in the old lady's face whenever she looked at Marie-Madeleine. The love needed no explaining, for who could not love such a girl? But as for the pity, he did not understand that at all. "Madame, I would never do anything to hurt Mademoiselle Perrault. If you believe I'm capable of such an act, say now, and though it would be a mortal blow," once again he glanced towards the door, "I'll bid her farewell."

"What I say is, it's a misfortune that the proof of the pudding can only be found in the eating of it," declared Norik. She sniffed, and seemed about to launch on another tirade when Marie-Madeleine took out a piece of paper folded very small.

"Come now, Granny, you've had your say—"

"There's more."

"Lew has endured your sharp tongue for long enough. Let him be. Or would you rather not hear my tale?"

The needle ceased its stabbing. Her severe expression softened. "A story is always welcome, *ma chère*," said the shrew, in a voice less harsh than hitherto. Her rummaging in a small box produced a pastille, which the odious creature sucked noisily and with a great smacking of lips.

It seemed the inquisition was over. Certainly the atmosphere within the chamber changed abruptly; it was as though the last quarter hour of baiting and taunting had never been endured. Lew exhaled, straightened his shoulders and nodded at the chair he'd previously been invited to sit on. "May I?"

"You should hear her tale of Bella and the brute," the old lady said proudly, her wrinkled features cracking open, sweet as a nut, to reveal an unexpected smile. "I swear it would bring a tear even to your manly eye. What shall it be today, my pretty one? Speaking for myself, I'd like to hear more about the girl who sat on the cinder board."

"Not this time," said Marie-Madeleine, holding Lew's gaze for sweet moments. Today her eyes were more blue than grey, and he was almost sure tiny flecks of amber surrounded the pupils. "No, this one is an old, old tale remade. Are we ready? Shall I begin?

> *Il était une fois a very beautiful princess, the prettiest ever seen, whose parents loved her dearly. Her christening, which was a splendid affair, was attended by six good fairies who blessed the little princess with the usual gifts: a sweet nature, charm, a small waist, fine hands, blue eyes, golden hair. But, as is often the way when fathers arrange these things, the kingdom's seventh fairy had been forgotten. She came anyway, her face black as thunder, her mood mad as a kicked hornet's nest. Standing over the royal cradle she muttered a*

Once Upon a Time in Paris

long string of words. Nobody could make out a syllable; however the little princess immediately began to wail. The other fairies hastily piled more good wishes onto the child, hoping that this would counteract the evil spell. One gave her intelligence, another wit, yet another presented her with self-reliance, this one gave her curiosity, that one, steadfastness...and the last one gave her the ability to make up stories. Years went by and the seventh fairy's curse was forgotten until one day it was noticed that the princess's feet were several sizes larger than those of her brothers. Moreover, they were extraordinarily wide, hideously flat, and webbed like those of a goose. In those far off days, it was thought that such feet were the mark of a witch, so naturally every effort was made to conceal their existence. Extra long skirts were declared à la mode. High heels and dainty footwear were banned. The king brought shoemakers from other countries to stitch extra-large shoes for his daughter, a dozen pairs at a time, and swore them to secrecy. As soon as the shoes were finished, the shoemakers disappeared and no one could say for sure whether they had been thrown into the castle's deepest dungeon or allowed to return to their homes. A year and a day later, when the princess had quite worn out every last one of the shoes – for her strange feet grew apace – another foreign shoemaker would be summoned and the hides of twenty oxen brought into the castle under cover of night for him to work with. But no matter what measures the king took, it was impossible to stop tongues wagging and all too soon courtiers began to whisper and point. After that, it was no time at all before everyone in the city knew of the princess's shame. For fear of the king's wrath, there was no jeering or calling of names in the streets, but wherever she walked, even when accompanied by the royal guards, a soft hissing – as of a flock of geese disturbed – began to swell behind the common people's teeth. And sometimes, small boys dared each other to cackle from their hiding places as the princess passed by."

Marie-Madeleine paused, but didn't raise her eyes from the paper. A spot of high colour, which Lew thought very becoming, had stained each of her cheeks. He waited in silence, anxious for the story to continue, not the least because she possessed a sweet, low voice which he couldn't imagine ever growing tired of hearing.

After a moment or two, the old woman patted the girl's hand. "Go on, my dear. Tell it to the end. For as you should know, ill luck follows abandoning a story in the middle of its life."

"The princess became very sad. There came a day when she refused to leave the castle grounds. Thereafter, she spent her days hidden away in a little shepherd's hut, spinning silk with a silver distaff and a golden spindle while telling stories to children still too young to have learned unkindness. And although an old fée she chanced upon while walking in the wild places at the edge of the forest foretold that one day she'd find true love with a man who cared not a jot for her strange affliction, the princess was not comforted, for who would ever discover her hidden away in the loneliest corner of the castle grounds? Soon she lost all hope. But it so happened that a prince, whose horse had bolted while out hunting, and who was making his way to the castle on foot, passed close by the hut, saw the beautiful princess at her spinning and storytelling, and fell in love with her. Before long he went to her father to ask for the hand of Bertrada – for that was her name – in marriage. The king hummed and he hawed and he would

not give an answer. Eventually, one of his counsellors took Prince Pippin aside and explained the difficulty. 'It makes no difference to me,' said the prince, who loved Bertrada for her pretty face and gentle nature. 'As a wise woman once told me, better a flaw on the outside than one in the soul.' They were married soon afterwards and lived in great happiness for many years."

"A very good story," said Lew, wondering why Marie-Madeleine's eyes were still fixed on her page – though he noticed Norik was now craned forward to stare at him, as if gauging his reaction. He dutifully piled more praise on both the teller and the tale, ending with: "And is it true?"

The old woman clicked her tongue with annoyance. "All stories are true, my fine fellow, even when they're not."

"It is a true tale," said Marie-Madeleine, nervously pleating the fabric of her skirt, "for Pippin and Bertrada became King and Queen of the Franks. Charlemagne was their firstborn son."

Lew willed her to look his way. "I believe their effigies lie in the Basilica of Saint Denis." A long silence followed during which he heartily wished for the old woman to disappear in a puff of smoke. In the meantime, at least he could feast his eyes on Marie-Madeleine. Today she wore a simple gown – again old-fashioned in style but pretty nonetheless – of fine linen embroidered with clusters of roses. As a result of her pinching pleats in the skirt, it had risen up slightly, allowing a glimpse of snowy-white lace beneath. He watched, entranced, as her fingers continued to pluck at the fabric, so that both skirt and under-garment rose, inch by inch by breathtaking inch, until he felt Norik's eyes upon him, whereupon he cleared his throat and desisted, fixing his gaze instead on the rose-coloured ribbons in the girl's hair – before realising that both women were now staring expectantly at him.

"Perhaps you've seen them," he asked, slightly unnerved. "The uh tombs, I mean."

Marie-Madeleine shook her head. "I haven't left this place in many years."

"Such a pretty face," Lew said gallantly, "should be seen everywhere."

"I've found the world can be unkind, sir."

"How so?" The girl didn't answer. "It wouldn't dare if I was at your side," he said stoutly, and intercepted the glance that passed between them. "Mademoiselle, if only you would allow it, I'd gladly—"

"My, how the day marches on," announced Norik, hauling herself upright. "I'm sure *all of us* have plenty of work to do. As for me, by now those laundry women must have finished their beating and paddling and scrubbing and gossiping and will be draping the linen wherever they can find space. It behoves me to see that the job's been well done and to make sure they don't make off with any leftover soap. I close my eyes to them selling our used wash water, for precious few can afford good *savon de Marseilles*." A sharp look was directed at Lew. "The door, if you please."

"Of course, Madame." He hurried to hold it open for her – even though the wider space seemed entirely unnecessary for such a tiny personage. It was a ruse: once over the threshold, she stopped and beckoned.

"The telling of that story was a very painful thing for her."

Lew frowned. "I don't understand."

"Ah, that's the pity of it." In a louder voice she added: "Give me a few moments – no more, or mark my words, I'll raise a hue and cry – to get my poor old bones down these Godforsaken steps and out of your way, and then follow after, quick as you like."

He turned back into the room to find Marie-Madeleine seated

in the carved chair, the half-stitched coverlet over her knees, her skirt once more wrapped under her feet. They looked at each other; looked away. There was suddenly so much Lew wanted to tell her that he found himself almost incapable of speech.

"Listening to your tale brought me great pleasure, Mademoiselle," was all he could come up with. "Have you written others? I would love to hear more."

"There are two more." She pointed to the sheets of paper he'd moved yesterday. "You're welcome to read them."

Lew looked away, embarrassed, for reading had always presented him with difficulties. More often than not, the letters jumped around on the page so that words became jumbled and the lines would not be marshalled, no matter how hard he tried. "I'd rather hear you read them."

A short silence followed. Then she said: "I enjoyed your descriptions of the Normandy countryside."

He smiled at her, glad to be back on safer ground. "When it was too late, I remembered a quaint custom of ours that takes place in the orchards at midwinter. Little boys with lighted firebrands run around the apple trees singing '*Taupes et mulots, sortez de vos clos, Sinon vous brulerai et la barbe et les os.*' Naturally, afterwards, the scamps expected to be well rewarded."

The rhyme was greeted with a small moue. "Moles and voles – come out of your holes. Poor little persecuted creatures to be threatened with having their whiskers and bones burned."

"I don't recall the boys ever catching any," Lew said dryly. A far-off banging coiled its way up the stairs. He guessed the old hag had reached the bottom and was now summoning him by beating on the ironwork covering the door below. It couldn't be time to depart. There was so much more he wanted to say. In particular, he wanted to share the joys of his own work with her. "I take it you know about the transformations going on below?"

"You mean in the old ballroom? Yes, it's been described to me. I've also seen the drawing you made of the wi…of our old friend. It was a little kind, I think." She hesitated, biting her lip. "Are you always so forgiving of unsightly features?"

Unwilling to admit the considerable pecuniary advantage in flattering the aged, Lew simply shrugged. "It's just a question of emphasising the better features and underplaying the rest." This was not what he wanted to speak of. "However some subjects," he said, looking her full in the face, "being perfect in every way, need no—"

"Nobody is perfect, sir." Marie-Madeleine sighed. "And some of us are far less perfect than others." The hammering from below recommenced with a vengeance.

"I'd better go," Lew took her hand and raised it to his lips, "but only in the hope of seeing you again soon." He ran down the stairs, only a little put out by her lukewarm response.

"I don't know what you've got to look so pleased about," growled the old woman at the door. "Her father will have the skin off your back if he finds out."

Sooner or later, Lew knew – for he remembered all too well the dismally protracted procedures his father considered necessary if they were ever to approach Angelique's sire with a view to marriage arrangements – it would be necessary to request formally Monsieur Perrault's permission to call on his daughter. Although the old man seemed a little more cordially inclined towards him of late, Lew was painfully conscious of being regarded as socially inferior. Artistic acclaim would change all that. One only had to look at the great, now unfortunately deceased, royal painter Charles Le Brun to see how far it was possible to ascend. However, such recognition would only be possible when the octagonal ballroom, finished in its glorious entirety, could be displayed to Monsieur Perrault's influential friends and colleagues.

With an early completion in mind, he examined his assistants' progress with meticulous care before recommencing his own work, sharing his greater knowledge and giving praise wherever it was deserved. After ascertaining that the red chalk guides used to transfer his original sketches to the walls were still sharp and clear, Lew decided to take a chance on the two younger men. When their present tasks were satisfactorily completed, they'd be allowed to tackle one of the main set pieces. It was a move designed to benefit them all.

Thankfully, it wasn't until much later, when the natural light was beginning to fade that Poucet appeared. The valet, dragging his dejection after like a fallen banner, peered disconsolately at the artist, who was humming as he painted. "You've seen her again." It was a statement rather than a question.

"That's right." Lew had just loaded his brush with ultramarine, the most expensive pigment he possessed. "Sorry, I must carry on." Glancing over his shoulder, he saw Poucet's face fall still further, and in an effort to soften the small rejection added: "This colour's far too costly to waste. It's made from crushed lapis lazuli."

"Should I care? More broken promises on your part – you said I could come with you next time."

"It's from remote mines in the northernmost part of Afghanistan. Think how far it's travelled to decorate this.... My friend, you weren't around, so I went alone."

"You can't have looked for me very hard. I've been nowhere today." Poucet pushed at a pile of discarded rags, first with the toe of one small shoe, then the other. "What happened?"

"As you can see, it's the perfect blue of the Virgin's robes—"

"What happened?" repeated Poucet, this time a little more loudly.

"Nothing happened." Lew hunched his shoulders and continued to apply paint.

"What kind of nothing?"

"Madame Norik was there." With a deep sigh of exasperation, Lew gave up and turned, clenching the brush in his fist. "Does that answer your question?"

"And she didn't see you off?"

"The old lady gave me a tongue-lashing, all right. All I can say is, her poor departed husband must have lived in holy terror of such a woman. *Une mégère* – a scold and a shrew," he forced a smile, "but eventually she relented. Marie-Madeleine read aloud a sweet tale she'd composed, and afterwards I was even allowed a few moments alone with her."

"Oh," said Poucet. "It's like that, is it? I see."

Lew's feelings were so new, so fragile, that he was tempted to continue holding them close to his heart, but the need to confide in someone, anyone, triumphed. "I think I'm in love, my friend. Be glad for me."

"But what about us?" the valet demanded. "What about us? We planned to leave this place together…to be together. Can you not remember how, when I suggested we travelled to my little house in Spain, you invited me to accompany you to your home instead."

"No, I didn't," Lew retorted, "but even if I had – and I really did not – everything's changed."

"Has it indeed?" Poucet's voice rose. "Does Marie-Madeleine know you lay naked beside me in my bed?"

Lew flinched. There was no missing Agrippa and Jean-Baptiste rolling their eyes and smirking on the upper level. One glare from him and the boys bent more assiduously to their tasks, but the damage was done. "For God's sake, Poucet – shut your nasty mouth."

"True though, isn't it, and not just once, but every night. Now

I'm to be cast off. I wonder what your new lady love will think about that."

"Does your master yet know that you dosed his guests with noxious weeds and deadly toadstools?" demanded Lew, grabbing hold of the small figure, and marching out of the door. "If you want to play games of this sort, *Judith*, think about how well that information would be received."

"You can't prove anything." The valet stood in the corridor with clenched fists, her eyes brimming with tears.

"Perhaps not," Lew said, more gently, "and I don't want to. I swore to stay silent, and whatever you think, I try to keep my promises. Come now, don't let's quarrel."

"I take it you didn't read *Donkeyskin*." Poucet's lips were drawn back and Lew caught a glimpse of long sharp dogteeth.

"It's a tale? I didn't realise. No. With so much to get done, what time do I have for reading?"

"You make time to visit *her*."

"*Oh mon Dieu*…. Twice only I've visited her." Lew clutched his aching head with both hands. "I swear to you – next time we'll go together."

"It's too late. I don't want to. I'm not interested in either of you. And I no longer care if her father wanted to marry her—"

"*What!*"

"In fact, I hope he did, if it means you can't have her. And even if he didn't, I'll see to it that she'll never be yours." Poucet's eyes narrowed. "You know what I'm capable of. Everyone that injures me or mine pays in the end. I'm warning you, paint-dauber – you're going to rue the day you treated me so badly."

Lew spent a restless night, his sleep disturbed by wild dreams of witches, shape-changers and poisonous toadstools. His first thought on waking was of the damage Poucet could wreak upon his life. His second, that he regretted their falling-out. He dozed for a while, woke in a state of alarm, and hurried to the kitchen shortly after daybreak in the hope of making things right before the valet disappeared upstairs to attend to his master's *toilette*. Poucet was already at the fire, filling jugs with hot water, and pointedly ignored Lew's greeting.

"A hearty breakfast," announced Jacques, reaching for a ladle, "is God's way of healing the damage done by whatever the Devil forced down our unwilling throats the night before."

Lew ducked under the cook's arm. "Poucet, my friend," he muttered, undeterred by the ferocious scowl directed at him, "listen, please. I'm really sorry about—"

"Hoi," yelled Jacques. "You two should know better than to play around by boiling pans. And mind that braising bell. Oh, for the love of God, Leonardo, get out of there."

"All right," said Lew. He ducked again, this time to avoid the irate cook's viciously swung ladle, slipped on some grease, and only managed to save himself from falling onto the red-hot stove by grabbing hold of the shelf where platters and trenchers were stacked. One leg slid in front of Poucet, almost tripping him up. Hot water slopped from the jugs. The clatter of metal hitting the floor seemed to go on forever.

"Bloody watch where you're putting your ugly great feet," snarled the valet. "Damn blockhead."

"Hoi, what's got into you, kid?" bellowed Jacques. "In all the months of trial and tribulation that living under this roof brings, I've never before known you turn nasty."

But Lew stared open-mouthed. "That's *it*," he cried, slapping himself on the forehead before sprinting from the kitchen.

"Here, what about your breakfast?" demanded Jacques, holding out a brimming bowl of broth. He shook his head. "I've never known Leonardo not start the day without several helpings of my very fine *pottage*. Oh, well, that's two first-time-for-everything happenings today and it's not yet seven of the clock. It must be to do with where the moon rode in the heavens last night. What rhymes with moon? Loon, spoon, and boon…. Ah – lunch served at noon, not a moment too soon."

Chapter Thirteen

Many years have passed since my good fairy made her promises to me. Time has proved us both right, for in spite of the jibes and taunts and threats from certain parties, I never stopped believing that some day the kind and handsome prince would find me, wherever I might be, and however carefully I was hidden away. Lew might not be a prince, but he's tall and very handsome, soft-spoken too. More than that, his eyes shone like a boy's while listening to my tale. It's true, he is a little slow on the uptake, but the witch says this is often the way with young men, so I've yet to see if my terrible affliction will drive him away.

"No good dwelling on it," says the witch. "We'll just have to wait and see."

"But what if—"

She's no help at all. "You'd survive, *ma chère fille*, even if the worst came to the worst. That's how we women live in this world – when some blackguard knocks us down nine times we confound him by getting up ten."

"Lew's not a—"

"That remains to be seen." The witch screws up her mouth. "Mind what you're doing with that bread. My poor back's not what it was. We'll have the place overrun by rats and mice if you keep dropping crumbs all over the floor with no one able or willing to sweep them up."

Once Upon a Time in Paris

"Stop fussing, Granny." I carefully tip the scraps onto the window ledge, though a visit from Reims has become a rarity and no doubt he's forgotten about learning to say *happily ever after*. With summer fast approaching there are probably better pickings to be had in the surrounding countryside.

The sun is low on the horizon, turning the clouds apricot, gold, violet and rose. Everything seems very still, but there must be a wind high above for one minute a splendid ceremonial coach drawn by griffins rides the sky and the next it melts to become a benign dragon, then a snake...and finally a string of pearls.

"Leave off your daydreaming and close the window, *ma petite*. It's almost time to light the candles."

"Not yet, Mamie – I'm waiting for the stars to come out. Let me be." Twilight thickens round me. There's the evening star – Venus smiling down on all lovers everywhere. The last glow of the setting sun turns into Cinderella's fireplace.

> *Cinderella dried her tears. "But however could I get to the ball." "Oh," said the fairy, "don't worry about that. Women like me always have a few tricks up our sleeves. Go into the garden, my dear, and bring me the largest pumpkin you can find." Cinderella did so. She came back staggering under its weight and the fairy pronounced it perfect. Taking a sharp knife, the fairy hollowed it out, cutting doors and windows in its sides. Then she tapped it with her magic wand and the pumpkin shell was instantly transformed into a beautiful gilded coach fit for royalty. "Now we must have horses. Six will suffice. I think the cat, the dog, and four red hens might do very nicely."*

No, that isn't right.

I'll tell Lew everything when he finally understands my strangeness, beginning with the move to this house. I was twelve years old. And that was when my peculiarity began to show. Soon, there was no missing it.

As for Cinderella, perhaps—

"Now we need horses. No less than six will do, and perfectly matched." They went together to look at the mousetrap in the pantry and discovered six mice, grown sleek and fat on butter and cheese and piecrust and all manner of good things that were stored there. As each mouse was struck with the magic wand it immediately became a prancing, dancing dappled-grey horse. "And now for a coachman," said the fairy. Cinderella looked around the kitchen, from the kettle to the besom....

Would she select a pot-bellied cauldron, or the stiffly upright fire irons, perhaps? It should be something that's very much part and parcel of kitchen life.

I'll tell him about the racket – far worse than the name-calling – that started up every time my little brother Pierre and his friends caught sight of me. The hissing and honking, the cackling and barking – even Charles-Samuel, who took life so seriously that he rarely played games, ran away covering his ears, laughing at their din. And once I even saw father smiling behind his hand at what he called *the boys' nonsense*.

The answer's a rat, of course. With breadcrumbs everywhere, and all the chicken bones, fishtails and oyster shells tossed onto the kitchen midden, rats would be regular diners there. Cinderella would choose a rat.

"And now for a coachman," said the fairy. They chose the plumpest glossiest rat from the rattrap hidden in the wood

> *store, one moreover with a fine set of whiskers. He was very content to be turned into a stout coachman with a beautiful twirled moustache. When it came to lackeys, a pot boy and the hump-backed spit-turner were pressed into service....*

They won't do at all. I haven't made the kitchen grand enough for an extra pair of scullions. Cinderella turned her hand to every task.

At Michaelmas we always had a stubble goose for our dinner, grown fat almost beyond being able to waddle from gleaning the harvested fields. The last one that ever came into this house was very large indeed. Lew shall hear how Pierre took the creature's wings and head, fastened them to a cloak and came flapping into my chamber in the middle of the night, honking and whistling, terrifying me.

Was he ever punished? Not by our father. In fact, it was father who brought the Royal Game of the Goose home, occasioning more mirth at my expense. The game's played on a board marked with numbered goose eggs laid out in a spiral. Each player has two dice. The object is to reach the centre before the other players. I refused to play, but it was impossible to avoid the noise of them honking whenever a player landed on a space marked with a goose, hissing when someone landed on one marked with a penalty.

Lizards can serve as lackeys – slippery creatures that spend their days basking in the sun. One might think them dead but for a knowing gleam in their eyes and the quick-flicking of their tongues.

> *"Back to the garden," commanded the fairy, "you're sure to find some lizards hiding behind the watering can. Bring me half a dozen." As soon as Cinderella came back, the fairy changed them into lackeys, resplendent in braid-covered*

uniforms, who immediately climbed onto the back of the coach. "You see?" said the fairy. "That's how we women live in this world. Nine times we're told we can't do something, and ten times we prove that we can. Oh – what's the matter now?" Cinderella hung her head. She did not like to complain again but there remained the matter of her clothes. "I still can't go," she said, "because I don't have anything suitable to wear. This dress belonged to my dear mother. It's ragged and old-fashioned and stained – and I'm tired of always being laughed at." The fairy touched Cinderella with her magic wand and at once the rags were transformed into a most beautiful cloth of gold gown set all over with precious stones – rubies, sapphires, and diamonds. Her hair was instantly arranged in the latest style and adorned with more diamonds, arranged so as to catch the light. And for her feet the fairy godmother gave her the prettiest little pair of dancing slippers, made of fur, pure-white ermine, trimmed with swansdown.

After all, if the fairy can do so much else, wouldn't she also correct Cinderella's peculiar defects?

Lew would have to know why I retreated to my tower. It was after being promised in marriage to an old man of fifty with the face of a toad, probably willing to overlook my curious affliction in exchange for a generous dowry. And that was *la goutte qui a fait déborder le vase*: in other words, the last straw.

When Cinderella arrived at the palace, the king's son himself ran out to hand her down from the coach.

The prince came running down the palace steps to welcome Cinderella, but Lew had to climb far steeper ones to find me. Should I tell him about the day I threatened to poison myself – it's not difficult to come by noxious ingredients in Paris – and almost went through with it?

When she entered the great ballroom on the prince's arm everyone fell silent. The musicians ceased playing. The dancers stopped dancing. The maids ceased their waiting and even the ladies of court stopped gossiping.

Time itself seemed to stand still when Lew pushed open my chamber door. At first I imagined myself dream-fasted. And then thought I might die from joy.

My father backed down in the end, not knowing that my life was never in danger. No bane could have killed me. I have his precious bezoar stone, an antidote for any poison, hidden inside poor Mama's dowry chest.

And even the king himself, an old greybeard, could not take his eyes off her.

However, if the rest of my good fairy's prophecy turns out to be correct, my happiness will be so great that perhaps I'll shed the past as a snake sloughs its skin, never speak of it to Lew and never think of it again.

"If you want a thing done," grumbles the witch, making me jump as she slams the window against the pestilent miasmas of night. "Can't you feel the nip in the air – a late frost, I shouldn't wonder. Oh, how cold your hands are. Sit here, *ma petite*, put this coverlet of yours, all stitched and mended, good as new, over your knees."

"Please stop fussing, Granny," I say, for the tenth time since rising. "I'm not an invalid."

"That's as maybe, but you don't look after yourself." Head on one side, she peers at me from her little witch eyes. "Now, would you like to know what I saw today, *ma chère?* Shall I describe the splendid sight to you? Or will we go down the steps and out into the world together, so that you can see for yourself?"

Without a word I set the dish of candied orange peel between us. And the witch nibbles and chews, describing the ceiling: "Oh, you should see it – domed like the sky above us, as blue as the approach to the gates of Heaven, I swear, and all spangled with stars. At the centre, the sun, and down each side of his rays are painted little fleurs-de-lys, which they say are lilies but which always look to me like the iris flowers growing wild along our River Isole. And that isn't the end of it. Below the stars hover all the birds of creation from the sacred wren to the mournful storm petrel – which as everyone knows are the souls of our poor dead fishermen – hawks and owls, finches and wagtails, and small birds without names looking like flying jewels."

"How beautiful it sounds."

"*Ma chère fille*, it is a sight not to be missed. I doubt even Versailles boasts a room more splendid than the one being fashioned under this very roof." And on she chatters, telling me about the portly rats, the sly dog fox and the gullible crow, the incautious crane, the tortoise and the hare, crickets and butterflies, ants and bees, trees and flowers.

In return, I read aloud my newest tale about a prince born so ugly and so misshapen that he was hardly considered human. As it turned out, this unfortunate boy was witty and intelligent; what was more, a kindly fairy bestowed on Prince Riquet the gift of being able to share his intelligence with the woman he loved best. A few years later, another queen gave birth to a daughter who was truly beautiful and totally stupid. However the same fairy bestowed on this princess the gift of being able to make anyone she loved handsome. It only remained for the two young people to come together. The witch found this a very satisfactory tale, though she did express some sympathy for the beautiful princess's ugly but clever sister who, truth to tell, I had quite forgotten.

Tomorrow, this story will go the way of all the rest, carried away on the back of the wind, as will the other, about a boy born disadvantaged by his small stature – one not for the witch's ears, being so tiny herself, and it's quite nasty withal – but for now they can stay on my chair.

Thus our evening was spent. But tonight I can't sleep.

Where is Lew now? What is he doing? Is he thinking of me? One minute my heart threatens to burst with joy, the next it shrinks with fear of what might yet be.

It's easy enough to tell which of my few visitors has entered the tower. They each have their particular noises. The witch grumbles and groans as she hauls herself up the cold stone staircase, the ogre puffs, pants, blows and wheezes, while Lew, who has only mounted those steps on two occasions, ascends quickly and quietly, not even letting the iron-clad door slam shut to announce his imminent arrival. This morning he takes the stairs at a run and arrives flushed of face and gasping.

"Lew – what's happened?" Not yet dressed, I quickly wrap my newly rejuvenated coverlet around me. "Why are you here so early?"

"Forgive me." He clings to the doorjamb, catching his breath. With no wig, his dark hair lies tousled and mussed around his shoulders – elflocks, the witch would say, and seize a comb, but she's not me – and even at this distance I can make out the tiny dew beads of perspiration on his forehead. His chemise is crumpled, streaked with every colour of paint, torn at one wrist, and only partially tucked inside his breeches. "Tidy yourself," the witch would shriek, whereas I'd fain do it for him. Something's wrong. He doesn't smile today, nor attempt the proper courtesies, but there's such intensity in his gaze.

"You shouldn't be here, Lew." The first time couldn't be helped, but the witch has laid down the law about a chaperon being present and in some things I dare not cross her. "Not at this hour."

"I had to see you." His eyes are still fixed on mine. "It couldn't wait. I wanted to say—"

"Yes?"

"How can I...? Listen – there was once a princess, the most beautiful the world has ever seen...." He stops. "No, that won't do."

"What is it, Lew? What are you trying to tell me?"

"I didn't..." he swallows hard. "That is to say...."

"Now you're alarming me." My heart is pounding so hard I fear for my rib cage. I want to run...but away from him? Towards him? I can't tell.

"Forgive me." Lew bounds across the room. He falls to his knees, takes hold of the hem of my overlong bed gown, and gently folds it back.

"What are you doing? No! Don't! Stop! You mustn't see." Before I know it he is dropping a kiss on each of my big flat shameful ugly, ugly, *ugly* goose feet. Then he stands up, takes my hands and pulls me towards him, planting the softest kisses imaginable on my ear, my jaw, my cheek, and finally, on my lips.

"Forgive me," he says, for the third time, "for not understanding. I've been a thick-skinned, unseeing, stupid beast." He kisses me again. "I loved you from the moment we met. Nothing else matters. Will you marry me, beautiful Marie-Madeleine?"

"Of course I will marry you, dear beast." Even as the words leave my mouth, I hear the deep boom from below that is the tower door slamming. The noise reverberates in the stairwell, holding its note, hardly seeming to diminish. "It's the ogre," I whisper, and Lew holds me tighter, not realising that makes everything twice as dangerous.

What a monstrous sight the ogre is, to be sure; clearly the man who renders him fit to be seen hasn't done any work today. Rage and the steep climb have turned his ogreish face the colour of beets, while his eyes look about to start from his head. Without the luxuriant wig, his near-bald skull is revealed – a moth-grazed tonsure with an additional grey tuft on top. It's only now that I realise my repulsive prince in last night's tale is based on the ogre, from his big red nose and enormous paunch to the stooped shoulders.

And what a din he makes getting his breath back, rasping and sawing and blowing, all the while beating his cane against the floor – especially when he tries to shout at the same time. "What's this? What's this, I say? Take your hands off her, you spawn of the gutter."

Lew steps forward. "Sir—"

"He was right," pants the ogre, brandishing his stick. "He warned me of what was going on. He said you weren't to be trusted."

"If you mean Poucet, he's a...." Lew hesitates, glances at me, and tries again. "Poucet is not a reliable person. Your valet, sir, is not what you think."

"And you, sir, are a blackguard, a scoundrel, a dastard, a knave." The ogre's cane slices the air. Lew ducks. A vase tips onto its side, spilling gillyflowers one by one by one.

"Lew – be careful!" I won't weep. I won't humiliate myself by backing into a corner and crouching there like a wounded animal as happened last time the ogre lost his temper.

The tower door slams again.

In the gaps between the ogre's endless bawling and blustering I hear the witch muttering and groaning as she hauls her old bones up the stairs to join us. She arrives, gasping like a hunted hare, and drops onto the nearest chair.

"You're a wretch, a limb of Satan," bellows the ogre, stamping backwards and forwards across the small space, "a varlet, reprobate, philanderer—"

"Sir, please be assured that I've done nothing wrong," protested Lew. "I have treated Marie-Madeleine with every courtesy."

Crash – over goes a side table: strawberries and pastilles everywhere.

"What would riffraff like you know about courtesy?"

"Granny," I cry, for even now nothing will induce me to speak to the ogre, "tell him that Lew's wellborn."

The witch tries but fails. "His father is—" It's not her fault. She's still struggling to get her breath. Anyway, who can make their voice heard over an ogre's roaring and shouting of insults?

"A viper, a rogue, wastrel—" The next swing of his stick sets a chest juddering. A wooden doll, a treasured once-upon-a-time birthday gift, wearing a dress as old-fashioned as mine and with its beribboned hair arranged in an elaborately careless *fontange* style, shoots into the air and cracks clean in half as it hits the floor.

"For the love of God," shrieks the witch, jumping up and wrenching the stick from the ogre's hand. "Compose yourself!"

The ogre stares down at her. His mouth shuts like a trap. "Harrumph." He looks at the doll, takes back his cane, and glances towards me. I stare straight ahead.

"Never mind my father," said Lew, raising his chin, "even those you dismiss as riffraff are capable of understanding common courtesy."

"Harrumph." Finally the ogre seems to have run out of harsh words. He takes a deep breath. "Le Sauvage, you will leave my house immediately. And never return."

There's a moment of stillness in the room. Lew reaches for my hand. Maybe he feels my heart sink, for his fingers tighten. "Sir, I wish to marry your daughter. And she has consented to marry me."

"Was I consulted about this nonsense?" snarls the ogre. "I have long feared the girl was mad. Now she seeks to prove it by attempting to wed a down-at-heel itinerant dauber. You seek my permission. I refuse it. The answer is no. It can never be. Now, get out of my house. Begone, I say."

"Sir, my project isn't complete." Lew speaks to the ogre, but he looks at me. "Two entire panels remain."

"The room must be finished," I tell the witch. "How can the ball he promised be held there with walls left unpainted?"

"Are those rooms to be locked up again, given back to the damp and the mice?" croaks the witch, massaging her throat. "A pity for something set to be the talk of Paris."

"This scoundrel is certainly not indispensable," the ogre informs me. "Someone else can paint the room. Finished it will be, whatever the expense. If necessary, I'll employ the finest artists in Paris."

"But," Lew objects, "the designs are mine, from my drawings."

"Not any more," says the ogre, his humour ice cold where before it was blowing furnace hot. "For the last time, leave now of your own accord or be thrown out onto the street."

"By you?" asks Lew, incredulous.

In response, the ogre steps out onto the landing and deals the side of the stairwell three mighty blows. And I hear another step on the stairs, the heavy step – slow and steady – of a fourth visitor, *fie, foh and fum*, one who hasn't strayed into my tower for many years. "It's the giant."

Lew looks at me with anguished eyes. "Marie-Madeleine—"

A moment later, the giant fills the doorway, stooping so as not to hit his head on the lintel. He says not a word. One great arm sweeps Lew out of the room, out of the tower, out of my life. I snatch up a book, my shawl, and search for my shoes.

"Wait, I'll come with you."

"You're going nowhere, miss," the ogre declares.

"Stop that noise, *ma chère.*" The witch clutches me with her spindly arms, holding me back as I fight to make for the door. "It'll do you no good. Hush now. Dry your eyes. Bide your time."

Oh, how I hate her. How I hate them both.

Now the ogre turns his vitriol on the witch. "As for you, Madame, having betrayed my trust, get out, clear off – go back to where you came from."

She gasps. "You're sending me packing?"

"Naturally – and why would I not? Be off with you, I say. You've allowed a philanderer access to my daughter's private apartment. It's a scandalous situation. If word should ever get out, what chance would there be of a suitable match?"

"Tell him I've chosen my own husband."

I might as well not have spoken. The witch is silent for a moment, and I consider repeating myself very loudly, but then she surprises me by standing up to him. I'm reminded of a fierce little robin defending her nestlings against a marauding tomcat.

"Now you listen to me, young Charles," she shrills, arms akimbo as if fluffing up her feathers to increase her size. "Was you sought me out, not the other way around. And why was that, pray? Because I'm family – Azenor Perrot as was – and that means something where we both come from. Ah, no good denying it – all the Perrots were simple Breton fisher folk from Concarneau. Our twice-great-grandmothers were sisters. Your great-grandfather was a Perrot, too. Old Pierre's father changed the family name when he set up as a lawyer in Touraine and it was fancified again when Pierre's son brought his family to Paris."

"Yes, yes," the ogre says impatiently, "this is old news." He takes one small step towards the door. I swear the witch's eyes flash scarlet.

"You brought me here. Remember that. You begged me to come and care for a daughter who'd shut herself away from the world – for no good reason you said, leading me to believe the worst. Instead, I found a girl lonely, heartsore, tormented almost beyond endurance." She prods his chest with her skinny witch finger. "And I soon discovered the truth of the matter – on top of everything else you'd tried marrying her off to a man nearer your age than hers."

"A repulsive old man," I say.

The ogre shuffles backwards in an effort to escape that prodding finger. "Far from being repulsive he was about to become the Vicomte de—"

"Who'd already buried four young wives."

"It was a very good match," the ogre says defensively.

"I've said it before. I'll say it again. I'm the nearest thing to a grandmother she's got. And I will continue to care for her," continues the witch, jabbing him one last time, "for as long as I see fit. As for the artist, you brought him into the house and let him roam unsupervised. Blame yourself. Two young people – what did you expect would happen?"

His mouth opens...closes again. It seems there are times when an ogre is no match for a witch. It's only after he's slunk away that I realise he's stolen my stories.

What would my good fairy say to this? I've found love and lost it in the space of a morning. But since no proper fairytale concludes without a happy-ever-after ending, it's clear that there's more of the story to come.

The king flew into a terrible rage on finding out that his daughter had fallen in love with a beggar. He summoned the court executioner and ordered the young man dragged before him in chains. "Prepare to die, varlet, reprobate, wretch, philanderer," he roared. Weeping bitterly, the princess threw herself onto her knees and pleaded for her lover's life. The executioner, moved by her tears, laid down his axe. The ladies of court wailed and tore their hair. The cooks blew out the fires and refused to prepare dinner. Even the scullions left off their sanding and scrubbing. Eventually the king relented and banished the beggar from the realm. The very next day he announced that the princess was to be married. Suitors arrived from near and far. Among them was a handsome young prince, mounted on a sleek black horse caparisoned in gold and flanked by a dozen attendants in gold livery. As for the prince himself, he was dressed in such diamond-studded finery that it dazzled the eyes. The ogre was delighted to receive him and was courtesy itself. But when the princess was brought in to be introduced, she recognised the young man immediately as her beloved beggar. "Dear princess," said he, "I wanted to be loved for myself and not on account of my father's great wealth and vast estates. That is why I came here disguised as a pauper. Let us be married without delay."

Chapter Fourteen

"You knew about Marie-Madeleine all along, didn't you?" asked Lew, as he was firmly shepherded back through the panelled wall. He surreptitiously pinched himself, hoping to wake from a bad dream.

Jacques grinned and flexed his muscles in a manner that seemed as much warning as boast. "Who else do you think hauled all those chattels up them steps? Books, carpets, pots, beds – that damn carved chair nearly broke my back but up it had to go, being her mother's. Anyway, nothing I wouldn't do for the poor little mite, though until today it's been a long while since I clapped eyes on her."

"I love her."

"Who would not?" agreed the cook.

"And she loves me. Stop pushing – I can't leave. Surely you can see that. Go back to the kitchen, Jacques. Let me get on with my work. He'll change his mind once he's calmed down."

"Not where his daughter's concerned, he won't. You shouldn't have started nosing around—"

"And you might have said something," Lew said reproachfully, "to stop me going off on a wild goose chase looking for a crippled soldier."

"I was sworn to secrecy, Leonardo. But you could have worked things out for yourself. Why would I be making little pink and white meringues for a battle-hardened old warrior? Or lemon possets scattered with sugared violets and rose petals? Or jellies and marzipan fruits and macaroons – all sorts of dainties fit for a princess, many prepared right under your nose. *Pardieu*, if you didn't notice me practising my supreme art in the cause of beauty, you should have." The cook set Lew walking again, pointing him towards the ballroom. "Get your things. Quick as you can. The master wants you gone before he comes back down." He watched impassively as Lew retrieved his bag, a few paintbrushes, and the likeness of Marie-Madeleine's mother. "Is that everything? Let's be going then."

"Three days," said Lew. "I've only known Marie-Madeleine for three days."

"You know, none of this is of my choosing, young Leonardo," Jacques said, as they were descending to the kitchen. "Her father being who he is, she'll go to a rich man. This world's a cruel place for those of us not born between silk sheets." He was silent for a moment. "How did the master find out about the pair of you?"

"Poucet told him," Lew said bitterly.

Jacques looked at him, surprised. "I thought you two were friends."

"Not such close friends as Poucet wished us to be."

"You mean he desired an unnatural friendship?" The cook's nostrils flared.

"Poucet is not what everyone in this house has been led to believe." Damn it all, thought Lew, such a betrayal negated any promises. "Poucet is a woman whose mother was a nurse in the Perrault household many years ago. Her real name's Judith and she came back in disguise to make trouble."

"What sort of trouble?" demanded Jacques, clenching his great fists.

Lew shrugged. "Why not ask her?" He'd said enough. Besides, here was the kitchen, there was the back entrance, and now the real misery of his situation hit home.

Once Upon a Time in Paris

"I have been instructed to see you out of the house," said the cook, holding wide the door and giving him a light blow between the shoulder blades, "and so I must. Good luck to you, young Leonardo. God go with you. Like me, you have great skills and men of our calibre generally fall upon our feet."

"What's happening, Lew?" cried Blanche, running in from the scullery, her hands crusted with scouring sand. "Where are you going?"

Escarlatta stared. "He's lost his position, by the sound of it."

Blanche looked stricken. "I'll always treasure my likeness, Lew." She dabbed her eyes with a corner of apron. "Promise you'll come back and see us."

"That's right, Leonardo," said Jacques, "come back and see us one day – when you've made a name for yourself."

Lew got no further than the front steps of the house, where he sank down, shocked and suddenly very cold in spite of the warm sunshine. Time ceased to have any meaning: he might have been sitting there for a few minutes or several hours when a carriage drew up and a priest alighted.

"A beautiful morning, is it not, Monsieur le Sauvage?"

Lew hauled himself to his feet. "I don't believe I've—"

"We have met," said the abbé, "but I did not appear then as you see me now, the humble abbé de Choisy. I confess, my greatest pleasure is to adorn myself with the garments and accoutrements of the fairer sex. I was introduced to you as Madame de Sancy, and was in the company of Mademoiselle Marie-Jeanne L'Héritier de Villandon, Monsieur Perrault's niece."

"I remember." Lew almost laughed in spite of his misery. First Poucet turned out to be a girl disguised as a man, now this fellow – who from his present appearance must have taken holy orders – admitted to dressing in women's clothing. What a story this

361

would make, had he the heart to tell it. "You were kind enough to compliment me on my work."

"I simply gave praise where praise was due." The abbé nodded towards the entrance. "Shall we go in together?"

"Alas, I have been thrown out."

The abbé de Choisy's well-groomed eyebrows shot up. "Thrown out? Good gracious – on what account?"

"That of," Lew looked away, "being discovered alone with Marie-Madeleine Perrault."

"Ah," said the abbé. "Thereby hangs a tale. Step into my carriage, young man. We'll take a turn around the streets."

There seemed no reason to refuse. "Since it sounds as if you know of Marie-Madeleine's existence, perhaps you can explain why she's been hidden away from the world – in that grim watchtower, behind fabrications about a monstrously maimed cripple."

"Nobody but Marie-Madeleine is responsible for her living arrangements." The carriage slowed as it turned into the rue du Faubourg Saint Jacques. "It was her sanctuary in a time of trouble. Gradually she became...well, what amounts to a hermit, refusing to leave the place or to receive visitors. Nobody is allowed in, not her brothers, though that's understandable in view of their behaviour – particularly Pierre who tormented her unmercifully – or even Marie-Jeanne, who is her cousin. Though as to the latter," he grimaced, "who can blame her? What's more—"

"Yes?" prompted Lew, for the abbé had paused as if selecting his words with more care than hitherto.

"The young woman won't utter a word to her father, doesn't even acknowledge his presence. It causes him a great deal of heartache." The abbé glanced sideways, as if gauging Lew's reaction. "He fears for her sanity."

"That's preposterous, Father. Marie-Madeleine read me one of her stories. It was cunningly written to make a point – though I didn't understand at the time. I saw no sign of madness." Lew found he was twisting his fingers together, one of Poucet's nervous tricks, and stopped immediately. "However, some might describe Monsieur Perrault's fury this morning as insane – I've never seen such rage among gentlefolk. To my mind, such an outburst belonged in the roughest of taverns at full moon on a feast day."

The abbé de Choisy smiled. "There are those among Charles' detractors who still speak of his furious argument with the great artist, Gian Lorenzo Bernini."

"I've seen Bernini's work," Lew said glumly.

"We're talking about thirty years ago," the abbé reminded him, "and that's a long time for an ordinary disagreement to be remembered…even by one's enemies. One must presume therefore that what took place was *extra*ordinary. At any rate, they say – in response to a stream of invective – Cavaliere Bernini retorted that Charles was not worthy to scrape filth from the soles of his shoes; furthermore, he threatened to complain both to the king and the papal nuncio."

"And did he?" Lew peered through the window, trying to work out where the carriage was taking them. They were, he thought, somewhere near the Champs du Capucins. For the sake of his pride, he would descend before what was undoubtedly a circular route returned them to the Perrault residence.

"Some say his anger was sparked by nepotism. As it turned out his brother – Claude, not an architect but a physician – snatched the job of designing the Louvre's colonnade from under Bernini's nose." The abbé leaned over and tapped Lew's knee as if suspecting his attention had wandered. "Perhaps it's only family issues that make his blood boil."

"Perhaps," agreed Lew, failing to find any comfort in the priest's conclusion. He was still cold, but at least he'd stopped shivering. "Would you be so kind as to stop and let me out here?" His request was ignored.

"Young man, it's your duty to return and finish those captivating murals."

Lew shook his head. "He won't allow me to complete my paintings," it was hard to get the words past the lump in his throat, "that's...that's bad enough, but it's nothing compared to the prospect of never seeing Marie-Madeleine again. We love each other. This morning I asked her to marry me. She agreed. And now—"

"Forgive my bluntness, but what made you imagine that a young man with – I presume – so little to his name, would be an acceptable match for the only daughter of Charles Perrault, distinguished author, a member of the academy, and previously the Controller-General of his Majesty's Buildings and Gardens?"

"We are descended of a noble family – there are extensive estates in Normandy." Lew briefly explained his background and the reasons for adopting a false identity, ending with: "Which is just as well, now that my father's fears are realised and I'm disgraced."

"Have you explained all this to Charles?"

"Monsieur Perrault," Lew said dryly, "was not in the mood to listen."

"Hmm, and what would your father think of this proposed union?"

Lew thought of Angelique and her vast inheritance. His father might be disappointed, but since his own marriage had been a matter of heart not head he'd understand. "He'd love Marie-Madeleine. I know he would." And so would little Fleurance.

"One last question – are you aware," the abbé coughed discreetly, "of Marie-Madeleine's imperfection?"

"You mean her feet?" Lew shrugged. "So they're large. I don't see what all the fuss is about. It makes no difference to how I feel about her." He held up his right hand. "Look, I have an imperfection, a crooked little finger. It can't be straightened. My grandfather's is just the same. In addition, I wasn't able to learn my letters as other boys could." Lew gripped the abbé's hand. "Please, I beg of you, ask Madame Norik, Marie-Madeleine's custodian, to take a message. Tell her I will return." He thought for a moment. "Tell her to look for the turtledoves. When a gold ring appears between them, she'll know I'm coming to claim her. Will you do that, Father? Please? God help me, I love her, I adore her. I can't live without her. There can be no happiness unless she's at my side. I must find a way."

"May I offer some advice? Go home, young man. Take up your rightful place within your family. Confide in your father and your grandfather – and seek their help."

"Yes." Lew suddenly felt some of the weight lifted from his shoulders. "Yes, that's what I'll do. The truth is, Father, I've been homesick for a very long time."

"In the meantime, though there's no guarantee of success, I'll speak to Charles on your behalf."

"You will?"

"I am ever at the service of true love," said the abbé. "There's so little of it in the world." He gathered the skirts of his cassock in one hand. "Now – it's I who will alight, leaving the carriage at your disposal. My coachman will take you to Saint Denis and set you on the road westward."

Of the three stories that he'd snatched from the tower, the one Charles found most appealing was *Little Thumbling*.

Il était une fois a woodcutter and his wife who had seven children, all of them boys. The oldest one was only ten and the youngest just seven. The parents were extremely poor and the children were a great burden since not one of them was old enough to earn his living. It was also of great concern that the youngest child was frail and never spoke a word. However, what they saw as stupidity was actually a sign of his superior intelligence. He was very small at birth, hardly bigger than a person's thumb, and for that reason he was called Little Thumbling.

The tale seemed to be set in 1650–52, or 1661, perhaps even 1693—

There came a terrible year in which the famine was so bad that the poor couple decided they must abandon their children.

It was a spirited adventure: he'd almost fainted when the bloodthirsty ogre cut the throats of his seven small-eyed, hook-nosed, big-mouthed and pointy-teeth daughters; his heart threatened to fail him as Little Thumbling and his brothers fled afterwards, blundering through the forest all night, terrified, not knowing where they were going. At the same time the tale spoke of wit and intelligence elevating a man from a humble background into the highest of social spheres.

Clearly this was a writer well aware of the wizened manikin he'd purchased long ago from the failed gambler, and if Marie-Madeleine had been through his curio chest – was it possible to keep anything secret where there was a female in the house? – it was likely that she'd also handled his bezoar stone. Ah, yes – at last Charles was able to fit together the pieces of a several-years-old puzzle. She'd threatened to poison herself. No idle threat as it turned out, for someone had assisted his daughter in purchasing arsenic. He'd been forced to abandon very advantageous betrothal plans while she, wicked and disobedient creature, being in possession of the genuine bezoar – unicorn, not goat – could have swallowed any poison with impunity.

Once Upon a Time in Paris

The story of Charlemagne's mother was rather dull, Charles thought. He'd come across a reference to the queen's feet before, and could understand Marie-Madeleine's interest in Bertrada's history. As for *Riquet à la Houppe*, though the prince was almost unbearably ugly – lame, hunch-shouldered, cross-eyed, and with the red nose that suggested an habitual drunkard – the tale confirmed his suspicions that women are stupid, or avaricious, enough to find all rich men attractive.

He sighed and locked the stories away with the others. If, or rather when, Pierre was granted the *privilege* to publish, the addition of these tales would make a reasonably sized volume. And it was to be hoped that by that date Marie-Madeleine would have claimed them as her own work.

The stories had been a welcome distraction, but what now?

His day lay in tatters. It had started with Poucet, grey-faced, wringing his hands, spluttering and stumbling over every syllable, apprising him of Lew's disgraceful behaviour. As behoves any father, he'd raced to defend his daughter's honour, verbally flayed the miscreant and sent him packing – receiving no thanks whatsoever, quite the reverse. And now Poucet seemed to have gone into hiding, afraid no doubt of meeting violence at the coarse and hirsute artist's hands. It wouldn't do.

For the tenth time Charles left the library and made a tour of the house, calling for his valet. Poucet didn't appear. Instead, the abbé de Choisy came gliding up the stairs with all the airs of a fine lady garbed in silk and satin.

"I must ask you to excuse my unkempt appearance," said Charles, immediately returning to his writing table. How was it that, even wearing his dusty black, François made him feel seriously disadvantaged? With luck this would be a brief visit. "My good-for-nothing manservant has disappeared. Woe betide the fellow when he returns."

Eliza Granville

"I've heard strange claims made about your valet."

"Oh?" said Charles, and waited, but the abbé seemed unwilling to say more. Instead he broached a subject better left alone.

"I've been speaking to your artist—"

"That wretch," Charles ground his teeth and fought to master a rage he'd thought already spent. "He's nothing but a limb of Satan, a reprobate, a viper I took to my bosom, a rogue, a wastrel, a philanderer and a rakehell." He carefully placed the button wrenched off during this outburst next to his inkwell. There was another job for Poucet, damn him. "I had Jacques throw the reprobate onto the street."

"A great pity," murmured François. "I so looked forward to seeing the room completed. Perhaps even to attending some delightful occasion there."

"And so you will. I've instructed the scoundrel's assistants to carry on with the work. It's straightforward enough. His cartoons are still lying on the table for reference. The designs have all been transferred to the walls. The drawing's the important part. Now it's only a matter of slapping on some colour. Any fool can manage that."

"Perhaps you're right," said François, though his tone said otherwise. The abbé made a steeple of his fingers and rested his chin upon it. "However, on my last visit I believe we agreed that Lew was a young man with exceptional gifts. May I ask why he was dismissed?"

Charles scowled. "The miscreant abused the freedom I gave him within this house. He discovered the way into my daughter's living quarters and made overtures of romantic friendship. She, poor frail-minded fool, did nothing to discourage him." Off came a second button. "And that useless old woman was privy to it."

"I understand that the two young people wish to be wed and—"

"Wed! Impossible! The fellow has nothing, less than nothing. Not even decent clothes to his back. He's homeless, rootless, little better than a *bohémien*."

"That may not be true," the abbé said carefully. "If it were otherwise, would you consider him a suitable husband for Marie Madeleine?"

"My dearest wish is to see my daughter settled and secure before—" Charles gripped the edge of his bureau. "After all, one can only live so long."

"You're a man still in your prime," murmured François. They avoided looking at each other.

"That's as maybe. One has to be careful. Better sooner than later. Of course such a match must be to a man I judge suitable. Le Sauvage is not that man." Charles carefully lined up the edge of the inkwell with that of his sander, placing the buttons between them. "I have certain candidates in mind and remain hopeful in spite of everything that's happened."

"And what of Marie-Madeleine's feelings?" enquired the abbé. "Don't they deserve consideration? What about love…affection?"

"What about them?" Charles flicked his fingers. "Such emotions come after the wedding. I grew fond of her mother – Marie Guichon – despite having seen her on a single occasion previous to the match being arranged. She was nineteen – three years younger than my daughter is now – and fresh from the convent." He returned the inkwell to its original position. "The dowry was 70,000 livres, which incidentally, Monsieur Colbert – my superior at that time – thought far too little."

"And did your wife return your feelings?"

Charles looked at him askance. "Naturally – she was my wife."

"Hmm," said François. "And yet you were so eloquent in your praise of true love between the little marquise and the Marquis de Bercourt in our collaborative work. You must remember the part where the marquis avows that they are made for one another. And – don't deny it – 'nature is wise, and her impulses are reasonable', are words that you put into the marquise's beautiful mouth. You also had a hand in this, from the marquis: '*I love her, I adore her, I can't live without her, my heart tells me that she would make me happy.*' These are practically the same words that Lew used to me today. What do you say to that, my old friend?"

"That's a story, François, make-believe. What we're talking about is real life." A small noise beyond the door alerted him: Poucet, no doubt. Seizing his cane, Charles ventured out onto the landing where he found the dark-haired maid – whatever her name was – polishing the floor. "Where's Poucet?"

"Don't know, sir."

"Well, find him. Tell him we need refreshments. If you can't find him, bring them yourself and be quick about it." On reseating himself before his writing table, Charles raised the question of his absent valet. "François, you mentioned rumours regarding Poucet. What have you heard?"

"Are you sure you wish to know? Very well – it seems Poucet has taken a leaf out of my book and elected to appear in disguise throughout her employment, though in her case it was not done for pleasure."

Charles stared. "You mean he...she...Poucet is a woman?" Several embarrassing thoughts occurred to him. One trusted a manservant to perform a great many intimate services. Damned if he'd have him – *her* – back, in that case.

"So I was informed. What did Lew say? Ah, yes – Poucet is the daughter of the nurse you engaged at your previous residence."

"Anne Goubert's girl?" Charles remembered her: an attractive woman, kindly, and with a lively mind for a peasant. She'd been such a great comfort to the children that he'd felt moved to help her financially when the crisis came.

"Apparently so."

"But why?"

"You'll have to ask her that."

The maid blundered in without knocking and set down a tray: wine and a platter heaped with small fritters the size of hazelnuts, still warm, and redolent of lemons.

Charles frowned. Delicious though they always were, it seemed no coincidence that Jacques, who'd been loud in his praise of Lew's work and obviously unwilling to evict him, had chosen to provide *pets d'âne* this morning. *Chanter à l'âne,* as the proverb went – speaking of the consequences of presenting things of beauty to an unappreciative audience – sing to the donkey and he will only—

"Ah, donkey's farts," said François, helping himself to a handful. He drew his chair closer. "Now, Charles, let's return to the subject of Marie-Madeleine. Whoever your daughter is to marry, it's time for her to rejoin the world. Since she refuses to communicate with you, the intervention of a third party is necessary. I know she refuses to see a priest. But I wonder – might she accept advice and friendship from a long-lost godmother?"

Chapter Fifteen

The witch finally ditches all sympathy and shows her true colours. "Look at yourself," she shrieks, holding the mirror a hand's breadth from my face. "What a sight, to be sure! Swollen eyes, red nose, and hair hanging like rat's tails – you've been bawling for hours. And what good has it done you, pray?"

"Two whole days," I sob, "and still no word."

"If the young fool's got a pinch of sense he'll be making for home. It's a long way to Saint-Lô and if he wasn't paid I doubt he's got the coin for a diligence. On foot, it'll take him the rest of the week – if he's lucky, and if his boots hold out. And if there are no Dutchmen, mad dogs, cutthroats – or cutpurses – maybe worse, on the road. Oh, for the love of Heaven, don't start up again. A fine thing it would be if he walked in and saw you in that state."

"All right, Granny."

"It would probably frighten him straight back out again."

"Yes – all right."

"Tumbling down those stairs in his hurry to be gone—"

"I *said*, all right."

"And keep running until he plunged into the sea and was lost forever."

"Granny, I've stopped. Don't go on."

"And about time, too, if you ask me," she crows, as if at a great victory. "Now, my sweet, while you're setting your appearance to rights, I'll fetch some dainties. A glass of wine each will hearten us...and then we'll see what we shall see."

She's a sly one, but that's in the nature of witches. I catch the rustling of silken skirts, the clop of high heels ascending the steps long before the stranger follows her into my chamber. The lady who enters is rather grand – grand enough that I feel obliged to drop a curtsey – powdered and perfumed, and wearing what is probably a very fashionable gown. I wouldn't know. But there's an air about her which suggests she'd wear nothing less than the best.

The witch sets out glasses and pours wine. "Weeping and wailing all day and all night," she claims, which is an exaggeration. And with that, they start talking about me as if I'm not here.

"One must be attentive in such situations," announces the fine lady. "I heard recently of a little marquise who, deprived of her loved one's presence, fell into a languor more dangerous than the most violent illness, until it was feared she would succumb—"

"There's no danger of that sort of decline here," the witch says sharply.

"Indeed, no. I can see that." Our guest sips her wine, takes one of the small cornet-shaped pastries filled with pistachios and nibbles it daintily. "This young man, Lew, seems a pleasant enough young fellow."

"Aren't you going to introduce us, Granny?" I ask, very forcibly, accompanying the question with the blackest scowl it's possible to muster in company. The witch mutters her usual threat about the wind changing, leaving our guest to speak for herself.

"Dear Marie-Madeleine, I'm Madame de Sancy, here as your godmother."

I look at the witch, who's nodding vigorously. "Both of my godmothers died of smallpox in the same year as my mother. I don't remember being told about you. Why have I never seen you before?"

Madame de Sancy just smiles. She eats another pastry. "Perhaps, as in the old tales, I am the godmother whose invitation was forgotten. Don't worry – I'm not full of anger and spite. Or perhaps it is because I was in Siam with the Chevalier de Chaumont at that juncture. Whatever the reason, I'm here just in time for you to meet your prince at the ball."

"Why ever would I attend any ball," I retort, "when Lew has been banished and told never to set foot in this house again?"

"Only listen, my dear," says the godmother. "I bring a message from him. Lew assures you that he'll return. 'God help me,' he said, 'I love her, I adore her. I can't live without her. There can be no happiness unless she's at my side. I will find a way.'"

"Oh." The world is suddenly a much brighter place.

"There's more." She leans forward and the air between us is suddenly suffused with the sweet scent of wood lilies. "Tell her, he said, to look for the turtledoves. When a gold ring appears between them, she'll know I'm coming to claim her."

"Is it a riddle?" asks the witch.

"Maybe," I say cautiously, for last time we spoke on the subject of riddles I flaunted my ability to produce all the answers. "I'll think about it." The godmother smiles encouragingly. "But," I add, "what's the point of him returning if the og— if my father won't give his consent to our marriage? Lew's father is a gentleman – tell her, Granny."

"I already know, dear. Lew confided in me."

"If it's a riddle," pipes up the witch, her smile pure malice, I swear, "she'll have the answer hidden away somewhere in that clever little head of hers."

"Godmother," I say quickly, "is it true that in Siam every street and building is made of gold?"

"I saw many curious things," the godmother produces what at first glance I take to be her wand, but which opens into a large fan, "and would be glad to speak of my travels, Marie-Madeleine, but there are other matters to resolve first. Since your father is so firmly opposed to your choice of husband, we'll need both a peck of good old-fashioned common sense and a great deal of magic to change his mind. Madame Norik will provide the first and I'll summon up as much as I can of the other." The room was growing uncomfortably warm with the sun now shining directly through my window; in different circumstances I would have thrown off my gown and sat in my shift. Today I'm forced to sit and simmer, grateful for the cool air produced by the godmother fanning herself. "And what will you contribute?" she asks.

"Granny tells me I have no common sense whatsoever," I say, uneasily – for I sense a trap closing. "And I know nothing of magic."

"Then allow two older and wiser heads to advise you. Shall I speak for us, Madame?"

"You might as well," cackles the witch. "Heaven knows I've wasted enough breath trying to persuade her to see sense." And from the look on her face, I know exactly what's coming.

"Even a country gentleman," says the godmother, averting her eyes, "would baulk at the idea of his son taking a wife who, though exceedingly pretty, dresses like a kitchen wench—"

"A cinder-arse," adds the witch, earning a look of distaste from her new friend, "or cinder-bottom, if we're being polite."

"And who doesn't know how to conduct herself in society." The godmother lays down a *tablette*, its leather cover stamped with red and gold fleurs-de-lys. A miniature pencil is attached by a scarlet ribbon. It appears she's about to make notes of what changes are necessary, not realising the whole point is that Lew loves me exactly as I am. I deem it wise to stay silent.

Truth to tell it's hard to get a word in edgeways as for the next goodness-knows-how-long they go at it hammer and tongs, until it's decreed that I must move back into my old chamber in the ogre's house immediately, civilly converse and take meals with him, receive dancing lessons, be tortured by *corsetières*, and fitted for garments of the very latest fashion – in short, learn to behave like every other young lady of refinement and quality. I'm forced to agree, since that's the price of the godmother's magical intervention. I'll *yes* and *no, please* and *thank you* in all the right places, allow myself to be buttoned and laced, perfumed and coiffed, but my thoughts will stay my own.

I reflect that refinement and graciousness come naturally to Cinderella. Perhaps that's because I've made her far more beautiful than I can ever be.

The king's son seated her in the place of honour. Cinderella conversed with wit and intelligence on subjects as diverse as the work of the royal artist and the latest battle news. When he led her out onto the dance floor, she moved with such grace that every other couple stopped to watch. A beautiful supper was brought in. The prince ate nothing, for he was too busy feasting on Cinderella's beauty, but she tasted a few dainty morsels and graciously sent her compliments to the cooks, who were forever afterwards at her service.

"Daydreaming again," says the witch, but not unkindly. She breathes a sigh of relief. "Well, that's that settled. My thanks, Madame de Sancy – now *ma chère fille* can take her place in the world and I will no longer have to drag my poor unwilling bones up and down those terrible stairs."

"One more night," I insist, for dreams inside a house are likely to be very different from those at the top of a tower. "It would be unkind not to bid farewell to Reims, my jackdaw." The two women exchange glances.

"One night, no more," agrees the witch.

"You asked about Siamese buildings." Madame de Sancy puts away her notebook. "My dear, gold is the be all and end all there. The palaces and pagodas – many statues, too – are completely covered in gold foil. Even the howdahs on the backs of elephants are gilded, and so were the serpent-headed barges on which we were transported to the capital. At court, important officials wear tall cone-shaped hats whose golden rims are encrusted with precious stones, and King Phra Narai, a man so powerful that it was forbidden to utter his name, wrote letters on sheets of beaten gold."

As the godmother continues to describe the sights – houses on stilts, the many varieties of venomous snakes, the brilliantly coloured flowerpeckers, kingfishers and sunbirds, and extraordinary plants growing in the mossy elbows of trees, their flowers hanging in the air like so many moths and butterflies – my thoughts turn to the ogre's library. It may be possible to find a map there showing the long route Lew has taken towards the west. Perhaps it will indicate any dense dark forests he must traverse, but not the brigands, wild beasts, witches and demons that pose such threats to travellers. Those are the dangers that old tales warn of, things whose menace can never properly be understood from books.

> *Soon the beggar prince came to the edge of the darkest forest imaginable. The trees' branches met overhead, letting in very little sunlight. Large and unseen beasts crashed through the undergrowth on either side of the track and in the distance he heard a terrible, unearthly baying. His courage almost failed. But then the thought of his beautiful princess heartened him. Hoisting his bag onto his shoulder, whistling a merry tune, he*

stepped forward into the gloom. Night fell. For a while, a single star lit his path, but as the moon rose he saw hundreds of eyes gleaming among the trees, and heard the snapping and snarling and slavering—

Later, when I'm alone, there's Lew's message to savour – and his riddle to solve. But for now, I nod and gasp with the witch at the idea of men employed to entertain the King of Siam by jumping off high cliffs, a *parapluie* in each hand, drifting slowly earthward like the little seeds of dandelions.

The two kitchen maids look at me, look at each other, and then turn to Jacques for enlightenment, but he's too preoccupied with his own guilt. It's hard to know what to say to him. We used to be friends in the old days. Before discovering my tower, the kitchen was a favourite hiding place, one where I was allowed to dip my fingers into containers of sugar and dried fruit, to lick spoons and sample trimmings, knowing my kindly giant would brook no hissing or cackling or name-calling there. And yet he was the one who marched Lew from the building.

"How could you?"

"I'm sorry, miss," Jacques throws a cloth over whatever he's been butchering and wipes his hands on a bundle of rags, "but what choice did I have? Anyway, it's probably for the best. Young Leonardo might be as skilled as me but he's poor as a church rat – head stuffed with fine dreams and pockets full of nothing but holes. Forget him, is my advice. Your pa will make you a fine match by and by."

My only response is to narrow my eyes and glare. This makes him even more uncomfortable; he shifts his weight from one foot to the other while a small tic pulls repeatedly at the corner of his mouth. Finally Jacques decides to appeal to my sweet tooth.

Once Upon a Time in Paris

"What can I prepare for you, miss?" he pleads, his great hands outspread to encompass everything the kitchen has to offer. "Macaroons, *talmouses*, waffles with rose-petal preserve, *petits choux*...only say the word. Or there is some *pain de gaulderye*, rich in honey and spice, recently arrived from Dijon, where the finest dough sleeps, they say, for a hundred years before being gently woken and baked."

The mention of spiced bread is tempting, but there's no time. I can hear the witch clack-clacking down the kitchen stairs in hot pursuit of me.

"No," I say, "instead I'll have the cook's head on a silver platter." His jaw drops. Then deep belly roars of laughter follow me as I slip out of the kitchen door and stand breathing in the dusty hot smells of summer.

I'm convinced that the answer to the riddle must lie in our small dovecot, situated between the courtyard and the *potager* – which the ogre prides himself was laid out in homage to the vast fruit and vegetable gardens at Versailles, a ridiculous conceit. Curiously enough, the dovecot is octagonal in shape, exactly like the ballroom which Lew was engaged in transforming. The witch trots after me, unimpressed by this fact, grumbling about the heat, the flies, and the overpowering smell of guano; it's not my fault that she doesn't want to let me out of her sight.

It's strange to be in the open air after all this time. Little has changed. In the distance, the same nameless old man, dressed – I swear – in the same leather breeches and jerkin, runs his hoe along the rows. He talks to the plants, tolerates small birds, but wages war on all the cats in Christendom, as is evidenced by a crude gibbet from which swings the remains of a brindled tom. Netted fruit trees link arms along the walls. And there's a pumpkin patch, though none of the orange globes are yet large enough for Cinderella's purpose. I wish the gardener a cheerful good day, but the witch, who suspects him of possessing the evil eye, only grunts.

If the smell was bad outside the dovecot, inside it's overpowering. The floor is deep in droppings, and more are piled up against the central potence, the upright pole to which a revolving ladder is attached. It seems a pity that saltpetermen never exercise their *droit de fouille* here, carrying away every last scrap of dung and fouled earth to make gunpowder, as they do in rural places. There are cast feathers everywhere, too, even floating on the still air, but only three or four birds anxiously watching from their tiny nesting spaces, and no pairs at all. I reach up to feel inside one of the nesting holes, but it's empty save for a few wisps of dried grass.

"Oh, good Lord above," the witch's complaint is muffled by the apron held over her face, "what call have you got to rummage around in such a filthy stinking place on your first day of freedom?" One sharp little elbow jabs at my side. "Out we go."

"All right, Granny." After refastening the door, I stand and fill my lungs with fresh air, my eyes searching in vain for a billing, cooing twosome of doves in the surrounding trees. Perhaps it's time to think again.

"That's the last place any decent young man would want you to go looking for answers," says the witch, as if in confirmation. "So I'm guessing you've finally been set a riddle you can't solve."

First there was lunch to be endured – for even an ogre so wreathed in smiles is still an ogre – then much fussing over updating the drapes and linens within my chamber. Afterwards I planned to visit the ballroom alone, quietly lingering over Lew's handiwork, which I've still not seen, but it appears that his two young assistants have taken on the task of finishing the remaining panels and, artists being what they are, I must be chaperoned.

My protests come to nothing. The witch is adamant.

"We'll go together."

"Oh, do let's," says the godmother. "Although I've now viewed Monsieur le Sauvage's paintings on several occasions, I don't think one could ever tire of them. There's something new to be discovered each time. He's captured the spirit of La Fontaine's work so well and in such a beautifully rustic way that, if it wasn't for fear of mud, I'd be off to the countryside right away to see all those charming birds and animals for myself."

I force a smile. "I've always enjoyed the fables."

"Most are retellings of ancient stories from Brittany," declares the witch.

"Are they indeed?" says the godmother. "Well, perhaps you're correct. In any case, dear Madame de Sévigné described them as being like a basket of strawberries. 'You begin by selecting the largest and best', she wrote, 'but, little by little, you eat first one, then another, till at last the basket is empty.'" She sighs. "For all his frailties, poor Jean will be sorely missed."

We push open the doors to a sorry sight: both young men are stretched out on cushions, snoring loudly, with an empty jug lying between them. The witch is on them in a flash. Never have I seen her so incensed. Thwack. Thump. A stream of unintelligible words descends on their heads – Breton, of course, and undoubtedly abusive, though the only word I pick out is *sus*, pigs.

"Oh, my," murmurs the godmother and draws me away. We pace the corridor, conversing about La Fontaine's fables, until an ominous silence falls.

On our return, the witch is calmly inspecting the domed ceiling, while the assistants – Agrippa and Jean-Baptiste – are hard at work, though I note several anxious sidelong glances cast her way. What a funny fearless little creature she is, to be sure. After witnessing such a ferocious reaction to drunken idleness, it fleetingly occurs to me that her fisherman husband was probably not the saint she portrays him as. But there's no time to dwell on such thoughts, for here I am surrounded by the outpourings of Lew's imagination, allowing me a further glimpse of his soul. Above me the azure dome with its sun, stars and birds, exactly as my witch described it, and below such a glorious riot of colours that it's hard to know where to let my eyes rest first.

"Magnificent," breathes the godmother.

"Ah," says the witch, "mark my words, this room will be the talk of Paris."

I can't bring myself to speak.

Each of the eight walls is decorated with a composite picture, arranged to include several of the best-loved fables linked by natural backgrounds. The one nearest to me shows *The Wolf and the Stork*, with the stork standing in the shallow ripples of a pond. Near his spindly legs is depicted *The Frogs Who Wanted a King*, the foolish amphibians squatting on their despised log monarch, unaware of the regal water snake coiled ready to strike. The pond itself is fringed by reeds, kingcups, yellow iris and the drooping branches of willow trees. Dragonflies hover over pink-flushed water lilies. And closer examination reveals *La colombe et la fourmi* – a pigeon crouched at the water's edge, extending a blade of grass so that the drowning ant may save itself.

I move on to a view of a vegetable garden – it might even be ours – with, at its centre, *The Jay Dressed in Peacock Feathers*. The high-stepping bird in question, dowdy beneath its borrowed plumes, is haughtily battering down a bed of plump asparagus spears. Marigolds, heartsease and camomile bloom in profusion. Here's *The Acorn and the Pumpkin*, though the gardener is long gone, and there's *The Fox and the Grapes*, with Monsieur Reynard staring longingly at a luscious bunch of grapes, forever out of reach. More branches, laden with gooseberries and *cassis*, point to a portly cat hunched between the rows of herbs, preparing to pounce on a sleek young mouse.

The godmother peers over my shoulder. "*The Old Cat and the Young Mouse.* And look," she points to an iron cauldron lying bottom-up among the shards of a broken clay pot, "there's *The Earthenware Pot and the Iron Pot.* I hadn't noticed it before."

I wish she'd stop talking. I'm busy with my own thoughts, and there's so much more to see. Finally, I plead a slight headache and escape to my room. Once there, I want to cry – at the beauty of Lew's work – and at the fear that he may never return, or that if he does, the ogre will turn him away, but I don't. None of the old tales ends that way. Neither will mine.

> *"Have courage," says the fairy, "for the road the prince must take is a magical one and for every tear shed by the princess who must wait for him it will become a man's-length longer."*

The days drag by, filled with the godmother's strictly imposed busyness, but still no word comes from Lew. Every morning the witch and I visit the ballroom. And every morning we find something new to marvel at. Sometimes a hitherto unremarked fable is revealed. Sometimes a depiction will trigger a memory or a fresh story which, as always, helps to take my mind off the endless waiting. Today, the witch catches sight of a jenny wren clinging to a trail of ivy and tells me later – over a dish of spiced bread – of a strange Breton custom called 'plucking the wren'.

"*Nin' ziblus bec al laouenanic, rac henès a zo bihanic,*" she chants. "We will pluck the beak of the wren, for he is very small. We will pluck the left eye of the wren, for he is very small. Ah, and so it goes on, right eye, left ear, right ear, every single part of the bird, first claw of the left foot, second claw, and so on and so on, ending with: We will pluck the tail of the wren, for he is very small."

I carefully divide the last slice of *pain de gaulderye* into two pieces. "All this chanting must take a long time."

"A very long time," agrees the witch, "on a bitterly cold midwinter night. But that isn't the end of it. You see, after the plucking of the tail, the chant must be recited in reverse, from the tail back to the beak again. The final line is: We will pluck the beak of the wren for he is very small, and now we have plucked him one and all. Then the wren must be killed, butchered, and shared round."

"I thought you said wrens were sacred in Brittany." And when, to my surprise, the witch concurs, I ask: "Have you ever witnessed this ceremony?"

She nods vigorously. "And there was great feasting afterwards."

I'm not convinced, but then this is the old dame who told Lew that all stories were true, even when they weren't. It hardly matters. Tomorrow we'll look again, hoping to find something equally diverting.

When he's sent to apologise, I hardly recognise tall and handsomely attired Pierre as the nasty little brother who once made life so miserable for me. He's seventeen, still the baby of the family. Someone, at some time, has attempted to teach him a lesson or two: I'm almost sure that his nose has been broken, and he's definitely lost a front tooth.

> *In addition to being assigned the most unpleasant jobs in the house, Cinderella's life was made more miserable by her two brothers. Both were extremely ugly, hardly fit to be seen, but since they would grow up to be men this was deemed unimportant. They also possessed nasty dispositions. The youngest pinched her and pulled her hair, calling her by all kinds of hurtful names. The older brother, who should have*

stuck up for her, simply laughed and went back to reading his books.

"What am I forgiving you for?" I ask, producing an expression meant to suggest total mystification. The witch sends me a warning look and shakes her head. Pierre's face, already flushed with embarrassment, seems about to burst into flame.

"For all those names I called you, and for making fun…and for the thing with the goo— that dead bird. I never meant to—"

"Of course I forgive you, Pierre."

Then Cinderella's sisters recognised her as the beautiful girl they'd so admired at the ball. Mortified, they threw themselves at her feet, begging forgiveness for all the unkind things they'd said and done and all the unhappiness they'd caused her. Cinderella readily forgave them with all her heart, for now that her dreams had come true what was past no longer mattered to her.

My meeting with Charles-Samuel is far more solemn. Tall and thin, already stooped by constant study, he's two years younger than me but, even at an early age, felt far older. There's no apology from him – I never expected one – and not a trace of a smile. Instead he bends over my hand, stiff as a sharply folded *ordonnance restrictive*.

"It is extremely gratifying," he pronounces, with the air of one measuring every word, "to see you have once again taken full possession of your senses, sister."

"I've already forgiven you, Charles-Samuel."

He drops my hand quickly. "Forgiven me for what?" His long nose twitches as if catching a whiff of possible litigation. I find it hard not to laugh.

"Doesn't a brother have a duty to protect his sister from mockery?"

But it's at this point that I realise the real villain – the one person who should have protected Cinderella – isn't mentioned in my story after the first sentence.

Il était une fois un gentilhomme whose second marriage....

My father declared, and I remember it very clearly, that he intended to devote more time to his children now that his onerous work for the king had finally come to an end. Of course, what he meant to say was that he'd devote more time to his sons.

Cinderella, who was as good-hearted as she was beautiful, procured for her father a fine position at court on the very day of her marriage.

But not even Cinderella could forgive an ogre.

"When you were a little girl," he says wistfully, "our love for each other was a very joyful affair. 'Papa,' you used to whisper, 'I love you as sour lemons love white salt.' This was after I'd told you white salt was the ancient name for sugar in the days when real salt was always grey in colour." His laugh is a mournful sound, but I harden my heart against it. "You'd heard a tale – *The Dirty Shepherdess* – in which the youngest daughter tells her father she loves him as fresh meat loves salt, and already you were changing stories to suit your purposes." His eyes are fixed on my face. He sighs at my lack of response. "I thought – once you agreed to leave your lonely tower – that things might go back to being at least a shadow of what they were. But no, still you hardly spare me a kind word, and never a smile."

"You sent Lew away." I stare at the tapestry above the fireplace, depicting of all things a visit to a tapestry factory. A peculiarly dull subject for a wall decoration – especially when compared with those the witch and I viewed earlier. "We love each other and yet you banished him."

"Of course I did, Marie-Madeleine. The fellow's an opportunist."

"No, Lew's the man my good fairy foretold. She said my true love would find me, wherever I might be, and however carefully I was hidden away. That's exactly what happened."

"Who is this good fairy person?" The ogre looks puzzled. "Surely you don't mean Goubert, the nursemaid. That was a very long time ago."

"She also said my peculiar feet wouldn't matter to him. And they don't."

The ogre starts at such a direct description of my affliction. He clears his throat and fiddles with the bits and pieces on his writing table. "Yes, well, Ann Goubert was a great one for imagining she could see into the future. Quite alarming, some of the things she came out with. Warned me not to let your brothers enter upon a military career for a start – as if any Perrault ever would – and told me I'd be remembered for centuries for something I didn't do." He peers at me. "You never met Poucet, my last manservant, did you?"

"No, why do you ask?"

"Because he.... Oh never mind. It doesn't matter now." The ogre heaves his corpulent self upright and paces from the chimneybreast to the window, stares up at the sky for a few moments, and paces back again. He shuffles through some papers. "I've misplaced a letter to you from your cousin, Marie-Jeanne. It will turn up, given time, have no fear." The search is abandoned. "Listen, my dear, I want to talk to you about your stories."

"You stole them."

He laughs. "As I believe you have stolen my bezoar stone."

"It was only borrowed. I'll return it within the hour, whereupon you must give *Little Thumbling* and *Riquet à la Houppe* back to me."

"Just those two?" asks the ogre, and from his expression, that's a question he's already regretting. My fists clench of their own accord.

"Does that mean you have others?"

"My dear girl, if only you knew of the hours, the days, weeks, I've spent searching high and low for the tales you tossed from your window," he says haltingly, "combing the grounds and the streets, visiting the dens of rag-pickers, rubbish collectors...sometimes finding complete pages, more often retrieving fragments and painstakingly piecing them together—"

"You had no right." I might as well not have spoken. He carries on regardless.

"It still grieves me that so many were beyond saving. And as for the thought that others may have been lost forever...." He groans, and one ogreish hand creeps to the middle drawer of his writing table revealing his hiding place. "I consider your stories to be masterpieces of wit and brilliance, Marie-Madeleine. It's a tragedy that only five survive...plus, of course, those I carried away yesterday."

"You had no right," I repeat, keeping a tight rein on my mounting indignation. "They weren't written down for you to lock away. They can't be owned by anyone – not by me, certainly not by you – because they belong to everyone." The ogre looks uncomprehendingly at me. "Don't you see? They're old tales that have travelled the world from the beginning of time – pausing here, alighting there, lingering long enough to work themselves into people's hearts and minds – always willing to let someone refashion them, thereby imbuing them with new life and ensuring their survival. But undertaking to do that refashioning brings with it a duty to give them back to the world." I extend my hand. "My stories, if you please."

He doesn't move. "Perhaps you might allow me to give them back to the world on your behalf."

"That task is mine." It's unwise to tell an ogre you don't trust him.

"Marie-Madeleine, it's too late. Five of your tales have already been copied and sent to the royal court."

"Not in my name, I hope." I beam hate at him, squeezing the words between my gritted teeth. Indignation has grown into rage, stiffening my spine until I fear it might snap.

"As a matter of fact, no," the ogre shakes his head, but won't look at me, "though I hoped you would lay claim to them, given time. They were well received. From what I hear, Madame de Maintenon has read them to the king himself. What greater honour could an author wish for?" In the face of my silence, he continues to stare at the carpet. "All that I ever did was with the best of intentions."

It's my turn to rise and walk to the window; the view from here is much inferior to the one from my tower. A storm threatens. Dark clouds are gathering, strung along the horizon like the black knight and his pack of hounds from my witch's tale of the loathly lady.

"Father," I say very calmly, turning to face him. "You have taken my work and done with it as you saw fit. You denied me the education my brothers enjoyed. You once tried to inflict a decrepit old husband on me. Can you not grant me sovereignty over any part of my own life? Don't forget that I read your *Vindication of Wives*, where you say of marriage: *the choice of each one must be left free*. Does that apply to everyone but your daughter? My choice is to marry Lew."

"My dear, it's not as simple as that," the ogre laughs at the notion. "The poem was a humorous response to a piece by a colleague...no matter. But rest assured that the suitors I find for you will be young and well favoured enough to please—"

"On the contrary, father, it's very simple." I grip the back of a chair so tightly that my knuckles shine white. "If you don't permit me to marry Lew, then I'll become a nun. After all, God won't care about my feet: it was His mistake anyway."

Autumn is fast approaching and there's still no word from Lew. I continue to believe he'll return; tears are reserved for my pillow.

All the greys of summer's end are gathering across the sky. The garden apples have been picked and laid away; already the trees have a bronze tinge to their leaves. This morning a few wild geese flew overhead, lamenting the loss of summer feeding grounds, and soon the swallows will return to the depths of their ponds to sleep away the cold months.

I've escaped the witch – a rare event – and am on my way to the dovecot for one last attempt at solving the riddle. Jacques, who is rolling pastry, starts singing, if one can call it that, the moment I appear in the kitchen, which only makes me wonder what he's been up to. Blanche smiles happily at me, and so, for once, does Escarlatta, the sulky, dark-haired maid. In passing, I notice she's attached a likeness of herself to the wall, immediately below that of Jacques. It's unmistakably one of Lew's sketches: he's made her even prettier than she is in real life.

The kitchen cat accompanies me, mincing along the path in a manner which is totally at odds with those rag-edged ears and the scars of affray covering his lean form. Today the doves are silent. Many are moulting. None look in the mood for courtship. I return to the ballroom, the only place still offering comfort. Agrippa and Jean-Baptiste have long since finished painting, packed up, and left; I can see where Lew's work ends and theirs begins, but the ogre seems satisfied. Splendid English chandeliers now illuminate both adjoining rooms. New furniture has been purchased, and the old pieces polished to within an inch of their lives. The day of the ball is almost upon us.

Today, the space smells strongly of paint, which is probably due to warmth from the hundreds of candles lit to test the chandeliers' safety. I'm drawn to the panel depicting *The Hare and the Tortoise* – although it's my least favourite fable and consequently the one I've spent the least time admiring. In the background a mouse is painstakingly freeing the mighty lion from the hunters' net and, on looking more closely, I discover *The Ant and the Grasshopper* next to a stand of wheat stalks and poppies. Above them all, robust branches intertwine forming a bower covered with pink and white apple blossom. Something glints among them. And oh! There they are – right there, enclosed by flowering twigs roughly forming the shape of a heart – the two turtledoves reunited, with a golden ring held between their beaks.

The godmother has already announced that she's ordered an ensemble of deep blue velvet for the occasion and there's been much fussing about the difficulty of having matching shoes made for feet which, though I'd never say so to her face, are far longer than mine, though nowhere near as splayed. I've seen to it that the witch – who intends to watch proceedings from a quiet corner of the gallery – has received a new gown; it's black of course, but with a deep collar of the finest, most costly lace, Venetian-style.

As for me, I've been digging my heels in, refusing to countenance finery to be worn at a ball I've had no interest in attending. Now everything's changed. After hugging the news to myself for a night and a day, I finally confide in the godmother.

"You see what this means, godmother?"

"I do indeed. Somehow," and here the godmother pretends to

look puzzled, "Lew's received an invitation to the ball. My dear, we must immediately summon the best couturiers. And I'll send a note to Madame Potiers, who is the best coiffeur on the rue Saint-Honoré, bidding her to attend on the day." She laughs. "It's time to work some magic."

> *The fairy touched Cinderella with her magic wand and at once the rags were transformed into a most beautiful cloth of gold gown set all over with precious stones – rubies, sapphires, and diamonds.*

"I must have a gown of cloth of gold, covered all over with precious stones."

"It shall be done," says the godmother, tapping my shoulder with her fan.

And in only three days the gown is ready for its first fitting.

> *And for her feet the fairy godmother gave her the prettiest pair of dancing slippers, made of fur, pure white ermine trimmed with swansdown.*

"I'd like dancing slippers," I declare, for have them I will, even if the shoemakers laugh outright at my strange feet, "of pure white fur trimmed with swansdown."

"It shall be done," says the godmother, touching my elbow with her fan.

Nobody laughs. And the dancing slippers arrive as if by magic.

"And a stole of swansdown in case the air turn chilly."

"It shall be done," says my godmother, and puts the fan into my hand.

And the beautiful wrap, made of the feathers of seven times seven swans, was only a week in the making.

In the meantime, the witch brings out my chest of previously rejected treasures and carefully unearths the ogre's diamond necklace from its silk wrappings. Without a word, she lays before me the aigrettes dripping with diamond *briolettes* and opens the pretty fan with its delicately carved ivory sticks, its leaves painted with roses, forget-me-nots, and small blue birds. And my little witch never once says: "I told you so."

Here I am, in my finery, on the ogre's arm as the music strikes up. I know very few of the guests, and yet they all greet me by name. There's no sign of Lew, but his paintings are being admired, and the ogre congratulated for commissioning them. The air buzzes with excitement. I'm being admired, too.

Ah, qu'elle est belle! Oh, she's very beautiful!

Nobody's clothes and jewels are as splendid as mine. And nobody laughs at, or even seems to notice, my feet.

When she entered the great ballroom on the prince's arm everyone fell silent. The musicians ceased playing. The dancers stopped dancing. The maids ceased waiting and even the ladies of court desisted from their gossiping. All eyes were fixed on the great beauty of this unknown lady.

Young and not so young men that I'm sure are possible suitors lined up by the ogre, press close, paying me extravagant compliments and making conversation. The godmother stands at my shoulder, and after a while she directs me to dance with my father. I do, despite his great clumsiness. Rarely have I seen him so happy, so puffed up with pride, and I might have forgiven him everything right then and there, if it wasn't for my fear of him throwing Lew out the moment he shows his face. When the dance ends, the ogre makes a low bow before returning me to my godmother's side, and then decides he must inspect the collation being laid out for our guests.

"Perhaps Lew isn't coming," I whisper, as the godmother pulls and pokes at stray tendrils of my hair. "Perhaps he's changed his mind." I scan the faces for the hundredth time. "Perhaps he isn't coming." Somewhere a clock begins to strike the hour, but the noise within the ballroom steadily increases, making it impossible to count the strokes. "He isn't coming."

"He's coming," the godmother says with conviction, and takes my arm. "Have patience, my dear. Let's partake of some refreshments."

I follow her blindly, suddenly aware of my great flat feet. It's likely that everyone's been warned not to stare at them. What if I trip and fall?

Lew isn't here. He isn't coming.

At times like these I need the sharp tongue and rough comfort of my little witch. And there she is, up in the gallery, not alone as I would have supposed, but surrounded by pretty young girls, hanging on her every word. The witch glances down, as if feeling my gaze upon her. She frowns, taking in my situation. Her eyes flash red. I can hear her voice inside my head as clearly as if we were back in the tower and she was bawling at me from an arm's length away. "Set to and finish the tale, girl. Finish it as you'd wish it to turn out in real life. Get on with it. What are your tales for if it isn't to sneak inside them and discover a cure for your situation?"

The king flew into a terrible rage on finding out that his only daughter had fallen in love with a beggar. He summoned the court executioner and ordered the young man dragged before him in chains. "Prepare to die, varlet, reprobate, wretch, pauper," he roared. Weeping bitterly, the princess threw herself onto her knees and pleaded for her lover's life. The executioner, moved by her tears, laid down his axe. The ladies of court wailed and tore their hair. The godmother went in search of her wand. The cooks blew out the fires and refused to prepare dinner. Even the scullions left off their scouring and scrubbing. Eventually the king relented and banished the beggar from the realm instead of beheading him.

The very next day he announced that the princess must be married. A great ball would be held two days hence. Suitors, old and young, ugly and well favoured, always rich – but never poor – began to arrive from near and far. On the evening of the ball a handsome young prince came to the palace late, mounted on a sleek black horse caparisoned in gold, preceded by a high-ranking official and flanked by a dozen attendants in gold livery. As for the prince himself, he was dressed in such diamond-studded finery that it dazzled the eyes. The ogre was delighted to welcome such a guest and was courtesy itself. Summoning the princess, he insisted she dance with this pleasingly wealthy suitor. But she recognised the young man immediately as her beloved beggar. "Dearest Princess," said he, "I came to you penniless and in rags because I wanted to be loved for myself and not on account of my father's great wealth and vast estates. You have shown that you love me for what I am and not what I have. As for me, I love you exactly as you are. Let us be married without delay."

"Marie-Madeleine," chides the godmother, "this is no time for daydreaming."

I blink, and find the ogre offering me a glass of cordial.

"You look very beautiful, my dear daughter," he says, yet again.

And again, I begin to thank him as prettily as I can. But somewhere in the middle of my sentence the room falls silent. Or seems to, because it decidedly isn't: mouths continue to move, fans beat the warm air, the violinists' arms go on sawing, someone drops a glass and I see it shatter against the floor. An elderly gentleman, fine-looking in spite of his years, has approached the godmother and is waiting to be introduced to the ogre. My godmother's lips move: sound rushes back into the void.

"Comte de Courcy," she is saying, "and this is Monsieur Charles Perrault, of the French Academy, about whom we've already spoken at great length."

I try to concentrate as the formalities continue. It feels important. But now someone has moved forward to stand beside the count, and my heart is pounding so hard that it's all I can do to raise my eyes and look at him.

"And Charles," concludes my fairy godmother, "I believe you're already acquainted with the count's grandson, Louis le Gentil?"

"Harrumph," says the ogre, scrutinising the tall, handsome and immaculately dressed young man standing before him, "I uh, Lew – yes, of course."

Lew bows very low. "May I dance with your daughter, sir?"

The ogre looks at him, and then he looks at me. He says nothing for a very long moment. And then my father surprises me by taking my hand and placing it in Lew's. What's more, he places his own hand on top as if in blessing. "Indeed you may, Lew."

Cinderella was taken to the prince, who found her even more beautiful than he remembered. He led her onto the dance floor and danced with no one else for the rest of the evening. She did not think it was possible to be any happier. They were married a few days later and retired to his country château where they lived happily ever afterwards.

Chapter Sixteen

It wasn't until two days after the wedding that Charles found the story on his writing table. He read it through carefully, and with great enjoyment. And then reread it, sighing as he remembered his once-upon-a-time passion for Marie Mancini, his youthful yearning to have glass slippers made for her adorable little feet, the better to admire them. To his mind, *Cinderella and the Little Glass Slipper* was a far more appealing title than *Cinderella and the Little Fur Slipper.* Both were a trifle long.

He might make a few additional changes later; a word here, a word there couldn't hurt. And then there was the matter of the moral. Something like—

> *My dear, it is without doubt a great advantage*
> *To possess spirit and courage,*
> *To be wellborn, to have good sense*
> *As well as your truly admirable talent –*
> *But all the beauty heaven has showered upon you*
> *Would have been in vain without the assistance*
> *Of your loving father and the fairy godmother.*

Charles locked the tale away. There'd be plenty of time to work on it later. Marie-Madeleine wanted her stories given to the world so that everyone could share them. His task was to see it done.

Historical Notes

Scholars still disagree about the authorship of *The Story of the Marquise-Marquis de Banneville*, though a 2004 edition attributes it to François-Timoléon de Choisy, Marie-Jeanne l'Héritier and Charles Perrault.

In real life, Marie-Madeleine Perrault and Louis le Gentile were married on 26 January 1701, in the presence of Charles Perrault, Marie-Anne de Harlay – the Abbess of the Abbey Port-Royal of Paris – and Thomas Corneille, the dramatist, a member of the *Académie française*. I've not been able to find more information about the real Louis le Gentile or about any children from the marriage, however I like to think the astronomer Guillaume Joseph Hyacinthe Jean-Baptiste Le Gentil, who was born in Coutances, Normandy, *might* be related.

More About the Press

CentreHouse Press is an independent publisher, specialising in memoirs, travel books, plays, literary fiction, children's books and non-fiction. The press also publishes ebooks. We have published, in either paper or electronic form, the following writers: Garry O'Connor, G. K. Chesterton, Peter Cowlam, Tony Phillips, Andrew Elsby, Jon Elsby, Eliza Granville, Harry Greenberg, and Sam Richards. The press has also featured the work of artists Anne Boulting and Julie Oxenforth, and has worked with artists Thierry Naiglin, Dawn Hunter and Elena Rosillo.

For the latest news, visit our website, centrehousepress.com, or catch up with opinion and reviews at our blogs and social media—

chpblog.centrehousepress.com
facebook.com/centrehousepress
@centrehouse

The Curious Ones
Eliza Granville

For more than fifteen years, Isabelle has been tormented by guilt over the disappearance of her youngest daughter. If only she'd been at the school gate to meet her. If only she hadn't been so engrossed in her painting. If only….

But now there's a granddaughter. In the hope that this new baby may heal what time, drugs and doctors never could, Isabelle drives the length of France to meet her. On the way she stops in a quiet patch of woodland and comes across a small child who looks like, but surely can't be, her lost daughter. The girl vanishes. Perhaps. And Isabelle gradually becomes convinced that unknown forces are at work, in which case her granddaughter may also be in danger.

The Vagabond Lover
Garry O'Connor

Cavan O'Connor was born into near destitution in Nottingham in 1899, but quickly rose to become the legendary 'Vagabond of Song'. He was one of the most famous singing legends of his era. He topped Variety bills. He was an adventurer, who cut a swashbuckling figure. In the golden age of radio, his broadcasts reached listening figures of over thirteen million. With his flawless tenor voice his status was as latter-day troubadour, a star of stage imitated by romantics young and old all over the civilised world. But what lay behind the idealised celebrity? Was he a gift from God, or a flawed, vulnerable being like the rest of us? Enter the writer son Garry O'Connor, who answers that question emphatically. In his memoir *The Vagabond Lover*, the father-son dispute unveils without sentimentality the general mess of domestic and family life, of which Cavan was the head. Revealed – in this searing, honest, dark revelation – are the miserable depths the sweet singer of lyrical song plumbed, and remorselessly so. O'Connor *fils* does not spare the reader, refusing to gloss over the traumas and crises of family conflict, as they run in parallel to his own fortunes and vicissitudes. He is dispassionate with the biographical detail, yet impassioned enough to recall one of his own plays, penned in his Cambridge youth, where the father Cavan is reimagined. In fiction as in life he is cast as the pivotal character in a family drama painful in its climaxes. Overarching is a first ever account of those Cambridge years, peopled with familiar icons of twenty-first-century culture. It's a fast-moving, two-pronged probe into the nature of celebrity, arriving at a profound resolution as the author shrugs off the flaws and setbacks packaged as part of the celebrity deal.

'A racy, opinionated and very readable account of life and loves in the English theatre since the 1960s.' **Bamber Gascoigne**

'A real page-turner. I couldn't put this one down.' **John Tydeman**

'An enthralling family biography, full of gossip, wise insights and fascinating revelations.' **Sir Ian McKellen**

'A delightful journey – probably O'Connor's best.' **Sir Derek Jacobi**

Prince Sigmund
Peter Cowlam

A modern-day fairy-tale of sibling and gender rivalry set in the fantasy kingdoms of Eede and Amateria. Will Prince Sigmund succeed his father as King of the patriarchal Eede, or will he be defeated by Queen Hilda, the head of state in the neighbouring Amateria?

Letters to Kafka
Harry Greenberg

The funny, tragic, sometimes hilarious letters to a latterday Franz Kafka, whose insights into the existential dilemmas of contemporary being continue to be misunderstood, and sometimes dangerously so.

Lightning Source UK Ltd.
Milton Keynes UK
UKHW022020060119
335063UK00006B/183/P